The Lady's Arrangement

by

Colleen L. Donnelly

Help Wanted Series

The Lady's Arrangement

Cover Art by *Diana Carlile*

The Wild Rose Press, Inc.
PO Box 708
Adams Basin, NY 14410-0708
Visit us at www.thewildrosepress.com

Publishing History
First Cactus Rose Edition, 2017
Print ISBN 978-1-5092-1324-5
Digital ISBN 978-1-5092-1325-2

Help Wanted Series
Published in the United States of America

Ben was tall, and he felt even taller as he took a step closer and leaned my way. "It takes two to bind a contract, and since I've just withdrawn, your arrangement is null and void. And just so you know, you can thank your lucky stars I'm not staying to marry you, because I take surprises a lot better than I take orders." His eyes stayed on mine until his gaze traveled from my face down to my boots. "And wearing trousers doesn't make you any more suited to giving orders than wearing a skirt would make me fit for giving birth."

My nails dug into my palms as I rolled my hands into fists. A word I'd heard Ted say when a pail slid off his bad arm came to mind. The word was immoral, but probably not too immoral for Ben Miller. "Just so you know, Mr. Miller, I've been running this ranch for three weeks now, in pants. I find skirts get in the way of things you'd probably be surprised I can do."

The half-smile returned. "I won't argue that. Skirts surely do get in the way." Ben straightened and slapped his hat tighter on his head. "Been my experience, too. Fortunately, neither one of us has to put up with one, since you can keep right on doing things the way you have been. I'm giving you an early parting. I'm leaving."

Praise for Colleen L. Donnelly

Amazon #1 Bestselling Author
RomCon 2014 Reader's Crown Finalist

~*~

"Colleen has the unique ability to draw the reader into her characters' lives and you become somewhat of an eye witness. I enjoy each of her books and eagerly look forward to the next one. Each story is different but at the same time another chapter into real life."

~*Judy Faunce, teacher and avid reader*

"Colleen Donnelly has outdone herself with a fast-paced story and characters! *THE LADY'S ARRANGEMENT* is a well-crafted dilemma, one that kept me quickly turning pages!"

~*Ericca Thornhill, author and teacher*

Dedication

To my dad,
who taught me about farming in Kansas,
my mom,
who taught me how to craft a good story,
my critique partners,
who helped me polish this one until it shone,
and my editor, Nan Swanson,
who has helped me find my author legs.

"Goodbye."
One word.
And we parted.
I glanced back only once.
~R

Chapter 1

New assignment: Tossed out of heaven, being sent to hell. Long before I was ready. ~Rex

Tiny flickers sputtered between the toes of my boots, the heap of dry grass and twigs catching. At last. "Sorry, Pop." I stared at the fiery glints, then straightened, rose from my crouch in one steady motion, and looked down, slid the flint and steel back into my pocket, and waited. Waited for the fire to grow…and destroy my boyhood home.

It waited, too. Sizzling while it sputtered, giving me the chance to change my mind and save everything else my pop had built that waited behind me—his enormous barn with a shed to its side, a smokehouse and outhouse not far away. But the house—the ranch house, the heart of our Red Rock Ranch—stood in front of me. Inches from the smoldering fire I'd started. I couldn't change my mind. There wasn't time. Thanks to some widow I'd never seen or heard of until today.

I dropped a knee to the ground, cupped my hands, and blew, sending embers upward along with a little spray of sparks, several stinging my face. I drew back. Gunpowder always meant business. And flint and steel meant reliable. That's why I chose them. I knew this job was going to hurt.

Flames and sparks gobbled away at the grass and

kindling I'd laid near the base of our house. I watched them rally, still small enough I could spit them out before they ripened into more of a fire. Leave everything standing until I could come back and use the law—like I was paid to, like I'd tried to—to set things right between my pop, Adler Duncan, and Matt Morrissey, the lowdown swindler who'd stolen this ranch from him. I could hunt Morrissey down the way a Ranger should, sniff him out from wherever he'd hidden himself in this Oklahoma section of Indian Territory, and make him pay for the way he cheated my father. I could. I should. But there wasn't time. I blew on the flames again.

"Morrissey, you won't be laying your head in my pop's house or stabling a horse in his barn." I leaned back on my haunches and waited some more.

Tiny ripples of heat rose above the flame's orange tips, luring the fire upward until it caught, stretching and gaining momentum like an angry rattler snaking along the bottom of the house my father had built for him and for me—Rex, his oldest son—while I was too little to do more than drag boards or fetch nails. Or to understand. I watched, hating the greedy flame as it roped what he had built for the two of us, claiming that simple square of one or two rooms for itself. Those boards he and I had put together had a different color from the ones the fire was racing toward, ones he added later when he married and built on, turning it into a house large enough to accommodate the woman who became my stepmother and the boy they had together. Little Brother. I always called him that, only half-brother meaning more to him than it ever did to me.

I stood as the fire hurried past the original square

and on to the different shade of wood that had held us all together as a family. I wallowed spittle in my mouth. Not enough to stop what I had started, now.

"You won't be sitting in our outhouse, either. Not after I'm done."

There was no reply other than the crackling, the biting and devouring of the wood. No one to respond to anything I said. But I said it anyway, and I meant it, wishing Morrissey were here to wrangle over what he wrongfully claimed was his. He hadn't been man enough to face me about what he'd done, knowing I had hold of the law's end of a waiting noose. One that said he'd come by this ranch crooked, a form of thievery worthy of death. A different sort of thievery than burning to the ground everything he'd stolen.

I ran my fingers over my trousers' pocket, feeling the flint and steel, their combination more of a weapon than my pistol had ever been. I understood fire. It had been a part of my life out here in the middle of Indian Territory and had meant a lot of things to me growing up on Red Rock Ranch. It had meant warmth and food. And it meant red—I'd always been partial to red. It also meant new growth for what prairie we had. It meant life out of death.

But not this one. This fire meant death.

Loose blades of grass and broken sticks tumbled out of what was left of my pile of kindling. They lay in the dirt at the toes of my boots, their tips smoldering. I stared at them, watched their dying sputters. Another chance to stomp out the growing flames, fight what was creeping along the base of the house, and leave everything my father had built intact. Leave it for that lowdown swindler, Morrissey, until I could get back and do things the way they should be done.

I wouldn't do that. My pop built this place. It was his and ours. I kicked the grass and twigs back to the fire and held them there with my boot. More sparks shot upward around the dry, worn leather, flames jumping higher up the ranch house's boards, their heat penetrating the front of my trousers and even my shirt as they grew—clothing adequate for a spring evening like this, but nothing against the fire's increasing fervor. Everything on me, from my toes to my shoulders, burned against my skin. I let it. I stayed right where I was—close to our old home, taking some of the heat from the last seconds of its life and holding on to memories as it let go. I was a part of this place, and it was a part of me. I would stay with it as long as I could.

The flames licked fast along the wood as I drew my toe from their base. Their hunger and the way they lapped up the weathered boards made my stomach churn. They spread, stretching out in fingers long and thin, and then into hands—broad hands that hurried to destroy this place. Different from my father's hands. His had created; his had embraced our home.

"If you'd been keeping a better eye on things, Little Brother…" I spat to the side, the heat searing my cheek as I did. Luke. He called me part-brother instead of Big Brother, or even half-brother. I stared at the wet ball of dirt. He kept me on the outside all of our lives, never doing his part when he left himself within. I ground the spit with the toe of my boot.

I ducked my head, forcing each boot a half step back. "Sorry it had to be this way, Pop." My voice came out wrong this time as I spoke into the flames. Maybe it was the heat making me sound nothing like the thirty-three-year-old man I was. A man who'd traversed the red dirt of Indian Territory on horseback day after day, swallowed dust and hot rays, icy wind and hard rain, and still spoke with the strength of a Ranger. What came from my throat just now was the tenor of a child. A boy who loved what his pop had built. Enough to destroy it rather than leave it in a crooked man's hands.

The heat pressed harder against my clothing and face. I latched onto the brim of my hat, lifted it, and ran a hand through my hair, straight hair, as black as the hat itself. Just like my father used to do, through hair the same color as mine until the gray set in on him. I stepped back farther, settled the hat on my head, and stared at the destruction I'd created. No Ranger would do something like this. Break his promise to uphold what little law there was—the law I was paid to instill. Set a ranch on fire and burn it to the ground to take back from Morrissey the only way I could. For now. I'd get it all back someday. At least what was left of it.

My father's face appeared in the flickering flames I stared into. Creases and grooves, dug deep from thoughts he had never shared, from steady devotion, and from working hard all his life, turned to channels where tears began to flow. I'd never seen my father cry. He stared back at me, his face rippling in the flare, his burning resemblance crying itself out until at last it disappeared. "I'm sorry, Pop…" My voice strained, its usual tenor still not there. "It's going to hurt when you find out everything you built is gone. As soon as I get back, I'll explain it was me that did this to your ranch, and I'll tell you why, so you'll understand. Someday when it all hurts a little less. And when Morrissey is hanging from a tree."

The flames continued to spread, their reach higher and broader as I stood there. I glanced down at the fire's base.

"You understand, don't you?" I looked up. My voice more like my own again, but softer. I waited for her, the one "her" I knew was in heaven and most likely watching what I'd done. The woman Adler married when I was six. Luke's mother, the woman who took me into her heart and raised me as if I were her own, the only mother I'd ever known.

I listened for some sort of assurance from her, strained above the crackling flames to hear the voice of the one person who surely understood what I was doing and why. I could imagine her, even after all these years, looking down at me—her soft brown hair, blue eyes, a half-smile I'd never forget. Luke was the best reminder of what she'd been like. He looked so much like her, even down to her not-so-tall stature, the opposite of me—his half-brother, the boy he resented for being so much like our father. I stared back at the flames, the heat burning my eyes. "It's okay, Ma. You know I'll make it up to Pop. Even to Luke, as soon as I get the chance."

Flames whipped around the windows as I waited and listened. I heard them eating up everything that said Duncan, everything all of us loved.

Pop kept buckets near the well he'd dug, not far behind me. If he were here, he'd be filling them. Luke would be condemning me, while Pop fought the fire and what I thought was the right thing to do. I turned…looking toward the pails that held far more than a mouthful of spittle as I heard the glass pop—

panes our father had been so proud of, and had protected from me and Luke when we were rock-throwing boys. They splintered and shattered in agonizing cracks. Endless explosions like a thousand gunshot wounds. That's how they would feel to Pop. I turned back toward our home. What used to be windows were now gaping holes, black and empty squares in a glowing house, all encased in a roll of smoke that plumed upward above a fiery red ball.

The sound of two boys broke above the crackling and the exploding of the panes, their mother's warnings trailing behind them. I heard footsteps, too, of Luke and me, running through smoke, the way we used to when we were young. I was always bigger and stronger. I could hold my breath and make it through to the clean air on the other side, while Luke staggered behind, coughing and sometimes crying as our mother shouted my name. "Rex, you stop that! Your little brother can't keep up with you. And what if you tripped and fell? Luke could never save you." Luke hated me for the games he loved but always lost. I don't know that he would have tried to save me if I fell, but I never took the chance he'd try and fail and walk away even more miserable than he already was. I also would never have let him succumb to the smoke. I stayed on my feet and ahead of him just enough to make him try harder. To turn him into Adler's son, the way I was and he wanted to be.

The smoke billowed upward above the curl it formed at the ground. It and the blaze beneath it were staggering—powerful—far more than I'd figured on in the dusky evening. I glanced across the land at the red rocks and hills surrounding what had been the Duncan homestead. It was late enough in the day I'd never pick out a rider coming to see what was happening. They'd be on me before I knew they were there, put a stop to me and what I was doing, or at least be able to describe me well enough Pop would be devastated. He'd buckle under the loss and betrayal before I had a chance to explain.

I glanced at the barn. I intended to burn everything. Nothing was to be left when I was done. The barn, then the smokehouse, the outhouse, and last of all the small shed, the place Ma always hid little treasures just for me, things no one else ever knew about or needed to see. Especially Luke. She buried them in an old tin, sometimes once a month, sometimes more often. As a boy, I'd dig them up and see what surprises she'd left for me. She'd watch, on occasion, and talk about them. She'd make me feel special when she explained how important those little treasures were. I hadn't dug into that dirt or touched the tin since before she died. I couldn't. But I would now. I'd retrieve that box and take it with me, finally look at the last bit of significance she may have set aside for her stepson. Burn the shed, and be gone.

Flames exploded inside the house, danced behind the empty windows as they gutted our home, consuming everything my father and Luke had left behind. The barn waited behind me. I turned and started toward the monstrosity Pop had been so proud of. Different sorts of memories lived there. Boy and man memories, pieces I'd never let Morrissey claim. I walked to the front of the barn, stopped near the door, and laid a hand against its rough, gray planks. "You'll never really be gone," I whispered, the heat from the house warming my back. "I won't let you." I pressed hard and ran the flat of my palm down the boards, splinters gathering in my skin like needles, each one an embedded memory. Something Morrissey could never have.

I stared at the gray slivers jutting from my palm, then swiped my hand across my trousers, fixing every sting as a permanent recollection. I gave the barn one last glance, then turned to the mound of kindling and bundles of dried and broken switchgrass I'd brought, toted and stacked an armload at each of its sides. I sprinkled gunpowder on each pile, a little more than I had at the house. Enough to catch, and do the job quickly. I circled the building, bent at each heap, and struck the flint until it sparked. As the powder ignited, I stood back, watched each bundle sputter, its grasses wilting like lit fuses, orange heat traveling up their stems.

The kindling began to glow, little flames climbing higher, but the barn stayed as it was—stubborn. It refused to catch. I ran a finger over the splinters in my palm. This building wanted to live forever. All of it, not just the little fragments under my skin. And it should. It was too striking to give in and die. I glanced back at the buckets. I could just let the house go, run around the barn and kick the burning kindling aside. I looked at what was left of our home, nothing more than a glowing frame in the waning light. Morrissey would keep his horse in this barn while he built a new house. I walked to each side of the barn, knelt, cupped my hands around the tiny flames, and blew.

"Enjoy living in ashes and dirt, Morrissey. It's far more than you deserve."

The barn caught and began to light up the sky, faster and brighter than the house had, turning our ranch into a beacon. Someone would surely notice. Another settler, even though far away, could spot a fire this size. Or maybe Morrissey, if he was around. He'd been lying low enough I hadn't been able to find him. But if he was close, and foolish enough to come here and try to stop me, I'd be glad, and I would have him. Make him regret pretending to be a ranch manager so he could steal into my father's funds. Morrissey would suffer. I'd make sure of it. Then I'd take him in. See that he hanged before I left for Kansas. The last place on earth I wanted to go.

"I need you to go up north, to Kansas. A place called Liberal."

The orders from my boss, Jim Handling, rang in my head—up north, to Kansas. I marched toward the smokehouse. If it wasn't for Jim's edict, I wouldn't be here now.

I scooped up and dropped another bundle of grass and kindling at the corner of the small building. I sprinkled the pile with gunpowder, lit it, and waited for it to catch. It sputtered. I was going to have to kneel again. "Not funny, Ma." I shot a glance at heaven, where the woman who had drilled repentance into me and Luke no doubt watched me drop to my knees with her little half-smile. I bent over the small flame, cupped my hands, and blew until it shot up close to my face. I rolled back on my haunches and watched it leap toward the broad surface of the smokehouse's dried wood and begin to climb upward.

The flame grew, creating an orange background to what I remembered from this afternoon. Jim, sitting at his desk, leaning back in his seat as I argued with what he'd said. "I have plenty of work here. I can't go to Kansas." I was looking not only for Matt Morrissey but also for a couple of other hoodlums who had swindled neighboring ranchers in the area out of all that was theirs.

"Turns out the work here might be tied to something bigger. A ring of thieves, by the looks of it." Jim leaned forward, stared up to where I planted myself at the opposite side of his desk. "Not just a couple of local crooks down here. Seems the same pattern's going on up north. Ranch managers somehow able to foot loans, take advantage of the owners, ruin their finances, and send them off penniless. Or in a casket."

"Let Kansas handle them." What I said was right, my kind of right, but not right for Jim. No one ever argued with him and won. He was the boss, his face a weathered roadmap of the work he'd done, proof of all he had accomplished in this section of Indian Territory, bringing it from a lawless piece of red dirt to a semi-civilized land. His way. A way that shaved a little off the edge of right to undo everything that was wrong. A way I always swore I'd never copy. Until today.

"I'll stay down here and catch this gang." I crossed my arms.

"There might be a main man somewhere. Maybe up there. Someone calling the shots, supporting these loans to floundering ranches. We need a man no one's seen before to go up there and nose around without looking like the law. That someone has to be you."

"Has to be me? It can be anyone. You have a half dozen good men you could send."

Jim scooted a newspaper across his desk and

tapped on a few lines of print he had circled.

I read what he had drawn a ring around. More of his little bit of wrong to make a right. "No." I shook my head, my voice sounding like I'd been gut-punched. "Nothing can make me do that."

And I'd meant it. The determination in what I'd said to him earlier today was still there as I backed away from my father's burning smokehouse. But the circle Jim had drawn was even stronger, tighter, like a rope looped all the way around me. Jim's staid expression and what he'd mandated turned everything inside me cold, even in the escalating heat. I slapped the back pocket of my trousers, tugged at the newspaper, the one Jim had shown me, until it came out. I tipped it toward the orange-and-yellow blaze, let the inferno illuminate the tiny print in Jim's circle. I re-read the words. Words that had sealed my father's ranch buildings' fate.

A gunshot exploded the air around me. Louder than Pop's window panes, and far more deadly. I dropped low, hunched down in the dirt, crumpling the paper in one fist while my other hand went toward the pistol in my holster. The echoing ring of the explosion faded. I waited, but no other shot followed. I half crawled, half ran to the woodpile, logs I had cut for my father late last year. I pressed low against the base of the pile, more splinters scratching through the shirt at my back. I stared into the dark, trying to see or feel who had fired the shot, hoping it was too dark for them to see me. I stayed low and to the far side of the pile, listening, waiting for the next round of gunfire, or a horse riding into the barnyard. The nose end of someone else's gun was never a place I liked to be, but I hoped it was

Morrissey's this time, if that's where I ended up. I'd have him, if so. The land lay silent; the only sounds the protests of my family home, the buildings succumbing to the fires I had set.

I glanced from where I crouched to the two buildings beyond me. The outhouse. And the shed with Ma's and my buried relics. Those buildings wouldn't mean much to Morrissey if I left them, but they meant everything to me. And Pop. And even to Luke. I studied the buildings' faces, weathered boards lit up with the orange glow of what was to come. Gunfire or not, those had to burn too. Even, and especially, the shed. I tore the newspaper into thirds. "No disrespect, Mrs. Howard." I stuffed one part, the part with what the widow had to say, into the woodpile. "Well, maybe just a tad of disrespect. No, make that a lot." I scraped the flint and steel. The newspaper caught, sucking the flame deep into the dry logs, the fire devouring Jim's ringed words.

"Wanted: Husband to co-own a ranch immediately. Purely business arrangement, and will be well compensated. Able to take orders. Contact Mrs. R. Howard, Liberal, Kansas."

Another shot split the air. A warning, if it was one of Pop's neighbors, a threat, if it was Morrissey. I hunkered even closer to the pile, snapped bark and twigs from the nearest logs, and fed them into the newspaper's flickers until flames sprouted and began to lick up the woodpile. I scuttled around the dark side of the wood to the outhouse and dropped low against its side. The shot had come from the same direction as the first. One man. Closer. Near enough to take me, but not close enough to identify me. No one was going to drop or find me in the middle of what I knew had to be done. I stuffed another section of the paper that held the widow's ad between two of the outhouse's boards, struck the flint hard enough it popped like a tiny gunshot, and lit it. "Come on," I whispered. Flames sprouted and devoured what was printed beneath the edict I hadn't been able to argue my way out of, sending red hot heat through my craw and up the edge of the splintered wood.

"You're the only single man I have." Jim's explanation roared louder in my head than the crackling of the outhouse. It had silenced me the way one well-aimed bullet would stop me now. At least Jim hadn't said what he could have—that I should have married years ago. Married Becky Landon. I'd meant to marry her. I'd wanted to. I just didn't get it done like I should have. Now she was Becky Carson.

But even not saying it, he and Mrs. Howard's blasted ad had set me wondering again if Becky was the first or second woman I'd lost by my own doing, since I never knew my real Ma or what happened. That wondering had fired right up as I stood in front of Jim's desk, praying he couldn't see the gnawing stuck in my insides.

"I'll make sure Mrs. Howard ends up with her ranch," he said, instead of what was worrying around in my head. "All you have to do is agree to the business arrangement until we catch the ring leader, if he's there. Just don't let her or anyone else know who you really are or what you're doing. When you're done, you can come back here."

Jim said everything was already arranged. Mrs. Howard was expecting me in five days. Five brief days that shortened the life of this ranch. Not enough time to find Morrissey so he could hang, not enough time for my family to have a chance of getting this place back, or for me to explain that burning it was the best thing to do under the circumstances. "You'll be married right away." Jim had said it the same way he gave any order: Here's your job, go do it. Not giving me enough time to make it right or say it was wrong.

"All she wants is a husband's name so she can keep her ranch. Seems her husband left the ranch's finances somewhat unclear when he died. Apparently died in some sort of accident. The bank doesn't want to leave the operation in a woman's name, even though she claims she's quite capable of satisfying them, were they to give her enough time. All you have to do is marry her so she can show your name to the bank. And like I said, when you've done your part in trying to locate this thief, we'll settle with her, sew it up tight as if she's still married to the fake name I'm giving you, so she can keep the place."

Jim's words, the thought of marrying some widow, jammed up my insides, turning them into ice. I glanced from where I crouched near the outhouse toward the shed, the last building still standing. I needed time. Enough to dig into the dirt in the back corner to get what had been hidden by the one woman who at least had wanted to stick around for me.

"Stop right where you are, or I'll shoot."

Tiny fissures snaked through the block of ice in my gut. I knew that voice as well as I knew my own. I heard the tremor in it, the sputter of a boy racing through smoke, the same childlike tone of my own voice earlier. He'd spotted an enemy burning down the

15

family home, even if it wasn't ours anymore. Luke. Why was he way out here instead of at the settlement, at the poor little house he and Pop were stuck in? Luke wouldn't understand what I was doing, even if I let him know it was me. Not while the flames were hotter than hell itself, the violence of the destruction we'd suffered lighting up the sky. I dropped to the ground and rolled, rolled beyond the next shot my brother fired.

"I said stop right there!" Luke's voice was tight, full of smoke, full of horror. "Stand up and face me like a man!"

Go home, Luke. Go away. I kept my head low and my face hidden, stayed to the dark as much as I could, crouched, and ran to the lone gum tree not far from the shed. Luke shot again. And missed again. Thank God Luke never was a good shot. Tomorrow Luke would report all of this to Jim. I'd be well on my way to Liberal by then. Too far away for anyone, especially Pop, to think it was me that had done this.

I stayed tight against the tree, gauged the shed, the distance from me to it with Luke somewhere in between. I rubbed my palm, the one I thought would hurt more than anything else until I heard my half-brother's voice, counting the steps to the corner where my stepmother would have last left that buried tin.

"Come out from there like I said. Slow and easy." Luke was near. Too near. The angst in his tone didn't tell me whether he was shooting at a villain or at the brother he'd always envied.

I dropped low and ran, ducked away from the fire's glow, and headed to the safety of the dark.

"Stop! I see you!"

I heard Luke behind me. Not just his voice, but his

boots, running in the dirt, his grunts of anger and breathlessness as he tried to keep up. I wouldn't fall. I never did. Neither would I stay just out of his reach to make him a little better. This time I ran and ran hard, but so did he. *Damn it, Little Brother, it's too late to be a hero now. Where were you when Morrissey was robbing Pop blind?* He shot again, wild as he ran, or maybe keener than I gave him credit for.

He stopped after that. Suddenly. The night was silent except for the fiery destruction behind us, and my own breath and boots as I ran.

"You won't get away with this, you know." He broke the silence and called from behind. I listened for "part-brother" as I ran. I didn't like the way he stopped. I didn't like how close that last shot actually came.

It was just me now, Luke still standing somewhere back in the dark. I could imagine him watching and listening as I disappeared in the night, then going back to the ranch and standing in the inferno that had been our home until nothing was left but that shed. And my tin box beneath the ground. Luke would cry even though he was twenty-six years old—it was in his voice when he told me to stop, in the tremor that weakened his threats. He'd stand there and cry just like I wanted to, but never would. Like Pop.

I slowed and glanced back. "I'm sorry, Little Brother." Something else he wouldn't accept or understand. I turned and ran the rest of the way to the pecan grove where my horse was tied—black as the night itself, but he and I always knew where the other was. Our trip to Kansas was going to be much faster than five days. Fast enough for me to disappear in case Luke thought it was me he saw. Fast enough to get done and get back as quick as I could.

I gripped the reins, and once I hit the saddle I turned my horse toward what was left of the family home. "I'll settle with you when I get back, Mr. Morrissey. You'll pay for every tear my brother is spilling right now, and all the heartache you've caused my pop." I tapped my horse's sides with my heels and spun him hard to the left, leaving the blazing ranch behind. "And I'll marry you, Mrs. Howard of Liberal, Kansas. But I sure don't want to."

Chapter 2

Shakespeare spoke of a deed without a name. I have a deed, somewhere. I need a name to make it mine. A man's name, and nothing else. ~Regina

Red curls fluttered across the front of my face, catching on my eyelashes and blocking what I could see of my son, of his rounded back as he knelt in the dirt. Twelve years old. My only child. And the reason the hard decisions I'd made had to be right.

"Jess..." I looped the ringlets behind my ear. He wasn't going to like what I had to say any better than I did. But it had to be said—now that we were down to two days.

I watched Jess as he smoothed the ground around his knees with the flat of one hand, and stood quietly as his narrow back flattened, stretching to plow clumps and clods aside, scooping them off the mound he was kneeling on—his father's grave, my husband's. Flynn Howard's.

He straightened once the lumps had been cleared. Both of us stared at ground now cleaner than the dormant fields scattered around our ranch, Jess's light brown hair, identical to Flynn's, swinging into place over his forehead and ears. With one hand he traced the edges of the boards that made up his father's marker, a simple wooden cross, unfortunately, all I could afford. I followed the course of his finger and read for the hundredth time in the three weeks since Flynn's death the dates I'd had carved beneath his name. February 16, 1851 to March 30, 1887. Thirty-six years, altogether. Old enough to die, yet still too young. What Flynn wasn't, was ready. And he hadn't made Jess or me ready, either. I stared at the dirt in front of my feet and shook my head. *Doggone you, Flynn.*

"Pa needs a better marker." Jess gripped the arms of the cross with both hands. "This one's not good enough for him. You can barely read his name or the years he was alive. It's like he's more gone than he already is." Long, thin arms stretched to the ends of the board, white showing on Jess's knuckles—emotion crowning the dedication I was determined my son would keep.

"We'll get a better one. Soon." Real soon.

Jess held onto the marker I knew Flynn would be ashamed of. He certainly would have spent for something grander if he'd planned for this. I would have spent more for him myself, gladly, if he'd ever let me know where our money was and how he tended to it.

"Ted said stone is better and lasts longer. He would help chisel Pa's name in it, if I asked."

I stared at my husband's name and thought of Ted Morgan and how quiet he had been the day we buried Flynn. Solemn, stolid, no expression or offer of support at all as he stood alongside me when they lowered my husband into the ground.

There never would have been a Ted here on our place if Flynn hadn't ignored my suggestions on how we could get our floundering ranch on its feet. Flynn's own efforts had failed, and my suggestions weren't what he wanted to hear, but when he stumbled onto Ted, he deemed it a stroke of good fortune and took him on as our ranch manager, swearing it was a miracle someone with Ted's experience would consider a small spread like ours.

Ted was compact and solid, slightly older than Flynn and me, and weathered in a way that bolstered Flynn's confidence Ted was capable in spite of his missing left hand. Lost it in a roping accident, Ted had explained, keeping the arm mostly out of our view. I learned later he'd cut it off himself. It was lose a hand or lose his life. "I trust him just because of that," Flynn told me when he related the story. Flynn had devoured Ted's every word, confident that a man who was willing to sever something significant to hold onto something grander, was a man he could trust with his ranch.

His ranch.

My ranch, now. Almost.

I cupped a hand at my brow and surveyed the piece of ground Flynn had bought and left behind. Left behind with enough complications I had a choice to make ahead of any tears and grief—either return to New York where we'd come from, penniless and in debt, or do the unthinkable in order to hold onto this place.

I chose the latter. I had a plan to manage the unthinkable.

Prairie swept around us, around my husband's grave where Jess knelt and I stood, bowing and waving in the wind, a dizzying swirl of grasses that never stopped moving. It made up most of what Flynn had bought and loved, less of it now than at the beginning, since Ted had convinced him field crops were the way to success. I looked beyond the immediate reedy flow at distant bare spots that interrupted the sea of blowing green—cold fields waiting for spring planting. Too many of them, in my opinion. All waiting for the first time for me to say what we would plant. And when. But most of all, and what Ted wouldn't like—if.

"Stone sounds good for your father's marker. What sort do you have in mind?" I looked down at my son.

Jess was on his haunches now, leaning back, tilting his head. "Has to be a smooth stone." He turned, straight hair swinging with the motion and falling into place over his brows as he looked at me. First at my feet, then up to my face, his mouth sealed shut by the time our eyes met.

"Well, we have lots to choose from around here." I dug my feet in near the edge of the dirt, holding onto my plan. "It should be easy to find one."

He shook his head, and craned his neck far enough back he could avoid what he didn't want to see. "No, Ma. Not just any old rock. It has to be big and last forever. Pa said this was Howard land from now on. Everything he bought and did was for me, for my kids, and then for my kids' kids. He had it all planned out, and I won't let anyone forget him." Jess turned from looking at my face back to the spindly cross. "The first Howard *man*."

His shoulders squared, the word "man" delivered with a punch. I joined him on the oval of dirt neither of us could get used to and laid the flat of my hand on the top of his head, then my fingertips as he tipped his head forward. Jess was twelve. He didn't need to know that the "everything" his father had bought amounted to this piece of land with a surprise debt hanging over it, and only rumors of there being more. He didn't need to hear that nothing was done, and not a thing taken care of. "There's a perfect stone for your father somewhere." My hand fell back at my side as Jess dropped his head even farther.

Jess did need to understand the predicament his father's death had left us in. And he needed to accept that what I was about to do to see us through it was the right decision. No matter what.

Two days. I glanced beyond the prairie at those pieces of ground Flynn and Ted had cleared for crops, stones turning up where they didn't want them, always causing trouble. We needed to find the right one for Flynn within two days, even though it had been three weeks since his death and in the flurry I hadn't been able to find or get my hands on anything else we needed. Things that were important and we were desperate for—like the money we'd brought from New York, and at least one deed.

It was Ted who suggested I talk to the bank before Flynn was even buried or grief had had time to set in, patting me on the shoulder without actually touching me, and insisting this was something that needed to be done. Flynn's death had been a shock, a horrible shock, his horse returning to the ranch without him one evening, his body found out on the trail the next day, a blow to his head on a rock.

Accidents happen, Flynn's banker, Mr. Gulliver, had tsked when I'd gone in at Ted's insistence. Mr. Gulliver added to my shock by saying Flynn's lands weren't mine, that bank policy and Kansas law forbid an unmarried woman to own property. Even a widow. *You'd best let all of the properties go, if you know someone to take them. We can extend a little leniency, give you a brief amount of time to get organized before you return to your family in New York. And of course, if you don't have someone who can take over your ranch, we'll handle that, too, since we possess the primary deed.* And he tsked again at the grievousness of my situation.

My name—I reminded Mr. Gulliver without the scream I felt roiling inside—was on the deed alongside Flynn's. We'd been on our ranch long enough to homestead it, even though we'd bought the land outright. I protested the law, argued the ridiculousness of it, asked why they held the deed, and why our money Flynn surely kept at the bank didn't account for something. Mr. Gulliver dismissed my arguments that day, going on to further dumbfound me with the news Flynn had no money, that he'd left his lands in financial trouble, borrowing against the acreage where we lived. Mr. Gulliver had no idea where or from whom Flynn was getting what little money he did to keep his loans alive, but it wasn't from the depleted account he'd once held at the bank.

"But we came here with an abundance of money," I exclaimed. And we had—all of our own, plus large contributions from his parents and mine—to secure and farm one piece of land…this ranch. Mr. Gulliver spoke over my floundering thoughts, over shock that was exploding in too many directions—the money we brought…was it gone? Kept at another bank, or in the tin box behind a hearthstone at our house, or somewhere else?

"Doesn't matter, anyway." Mr. Gulliver summed up my and Flynn's four years in Kansas. "No need to work yourself up when, as I said, it's not our policy to leave deeds in a woman's name." Deeds. Mr. Gulliver had said "deeds." He'd also said "lands and properties."

"Flynn bought more than just this ranch?" I plied Ted with more questions on the way home, my chest burning with tears that couldn't find their way out, tears that had too many reasons to be there.

He shrugged. "Must have. But I warned him not to."

I yanked open the tin box I'd already checked as soon as Ted brought me back to the ranch. I found it the same way I had the first time—empty. No money. No deeds. Ted had followed close as I'd scoured the house and the barn and found nothing in those places, either. Flynn hadn't said a word to me about owning anything else, especially other land, and he wouldn't have wasted our money, nor would he have lost it. Surely. He'd been a merchant back east, and he'd made the promise to himself, to me, and to our parents that we'd return to New York if ranching didn't work out. He'd spend only so much, then take us home with enough to restart him in his business and pay back those who'd invested in his dream. That was Flynn's plan. Before he died.

I glanced to the side of the nearest field—one I was letting go back to prairie so I could raise cattle instead of crops—and studied the house and barn Flynn had built when he began this venture. Flynn had never built a thing in his life until he came here, and it showed in their slack construction, obvious even at this distance. He'd been a businessman where we'd lived in New York—where we'd been introduced to each other by my father, married at his encouragement, and where we'd eventually given birth to Jess. It was Flynn's dream to ranch and his belief it would be profitable that had uprooted us and carried us all the way here four years ago. But it was my determination to stay that would keep us here now, as well as make us prosper, right where he'd planted us, not far from the small but growing town of Liberal, Kansas.

The wind teased my hair as I stared at Jess's back, and it wrested more red curls and strands from the leather strip I'd started using to tie it back only hours after Flynn was buried. One of my best combs, one of a pair Flynn had given me, lay out here somewhere, lost in this prairie after the service as I'd stood off to the side listening to Mr. Gulliver tell me he had good news—he had someone who would take over Flynn's properties so Jess and I could move on, return to New York City where we'd be taken care of. Mr. Gulliver had leaned close when he spoke, and rested a hand on my shoulder as he extracted Flynn's ranch from beneath my feet. *You just pack up your necessities, your fine apparel, and move back east to your real home and family. Lone, unmarried women aren't made to ranch, not even allowed to, especially an elegant woman like you.*

Elegant.

Ted had walked Jess away from us when Mr. Gulliver pulled me aside. I watched him and my son as Mr. Gulliver finished, caught Ted's glance back as I stood letting the banker's "good" news sink in.

"No." I'd said it with my eyes fixed on my son. Elegant wasn't the only thing I'd learned growing up. "My father's a banker, like you, Mr. Gulliver, but in

New York." I'd taken a step back and freed my shoulder from his touch. His genteel demeanor vanished as I looked at his face. "His attorney will review all of Flynn's financial paperwork and deeds for me. Send everything to him right away. Then you and I will talk."

Wild ringlets, freed from my leather strap, swiped across my eyes now the same way they had after Flynn's funeral, the wind ripping them loose that day from my arrangement of pins and combs. I'd let all of my finery go as I stood near Mr. Gulliver, instead holding onto the ranch and the four years we'd invested here. I'd learned my role here well, mastered what I needed to know and do while Flynn struggled to master his dream. I'd developed a knack, and I decided I'd use what I'd learned to turn Flynn's dream into a success as I stood on the prairie letting my pins and combs fall to the ground while listening to Mr. Gulliver and watching my son. Jess had stood in the prairie with Ted, halfway between our house and me, looking too much like Flynn, too much at home on a land that had done nothing but take. So far. That's when I'd said, "No," and sent Mr. Gulliver away.

I ran my hands over my head, corralling every lock I could as I thought of all that "No" had cost me in the past three weeks, knowing it was about to cost me and my son much, much more. I tipped my head forward as I held my curls back and loosened the leather to retie my hair. I twisted the rope of locks as I looked down toward my feet, at the toes of my deceased husband's boots stuffed full of socks so they'd stay on, worn leather tips peeking from beneath the bottom of Flynn's pants I had rolled up and cinched tight at my waist. His shirt billowed like a sail in the wind beneath my upraised arms, fluttering above where I had tucked it in his dungarees, and folded several times at the sleeves. Different from the finery I'd normally worn, dresses and as much elegance as I'd been able to manage while tending a ranch house, a garden, and barnyard chores. But not anymore. Jess had paled the first time I stepped out of our house in his deceased father's clothing instead of my nice dresses, while Ted had reddened, his eyes wide as I passed. I tugged the leather taut around my hair and shook my head. Larger changes than what I wore were about to come, and those two needed to be ready.

"Look at me, Jess. There's something we need to talk about."

Jess glanced up from the bare ground that circled us, oval like a rug around Flynn's boots and Jess's bent knees. He stared at Flynn's dungarees, then twisted in the dirt and staggered to his feet. "I know, Ma, and I already know what about."

"You do?"

"I do. I figured out what Pa would want me to do, and I aim to start doing it. He told me over and over he took care of everything ahead, and I just needed to watch and learn. I did that. And I'm going to do more as I take over being the man in this family. The first thing I'm going to do is get Pa a new marker. I'll find the stone all by myself, and Ted can help me chisel it. You can get back to what you're supposed to do." He glanced down at Flynn's pants and shirt. "The way you're supposed to do it."

I listened to Jess as I looked into eyes he'd inherited from his father. Blue eyes, dreamer's eyes that wanted things to go well. Smoothly, easily. Eyes that wouldn't fathom feeding Mr. Gulliver a string of stories to buy time the past three weeks. Eyes that couldn't grasp unexpected debt, missing deeds, lost money—or that in two days a man who had agreed to marry me so I could save this ranch would arrive.

Jess and I stood locked in silence. A silence I held against Flynn.

"I can do this, Ma," Jess said. "You don't need to do any of Pa's work…" He glanced down again. "Or wear his clothes."

"Jess, there's something you don't understand. Something even I didn't understand, at first."

Anything at all I can do for you now that you're on your own, you just let me know. The reverend who'd performed Flynn's service had approached and spoken to me here in the prairie after I sent Mr. Gulliver away.

I'd stared at the mound of dirt while the reverend made his offer, watched two neighboring ranchers shovel scoopfuls of Flynn's land on top of his pine box and pat it into place. I shook my head when the men finished, and then looked up into the reverend's face. "There's nothing, really, unless you know how a widow can survive out here."

"Well, the usual means, I suppose."

The fact he responded with anything other than a consoling pat on my shoulder and a sad shake of the head made me draw closer. "What usual means?"

"You'll have to remarry if you intend to stay on this ranch."

"Remarry?" That was the last thing I would do— add another man who wouldn't listen to a single idea I had, then leave me penniless and in shock, too overwhelmed to spare a moment for grief. I laughed after my outburst at the absurdity of the suggestion. It was an unladylike eruption, and I expected the reverend to do the same.

He responded as stoically as if he were still giving Flynn's eulogy, without any levity at all. "Performed many a quick wedding for widows left behind. And I do mean quick. Just let me know when arrangements have been made." He'd tipped his hat, then strolled away, leaving me alone with unthinkable arrangements fluttering in my mind.

Jess had to be told about those arrangements and the upcoming ceremony that was nothing more than a business deal. Far less civilized, even, than the pairing my father had suggested between Flynn and me. "I should have said this days ago."

He frowned. "Said what? I just said it all."

I glanced from his blue eyes back to the bare dirt beneath our feet. I wondered if Flynn knew, if he could hear, if he realized the mess he'd left me in. I considered stomping one of his boots to see if I could jar a reaction from him—a sign as to where our money was, what another deed might be to, whether he had known Kansas law wouldn't leave me the ranch if he fell off his horse and accidentally died.

Jess tilted his head, tall like his father, the same boyish features, but pinched tight, so tight he looked older than his twelve years. His hands, though, the balled fists at the ends of his long, thin arms, reminded me of myself. Determination, energy. A plan.

"It's the ranch, Jess. I have a plan."

"The ranch isn't for you to worry about, Ma. I just told you that. So quit acting like it's your problem. Pa never got the chance to show me everything, but I still learned a lot from him. I can figure out the rest. We'll be fine."

I bit my lip, thinking of what Jess may have learned from Flynn, methods that hadn't worked before and I intended to change anyway. "It actually is my job to worry, son. Things are going to be different from now on. Not exactly the same as when your pa was here. I'm going to test some new ideas…such as more cattle and fewer fields, hay instead of some of the crops your father tried."

Jess shook his head, his brows furrowing over the bridge of his nose. Ted's had furrowed also when I'd told him I wasn't buying seed from the neighbor. Ted, like Jess, but with a more mollifying demeanor, had suggested I not take on too much in my current state…or the state of the ranch. Neither one of them thought I should interfere with what they believed to be best. They didn't want my suggestions any more than Flynn had. Any more than my father had, either, when as a child I pored over numbers at his New York City bank and came up with bookkeeping strategies of my own. A smile was all the reward I received from him— the honor of being groomed as the next banker in the family going to my cousin Clyde. Clyde, who wrote me often behind my father's back, asking for advice.

Jess's furrow deepened. "Things don't have to be different. I don't like different. I don't like changes. I want everything to stay the way it is, the way it was before."

"I wish things didn't have to change, either, but they do. They would have to change anyway, even if your pa were still here. But now they have to change even more, and I want you to be ready."

"Have you talked to Ted? He knows what's best here. You should just let him take care of the big things while I keep learning."

I stared at my boy. According to Flynn, Ted knew more about ranching than any of us, but I knew from my garden this soil wasn't conducive to certain crops he suggested. It was a grass land, a dry land, a land that should support cattle. I shook my head. "Ted's not the boss of this ranch. I am."

Jess's eyes opened wide. "No...no, you're not the boss. That's not right."

"Listen to me, Jess. I need you to understand the changes we're going to make while I..." While I marry a perfect stranger, use his name to secure this ranch, then borrow or find enough of Flynn's money to pay him off and send him away so I can keep his name and this land for the two of us. An arranged parting. It was drawn up in the papers the stranger had agreed to. I swiped my hands down the front of Flynn's dungarees. "While I..."

"That's not how Ted said things would be now that Pa's gone. He didn't mention any changes."

"What? Ted? He talked to you about this?"

"He did. Especially when you became different. You know, when you started acting more like Pa than yourself. And looking like him, too."

"Okay, Jess. Just tell me what Ted said."

"He said boys make good sons and women make good wives. If I did my part and kept learning to ranch, you'd eventually get back to doing yours, and he'd fill in where we lacked. Where Pa used to be."

"No." There was that word, and I'd said it again.

Twice out here on my prairie in the past three weeks. "Ted is our help." Help I'd informed him I couldn't afford, but he insisted he would stay. It wasn't to "fill in where we lacked" that he'd offered me. He'd said he was doing it for Flynn, holding up his end of the bargain from when Flynn hired him on, until this ranch business was settled. "He's here to help, but Ted can't fill in. Not like we need."

"What we need is for you to cook, keep the house, go back to looking like my ma again. Ted said nothing graces a ranch better than a woman who's a lady."

"Ted said that? After your father was…gone?"

"No, Ma, before. But he's still right."

I stared at my son. Ted had offered me gardening and barnyard advice I didn't really need before Flynn's death, but he'd never mentioned roles he deemed unsuitable for women. His simple, "You should talk to the bank," I'd taken as evidence Ted recognized me as his new boss. When I'd turned to him that day at the bank, glanced to my side at the one-handed man Flynn had trusted, Ted had returned my look with a grim nod. I'd taken that, again, as saying I was the same as Flynn to him.

"Listen, Jess. A lady can grace a ranch in more ways than one. And, I'll have you know, I'm still your mother and Ted's boss for as long as he's here, no matter how I dress."

"As long as he's here?" Jess backed away. "Everything's changing. Now you're saying Ted's gonna go. I don't know who you are anymore."

"I didn't mean Ted's leaving. I offered to let him go if he wanted, but I've never asked him to." Yet.

"You can't ask him to. Pa hired him. You're not

the real boss." Jess twisted on the heel of his boot, spun in the direction of our house, then paused and glanced back. "I lost my pa, and it feels like I've lost you, too. I don't want Ted gone or more things to change. I want everything back the way it was. Now."

Jess raced across the prairie, rounded the house his father had built, and disappeared. The closest we'd ever get to the way things were before was for me to marry the perfect stranger who would be here in two days. A man I wanted nothing to do with, but who had agreed to my terms of letting me have his name and taking orders from me as long as he was here. I stared at the house and barn where Jess had run. If my boy wanted to raise a family on this ranch someday, and Ted wanted a job, they had to accept what I was going to do and the way I was going to do it. In two days. And from now on.

I stared at the ground. *Doggone you, Flynn.*

Chapter 3

Kansas dirt is brown, but I still see red. Red flames and red dirt. My father's life burning all the way to the ground. ~Rex

"That-away, mister." The farmer pointed to his left, a long forearm sticking out from what remained of a tattered sleeve. He made Kansas look even less like a place I wanted to be. I turned the direction he aimed his finger, toward a house that looked near broken-down. Maybe old. Maybe the widow was, too, making getting here two days early something I might regret. "Mrs. Howard lives that-away a short piece."

I gazed down a long narrow strip of dirt, beaten bare by hooves and wagon wheels, that stretched between where I sat on my horse and the place that was to be my new home. Temporarily.

"She's recently widowed. Nice service." The farmer dropped his arm to his side. "You kin?"

"Sort of. Thank you for your help. Obliged." I tipped my hat to the farmer's questioning nod and nudged my horse the direction the man had indicated, wishing this weary animal would refuse to go a step further. "Not really all that obliged." I muttered it so the farmer couldn't hear as my horse dragged one foot in front of the other and headed Mrs. Howard's way.

I leaned forward and patted my horse's neck. He

was a trooper, even though for once I wished he wouldn't be, and he was warm. We were both tired. His head bobbed up and down with each step while mine lolled from side to side. Tired and bored. Kansas was flat, flatter than what I was used to, with every direction offering up the same scenery.

"There ain't even a fit place to hide around here." I patted my horse's neck again. "Or a gully we could dip into to turn tail and run." I glanced behind and felt the wind on the back of my neck instead of my face for a change, a wind that hadn't stopped whistling since the terrain had stopped changing. I gazed where we'd come from, toward the southeast, back to red dirt and red rocks, where no widow woman would interfere with what I really needed to do.

The farmer's arm, long and thin, waved at me from the side of the road. He stood where I'd talked to him, his hand held high as he watched me go. I lifted a hand and waved back. *No, I haven't lost my way.* I dropped my arm and twisted forward in the saddle again, the wind once more against my face. "Like I said, ain't no place to hide around here." I tugged the brim of my hat low over my forehead.

From beneath the hat's lip, I peered at the brown swath of dirt stretching ahead. I loosened my jacket. It was warm for spring, almost too warm for early afternoon. I judged by the sprouts of grasses in unripe shades of green that Kansas springtime wasn't much different from what I was used to south of here. Just more of it. These young blades were spindly and waved like the farmer had, from both sides of the road, flowing the way I always imagined sea waves would if I ever saw an ocean. "Mrs. Howard most likely has cattle," I said to my horse. "Some of this grass and a couple of those patches of brown dirt might be hers." I never much cared for brown. I preferred red. Red dirt. I tugged my hat a little lower. Red flames. Their crimson heat and my brother's voice still dogging me. Both had chased me all the way from Indian Territory to here. Made me ride foolish. Hard and fast to brown dirt and flat land to marry a widow woman I didn't even know. Didn't want to, either.

I dug beneath the flap of my saddlebag and extracted a small flask. "Courage" caught my eye, the sun glinting off the word I'd scratched into the flask's side the night Becky Landon married and became Becky Carson instead of Becky Duncan, the name I thought she'd end up with. Now I was heading to a woman I knew wasn't going to be with me long even before I got started. "The Parting," she'd called it in her written description of our arrangement, according to Jim. I unstoppered the flask and took a small swig. I never needed Courage when I faced outlaws. I closed the top and dropped Courage back into my bag.

I slid my fingers through my horse's wiry black mane, the section nearest my saddle horn. "It's your fault we're early, you know. You ran too fast. Seeing Luke was hard on both of us." Especially there in the middle of our burning ranch. Seeing him that way made me ride as hard as I could so I wouldn't turn back and tell him he deserved to be left standing there shooting crazy and crying. He should have been smart enough to see what Morrissey was up to and do something about it. He was the one living on the ranch with Pop at the time, not me. I'd been long gone, giving Luke space to grow into something on his own, while I kept contact with our father, sending him an occasional letter from wherever I could. Blast that Luke. If I'd turned back that night I would have needed to punch him. For both of our sakes. And when he got up, his aim probably would have been better. Maybe I would have let it. I dug my fingers deeper into my horse's wiry hair. "It's just a couple of days. Mrs. Howard shouldn't mind. Two days early means two days sooner we get finished so we can go back home." *To what's left of it.*

I let the reins sag alongside my horse's neck as the house and barn became plain in my view. He moseyed at his own pace down the narrow strip of dust. Brown dust. The house was small. It wasn't old after all, but it looked weary, the barn a mite bigger, but no better. "I'd say we're at the right place." It looked like a woman had built it and was struggling to keep it up. "Has to be the widow Howard's home."

I made a low sound in my throat at the entrance to the homestead. My horse stopped, and I surveyed what lay ahead. A house, an outhouse, and a barn. That was all I could see, possibly all she had. A fence swayed around the nearside of the barn, barely substantial enough to be used as a corral, its posts struggling to hold upright. The barn itself was crude, nothing like my father's…the one I'd burnt to the ground…an act that might do this one a favor. I shoved my hat back and scratched where the band had been. This barn was not only small, it was built with wooden planks so uneven that gaps rippled between each board. It looked like a row of bad teeth, the kind meant for whistling or straining soup. I tugged my hat forward again and settled it back into place. At least the barn was suitable for sleeping in decent weather. I'd be gone by winter, so making that my bedroom for the next few months suited me just fine.

I studied the house next, a square, squat building surrounded by dirt. More brown dirt. The main level was small, and what appeared to be an upper berth, even smaller. Both buildings and the outhouse blended into the ground around them. "Stark. That's the word for this place." This place needed some life. Mrs. Howard truly needed a man. One who wasn't getting paid behind her back to be with her.

I made a clicking sound. My horse dragged first one hoof and then the other through the dirt, heading straight for a trough, a crude wooden structure beneath the mouth of a pump that stood between the barn and the house. "Thirsty?" I asked as we reached its edge and stared down into the trough's bone-dry bottom. "You're going to stay that way for a bit, it looks like." I threw my leg over the bundle tied behind my saddle, lit on the ground, and slid the bridle and bit from my horse's head. "Hang on. I'll pump you a drink. Pray this thing holds water."

"Mind telling me what you're doing?"

The voice came from behind. It was young, but cracking the way a boy's did when manhood was knocking at his door. I angled my arms out to the sides, let the boy see both hands. At the age I guessed him to be, it was wrong to trust that innocence still ruled. When manhood was that close, I could just as easily turn and look down the barrel of a rifle as into a freckled grin.

"My horse is pretty dry. Haven't seen much of a stream for hours, so I thought I'd get him a drink before I said hello." I kept my back to the boy, and my hands in plain sight. The boy said nothing. I waited and listened, not sure whether I'd hear a welcome or the click of a hammer being pulled back. My horse turned from nudging the dry wood and looked toward the barn. He tossed his nose into the air, gave a dry nicker, then swung back to the trough. "I was looking for the Howard place. If this isn't it, I'll be on my way. I didn't know of any boy supposed to be here. I mean, young man. You a hired hand, or am I at the wrong ranch?"

The boy's shadow appeared in the dirt to my left. Long and lean, easing my direction until it stopped. "I work this ranch, but not as a hired hand," the boy said, his voice solid this time. "I'm Jess Howard."

"Nice to meet you, Mr. Howard." I kept my tone level, gnawed the inside of my cheek. A boy. A woman and a young boy. Luke would get a chuckle out of that. He'd laugh at what a misfit I'd be again. All the useless plans I'd laid out for him back then just as useless with another boy now. There was no mention of a son in what Jim had told me. Or even a little brother. Surely Jim wouldn't have omitted a fact like that. Mrs. Howard might have, though. The woman must be a liar.

The pump let out a squeal. I turned to the side, slow, to where the boy stood lifting the pump's handle. He was tall and slender, straight brown hair flopping forward on his face. His build and strength reminded me of myself at that age, but the childlike look on his face was too much like Luke. The soft way Luke had looked when he didn't know I was watching.

"Thank you." Water dribbled from the spout, a trickle that soaked into the dry wood of the trough. My horse dipped his head, nuzzled the damp wood, then stuck his nose under the growing stream. "He's mighty thirsty." I nodded toward the horse, and let my hands fall against my sides.

The boy pumped harder. Water began to pool in the bottom of the trough. The breeze around us carried the squeal of the pump and the greedy slurps of my horse. I wanted to ask where Mrs. Howard was. Not that it mattered much, now. As far as I was concerned, this arrangement was over. If she had a son, this wasn't the deal I was signed on for. I was bad with women and worse with boys.

"What's his name?" the boy asked. The squeal slowed.

"What?"

"Your horse. What's his name?" Jess Howard looked at me, the sort of serious curiosity only boys could have.

"I never named him. Seemed like a wasted effort for an animal I just use for work. I mean, to ride." I looked down at the water filling the trough.

The boy pumped harder. Water surged until my horse tossed back his head and nuzzled my shirt. The wet circle he left on the front revived the smell of burning wood and old smoke. Of my father. Of Luke.

The boy stopped; the squeal disappeared. "There are things we do just because we have to, and others happen whether we want them to or not. But no matter what, giving and knowing a name is right. It's a sign of belonging."

I glanced at the boy. This had to be Mrs. Howard's son. Death was in his stare, regret in his words. The same vacancy that had devoured me and Luke when his mother died. I extended a hand. "My name's Ben. Ben Miller. I'm glad to meet you, Jess Howard."

Jess stepped away from the pump, walked to the other side of my horse. He put a hand on the horse's neck. "We have another horse here. Just one." The boy paused, chewed his lower lip as his hand ran down my horse's neck. "I call him Boss because he belongs to our ranch manager. I'd call this horse Walter, if I was you. It sounds like water, and he sure does like to drink." There was a smile somewhere in Jess's gaze. I leaned around Walter's head and took the boy's free hand.

"Walter it is. We're both glad to meet you."

Jess smiled, still caressing Walter's neck. "Why did you say you and Walter were here?" he asked.

"I didn't say." Ben Miller was the fake name Jim had told me to use. The boy hadn't flinched when I said it. Hadn't shown any sign of having heard it before. Clearly Jess knew as little about me as I did about him. "I'm…"

Jess's expression changed. He dropped his hand from Walter's neck and the other from my grip. He peered around the horse's nose, off toward the prairie.

I turned and glanced to where the boy stared. Over the small rise someone was walking. A slow and laden step coming our way. A man, by the look of the trousers, except they were cinched tight at the waist. They were far too large for him, and billowed at the hips. Even the shirt was too big, angling down behind the belt in a tight vee. With men like that on the ranch, no wonder Mrs. Howard needed help.

"That one of the hands?" I glanced back at Jess.

The boy snorted. "If she was a hand, I'd fire her. Send her back east so she can remember who she is."

"She?" I turned back around. The figure was

closer. Near enough I could see the hair now, a cloud of wisps and loose red curls escaping whatever knot she had it gathered in behind her head. Red. "Is that how women dress in Kansas?"

Jess snorted again. Louder this time. "That's no Kansas woman. That's my ma."

I'd never seen a woman in men's clothing before, and getting a closer look didn't appeal to me. I latched onto Walter's bridle and slid it back over his head. I'd rather face Jim, tell him the Howard situation didn't work out, and confess I'd burned my family's ranch to the ground, than get yoked with a woman in man's clothing, especially a woman that thought nothing of telling a lie. Mrs. Howard slowed as I watched her. She must have spotted me and Walter. I glanced back at her son, who was scowling at her approach. I considered leaving Courage with him. "I'm not supposed to be here after all. I need to get on down the road."

"Me, too," he responded. There was boyish determination in those eyes. It mingled with the hurt, pointing him places I could tell he wasn't ready to go.

"You're leaving, too? You work somewhere else besides here?" I saw then what I hadn't before. A small bundle lying in the dirt behind Jess. A tablecloth tied in a knot around whatever it was he thought he was going to need. I remembered tying one myself once. The night I left home to become a Ranger.

"We got more than what you see here. I know we do. More land, I'm betting. I aim to find it, if so, and if it needs worked, then I'm gonna work it. Myself." He turned and bent in one easy movement, the bundle he'd tied swept up off the ground and pinned under one arm.

I glanced back to where his ma was crossing the

prairie. She was hurrying now, tearing through grass too thick for her small stature. She was coming after one of us, and it was probably her son. I recalled that sort of motherly devotion. It was powerful, and it was coming our way. "Guess maybe Walter could use a little tending to, if you don't mind. Then I'll go." I looked back at Jess, extended the reins his direction. "Can you spare a minute, before you head out, to give me a hand?"

She was getting closer. I saw it in his eyes along with, "Dang," the younger version of the word I felt like saying. Neither one of us was going anywhere right now, and neither one of us wanted to stay.

Chapter 4

I have a boy who won't listen and a ranch manager who can't stay put. That man coming to marry me in two days had better know how to do as I say. ~Regina

The breeze turned my hair into a thousand whips. I ran a hand up my forehead, cupping the curly mass above my brow, and the other up from the base of my neck to corral what my leather strap seemed incapable of holding. My hands just weren't big enough to grasp the bulky rope of hair and retie it while I raced across the prairie toward my house. That wasn't Ted standing in our yard, and that wasn't his horse. It was some stranger, tall and dark like the animal next to him, watchful like the sort of men Ted had warned me about now that I was alone. I scanned the area around the barn and house, searching for Jess, praying Ted's accounts of local marauders had sunk into my boy.

"Drat!" I flung the leather strap into the grass, my red curls blowing free the way they wanted, billowing around my face as I ran, squinting between them at the man poised near our watering trough. I looked past him, around what I could see of the barnyard, wanting to spot Jess, yet not. Not out in the open where the stranger could see him, also. Blast Ted for not being there. Every time I sent him to Liberal lately, seemed he was slower and slower coming back. I had let it go, figuring we all needed a little time to heal. But I'd put a stop to it as soon as he got back, or he and this stranger both could take to the road.

The intruder didn't move as I plowed his way, the breeze raking the grass to the side, making it impossible to run in Flynn's oversized boots and pants. I glanced toward the house. If that man wasn't standing there staring at me, I could slip that way, duck inside, and grab Flynn's gun from near the front door—the place Flynn had always insisted we keep it, just in case.

I'd pondered these moments after Ted's accounts of hoodlums preying on women and children, rehearsed in my mind what I would do to protect us. Moments like this weren't supposed to happen when Ted was gone and I was out in the prairie and our only weapon propped where Flynn said it should be. *Doggone you again, Flynn.* The man looked too strong for me to take on without it. There were no trees between me and him, no chance to grab a fallen limb to take with me. I kicked through the web of prairie as he continued to watch me. God, don't let this be one of those fellows who thrives on trouble. Let him be some weary traveler, some woman's good husband who'll take a rest and then be on his way. Quick.

The black horse shifted, repositioned, and tossed his head to the left. The stranger shifted with him, and lifted the reins. I stopped. He was leaving. Thank God.

Before the black of the horse or the black of that hat had moved very far, my son appeared, Jess's fairer hair and his shorter stature both in stark contrast to the two he stood next to. One of my boy's hands ran up and down the animal's face, while the other reached for the reins. The black hat gave him a nod, turned, and glanced at me, then started toward the horse's other side.

"Jess! No!" My voice sailed away as if it was nothing but air, its sound too thin and too shrill to be heard over the Kansas wind. "Jess!" I rose to my toes, cupped my hands around my mouth, and shouted again as the man stopped at his horse's nose. I dropped to the flat of my feet and called again, the wind carrying off my screams. "Just let him go, Jess. Let him get on that horse and go." I willed him from where I stood. Silently, this time. Jess laid a hand on the reins. *Lord, if that boy isn't going to pay any attention to me, I pray he at least uses my good sense more than Flynn's good manners.* Jess and the stranger walked away, leading the horse toward the barn. "Jess!" The two of them and the horse disappeared inside.

I ran again, Flynn's boots sloshing on my feet, heavy and coming loose as I plowed through more grass. I hadn't run since I was a girl. Just like I hadn't learned to ride, or planned a crop, or figured out what to look for in a good cow or horse. Until Flynn left me on my own. I tugged up on the front of his dungarees, pulled them as high as I could to lengthen my stride. When at last I broke free of the edge of the prairie, I stumbled through the rectangle of dirt that was wired off to be our garden, hurried across the bare yard between the house and the barn, and stopped just outside the barn's open door, where I heard his voice— the stranger's voice—rumbling over my panting.

"That's a good way to end up with blisters…"

I dragged one more large breath into my burning lungs, stepped inside the barn's doorway, and stood as tall as I could. Latching onto the pitchfork at the wall beside me, I headed across the dirt floor toward Jess and the man.

The stranger dwarfed me in muscle and height, tall and lean, the wear and ruggedness of the outdoors on his skin and in his nearly black eyes as he took in every step of my advance. This was no woman's good husband. I planted the pitchfork's prongs in the dirt floor and faced the two of them.

"...if you hold it wrong." The stranger's voice, deep with the resonance of a man who'd weathered a few storms, faded as he stared at me, his last few words thinning to a whisper.

I glanced at Jess, then back to the stranger. The man was even more daunting than I'd guessed from a distance. He looked hardy, though handsome beneath the wear and tear and pinkish-brown dust I could see. Handsome didn't matter. It was his frown I didn't like. I gripped the pitchfork's handle tighter.

"Ma, what are you doing with that? I told you I'd take care of things around here." In four strides Jess was in front of me. He wrapped one hand close to mine around the fork's handle, a curry comb in his other.

In that one brief moment when my son's hand was safe next to mine, I glanced behind him at the stranger's unsaddled horse, at the faint grooves in its hair where the comb had been. A pack lay on the dirt floor to the side, pushed up against the low wall where a saddle I didn't recognize was slung over.

Flynn's good manners were clear on Jess's face as he freed the pitchfork's handle from my fingers. His warmth left my hand, a scowl that didn't know any better remaining behind. I tossed my head back as he carried the fork to the barn door. "I'm Mrs. Howard.

48

Regina Howard. I see you've met my son. This is our ranch, so I suppose you'll be on your way soon." The handle hit the wall as Jess stood it where it had been. I lifted my chin higher and stared up into the stranger's face.

The stranger gauged me the same way I scrutinized bags of flour. His brow puckered as his eyes traveled from my hair all the way down to Flynn's boots, his mouth twitching when his gaze passed over Flynn's shirt and pants.

"And your name is?" I stepped out of the man's gawk, made my way around his horse to where his saddle was slung. Flynn's spot, the place he'd always kept *his* saddle, right outside the first stall. I stared at the area that had always been Flynn's. I'd sold his horse for Jess's sake, never announcing I would, or explaining myself afterward. I didn't think Jess could ever ride the horse that had thrown his father. Even I couldn't. No one had touched these areas since. Not Jess. Not even Ted. No one would, not even after I replaced Flynn's horse with another. As soon as I had the money.

I placed a hand on the wood near the stranger's saddle, tapped the worn leather with a finger, as Jess headed our way. Jess stepped alongside the horse and began to glide the comb down its back.

"It's Ben, Ma. This is Ben Miller. He thought he was supposed to be here, but decided he was wrong. I'm tending to his horse, Walter, before they head on down the road. Comb him good, then put him in that stall over there and let him have some hay and water." Jess didn't look at me while he spoke. He was studying his hand and the position he held the comb—evidently to ward off blisters—while he curried the horse. "Ben said he'd show me how to check the hooves, too."

I stared at my son, watched a diligence I hadn't seen before, especially not in the past three weeks...stared until Ben was there, that is—standing right in front of me, blocking what I could see of Jess. Ben swallowed one of my hands in his and held it tight, mine disappearing in his large clasp. "Ma'am." That deep voice was back, one that would be able to make itself heard from out on the prairie.

I looked down at his hand, the way it closed over mine. Big and strong, with weathered skin that pricked against my own. I couldn't believe he was here. I yanked back with my arm, but he held tight. Ben Miller. He wasn't supposed to arrive for two more days. "But..."

"You're surprised." Ben's grip tightened even more. I winced, but kept it on the inside where he couldn't see it. I tried again to wriggle loose as a half-smile stretched one side of his mouth, the sort of smile I was certain shouldn't be trusted. "I'm surprised, too." The set of Ben's jaw, the look on his face...the stare that traveled over his shoulder to Jess—his surprise. I gave my hand a harder yank and pulled free.

"You know each other?" Jess turned our direction. I leaned to the side and peered around the tall obstacle in front of me to see Jess's hand fixed on the horse, and his brows fixed in a frown.

"Mind taking Walter out to the corral for some hay, instead of in here?" Ben stepped aside, lifted his hat and ran a hand through the darkest hair I'd ever seen. Hair that didn't flutter back into place the way Flynn's would have. Neither did it spiral upward in a coil like mine. Ben's hair was somewhere in between—dark and thick, undaunted by the long fingers combing through it. "He's probably hungry after hieing it like he did."

"Hieing?" I looked from his hair to his face. "That's not a word," I sputtered, expecting Jess to be surprised, too.

"Hightailing. 'Hie' means to hightail it." He turned to Jess as I opened my mouth to correct him. "I'll pay you for the feed and the trouble."

"Sure thing." Jess sprang with more enthusiasm than I'd seen even previous to the past three weeks. He took Walter by the halter and was gone, my "yes, you can" or "no, you can't" not even out of my mouth.

I watched my son disappear through the back of the barn. When he was gone, when the back end of that large black horse had disappeared with him, I wheeled to Ben. To eyes as dark as that hair that was back under his hat. Not just dark in color but also in tone.

"You're early." I spit the words. "I specifically said when you could arrive, and I had a reason for that particular day." I nodded the direction Jess had gone. "That was my reason. He needed to be ready, time to heal and to understand why you were coming. If you had arrived on the day we'd agreed, he would have been prepared, and I wouldn't be in a predicament now." Maybe. I stared at Ben, waited for him to apologize and promise he'd pay more attention from now on. He stared back, his dark eyes boring straight through me. I crossed my arms. "My advertisement was clear. I said a husband who could take orders. Maybe now you can see why that was so imperative."

"Imperative?" He frowned.

"It's a real word, as opposed to 'hie.' It means

vital. Important."

"Oh. I see. Guess you have your words and I have mine." He took a step back, his gaze never leaving my face. "I appreciate the surprise I gave you by showing up early, Mrs. Howard, but I consider that minor compared to the surprise I had, having a boy sprung on me."

"That boy…Jess…is not a surprise, and he wasn't sprung on anyone. He's *my* son, so he's none of your concern. He isn't a part of our arrangement."

"He has a name, something I've already learned your boy sets store by. He's here. And he's a young fellow with a load on his mind, something I guarantee I'd be no help with. He's a part of whatever arrangement you get yourself into, ma'am, this particular one no longer involving me."

"I'm the one who initiated this arrangement, and I'll be the one to say when it's done. It's my ranch, after all."

Ben was tall, and he felt even taller as he took a step closer and leaned my way. "It takes two to bind a contract, and since I've just withdrawn, your arrangement is null and void. And just so you know, you can thank your lucky stars I'm not staying to marry you, because I take surprises a lot better than I take orders." His eyes stayed on mine until his gaze traveled from my face down to my boots. "And wearing trousers doesn't make you any more suited to giving orders than wearing a skirt would make me fit for giving birth."

My nails dug into my palms as I rolled my hands into fists. A word I'd heard Ted say when a pail slid off his bad arm came to mind. The word was immoral, but probably not too immoral for Ben Miller. "Just so you know, Mr. Miller, I've been running this ranch for three weeks now, in pants. I find skirts get in the way of things you'd probably be surprised I can do."

The half-smile returned. "I won't argue that. Skirts surely do get in the way." Ben straightened and slapped his hat tighter on his head. "Been my experience, too. Fortunately, neither one of us has to put up with one, since you can keep right on doing things the way you have been. I'm giving you an early parting. I'm leaving."

My nails dug deeper. I stretched Mr. Miller's way. "I told you, this is my arrangement, and I decide when you leave, so don't think you can just ride away before I get the chance to throw you off this ranch. And it just so happens I was about to tell you to go, so you are hereby free to take your leave. Get out!"

There was no wind in the barn to sweep my words away, but still he just stood there as if he hadn't heard a thing, gauging me again, until he tipped his head forward and touched the brim of his hat. "Good luck to you, Mrs. Howard." He wrapped a hand around the horn of his saddle, a hand as tan and weathered as the leather he yanked off the rail. With the saddle in one hand, he scooped his pack off the barn floor with the other, tall and sure of himself, as he headed Jess's way.

"You're right that it's good I found out what sort of man you were early on. I had the perfect plan, and thank God I saw…"

"Mrs. Howard?"

I stopped. Ben continued his stalk toward the rear of the barn, as I turned to the voice behind me. "Ted? You're a little late, I'll have you know."

Ted stood to one side of the barn's wide doorway,

reins swaying from his good hand to his horse behind him. "Someone here to see you."

Mr. Gulliver stepped into the doorway and past Ted, stopping just inside the barn, looking every bit as fancy as he did at the bank. Or had at Flynn's funeral. "I hope this isn't a bad time. I ran into your manager, here, in town, and asked if you were home." Mr. Gulliver nodded at Ted, but his eyes weren't on him. Neither were they on me. His gaze traveled over the top of me, to the man who was supposed to be getting his horse and leaving.

I watched Mr. Gulliver's eyes and waited, giving Ben enough time to excuse himself and go retrieve Walter from Jess. Nothing came from behind me. Not a word, even his footsteps had stopped. By the silence in the barn, and by the direction of Mr. Gulliver's gaze, I knew Ben was still there. "Quite honestly, Mr. Gulliver," I said loudly enough to draw Flynn's banker's attention to me, "this isn't the best time. I'll come into town in a day or two, and…"

The sway left Ted's reins as he moved alongside Mr. Gulliver, looked from me to the man behind me, and stiffened. "Mrs. Howard's got business to attend to. We got a ranch to run. You leaving?"

"I had some business here, myself." By the resonance of Ben's voice, I knew he still hadn't moved.

"If it's done, kindly head on down the road. Mrs. Howard don't need no more troubles." Ted stepped more to the side, even closer to Mr. Gulliver, leaving a wider space in the barn's doorway for Ben to go.

"Ted, I'm handling this man." I caught the bulge of Ted's jaw as he glanced from Ben back to me, understanding far better than he did that seeing a stranger come and go was less upsetting than if I'd had to tell him this stranger was staying so I could marry him. I turned to Mr. Gulliver. "And I'll conduct any business you have for me in Liberal, at your bank. Not here, not now. As you can see…"

"There isn't enough time to wait until you come to town, and I can see it's a good thing there isn't." Mr. Gulliver's eyes were on me now, traveling from Flynn's boots to his dungarees, up to his shirt, and stopping at my loose hair. "Mrs. Howard, your husband would turn in his grave if he saw what this ranch has done to you. This won't do at all, so out of respect for the deceased, I'm right in saying that the new owner of this ranch is ready to take over. You and your son can pack up and be on your way to lives you're much more suited to."

"New owner? But I told you I was…"

"You told me lots of things, none of which matter in the eyes of Kansas law. You're out of time, I'm afraid, and clearly out of your realm. We've been very lenient, bending the law for you, and it's at the breaking point now. Breaking the law is something my bank just won't do." Mr. Gulliver had that tsking sound as he spoke, along with a slow shake of his head I didn't for one second believe was out of concern for me.

I stepped between him and Ted, tired of this man robbing me of the very ground Flynn was buried in. "Stealing a ranch from its rightful owner is breaking a law. Have you even sent copies of the paperwork to my father's attorney like I told you to?"

"If you're referring to yourself as the rightful owner, you're not." Mr. Gulliver barely concealed a twitch I wouldn't be surprised was the beginning of a sneer. "Women can't be entitled to land, no matter what the deed says. The new owner for your ranch is…"

"A man. That's what the law says, and the new owner *is* a man. He's right here, in fact." I spun in the dirt, looked into the dark eyes of Ben Miller, who'd made the mistake of standing in my barn a minute too long. I marched his way, daring him to move as I advanced. "You can keep your saddle over there." I tipped my head to where Ben's saddle had just been. Flynn's spot. I snaked a hand around Ben's arm and locked him in place as I turned to Mr. Gulliver, and the gaping stare of my ranch manager. "Meet my new husband. Or he will be soon. Probably tomorrow."

"Ma?" Jess. I heard the strain in his twelve-year-old voice. I turned to an even more sickly strain on his face.

"Jess…"

He was gone before I could say more, the slender back of my son leaning into a run that would take him even farther from me than earlier today when he left me standing at his father's grave.

I dropped Ben's arm. "Jess!"

"Giddy-up," was the only response I got. It came from the back of the barn, the twelve-year-old voice even tauter as it urged the horse to go. "Hyah," rang through the barn, followed by the unmistakable hammering of hooves through the outside gate.

"My horse!" Ben shouted. "Can that boy ride?"

I ran after Ben as he bolted away, following him through the back of the barn and into the corral where his horse should have been. A bunker of half-eaten hay was all that remained, while a cloud of dust behind racing hooves and a boy's urges to hurry faded down the road.

"Of course my son can ride, and I know the places he likes to go," I said, envisioning the happy places along with the sad, wondering to which this new shock would take him. "I'll go get him. You wait here."

Ben shook his head, glancing from Flynn's shirt to his boots, then back to my face. "No, ma'am, you're mistaken. You won't go get him, and I won't wait here."

Chapter 5

Skirts sure do get in the way. Mrs. Howard couldn't have said it better. ~Rex

It wasn't the barn I saw. It wasn't the memory of those two sour faces inside it, either. Or the recollection of my horse being led away by Regina's son. It was her face—rather striking, honestly, something I hadn't noticed over the pitchfork, over the saddle, or over her son—that I noticed as it disappeared behind me when with one quick stride I shot past her, heading back to where that other horse was. Her comeliness struck me in that fleeting second, almost making my next stride unsteady. But what nearly brought me to a dead halt was the look of a mother. A woman wanting her child back. Protective concern that enhanced her beauty even more.

I had to agree with her son. The mother beneath that mane of red hair and oversized men's clothing had at her core pure woman and all the breeding of the East. I heard it in the way she talked, saw it in the way she carried herself. Imagined it beneath the baggy pants and shirt. She was far better suited to having a dress cinched around that tiny waist than saggy trousers, slippers on her feet instead of oversized boots, and something fancy pinning that mountain of curls into some sort of style.

"Is that horse out front one I could use?" I called back over my shoulder.

"That's Ted's." She was in motion. I caught a glimpse of her arms pumping as she ran to catch up, one pointing toward the barn. "You stay here, I'll take it and get Jess."

"Boss."

"Yes. That's better." She glanced up as she drew closer.

I slowed as I looked back.

She narrowed the distance between us to a matter of paces as I reached the barn, and looked up at me as we hit the gate. "You don't have to call me Boss, but I'm glad you finally understand I make the rules around here."

"I meant the horse." I stared down at her, the thin beginnings of becoming levelheaded disappearing as her eyes went from too bright to narrow. "Jess told me, before you came into the barn earlier, that horse's name is Boss. He said he called the horse Boss because Ted manages your ranch."

"Neither that horse nor Ted is in charge here." Regina's face fired scarlet. It brought out the strawberry in her hair. "I'm the one in charge." She shot a glance the direction Ted would be with his horse. "I don't have time to stand here and explain everything to you. I need to get my boy."

She did need her boy. And I needed to get my horse. I intended to do both in one quick ride. I stepped into the barn. She did the same, the two of us hurrying side by side to find this fellow named Ted. We found him just where we'd left him, next to the perturbed banker, an even more cantankerous look tightening

Colleen L. Donnelly

Ted's face.

"Mind if I borrow your horse?" I eyed the animal next to Ted. One quick glance told me it was a rather expensive mount. Especially for a ranch hand. Good flanks, long span front to back. Might be able to catch up to Walter, since Walter was worn out and wouldn't run as hard as usual with a stranger on his back. "Got a young man on my horse I need to go find. I'll bring Boss right back."

"I ain't letting you take advantage of widows, and you sure ain't taking advantage of me. Mrs. Howard don't need your help getting her son. I'll do it. And she certainly don't need you for a husband. She's got me to watch out for her." Ted drew back the hand that held his horse's reins.

"You might take some of those notions up with her. In the meantime, I could still use your horse." I came close, near enough I would get a hand on those reins first chance I got.

"Ted, this is Ben Miller. He's not taking advantage of me. I'll explain later. Just let me have your horse for now. Jess is out there on a strange animal, running wild."

"Ben-Miller-Who" flickered in Ted's eyes, the sort of "Who" that meant he hadn't heard of me before this moment either, and didn't care or trust what the answer was. He was sizing me up—my height, my arms...two hands instead of just the one I realized he had. He was clever at the illusion of having two good hands. He'd been at this for a while.

"I'll be back with Boss as soon as I get Jess." Regina reached in front of me for the reins.

I raised a hand, blocking hers. "You're not riding

60

for me, or getting my horse. He's neither strange nor running wild, but he's more animal than you can handle, and he won't slow down for you. I'll go. And I'll take good care of your boy. You wait here." I looked down on her mountain of hair. Red. Like Oklahoma dirt.

She tossed her head back and glared up.

Ted held the reins away from both of us. "Ben Whoever-You-Are, you sit tight while Mrs. Howard and I go after Jess. We don't need no help, and I can handle any horse there is."

"Mrs. Howard." Mr. Gulliver stepped Regina's way. "Let your manager, Ted, here, go for your son while you and I discuss…"

"I said I'd see you in town, and this ranch is still mine since I have a husband now. Or will have soon." She snatched the reins from Ted's hand. "I'll be right back."

"No, I'll be right back." I reached for the reins. She yanked them high and behind her. Not so high I couldn't outstretch her much smaller frame, but out of reach where I had no right to lean. I stared down at her. I hadn't noticed how green her eyes were until now. Piercing green as they bored into mine. "All right. He's your son." I turned to Ted. "*We'll* be right back."

Her stretch relaxed enough that she let me take the reins. I looped them over the saddle horn and set the toe of my boot in the stirrup. As soon as I hit the saddle, she was at the horse's side, one arm, far too slender for the sleeve that bunched down near her elbow, extended my direction. I took her hand, let her foot have the stirrup, and lifted her up. She slung one leg over the horse's back and dropped into place behind me. "How

61

long you been wearing trousers?"

"Let's go."

"Mrs. Howard, I must insist that you consider..." Mr. Gulliver came near the horse.

Regina dug her legs into Boss behind me, and we were off.

I tipped my hat at Ted as Boss leapt forward. Both of his bosses leaving him behind. He missed, or ignored, my gesture as we sped off, his eyes on the woman behind me.

"Go northeast," she shouted near my ear. "It's where Jess always goes. It's where his father was...never mind. Just go northeast."

I let Boss have his head, reining him northeast, wondering if that was the direction Jess had intended to go look for land before the widow Howard found us both out. My shirt tightened against my ribs, hard knots I decided were Regina's fists gathering the material in handfuls at my back. I glanced down at the buttons straining in their holes. "Let go of my shirt and grab around my waist," I called over my shoulder.

"This is purely a business arrangement between you and me." She leaned to the side and yelled. "Nothing else."

"We have no arrangement, business or otherwise, in case you've forgotten."

"You're more than welcome to leave right after I get your name on my ranch, in fact I insist you do. I promise to pay you for your trouble. Eventually. Pay you well enough to help until you come up with a plan. I recall you saying in your letters that your cattle driving days were over, thanks to the railroads." She pulled tighter on my shirt.

Cattle driving days? I'd forgotten the story Jim had invented about me. Didn't matter anyway. I glanced over my shoulder. "I said hold on around my waist. You're about to rip my shirt, and I only have three. Unless you want to loan me a blouse you clearly don't use."

My shirt loosened, the buttonholes relaxed. If she was still behind me, she wasn't holding onto anything. I glanced back to make sure I hadn't lost her, my face meeting hers as she leaned to the side to look ahead. Long strands of red hair whipped up and down behind her, like a curly, determined flag.

"Hold on." I looked forward again.

She didn't. At least not to me. I had to give her credit. She rode better than most men. Not many could hold their own on the rump of a racing horse.

Her arm shot out from behind me, a slender finger aimed to the left. I saw her son, then, and my horse. The lanky figure bent tight over the back of the galloping black animal, brown dirt thrown up in occasional clouds and clods behind them. Walter's stride was powerful, impressive for a horse that had been ridden hard from Indian Territory to here.

"Hold on." I reined to the left, leaned closer to Boss's neck, and spurred the animal on. She must have leaned with me, I'd have to trust that she did. There was no use telling her to hang on again.

"There's a gully up ahead. Jess knows it's there, but your horse doesn't, and it looks like it's running amok."

"Amok?"

"Wild. Crazy."

"That's called hieing where I'm from. And I told

you, Walter won't run wild with your boy." I pictured her gully as a dip, nothing more than that in land laid out flatter than the bottom of a griddle.

"You've got to stop him! See it up ahead? That sharp drop into that old creek bed?"

I did see it, the change in the line of blowing prairie, the bend in the lay of the land. The widow was right. I urged Boss on. Walter was powerful, as tired as he had to be, running strong at Jess's insistence. But he'd slow when he heard me. We inched closer, close enough Walter could hear before he reached the gully I knew he'd handle just fine but the boy might not. I lifted my head into the wind and let out a whistle. Walter's rump dropped, his front legs stiffened. Jess flew over his head, a spindly ball of arms and legs rolling hard through the prairie.

Regina screamed. More shrill than my whistle, the wail of both echoing from my ears to my chest. A call of love. Like the sound a little brother made when he shouted, "Stop" at someone running from their burning ranch. Or the sound a stepmother made when she begged two boys to be careful around red things—like fire. Like the red-haired woman behind me crying out to her son. Another boy I'd somehow done wrong. Love always seemed to happen this way—so shrill, so harsh, so dire...so red.

Chapter 6

Whatever vile thing Ted spouted that day he dropped the bucket, I double it today. For Ben. ~Regina

I dug the heels of Flynn's boots into Boss's sides, hurrying the horse forward while Ben drew back on the reins to slow him down. I hurtled off the side, hit the ground very nearly as my son had, and floundered after him over hard earth and brittle grass, my skin and bones battered and burning as I tumbled. Jess lay just ahead, his body still, the angle wrong, his back arched my way for the second time today.

"Jess!" Brittle stems, skeletal survivors of winter's cold, speared and nicked at my skin as I righted myself and ran.

Ben's boots thundered behind me, then alongside me, and finally ran past as he stretched ahead. His stride powerful like his horse's, his surge great as he hit the ground, his height still evident as he plowed through grass and dirt on his knees until he came to a stop where Jess lay. I skidded to a stop behind him, hitting Ben's arm as it came up, blocking me from my son.

"Get out of my way!" I twisted, squirming under Ben's arm. He latched onto the shoulder of Flynn's shirt and held me back. I pawed at him, raked my hands through the air, threatening him over his shushes while his other hand traveled lightly over my son's body.

"What in the world are you doing?" I grabbed at everything, latching onto nothing. "For Pete's sake, Jess needs to know I'm here, and you barely touching him won't tell him that. Let go of me!" I jerked and squirmed at the end of his arm, dangling like a fish from a hook.

"You gonna be still?" Ben's dark eyes were on me, darker than before, the hand motionless he'd been running over Jess. The face I'd thought of as rugged earlier, maybe even handsome, held me in a glower. An unsteady glower, as well it should be after what he'd done.

I kicked all the more. "This is my son! Let me go."

He held me back with no more trouble than if I were a rag doll. "I need both hands to check your boy. You need to let me do it."

That look was there, that little bit of unsteady beneath the deepening threat. I didn't like that look. I knew I couldn't trust him. "He needs me more than he needs your hands right now, especially since this is your fault."

Ben's arm sagged, enough that I took a swipe at his shirt. He yanked me up again, his arm powerful and holding taut. "You don't want him needing some explaining how it was you made him worse by pawing all over him."

I stopped the clawing I'd been doing, dropped my hands, and forced my arms to stay at my sides. The only sound besides the wind around us was the air going in and out of my lungs. Hard. Loud and hard. Harder than I'd realized. Jess was the biggest reason I hadn't cried enough for Flynn. I'd let my boy cry for the both of us while I struggled to hang onto what was left of Flynn's dream. I looked at my boy. If I lost both of them, the tears would explode and never stop. "Okay," I whispered. "Finish. But remember, he's not some cow on the range, he's my son. Just do what you have to, and do it quick."

He let go, and I scooted nearer Jess's back. Thin stalks of grass spiked up between us as Ben leaned forward. His back stretched long, his arms making his reach even longer. I watched this cowhand who should have been in Liberal right now becoming my husband instead of here draped over my son he'd hurt. Walter stayed near while Boss wandered away, Ben's horse nuzzling Jess's bent knees as if he felt guilty—like his owner should.

Maybe it was all a dream. Maybe a nightmare. Ben's hands squeezed harder now, the tension of his fingers obvious as they traveled around Jess's head and down his back, stopping lastly at his legs. Splatters appeared on Jess's shirt. Small dark circles that spread and widened beneath where I leaned. I swiped my eyes against my shoulders, and wrapped my arms around my boy.

Ben's hand touched one of mine as I clasped my son. His hand traveled up my forearm, and over Flynn's sleeve. When it reached my upper arm, it stopped and squeezed. "You can't be putting pressure on him," he said. The dark of his eyes was swimming now, swimming from him to me as his squeeze tightened. "We don't know how hurt he is, and you might be making him worse."

"Me? I'm not his problem." I yanked my arm loose. "I didn't cause this. He needs me. He needs to know I'm here." I shrugged away and held tighter to

Jess.

With one hand on each of my arms, Ben broke my embrace on my son. In a single motion he had me on my feet as he rose to his.

"Let go of me! How many times do I have to say it? Clearly, taking orders isn't one of your qualities, if you even have any."

Ben towered above me. Over the wind, through my insults and tears, he held on. Close and tight. Too tight for me to swing at him.

"Listen, Regina. Get on Boss and go for help. You surely have some sort of doctor around these parts."

I nodded. In Liberal. Doc Harris. The answer rattled around with the storm I tried to contain—the deluge of tears that needed out. "I'm not leaving Jess."

Ben's fingers tightened more. If he lifted me like a child and set me on Boss, I'd kick him the moment my feet left the ground.

"It's better if you go." His head bent forward, the dark of his look lost now in the shadows of that deep complexion and the waning afternoon sun.

"No, it's better if you do. There's a doctor in Liberal." I wrenched my arms free. I rubbed them as I took a step back. "And don't bother to come back once you've sent him." I dropped my hands. "Never mind. I didn't mean that. You have to come back so we can get married."

His jaw swelled at both sides. The way Ted's did sometimes, the way it had at the barn when he first met Ben. "I can go for help," he said. "But it will take me longer than it would you. I'll leave Boss with Ted when I stop and explain where you and the boy are, and I'll have to get his or that banker's help, since I don't know where to go or who to ask. I'll have to saddle Walter while those two do what I expect they'll do—argue with me. Seems to be the Kansas way of doing things. And finally, you have to promise you'll stop squeezing your boy until I get back with the doctor. Can you manage that one thing if I do all of the rest?"

My palms itched. Itched for the sting of my hand against his face. The face that hurt my son and spoke to everything except the one thing he'd promised to do once he got here. "Surely a man who's driven cattle all his life doesn't need detailed directions. And from what I've seen, you are more than capable of handling Ted. Those are minor problems compared to—" I glanced down at my son. Compared to Jess. To me. To our future here on the ranch. The shallow lift and fall of Jess's ribs promised he was still with us. How long had Flynn lain this way? If help had been there for him, would he still be alive? We'd searched for him all night, Ted and a neighbor helping us, looking every direction except the one where Flynn lay. Dying or dead. "Liberal isn't far. I'll tell you how to get there and how to find Doc Harris. Just take Boss and leave Walter here."

Ben was quick. He didn't argue, for once. In three gigantic steps he was at the other side of Jess, and in several more he was where Boss nosed around in the grass. He whistled for Walter—gentler this time—as he reached for Boss's dangling reins.

"You ride that way." I pointed. Ben didn't even look the direction I indicated. "Straight that way," I said louder. "Maybe three miles."

With both horses beside him, Ben stared at me instead of the direction I pointed. His face was a blank, a look that said everything and nothing at the same time. At least Flynn's expressions had been easy to decipher, whether I liked what I saw there or not.

"Never mind. Just give Boss to Ted and tell Ted to go get the doctor. Then you can get on down the road. Seems that's what you want, to just get out of here." I knew it was. Wanting was so thick on him I could smell the desire to go. Break his promise. Leave all the pain he had caused behind.

Instead of going, he knelt at my boy, ran a hand over his hip and thigh. He stole a glance at my dungarees, then rose to his feet. He swung a long leg over the back of his horse, Boss's reins still in one hand. "I'll send Ted for your doctor, but I'm not going anywhere until we get this boy settled."

"I don't need your help getting Jess settled." I waited for him to argue, deny everything was his fault. I watched his jaw, expected to see the flex again, but nothing happened. He leaned the direction he wanted Walter to go, and the two of them pointed back toward my ranch.

As they turned, I heard it. My son's whisper. I saw it on Ben's face as he stopped Walter with a touch of the hand.

"Jess?" I dropped to the ground, leaned over my boy's back. "Jess?"

"Pa?" It was a whisper, but it felt like a shout. Jess's eyes were partway open. He was squinting upward toward Ben.

I rose. I looked at Boss, then back to Ben. "You stay." By the time I was on Boss, Ben was off Walter. I left the two of them behind with my son, using the end of the reins and the heels of Flynn's boots to hurry Boss to Liberal. The sun was sinking lower, the cool wind and the sound of my son's voice—the way he looked at Ben and called him Pa—were bringing water to my eyes faster than I could get away. Streams of it.

Pa.

I drove Boss harder.

Chapter 7

I'm not cut out for young boys, brown dirt, or bossy women. No matter what. ~Rex

I stared at Regina's boy lying quiet in the grass. His mother was right; this was my fault.

What if he falls? My stepmother's voice whispered with the wind. Her other worry had been what would happen to Little Brother and me if Luke fell and I couldn't save him. Regina'd ridden away with the same worry my stepmother always had in her tone. I looked to the northeast, the direction she'd gone, feeling what she'd left behind in her haste—the mark of a mother. The mark of a woman loving, running hard and scared.

Walter nickered. Air drained from my lungs, full of old smoke as I forced every bit of it out. I glanced Walter's direction. "Mind keeping yourself busy while I tend to things?" Things like this boy here, who'd given Walter his name, and who'd be hurting bad if he happened to wake up. Jess's rib cage barely moved, shallow breaths hardly noticeable. "You will wake up," I said. I'd stay until he did.

Walter tossed his nose in the air, then shoved it deep into last year's brown spikes of grass, searching out the newer, greener, tastier ones. I was good with horses, much better than I was with boys. At least I'd always thought so. But somehow I'd missed...or maybe

72

I'd just skipped...the naming part. How important that was, especially the belonging notion. The way it made a pact.

"Walter." He drew his head up, chewing his find, then drove his nose into the prairie grass again.

The sky and temperature changed as the sun sank lower, the late spring afternoon dimming and cooling fast, too fast for a boy with injuries to battle. I stepped around to his back and knelt with one knee close to him, watched for the telltale signs of shivering I'd seen with injuries in the past. Downed Rangers, dying criminals. A slight, almost invisible shudder traveled the boy's back and shoulders. I glanced up at Walter. Jess had ridden bareback. Nothing there but the halter. I fumbled with the buttons Regina had almost ripped loose, stripped my shirt off, and draped it over the boy.

Straight hair fell to the side over Jess's forehead. His face was so young. So much like Luke. I glanced along the lean curvature beneath my shirt. But Jess was built like me. Jess acted more like me, too. Or maybe it was his mother Jess acted like.

My shadow stretched across his hips and legs, the sun sinking at my back. I stood, moved to the boy's front side, and sat close, hoping between the lowering sun and my fairly near body warmth Jess would gather a little heat.

I laid a hand on the boy, studied the way he lay and the way his leg bent—the way it had felt in my hands. He wasn't going anywhere soon. I slid a hand to where his ribs were, beneath my shirt, to keep track of Jess's vitals. I glanced over my shoulder to the northeast again, where Regina had ridden, torn across the prairie like she couldn't get Boss to run fast enough. Her tiny frame rode like she was a piece of Ted's saddle, like she'd been doing that all of her life. I shook my head. That couldn't be true. Her smooth skin, the way she spoke and carried herself, told me she hadn't. I wondered what the Kansans there in Liberal would think when that tiny woman barreled into town in her dead husband's trousers and boots.

I snorted, glanced back at her son, drew my fingers off him. "Sorry. Didn't mean any disrespect by that. Thinking about your ma. She's special. In her own special way." I eyed her son. He still breathed, but he didn't react.

Walter moseyed in a circle around us. Jess was right about Walter's name. He was a good horse who loved a long drink. Like Jess was probably a good boy with his own wants and needs. Ones that sent him flying across the prairie on a strange horse when he heard his ma say she was marrying me. I snapped a brittle stem of grass off near the ground, broke it in halves, then into quarters as I stared over my right shoulder toward the northeast.

"Don't touch the boy," I said without turning. "We don't know how bad he's hurt."

Ted stepped from the left and walked where he could take a stand in front of me. He didn't continue around to Jess's front where I sat. I looked at the stocky man on the other side of the boy. I'd seen that sort of stance before, the spread of the feet that set the boots as far apart as a man's shoulders were wide.

"I'm guessing Mrs. Howard's gone on my horse for Doc Harris. She should have had me go. I would have, if I'd known."

I plucked another stem from the ground.

"I'll sit with the boy. You can git on down the road." Ted bent forward and lifted my shirt.

"Best leave my shirt where it is." I nodded at Jess. "Unless you're thinking on giving him yours." I knew Ted wouldn't do that. In the few minutes I'd been around the man, I'd seen that arm with the missing hand mere seconds. He wouldn't go without a shirt. The severed limb would be too obvious.

He dropped the shirt back where it was. "Like I said, you can git on. I'll take care of the boy and his ma."

"I'll wait."

I edged a little closer to Jess, gauged again the shallow lift and fall of his ribs beneath my shirt as a chorus of coyotes struck up across the prairie. The wind was dying down, the way winds often did toward sunset, stretching out the eerie wails as the breeze did nothing to interfere with their sound. Maybe some things didn't change no matter where you happened to be. Not just the wind, but mothers and stepmothers also, the way they saw the men in their lives, especially the young ones, like Jess. The coyote cries dwindled, thinned out to nothing, but the wind didn't completely stop. This Kansas wind just slowed, turning into more of a whisper than the whoosh I'd been hearing every day since I'd set foot in this state.

The evening changes ticked time away faster than I liked. I listened and watched, took note of everything around me without taking my eyes off the grass I toyed with and the boy that lay in it.

"They're family to me." Ted broke the quiet. "Been with them since before, and aim to stay on, too."

"As ranch manager?" I glanced up.

The sound of hoofbeats became more apparent, my heart joining their thuds, mine loud where theirs were muffled by distance and the carpet of grass. Ted finally heard them and looked up. Two horses. I turned. Regina was dwarfed on Boss, barely visible as she bore our direction. A more erectly postured figure sat on the horse running alongside her. A bag flopped at his side, his coat flapping with every stride.

I stood, staying close to Jess, and watched the pair riding our way. Boss reached us first, Regina on the ground before the large horse managed to stop. She did it without stumbling this time, even with those baggy trousers and oversized boots.

"How is he?" She dropped at her son's knees.

"Stable," Ted said. He came around the boy and stood near Regina.

"You covered him with a shirt," she said. She looked up at Ted. Then at me, at my bare chest. "Your shirt? Why?"

"Was he shaking?" The doctor was there now—a man who, in a glance, was everything this boy and his mother were going to need—hovering at Jess's back, his bag open on the ground.

"Yes," Ted answered without looking at me.

"Shock, maybe." The doctor felt the boy, much the way I had, his hands moving first around Jess's head, then his neck, then along his back and down his arms and legs. He did it the way I'd seen it done so many times, done it myself even, except for the little bit of extra tending I saw in his hands that I didn't have. It was in his posture, too, the way he bent over Regina's son, the way he was mindful of her nearby, and not holding her back. The doctor glanced at her as he dug what he needed from his bag. His hair fell over his forehead the same way Jess's did, but Doc's was darker. He was more my age than hers, but he wore his years in his heart instead of on his skin. This man would know how to do good for a family.

"Is he going to be all right, Doc?" Regina whispered.

The doctor felt around Jess's head one more time, paused at the back, used both hands in a circular motion as he stared at the horizon, then turned back to her. "Knot on his head. Bruise, I'd say, hopefully not more." He rested on his haunches. I waited for him to say, "Leg." I knew the leg was broken. It was Jess's backbone I wasn't sure of, the image of him tumbling off my horse and across the ground made him look fragile and me rash every time it ran through my mind. "We need to get him to your house, but carefully." The doctor laid a finger high on Jess's thigh. "His leg's broken here. Hard place to set, so we have to make sure we don't jar him as we go."

Regina gasped. I closed my eyes, pinched them shut, grateful the doc hadn't found more wrong. Regina was leaning into her son as I opened them again, Ted bending close over her. Too close.

"Try not to disturb him," the doctor said to Regina. He said the same thing I'd told her, but he said it different. Better. She pulled back from Jess, leaving her hands on his arm.

"You have any poles at your ranch? Blankets?" Doc Harris looked from her to Ted.

"I'll get them," I said. Her barn and homestead were small, little enough I could spot, or even concoct, what Doc needed in a short amount of time.

Ted straightened. I saw the fire in his eyes as he looked my way. Then I saw it fizzle as he glanced down at Regina.

"Be right back," I said. I was on Walter before anyone had a chance to argue. Regina and Jess were in good hands with the doctor, but that didn't make this ride any easier. The air was chilly as it swept over my chest and back, around my neck, and along my arms. The cold was uncomfortable, but so was heat. Fiery heat from a burning house, not to mention a jealous ranch manager's touch. My shirt had seen a lot the past few days. It had protected me, and now it protected Regina's boy from other things I'd done.

I saddled Walter fast once I reached Regina's barn, my mind racing with my hands, the way she had across the prairie. Walter could tote Jess back to the house on a stretcher, the way the doc would want him carried, if I rigged a sort of harness to his gear. I wasn't sure Boss could manage it, and I didn't want to waste time finding out. I grabbed an extra shirt from my roll, then scoured the barn as I slid it on. Two rough boards, long and narrow, would do. A discarded board lay along the side wall of the central open area. It was wider than we needed, but I found a hatchet in an alcove of tools and split it in half.

At the back of the barn, at the very corner, I found a room I hadn't noticed earlier. It was behind a closed door and looked used—Ted's, I assumed. I fumbled for a latch, a tricky setup that frustrated me enough I pondered bringing the door down with my boot. The door popped open with the first toe-tap. Ted had a cot to the side with a blanket fitted across its top. The right size to make a stretcher, and sturdy, but I'd prefer one

Ted wasn't using. I made a quick spin and eyed what Ted owned. Not much besides the cot. A large wooden box, a few grub utensils, a holster, a rifle, and a rope. I grabbed the rope. He probably wouldn't kick up too much of a fuss about me borrowing his private belongings, under the circumstances.

I lifted the lid of the box, hoping for another blanket. Ted was neat, if nothing else. Everything inside was arranged in perfect stacks, and at one side I saw what I needed—an extra blanket. I gave it a tug, an awful clatter following down inside the box. A small metal chest tumbled and rolled from the blanket. It landed on a book—a Bible, by the look of it. The chest popped open, papers spilling everywhere. I considered cursing as they slid to the bottom, but eyed the Bible and held back. I tossed the blanket on Ted's cot and gathered the papers…bank paperwork, maps, deposit slips, and a deed. I laid everything back in the metal chest, snapped it shut, and set it where the blanket had been.

I started to close the wooden box's lid when something glittery caught my eye. Too glittery for a one-handed ranchman. I leaned forward and touched what I saw, down low and to the side of the stack I'd just disrupted. Pointed tips and sparkly insets scratched across my skin. I latched onto the barbed contraption and lifted it out. A hair comb. I'd never seen one so fancy before. It had to be expensive, or at least it would have been at one time. Not now, though, with two of its teeth broken off and several others chipped at the ends. Evidently it was worth something to Ted in this condition—at least worth hiding.

I lifted the metal chest back out and wrapped it in

the blanket the way it had been before. I laid both atop the stack next to the comb. The fancy broken comb. Everything back in place just like I'd found them, I lowered the lid. I snatched the blanket off Ted's cot, mounted Walter with everything I'd found for the doctor, and headed east.

Chapter 8

Jess never looked so much like Flynn—pale, still, quiet. Just like Flynn—when we found him and brought him home. ~Regina

I stood, my son close at my feet, and glanced toward the ranch. Jess was still breathing, but too shallow. He hadn't stirred, even with Doc working on him, not like he had when he thought Ben was his pa.

"I can go," Ted said, appearing beside me. He was looking the same direction I was. "Don't know we can trust this fellow."

I glanced at Ted, then back toward my home. I squinted, peered hard through the fading light. "Hear anything?"

"I should go check."

I watched alongside Ted to the west. If Ben was really doing what he said he'd do—staying until Jess was settled—then the only good Ted would be was to help Ben find what he needed faster so he could leave sooner. Or argue enough—the Kansas way, according to Ben—to slow him down.

"I'm worried about moving him." Doc spoke from the ground, the way a man does when he's talking to himself. I turned and looked down. I was meant to hear. Doc was talking about my son.

"You mean we should leave him out here?" I

dropped down next to Doc and laid my hands on Jess's side, lightly, so as not to disturb him, as I stared at Doc. "Won't he get cold if we do that?"

"No, I didn't mean leave him out here. I meant I'm worried about moving him without at least trying to set that leg first. That bone, that large bone, is pretty important. I wish I'd thought of that before I sent your friend off. I would have suggested he bring something back for splints." Doc Harris looked around at the nearly treeless prairie, then back at me. "That fellow— he a friend of yours? Or maybe family?"

"Neither," Ted answered above me. Doc didn't look up at Ted when Ted answered out of place. Doc kept his eyes on me, telling me in his look that he understood. This was my son and my ranch, he wanted my response, my voice, and no one else's.

I opened my mouth to correct Ted and tell him I could manage my own answers when I heard him, heard the sound of Walter's hooves thundering across the prairie. That black horse had a way of running that Boss didn't have, or even Flynn's horse hadn't had— weightless, yet powerful.

Ben's silhouette appeared in the dusky light as I looked to the west. His and Walter's black outlines resembled warriors as he rode up on us and wheeled his horse to a stop. Two long poles wrapped in a blanket extended to the front and behind Ben's outline, like spears balanced under one arm. I stood as he swung both legs to the same side and dropped to the ground.

Doc joined me, stood close, and watched Ben alight, then hurried his way. "Wish I'd thought to have you get something we could use for splints."

Ben set the long poles on the ground, leaned over,

and unwound them from the blanket.

"Well, I'll be." Doc bent down and came up with two smaller, thinner boards. "Now, if we only had…"

Ben handed him some rope.

"You a doctor?" Doc looked at Ben.

"He was a cattleman." I stood out of the way, not saying what Ben was supposed to be, and watched the two men move in unison. Ben worked alongside Doc Harris as if he understood medicine, not just animals, anticipating the doctor's every move. Their harmony made it seem the two of them had been working together for years and I could relax. But I couldn't. I was grateful for their unity and appreciated their joint knowledge, but this was my son and the man who had caused his accident, so I stayed far enough back to allow the doctor to work freely over Jess, yet near enough I could monitor everything Ben did.

Doc paused and looked at his tall counterpart, then up at me, a tiny frown tightening his brows.

"Might move close to her," Ben said to Ted, tossing a nod my direction.

Ted didn't stir, but Jess did. He jerked. He let out a sound from deep within that rumbled like a buried scream. Mine followed his. A scream I never knew I had escaped, crying out sharp and clear as it rang across the prairie. Ben came to his feet, stood in front of me until the scream waned, and caught me as I dropped to be near my son when the scream finally died.

"Let me see him." My hands stretched and reached toward Jess while Ben's gripped my shoulders, keeping me off the ground, his body like a wall between my son and me. "Let me go. I'm tired of you being in my way!" I squirmed as Ben held on, glancing back at Ted.

"Come on, Regina. Let Doc do what he has to." Ted came to my side, his good hand touching my arm. "Next time give us a little more warning." He growled at Ben.

Ben let the desperation and fight go out of me before he let go of my shoulders and steadied me back on the ground. His hands stayed close as he remained in front of me, waiting for my next move.

"Was that supposed to happen?" I looked from him to my boy.

"Yes'm." Ben nodded. I stayed where I was, watching as Ben edged away and rejoined Doc Harris, dropping to the ground near my son.

"He'll be okay." Ted came to stand in front of me, taking the place where Ben had been.

I glanced at Ted's face, hoping Flynn's ranch manager was right…that he cared the way I did…and that I could see it there. "I'm just worried." I stepped around him, closer to Ben and Doc Harris, leaning over them as the two men put my son back together.

Jess moaned, he stiffened as the leg was formed to the splint, Ben binding it with a section of rope they'd cut from the longer piece.

"Are you sure this is right?" I cringed as Ben snugged the rope tight.

Doc and Ben looked up at the same moment, their hands still on my boy as they stared at each other.

"Was it done wrong?" I looked from Ben to Doc. "Did Ben tie it too tight?"

"He did fine." Doc glanced up at me. "Everything Ben has done has been correct."

"You're sure?" I rested my hand on Doc's shoulder. "I mean, everything's really going right?" I needed to be certain. I needed the face looking up at me to assure me Jess would be okay. He wanted to be just as certain. It was in his gaze just before he glanced down, from my face to my fingers gripping his shoulder.

"We need to move him now." Ben left where he'd knelt on the ground. I heard him stand, felt the quickness as he came to his feet, and his nearness as he stood at my side.

"Ben's right." Doc let go of Jess, and I let go of his shoulder as he stood. Things were happening too fast amidst looks that were too uncertain. "We'll know more about how he is when we get him settled."

Settled. Then Ben would go. Like he said. I glanced at the man next to me, then stepped away as he and Doc bent and eased Jess to his back, soft moans rumbling deep within him as they did. When my boy was flat, and his sounds stilled, Ben straightened and eyed what they'd done.

"You put a different shirt on while you were gone," I said.

His Adam's apple gave a little bob, his only response as he turned to Doc. "Ready?"

"Ready as we'll ever be."

Ben stretched the blanket over the grass and laid the boards a little way from each side. He folded the blanket's edges over the boards toward the center.

"You've done some doctoring somewhere," Doc said as he waited near Jess.

Ben carted the makeshift bed alongside Jess, took his first shirt from on top of Jess, and snaked it beneath him, worked it under Jess's ribs, hips, and thighs until it cradled him. "If we all lift at the same time, we can get him on the cot without disturbing him too much." Ben glanced up at us, then straightened.

I nodded and took Jess's head while Ted went to his feet. When we were all in position, we waited, listened to Doc breathe out numbers as he counted to three, and then we lifted. Together. Jess didn't moan. His hip didn't bend or his leg shift. In the most delicate of motions, he was on the blanket. I slipped my hands from beneath his head, brushing his hair from his forehead as I did.

Ben gathered the rest of the rope as I knelt there. He looped and knotted it until he'd crafted a makeshift harness and connected it to both sides of Walter's saddle. His cattleman side was coming out now; I saw the dexterity as he handled the rope, a rope that had something to do with my son.

"Here, use Boss, instead." Ted stepped up and took hold of the rope.

"Walter's used to me," Ben said. "He'll pay attention as I come along behind with the back of the cot."

I saw then what Ben was doing. One end of Jess's cot would be rigged behind Walter while Ben walked behind carrying the poles' other ends.

"But Boss has gear. He's a ranch horse, and Jess knows who we are. Boss and I should do this."

"No, Ted. Let Ben do it with Walter." I stood and stepped between the two of them, but it was Ben I turned to. I looked up into his tanned face where unsteadiness had hardened into a determination to see my boy settled. "You shouldn't have whistled at your horse when my boy was on his back. But I thank you, just the same. You've done well helping to settle Jess."

Ben said nothing. He returned to rigging the harness, the rope as lithe in his hands as if it were string. I watched his hands and arms, sure and dexterous, fast and strong. Before I knew it was happening, Jess's cot was off the ground, one end at Walter's rear, the other in Ben's hands. Ben made a noise, and Walter eased forward. Smooth as silk, the two of them, with my son, starting across the prairie.

"I'd be honored if you'd ride my horse." Doc's voice was soft at my side, his horse's reins extended in his hands.

"She can ride Boss." Ted brought his horse to me. "They know each other."

"I'm going to walk," I said, watching Ben's back as he followed his horse, straining to see my son toted between the two of them. "Thank you both, though." I hurried away and to Ben, following close behind as he and Walter carried my boy, their black silhouettes moving smooth and easy toward my ranch. "You've done well," I said, "enough to get my boy nicely settled."

"I ain't going yet, if that's what you keep trying to say," Ben said without looking back.

"I'm saying you've done plenty, though."

"And I said I'm not going until this boy is completely settled."

I stepped closer, opened my mouth, then closed it again. I wouldn't argue like a Kansan or say what I was thinking—God help whatever poor woman ended up married to this man.

Chapter 9

Kansas sure gets dark when the sun goes down. The wail of a coyote seems closer, and eerier. Varmints rarely travel alone. ~Rex

I straightened and took a step back, leaving Jess on his mother's bed with Ted's blanket and my shirt wrapped around him. He was quiet, Regina and the doctor huddled close by his side. He was well loved and well taken care of; all he had to do was wake up.

I moved farther back and took in the room. Mrs. Howard's bedroom. Heat rose around my collar as every wall and every corner breathed woman. Kansas and the outside of this home were stark, but here, on the inside, was color, fabric, and sweet smells that made my head spin. Mrs. Howard's room had so much lace, so much finery and womanly frills that her boy could never get well lying in a place like this.

"He did okay being carried here, right?" Regina was close to Doc. She spoke low, looked his way, a hand on her boy, while Ted watched from her other side. The three of them stood there, the two men oblivious to the rest of the room as the tiny redhead between them spoke.

"His leg is stable. It made the trip well." Doc glanced back at me. I caught his gratitude while, "Mister-Who?" flitted through his eyes.

"How about the rest of him?" Regina tugged at Doc's sleeve. "Why doesn't he wake up?"

Doc turned from me and looked at the woman next to him. "He took a blow to the head, and I don't know when he'll come to. I hope soon..." Doc's voice was soft, the comfort in it evident. Even from across the room I couldn't miss the kindness he offered. Special, was my guess, just for her.

"Your boy's tough." Ted ran a hand across Jess's head. "He'll be fine."

"We'll do our best to make sure he is." Doc looked tired, like evenings of this sort aged him more than time ever did. He watched Regina run her hand along Jess's arm. When she glanced up at him, his face colored, something bending over his bag and rearranging its contents didn't hide. At least not from me.

"When will we know if he'll be completely fine?" she asked.

Doc Harris looked up from his bag, the tinge still there. "Soon. I'd say soon. I'll come often. Daily. If that's all right."

"Please do." Regina nodded as she bent over her boy. Her hair fell like a cloud around her son and her face—a face I had to admit should be out where it could be seen. Not the sort of face I expected on a liar, or on a woman in trousers with a pitchfork in her fist. I glanced at the two men who flanked her. At least one of them saw the same thing I did in that fog of red hair.

Regina drew her curls to one side, looped the mass of them behind her neck, and let them fall over one shoulder. Becky had been pleasant, and pretty enough, but for all of her good qualities she never filled a room the way the widow did. Regina caressed Jess's face as she leaned his way. It was like looking at a painting—nothing like the woman I'd seen come stomping through the barn earlier—a painting my stepmother would have hung.

"Okay if I stay close to him tonight? Sit at the edge of the bed, if I'm careful?" She looked up at the doctor.

"Yes, certainly." He lifted a hand. I thought he would touch her, the way he held it close in the air, but he let it drop, burying it in a pocket, instead. "Talk to him some. That's what he needs. Let him know you're here. That may help him wake up." Doc glanced back at me. He missed the widow's I-told-you-that-earlier look she tossed at me as he walked my direction, his hand out and extended my way. "We haven't officially met, but I'm glad you were here. I'm Doc Harris from Liberal. Been doctoring several years, but never had help like you gave me tonight. Thank you for all you did."

"Ben Miller. Glad to help with the boy," I said. His handshake was firm, steady, but not hard.

Regina glanced up. "Doc, I'm sorry. I should have introduced the two of you sooner. But Ben isn't intending to be…"

"You had too much on your mind," Doc interjected and smiled her way, then turned back to me. "Miller. There are some Millers north of Liberal. Good people. You related to them? From around here?"

I shook my head. "No," I said, the same moment I heard, "No family in the area, but that's what he prefers. No family." I peered at the woman perched next to her son.

"As I was saying…" I looked at Doc again.

"He came with the intent of staying, though,"

Regina cut in again. "But that didn't last."

I leaned around Doc, making the frown on my face plain as day for a woman choosing to talk for me. I scanned the room, looking for a dress. She had to have at least one somewhere. And she needed to get it out and put it on. Wearing trousers was going to get her in a lot of trouble.

"But…" I tried again, not spotting any fine clothes.

"But he didn't like what he saw," she finished for me. "So he'll be leaving soon. To where everything's perfect."

I threw up my arms. "Well, there you have it, Doc. Whatever you need to know about me you can ask the…the…her." I jerked a thumb the widow's direction. I caught her eye and the glint in it that time, but I couldn't care less what that bossy woman thought. I turned and headed toward her bedroom door where more glint—a different sort of glint—stopped me. Sparkling trinkets, eastern trinkets, glittered in the candlelight. I glanced down at her dresser top, where dishes and small trays shimmered with lockets, perfume bottles, bracelets, combs, and more.

"I suggest you leave the lady's things alone." The brim of Ted's hat and his one good hand blocked what I could see. "She's had a rough evening. No call you getting sticky-fingered."

"Nothing sticky about me. Like she just told you and everyone, I ain't sticking around." I didn't need to re-announce my leaving, since the widow already had. Just said it nice and quiet to her ranch manager. Touching my hat, I went on through her bedroom door, on through the rest of her house, and on through the Kansas dark.

91

Chapter 10

If I have to swallow crow, then I might. But a little respect afterwards would certainly be in order. ~Regina

"Who is he?" Doc asked as Ben strode from the room.

"No one," Ted answered. He walked from my dresser, the sound of the kitchen door punctuating the last of Ben's footsteps. "Just someone trying to take advantage of a widow and her boy."

"Ted, I believe Doc was asking me. After all, this is…"

"I should have been here today. I warned you about fellows like that." Ted nodded toward the jewelry on my dresser top where Ben had stopped. Ted *had* warned me. Surely I'd have more sense than to invite one of those types here to marry me.

"We'll talk more about you being here, later. Please go take care of Boss now. The poor animal is probably unhappy standing out there still saddled up, after I rode him so hard." *We* rode him so hard. Me and Ben. I glanced at my dresser. Surely I had more sense…

"Well, I'm sorry again I wasn't here." Ted nodded at Doc and me, then left my room.

I looked at Doc as soon as Ted was gone, my kitchen door shutting more softly this time. "How much do I owe you for all you've done?"

"I won't discuss payment now." Doc stood over me. "When this is all settled, we'll talk."

Settled. I glanced at the empty doorway. "Is there something worse you haven't told me about my boy?"

Doc's eyes were blue like Jess's, like Flynn's. A warm blue that softened the air, almost taking the icy fear out of my question. "There's nothing more, other than the fact Jess may be confused and terribly sore when he wakes up. And I don't know how long either will last."

"I'm grateful you're willing to come back often while Jess is recovering." I glanced at my dresser, where my jewelry lay. "I may have to be creative in the way I pay you."

Doc's hand was warm—like his smile. His fingers were smooth and gentle, unlike the rough and calloused ones of Ben, as he patted my hand. "I won't talk payment with you, Mrs. Howard. Let's talk only of Jess."

"But I won't have it that way…"

"And speaking of Jess, you're going to need something for him when he does wake up." Doc dipped into his bag and came out with a tiny bottle he placed in my other hand. "This will help him with the pain. Just a little bit, though. Less than a spoonful, and only if he needs it, but no more than two times a day."

I looked at the bottle. If I paid Doc with money, it would likely take what little I'd found of Flynn's, plus the cash from selling Flynn's horse.

"What does this medicine cost?" I asked.

"Nothing tonight."

"Doc, I appreciate…"

"Okay, if it makes you happy. A bottle like that costs fifty cents, full. As you can see, the one I gave you is barely half."

"And your trip out here?"

"Mrs. Howard…"

"Doc, unless we do this right…"

He raised his hands. "All right. A trip might be the same. Probably less."

I dropped my hands, along with the bottle, into my lap.

"I said, don't worry," Doc repeated above me. "You have only one thing to think about." Doc nodded toward my son.

Doc Harris was right. If Flynn were still alive, Jess would be all I was thinking about. But since Flynn wasn't, I not only had Jess, but also his bills. And a ranch the bank wanted to take away from me, and some stranger outside in my barnyard who didn't mind eyeing my jewelry, but was stubborn enough to refuse to keep our agreement so I could tell Flynn's banker to go away and leave me alone.

The door to the kitchen opened and closed again, and footsteps I knew were Ted's came back to the room. He nodded at me, the scent of a weary horse wafting with him as he walked to the foot of the bed, and stood where he could see Jess.

"I'll bring you a little something as payment tomorrow morning." I said it low so Ted couldn't hear. I glanced at Ted, the ranch manager I also couldn't afford. Two men in my room, neither one of which I could pay what I owed him. That third man in my barnyard had to stay, no matter what, stay and marry me like he was supposed to; then he could go. "I'll be coming into town tomorrow with Ben while Ted stays with Jess."

"You'll be going into town on your own, I'm afraid." Ted heard me this time. He glanced up from watching Jess sleep. "If that was his horse I heard outside just now, you will." Ted jerked his head toward the window.

I looked at the dark panes behind my lace curtains. I heard nothing. Ted crossed his arms and repositioned his feet. I stared harder and listened more.

"Excuse me for a minute." I stood. "I'll be right back."

I burst through the kitchen door out into the stretch of dirt between the house and the barn. Surely someone I would choose to marry would at least have the decency to tell me he was going before he rode off into the night. The dark was palpable, tiny stars too high to do any good. I planted my fists on my hips and called into the dark. My voice carried well in the cool night air, almost a melody, but it brought no response other than the spring peepers'. I listened to the high-pitched little frogs chirping as if all was well, when it wasn't. I swam through the darkness and their songs to the barn, felt my way through its door. "Ben? Walter?" My face heated up. I couldn't believe I called for a horse as if he'd answer.

Only my voice came back to me from those four wooden walls. Ben was gone. Really gone. That vile word of Ted's came to mind again. This time I shouted it.

Chapter 11

Good news travels fast. Bad news travels on a black horse in the dark of night. ~Rex

I didn't need the fire I lit for heat, and certainly Walter didn't care. I was warm enough, even in the cool night air, thanks to too many hours with the sassy widow and the man she had for a ranch manager.

I estimated Liberal to be over the next rise. I'd been on a horse most of my life, especially since I'd left home, often in uncharted terrain. It was second nature to know where a man would settle, easy to judge the good land from the bad, even in an endless prairie where things all looked the same.

I stared at the tiny flames. They grew from flickers to blazes, but only in my thoughts. Big enough to destroy a house, a barn—everything except a shed. I wondered what Luke was doing, and whether my father knew his place had been burned. I'd rather tell Pop myself, but Luke wouldn't have the strength to keep the horror to himself. He'd run first to our father. Then to Jim. He needed someone to go to. It was the way Luke was.

I glanced at the blank pages lying on my knee. I sat cross-legged in front of the fire, a stub of a pencil in my hand. Shavings, tiny splinters and curls of wood lay scattered on my trousers, remnants from sharpening the pencil with my knife. Sharpening that hadn't helped. The words still wouldn't come.

Dear Pop,

I stared at the empty page, slid it to the bottom of the stack, and rested my pencil tip on the next.

Luke -

How could I explain that I did what I thought was right in a way Luke would understand?

Jim,

I knew what I had to say to him—I made it to Kansas, but was leaving right after I nosed around like he wanted. I'd have to explain about the part I wasn't going to do. How the widow had a son, so the marriage deal was off. Jim would figure out why having a boy in the picture made the arrangement too complicated when Luke came crying to him about the ranch. Jim was sharp. He'd see right through the flames Luke spewed about. He'd see me. And he'd see the mess that nipped at my heels. But he wouldn't let it affect his plans. And he wouldn't want it to affect mine.

I tapped the blunt end of the pencil on the page. Regina would be fine without me in her life. Her need for a man could be met by anyone who could sign his name, even by either of the two right under her nose. And if not them, she was pretty enough to nab another. I tapped my pencil on the page again.

Dear Becky,

I'd started this letter a thousand times, practiced it over every mile of Oklahoma Indian Territory, even over the trail I'd burned to Kansas. I never knew what to say, wasn't sure how or what to ask. I glanced up at the tiny stars dotting the sky. My stepmom knew all the answers. If only I'd asked her when I had the chance.

But I was too young, hoping all women were like her. Even my real mother, whoever she was.

I pressed the pencil to the page.

Jim—heading back. Deal fell through. Will check around first, then explain when I get there. Rex.

I folded the page and stuffed it in my shirt pocket to mail tomorrow. I stared at the next empty sheet. The fire was dying, getting too small for light.

Pop—See you soon. Rex.

I folded that one, also, and stuffed it into my pocket along with Jim's. The rest of the sheets, and the pencil, I put back into my pack.

"Goodnight, Walter." I stretched out near the fire, my pack jammed under my head for a pillow, and wondered how long it would take for Jess to wake up, how quick I could be at sniffing out any foul ranch shenanigans. I stared at the ceiling above me, black heaven with tiny pinpricks of light. Glitter. Sparkles. Like the twinkling on Regina's dresser as I'd raced through her bedroom door. I frowned at the sky. Vials, jewelry, snifters, and bottles. And combs—one comb in particular. Identical to the one in Ted's box. I sat straight up. *Dang.* That's how Jess would say it, and how I'd be saying it from now on. Neither one of us was leaving the widow Howard yet. Even though neither one of us wanted to stay. *Dang.*

Chapter 12

Mama always said, "No news is good news." At last I understand. ~Regina

Ben was gone. He hadn't come back during the night, and as far as I was concerned all of the "what-ifs" had gone with him. Except for the "what if I'd been quick enough to shout 'good riddance' before he rode away." That would have been worth saying.

I looked up from the ad I'd rewritten for a husband, tapped my pencil on my dresser top, and stared at a face I barely recognized. Flynn wouldn't even recognize me. The sun and wind had changed my skin and hair in a short amount of time, darkening one and highlighting the other. Maybe Ben didn't like what he saw. Maybe the slight wash of freckles broken out over my nose caused him to... I shook my head. Ben had been looking at cows for years; he could put up with a few freckles.

I folded my ad and slid it into Flynn's shirt pocket, glad I had color on my face so the reverend wouldn't see me blush when I asked him if he knew any eligible men who were willing to share their last name without a lot of...without any other wants or desires. If he said no, I'd advertise again. Then go tell Mr. Gulliver there'd been a slight delay. "Darn you, Ben Miller!"

"Ma?"

I glanced behind me in the mirror.

"Jess…" I hurried across the room and dropped to the edge of the bed. "You're awake!" I ran the back of my hand across his forehead. His skin was cool to the touch, and as white as the sheet he was lying on.

He closed his eyes, a wince pinching the corners.

"I'm sorry." I rose from the bed as gently as I could, wishing I could sit back down and wrap him in my arms. "Doc left medicine for the pain." I hurried across the room.

"Doc Harris? Was he here? Why do I hurt so much?" Jess groaned behind me.

I snatched the medicine from my dresser and returned to Jess's side. I'd placed a spoon next to it, trusting and believing he would awaken soon.

"You fell. Can I lift your head so I can give you this?" I held up the bottle and trickled a tiny amount into the spoon, lowered myself beside him, twisted, and slid one hand under his head, balancing the spoon in my other. "Just open your mouth. I'll do the rest." His face tightened as the golden liquid dribbled between his lips.

"Where did I fall?" He coughed as I settled his head back to the pillow.

"It will take a bit for the medicine to take effect. Don't cough, if it hurts. Don't laugh, either."

He peered at me through nearly closed eyes.

"Okay, you won't be laughing. You fell in the prairie. How much do you remember? Anything about yesterday at all?"

He frowned, cottony memories like shadows crossing his face, most of which I prayed wouldn't stay. "I don't. I don't remember anything."

"Do you remember you and me in the prairie

yesterday afternoon? Together out at your father's grave?"

Jess stared at my ceiling. "Maybe…I think so. Sort of. Did I trip? I must have hit hard. My hip hurts something awful."

"You broke your leg." I laid a hand on him. His eyes widened. "We set it last night, but you were unconscious."

Voices rose from outside the house. I glanced toward my bedroom window. It was closed, but men's voices were clear, loud, sharp, and growing stronger, powerful enough to penetrate my bedroom wall.

"I said there's no need you being here." It was Ted. His voice close to the house. Doc Harris said he would come by today. I thought it would be later, after I'd gone into town to pay him. Surely Ted wouldn't run the doctor off.

"I'm checking on the boy."

I stared at my son.

"Ma, let go of my shoulder. You're squeezing me."

I let go but kept my hand there and patted him, a tap for each footstep coming through the house.

"He's sleeping. He won't even know you're here." Ted was near my bedroom door.

Jess strained toward the commotion. I knew that other voice, and it wasn't Doc's. I stood and turned to face the doorway.

"He's awake, but he's not well. Not well enough for unexpected visitors." I stared at Ben. Unwelcome visitors, ones who'd run off during the night.

"Mrs. Howard." Ben tipped his head, and removed his hat.

"Son." Ted slid around Ben and came to the edge

of the bed, taking a spot alongside where I stood. He removed his hat, the same way Ben had, then dropped to one knee at Jess's side. "Glad to see you're awake. Sure was worried about you."

The glower I gave him did nothing to stop Ben from continuing across my room. He trailed Ted's path, coming to a stop behind him, the brim of his hat running through long fingers. Fingers attached to strong hands, to sturdy arms, and on to muscles that swelled beneath the fabric of his shirt. Muscles I'd seen yesterday.

Ben tipped his head my son's direction, and leaned high over Ted. "How you feeling?"

"The boy looks tired." Ted came to his feet, sending Ben a step back. "I say we wait till Doc's been here before we bother him with visitors."

"Yes. You're right. We should let him rest." I walked around Ben, marking a new trail I wanted him to follow toward the door. A curl fluttered loose just as I passed. I jabbed it back, blowing other stragglers out of my face.

"You look fine." Ben watched my hands. "Your hair's up today. Pretty combs."

"I'm going to town."

Ben's gaze traveled from my hair to Flynn's pants, and finally to his boots. "Really?"

"This talk is keeping the boy awake." Ted stepped into the space between Ben and me. "I say we all go outside."

"I saw you," Jess whispered. I looked around the two men and down at my son, at the face that blended with my sheet. "I remember seeing you." Jess's eyes were wide now, bluer against his washed out face, and steady on Ben.

Ben's hat stopped spinning as he turned to my boy.

"You kept telling me to hold on, to be brave. You told me not to cry, but to try harder, the way Pa'd be proud of me to do."

"Jess, you must have been dreaming."

"No, Ma. I wasn't dreaming. He was there. I saw him and heard him."

I looked up at Ben. At the color waning beneath his tan.

"Son, that fellow said no such things." Ted turned to Jess. "I was there the whole time. I heard everything he said, and there wasn't nothing like that. But holding on like you did was right. That's just what your pa would have wanted. I'm proud of you."

"No, it was him." Jess twisted his head to see Ben better, and his face pinched as he did. "You were tall, and it was so smoky, but I heard you. I followed you."

"Anybody home?" Doc Harris called from the kitchen door. It was my son we were listening to, not Doc. He was quiet for a moment, then called again. "Okay if I come in?"

Ben stepped around Ted, hat in hand, as I found my tongue and invited Doc in. His footsteps came through the house, more softly than these other two men had come, as Ben bent over my son.

"A boy has to learn his way through smoke. At least I always thought so."

"Well, I see our patient's awake." Doc's voice was light, like his step, as he came into the room. I heard him behind us as Ben straightened, then in front of us as Ben took a step back. Doc walked to the foot of Jess's bed as Ben moved away. "That's what I like to see."

Ma'am. I saw it in the way Ben tipped his head as he backed farther from my bed, and in his glance as he settled his hat on top of that black hair. He turned when halfway across the room and walked toward my bedroom's door. He paused before he went through it, stopped at my dresser like he had before, and glanced down at the combs and pins I kept in a dish.

"You absconding for real this time?" I set my fingers at the dish's edge and tugged it my way. My belongings were none of his concern, but his comings and goings were mine. Ben had come and gone too many times, and I had a ranch to save.

"Absconding?" Ben touched my favorite comb, the one whose mate lay out in the prairie somewhere. "Is that anything like taking something that isn't yours?"

"You'd best be on your way," Ted said from my side.

"Ted, I can manage."

"I should have been here when this fellow came the first time. He wouldn't be here now, if I was, touching things that ain't his."

"Ben came at my invite, Ted." I turned to Ben. "Ted knows I lost one of my favorite combs out in the prairie, the match to the one your finger's on. And just so you know, absconding means going. Going without reference to taking anything. So are you?"

"Not far." Ben kept his finger on the match to the comb I'd lost, then dropped his hand back to his side.

"Not far? My ad wasn't for a house guest."

"I don't intend to be one." He ducked his head at the doorway. "Ma'am." And he was gone. Again.

Chapter 13

The finer things in life aren't always fine. ~Rex

Liberal was more than I expected, but probably far less than what a woman like Regina was used to. Why she insisted on keeping her ranch was beyond me. She sat a horse amazingly well, but not with the same precision she'd fit a dress if she'd wear one. I could tell by her husband's cinched pants what she was cut out to wear, and I wasn't the only one in her room who'd noticed. Those other two men at her son's bed had also. Doc, in the way a gentleman would, and Ted the way I'd seen roosters behave. A rooster with a comb that wasn't his.

"How much to send a couple of letters?" I asked the clerk in the postal building I'd found. He was tall and thin, balding above the visor he touched and tugged at more than necessary.

"You new here?" he asked as I slipped my two letters his way. "Mr. Greene's my name, with an 'e' on the end." He glanced at the coins in my outstretched palm. "Only half that amount would be fine."

I dropped two of the coins onto the counter. "Thank you."

"We get lots of new folks out here." He scooped my money to the edge of the counter and into his other palm. "Liberal. It means what it says—generous. An oasis, and a real draw for people wanting to rest or stay."

"A growing town, then?" I asked.

"Booming. Well, maybe blooming's more accurate. But with the railroad coming this way and the reputation we have for being a comfort to the weary, things just keep changing. Booming is coming."

"Sounds like a right nice place." I smiled at Mr. Greene. "Like a man could make a life here. Settle down."

"Lots of them do. You thinking about settling here yourself?"

"Might look things over," I said. "Who would I talk to about that? About finding some land?"

"Oh, the bank's the place you want to go. That's where everyone goes. Even the railroad has dealings with them."

"The bank," I repeated. "Might have to pay them a visit." I tipped my hat. Jim sent me here to get married so I could search around for men like Matt Morrissey without being noticed. One out of two wasn't bad. I'd do Jim's rangering for him. Discreet, like, since I wasn't getting hitched. Then I'd make sure the widow was married decently before I went, for her sake. "Thank you again." I stepped out onto the boarded walkway.

Liberal was a blooming little town, the walks and street flowed with a steady stream of people and horses. I looked to the left and saw the sign for the bank. Mr. Gulliver. I wondered if he would be as friendly as Mr. Greene had been.

I strolled down the walk and stepped through an ornate wood-and-etched-glass door that smelled like money. The building was larger than I'd expected, with high ceilings and a lobby that hummed like a hive with customers and clerks. I closed the door behind me and scanned the room, a head above nearly everyone else.

"Thought I'd introduce myself officially." I extended a hand across Mr. Gulliver's large oak desk. "Ben. Ben Miller," I added before he had time to wipe the surprise off his face.

Mr. Gulliver's grip strengthened as the shock of seeing me waned. "Mr. Miller. Yes, we encountered each other yesterday." Mr. Gulliver was as accomplished as Ted. Ted did a decent job of hiding his one bad hand, and Mr. Gulliver did a fair job of disguising the gold-digging clink in his tone. "And if I remember right, according to Mrs. Howard, you're here to…" He raised his brows as he slid his hand away and leaned back in his chair.

"To say hello." There were things Jim would want to know that this man probably could, but never would, tell me. He was too slick, too paunched with self-assurance. "That's all. Have a good day." I turned.

"Mr. Miller, please, have a seat. A quick hello is hardly the way to make an acquaintance, and besides, there are things we need to discuss."

I glanced back at the man Jim would be curious about and Regina had been counting on me to satisfy. His arm swept in a low arc in front of him, pointing toward the two chairs I'd been standing between.

"Thank you kindly, but I'd best be going. When there's a lot to do, there's little time for discussing it."

"A lot to do. You mean here? Or do you mean you'd best be going somewhere else, say farther away?"

"Going home. Thank you for your time." I nodded and turned. This time I kept going as I walked across the lobby between customers and clerks, then out the door to the walkway. Mr. Gulliver wouldn't chase after me. Hurrying would be too obvious.

"Mr. Miller?"

I glanced to the right. Mr. Greene hightailed it my way—hied, no matter what the widow thought—a folded piece of paper in his hand, waving like a flag. "We got a wire for you just after you walked out. Wouldn't have known it was yours, except you'd just been there." Mr. Greene was slender and not that old, but still he panted as he reached me, my message flapping in the air.

"Thank you." I took the paper from his hand. "Owe you anything for your trouble?"

"No, sir. Just glad we found you. You staying in town in case we need to find you again?"

I glanced behind him, wondering who "we" was. "Don't worry about finding me. I'll find you. Thanks again."

I stepped to the edge of the boarded walk as Mr. Greene hurried back the way he had come. I leaned against a post and opened the wire.

Your brother paid a visit.

I crumpled the note in my fist. I didn't have to read more to know it was from Jim. I stared down the street. Luke. Little Brother. I opened the wire, and smoothed it out enough to read between the creases.

Shooting from both hips with his mouth. Aiming for Morrissey. Eventually, for you.

Jim was sharp. He'd figured far quicker than Luke it was me who burned our father's ranch. He'd also know soon enough from my letter that I was coming back with my assignment half done, so I'd best be sure the rangering half was done right, since it wouldn't be done his way. Pop would get his letter too, and he'd know I was still alive. That was enough for now. Pop didn't need to know more.

I glanced toward the south. Kansas had no obstructions. I should be able to see red. Red hills, red dirt, red-hot Luke.

Red curly hair.

I shoved my hat lower on my head.

Morrissey would be safe from Luke. He was too smart for Little Brother. I was too, but smart wasn't how I handled my half-brother.

"Oh, I thought you were going home."

"Mr. Gulliver," I said without turning. I continued to stare toward the south.

"I was just leaving for the day, I'm surprised to see you're still here."

I folded Jim's wire and stuffed it into my shirt pocket. "I'm surprised you're leaving so early."

"If it's land you want, Mr. Miller, I can assist you with that. Maybe in a simpler fashion than what you're considering. Land with fewer complications attached."

I turned and faced Regina's banker. He was nearly tall enough to look me in the eye, and he held himself with as much confidence as if he were. "Your bank has land?" I watched for the blink that wasn't there…the shuffle, the clearing of the throat, anything that would tell me Mr. Gulliver was uncomfortable.

"You're in the West, Mr. Miller. There is land in abundance out here."

"Just like that? Land for the taking?"

"Well, Mr. Miller, there's always a price tag. Time. Money. Some just not as pricey as others."

"So, a way to help with that price tag if a man wants to do more than just homestead?" I watched again for that shift, the nervous repositioning of the hands or feet.

"That's right. That's the business of a bank. Land and opportunity without complications—complications like a family and its problems attached. Unless it's too late for that. Is Mrs. Howard now Mrs. Miller?"

"You have a deed I could sign?"

"I have the deed. But her husband left the finances in such a shamble you're going to have to have some money up front, I'm afraid. Clean slate, new deed."

"I'd like to see the deed. And hear the story about the finances."

"First the marriage certificate, then we'll discuss her financial problems, and lastly we'll tend to the deed. Now, as I said, I must be going. When you have that certificate…" Mr. Gulliver turned.

"Seems pretty complicated out here to keep a ranch in the family it belongs to."

"Mr. Miller, if it's land you want, I can help you. If it's the widow you want, I'm warning you that you're in for some steep challenges."

"It's Regina's land this is about, not me."

Mr. Gulliver came closer. He stood in that almost eye-to-eye position. "Ted Morgan is her best solution, if she and her land are your concerns. He's local, he has a reputation, and he knows her ranch better than anyone around. His name on that deed would bail her and that boy out because we know he'd turn that ranch into profit. Then you'd be free to do as you wish."

110

"Without marrying her? Regina knows what you've said about Ted?"

"Well, she was a bit baffled by the mess her husband left her in, but she knows women can't own land in Kansas. Only men."

"Men. Like husbands, unless they're dead."

"Unfortunately, that happens. Good day, Mr. Miller."

Colleen L. Donnelly

Chapter 14

There are too many men in my life, and not a single one of them knows how to take an order. ~Regina

"Why are you here, Mr. Miller? I thought you were gone. For good this time." I dropped into the back of the wagon what was left of the wire Flynn had bought, and rubbed my palms down the front of his pants, dulling the sting from its thorny barbs.

From on top of Walter, Ben stared at the tools stacked next to the wire. "Told you I wouldn't go far. Ted need those things?"

"No, I do. I'm expanding the fence around my cow and calf so I can build up the herd." Instead of talking to the reverend or placing a new ad for a husband, like I would be if the men in my life hadn't confounded my morning. "If you were staying, I might let you help, you being a cattleman and all."

"Cattleman... That's right. Well, those cows didn't have fences."

"Look, Ben, I don't have time to waste, and I can't have you just loitering around."

"Loitering?" Ben repositioned his hat on his head.

"Sitting around on your horse."

"I'm not just sitting. I'm tending to things. You got posts?"

"If it's Jess you're tending to, Doc has that under

112

control." I hopped down out of the wagon, slapping dust and grime off my hands.

Ben glanced at the house. "What did Doc have to say when he was here?" Ben rose in the saddle, swung a leg over Walter's back end, and lit on the ground near where I stood.

"Get back on your horse. You just said you don't do fences, and we don't need tending."

"I can do posts, and it looks like you need some."

I glanced at the nearly treeless prairie and Flynn's axe in the back of the wagon. "I have the posts under control. I have a plan. And what Doc had to say is nothing you need to tend to, so you can be on your way."

"If your plan is for cutting posts, that isn't going to be…never mind. Just tell me what Doc said."

"If it means you'll get on down the road, he asked Jess questions, rather mundane questions like how many legs a rabbit has, what color the sky was, what was Jess's favorite food."

"Mundane?" One side of Ben's mouth kicked up. "Not sure what 'mundane' means, but Doc did right. Shows whether or not Jess remembers things he would have known a long time ago."

"You might be a bit shy on vocabulary, but you sure know an awful lot about doctoring for a cattleman."

Ben rolled his shoulder in a slow shrug. "More than just cattle out there. Got cowhands, too. How'd Jess do?"

"He had to think about his answers, but he was right every time."

Ben tossed the ends of the reins over Walter's

113

neck, flung the stirrup over the saddle, and began to undo the girth underneath. "Did Jess remember more recent things?"

"Why are you unsaddling your horse?" I marched to his side and stood close, where Ben could see me.

"Tending things wears Walter out. Did Jess remember…yesterday, for instance?"

"You mean real memories instead of the imaginary ones of you encouraging him?" I shook my head as Ben glanced over at me. "No. He doesn't remember much about yesterday, but he sticks to his story that you told him to keep going."

Ben tugged the saddle off Walter's back. It dangled between his arms, one end in each hand, as he turned to face me. "I did say those sorts of things once. But that was years ago. To a different boy. A young fellow who needed to try harder, so he'd hate me less. I didn't say them to Jess. I only thought them."

"He said it again after you walked out. He told Doc all about you."

"I imagine Doc would agree Jess just dreamed what he thought he heard. And I'm pretty sure when Jess gets his memory back he won't think so kindly of me. That other young fellow never did."

"Well, it won't matter much what Jess thinks, since you're done tending to him, and leaving. Is Walter recovered enough you can go?" I stretched an arm up and ran my hand down Walter's neck. "He feels recovered."

"We ain't done tending, yet, so I'd say no."

I stopped caressing Ben's horse's neck and planted my hands on my hips. "Let me say it again: I didn't invite you here to come and go at your leisure. I have a ranch to save and a boy to see to, not to mention…"

"The arrangement you've got to work out."

"A new one, since ours was a failure." I couldn't look at him. My ad, my cow standing idle, my boy on his sick bed, the ranch this cowhand refused to help me keep, and the tears still waiting to be shed got in the way.

"If I'd been told you had a boy, and he'd been told about…about your plans…things might have started out a whole lot better. Not that your stubbornness—I mean, our differences—wouldn't have sparked up enough trouble on their own." Ben's grip on that saddle whitened the crowns of his knuckles. Like peaks, covered with ice caps. Frigid ice caps. "Never mind all of that." One end of his saddle dropped toward the ground. "We're past starting out. We've got to tend to what we have so you can get on with your life and I can get on my way."

My life. His way. The cold of those caps swept around me. The air became thick, too heavy to breathe. It felt like losing Flynn all over again. I stared at Ben, at the black hair and the dark skin that was here, and then would go again. But he was supposed to. It was my other plan. It just wasn't supposed to happen with someone so complicated. "No." It was all I could think to say. "We're not tending to anything together. 'I should have' and 'you should have' no longer matter, except for your responsibility for what happened to Jess and for causing my plan to fall apart."

His saddle dangled by the horn as he looked down at me.

"Please put that saddle back on Walter and go." I meant it. It just didn't come out like I did.

115

"I told you, Mrs. Howard, I have things to tend to. One's your son, and another's you."

"Me?"

"Yep. You told me what Doc said about Jess. What did he say about you?"

"Me?" The question, the way I screeched it, sounded rangy and ridiculous. I closed my eyes. I knew better than to converse like a child or squawk like a hen, especially with a man whose vocabulary contained less than twenty words. "What I mean is, whatever is it to you if Doc said anything about me?"

"There's still that arrangement to be made. And it needs to be a good one." Ben stepped closer, dragging the saddle with him.

"Doc has nothing to do with any arrangement I make."

"He's a possibility."

"A possibility? How dare you! It's not like I'm some cow men barter over."

"One thing about cattle is they never give you any sass."

I balled my hands into fists. "I won't be herded like, compared to, or mated off like some cow, Mr. Miller. And that's not sass, that's the respect I deserve."

"Bred."

"Bread? You hungry?"

"You breed a cow, you don't mate it."

"Oh. Yes. I knew that. That's what I meant." I tossed my head back again, hoping the sun would hide the crimson burning my face, praying when I looked back, Ben Miller would be gone. For good this time.

Ben let go of the horn of his saddle. I looked back at him as it dropped to the ground, the top leaning against his leg. "Look, I'm no good at these man-and-woman things, but you need more than a business arrangement. You need a real husband. Why settle for some agreement with a stranger when there's a man close here who'd marry you right?"

"Mr. Miller...I..." No more words would come. They caught in my chest, where my heart struck up a chorus of eager beats as I stared up into eyes I could tell meant everything the man behind them said. If a cowhand ever proposed to me, that's exactly how I imagined it would sound.

He raised a finger in my silence. His hand came close, his finger at my lips.

"Please listen. I want you married the right way, with your property secure."

I nodded. His finger brushed against my mouth, the sensation delicate, yet firing all the way to my toes.

"I'm suggesting you consider Doc for a husband. Admittedly, you're too much of a wild thing for him, but he'll give you more than just a last name. He'll dote on you, watch out for you, and probably even take orders from you. And he'll be good to Jess."

Doc. My heart became silent, my chest an empty cavern. Ben lowered his finger before I could bite it off.

I felt red crescents forming where my nails dug into my palms. "I don't need your advice or that much of a husband, and Jess doesn't want another father."

"You need to get yourself wedded to someone before something worse happens. And Doc's a nice man, who actually seems to like you."

"Doc, or anyone else from around here that knows me, would have unwelcome notions about me as a wife, and fatherly ideas for Jess. We had Flynn. That was enough. All we need now is this ranch. And whatever else Flynn had. And a man's name to get them." I stretched taller so this cowhand would take me seriously. "Kansas law says I just need a name. A man's name. Any name will do, as long as that name stays out of my bedroom, my pocketbook, and Jess's life."

Ben straightened. "Ma'am, if something's empty, a good man would more than likely want to fill it." He lifted and tossed his saddle on Walter's back, and grabbed his dangling reins.

I reached above his hand and snatched the reins away. "Ben Miller, I'm tired of you coming and going. You need to…"

"Tend to things." The skin of his hand scratched mine as he peeled back the fingers I had clamped around Walter's reins.

"Your skin feels like a cactus. Let go." Red pinpricks showed on the palm of Ben's hand as I yanked mine away.

"Not cactus. Memories." He dropped his hand with the reins. "You and Jess both need a good man attached to your 'any-name' husband, and right this moment your best option is the doctor. Unless you've got some other neighbor interested in that red hair of yours."

"Of course not!"

"Well, you're a lady somewhere under those trousers, and you've got a boy to look out for. I'm not good with boys, but Doc's the sort that can tend to all of your boy's wounds. It's up to you, Mrs. Howard, to come up with a new husband. It won't be me. It doesn't have to be Doc, either, but you'd better make sure the man is at least as good as his name. Which brings me to the last thing I need to tend to." He looped the reins over Walter's saddle. "I want to have another look at those combs on your dresser."

"My combs are of no concern to you, and I wish you'd stay away from my things." I lifted a hand to touch my hair where the comb should have been. "I've already lost one of my favorites, as I said, and I don't care to lose any more."

"I'm here especially because of that comb. I don't want any more hurt to come because of it after I'm gone."

Chapter 15

Being a Ranger showed me how to see the black and white of living. That is why there are no women Rangers. ~Rex

"I thought you were gone." Ted stood in the barnyard behind the woman who was his boss, saying the one thing the two of them liked best to say. I'd seen him riding across the prairie, his stocky set on that horse of his heading this way. Regina turned toward her ranch manager, her fists back on those hips.

"Where were you?" Regina asked.

"I came from the north field. Looking it over before we plant."

"I told you we're not planting that field. You were to corral the cow and calf so I can extend the fence."

"You'd be smart to keep that field in crops, with the ranch in the situation it is."

I glanced at Regina's manager, the one man in Liberal I'd been told knew her land and business best. The name that would save her an arranged marriage and embarrassing debt. I patted Walter as he stuck his nose my direction. The one name I was pretty sure should never be allowed on her deed. I walked to the barn.

"Ted, I'm in charge of the ranch. For now, just go watch Jess while I start the fence. After *I* corner the cow and her calf, since you didn't."

I could picture her in the quiet that followed her orders, a finger tapping her lips as she glanced toward the prairie, churning up another of her plans. The same lips I'd touched earlier. I found other tools I knew the widow would need, even if she didn't, and stepped with them out of the barn.

"Maybe if he would go, you could think straighter about what this ranch needs," Ted said loud enough for me to hear.

"I'm tending to a couple of things." I tossed the tools into the back of the wagon and turned to Regina. Darn. There was no finger tapping on those lips.

"We don't need any tending. Just like she don't need a husband."

"Both of you! If I choose to marry again, it's my business. And Ben will be gone as soon as he understands I don't need him tending silly things like my combs."

"Your what?" Ted's eyes widened beneath the brim of a hat he wore far too low.

"My combs."

"Curry combs?" Ted asked.

"No, hair combs."

The sound of knuckles cracking came from Ted's one good hand. "I think your tending is done here."

That comb of hers he had in his box would probably disappear after this, but it wasn't worth a barnyard brawl now when there were bigger things at stake. Like her ranch, and my rather shaky permission to be on it. A buggy broke the silence, softly, as it entered the drive. Ted didn't flinch, and Regina didn't turn. I heard it pause at the mouth to the barnyard.

"Mrs. Howard?"

Regina rounded at the sound of his voice, the one voice I'd suggested she pay attention to, her face softening yet lighting with surprise. Maybe more than surprise. I caught the halt as she turned from Ted and me and said his name. "Doc…"

"Thought I'd drop by before heading back to Liberal. Been down the road looking in on the Calvin twins. Is it okay to see Jess again?"

Ted's knuckles fired another round, then went quiet. I thought about doing the same as I looked from Regina to Doc, noted that gentle demeanor he had that claimed to be here to check on her son.

"Yes. Of course. Please do." Regina pointed toward the house.

"He was faring pretty well earlier. But no harm checking him again…" Doc's voice softened even more, the smile behind it clear as he eased his horse and buggy forward.

Doc had Regina's attention as she watched him steer to the house and step down from his buggy. She was quiet for once, studying the man's every move. "Please come in."

Doc Harris lit on the ground, nodded at Ted and me, then strode to Regina's side. He kept a respectable distance between them as they went to the house together. He held the door for her with one hand, his bag…a bag he probably really didn't intend to use…dangling from the other. I stood alongside Ted until the kitchen door closed behind them.

"Time for you to go."

I glanced at Regina's one-armed manager. "When I'm done. Not before."

I hustled past Ted and went straight to the house,

leaving Walter saddled where he was. I covered the distance from the kitchen to her bedroom in four quick strides and stepped inside the room. Doc's and Regina's backs were to me. They stood side by side over a sleeping boy, Doc's bag hanging useless from one hand, as I'd suspected it would.

"How's the boy?" I strode further into the room.

"He's sleeping." Ted came around me from behind. He was sneaky, for such a stocky fellow. He hied it to Jess's bed, taking his place at Regina's other side. Doc leaned forward and glanced around the widow at her ranch manager.

I walked to the window instead of taking a place in her line, the window Jess could see from where he lay, and I slid open the fancy curtains and peered into the small barnyard. This room needed more air. I latched onto the sash and tugged the window up, sticking my head outside.

Before the Kansas breeze had a chance to waft past me, footsteps marched across the room and stopped at my back. Ted's, from the sound of them, and I saw I was right when his good hand settled on the window's sill. "Jess needs to stay warm, and you need to get on down the road."

"I'm tending." I ducked my head as I came back inside, and shouldered close to the pane.

"Like hell you are!"

The widow marched up behind him, her footsteps even harsher than Ted's in her deceased husband's boots. "Ted! Jess can hear you. And when Ben goes is up to me, not you."

I set the heel of one palm on the sill, leaned, and looked outside. "I'm the one says when I go."

I didn't have to see her to know Regina's hands were on her hips again. The good Lord gave her the perfect set for that. I wished he hadn't. "I have that say, not you."

I glanced beyond the barnyard, down what they called a road, and across the prairie on both sides. Ted's impatience pawed at the floor; I felt it in his stance. "I never leave a job until it's done."

Regina took me by the arm. There was power in that little hand as she nodded to Doc and steered me from the room. I let her. I wanted her away from the two of them. She led me to the kitchen door, but that's where she stopped. Not nearly as far from them as I'd hoped. "I don't need your help here, or your tending. I can take care of myself." She squared in front of me, tiny but full of spit, like a wet cat. "Next time I advertise for or choose a husband, I'll make clear all of the details involved. You've accomplished that much, so in my estimation the only thing left that you need to tend to is leaving." She opened the door and pointed outside. "Get on Walter and go."

Walter looked up. He was bright, but surely he didn't know his name this quick.

"Say it again," I looked at the widow. "Say Walter's name again."

"I'm not speaking to your horse, I'm speaking to you!"

I leaned out the door. "Walter," I called. He raised his head again. He nickered, different than he usually did when he heard my voice, and I grinned. "Your boy sure did right by my horse. He taught me something about the value of a name, Mrs…"

"Walter…" Jess's voice was rough, a feeble strain

as he called my horse from Regina's room. "Walter…"

Regina's face looked like mine felt. Except lots prettier. The two of us turned back to her room and hied it inside.

"You remember?" She pushed to his bed, dropped down to the floor, and knelt beside him. Jess's eyes were on the window, through which Walter's nicker could still be heard.

Doc Harris scooted close, leaned over Regina's back to the boy, eased Jess's eyes wide, and studied his pupils. "You remembering more?" he asked. "You remember Walter?"

Jess nodded, and winced when he did. "He was with me, wasn't he? He helped me."

"Yes, Jess. Walter helped you." Regina stretched closer to her son.

"Can I see him?" Jess looked from the window to his mother.

"Of course you can." She patted her boy and turned back toward me, peering around the doctor's legs. "Would you bring Walter to the window?"

"So he's getting better." I looked at Doc. "Might be up and around before you know it."

"Then you can leave," Ted muttered.

"I imagine he's talking to me, Doc." I turned to head outside, paused at the door, glanced down at Regina's finery, and touched the lone comb.

A burly hand stripped mine away. "I don't know who you are, but I aim to find out." Ted's voice was low. Raspy and coarse, like leaves over rocks. "The last thing you want is for her to find out she's been lied to. Which I suspect she has."

Chapter 16

I'm marrying for love. For love of my son, who's better, and who remembers that horse. ~Regina

Jess had stared at Walter's long black nose protruding through my lace curtains, shadowy memories bringing color to his face. "Walter," he'd said again before he finally drifted back to sleep. Ben had stood back, out of Jess's view, but I saw him watching from the side. Watching me. And Doc.

"It seems you came by at just the right moment," I said to Doc when it was just him and me left in the room with my sleeping son. I'd sent Ted out, and Ben never returned. I'd been listening for my wagon, daring either of those two to take over my fence. "I want to thank you properly for stopping by." I walked to my dresser, glanced at everything on its top, and promised myself I'd hide it in a drawer soon where no one could see it except me. I eased a drawer open and removed part of the little money I had, then returned to Doc's side.

"Here's a portion of what I owe you. I want to pay you something." I handed it to Doc.

Doc shook his head. "I confess, I hoped to talk to you this evening, but not about money." He raised his hand, pressed mine with the money away. "Stopping by like this is part of the care for the boy. It's not extra, and I wanted to drop in."

His hand stayed on mine, as did his eyes. Smoother than Ben's hand had felt against my skin, more like Flynn's. And it was different the way Doc looked at me. Ben's eyes had fire in them. Doc's were peaceful, pensive, more of what Ben had decided I needed. Doc's gaze flitted down at Jess, then at the bag he had set by the bed.

"You're going to need this boy's help. If you're intending to keep the ranch, that is." He glanced up from the bag. "You're going to need a lot of help. Someone beside you. Beside both of you."

I could see myself in the blue of his eyes. I could see Jess, also. Eyes blue like Flynn's, but more so. Features soft like Flynn's, but softer. Gentler. Not black, not powerful like the dark orbs that heated everything when Ben looked my way. Doc wasn't the sort of man I could say "I can take care of myself" to. He was the sort of man who would step aside and let me, if I did.

"I owe you…" I raised the money again.

"No, Regina." A blush splashed across his face. "I'm sorry. I shouldn't have addressed you by your first name. Unless…unless that's all right with you…"

I looked deeper into the blue, took in the handsome face that surrounded it. The sincerity. He was offering me more than a name, much more. Just as Ben had said. Ben. "Take this as partial payment. I insist."

"If it's business to you, you owe me no more than you would that Ben fellow out there. He did as much as I did. In fact, if you couldn't have found me, my guess is he could have handled everything your boy needed."

I stuffed the money into Doc's hand. "Take this. I

owe you far more than I owe him. If anything, that man owes me."

Doc laid the money on the quilt that was tented over my son. He bent for his bag. "I'll come again tomorrow," he said. "I want to."

Chapter 17

Red. Blue. Brown. There's too much color here, but all I can see is red. ~Rex

So, are you married yet? I couldn't shake the way Jim's voice would sound if he showed up in Liberal. The question rang in my head as I stood in Regina's barnyard, thought about her banker, and recalled the way Doc held himself when he was beside her.

I hesitated with Walter near the barn door. We'd been sleeping out under the stars every night, keeping some distance so I could keep some perspective. "Come on, boy. I mean, Walter." I patted the saddle on his back. He tossed his nose in the air; he was feeling good. The rest and attention here suited him. It would likely ruin him for the things that had always suited me. "Don't be thinking things would be easy just hanging around this ranch, because I can promise you chasing outlaws over cactus while unarmed and barefoot would be far better than tangling with that tornado of a woman Flynn Howard left behind." Walter ignored me. He tossed his head again like a young stallion.

I strode back into the barn for my bedroll, Jim's voice still dogging me. He might have my letter by now, but it wouldn't make any difference. I knew Jim. He'd given me an assignment—the hardest one he'd ever given me—and he would expect it to be done. If I hurried and got the widow married off, and did a quick scour of the area for ringleaders to these ranch schemes in a way that no one would suspect, I could hightail it back to Oklahoma Indian Territory before Jim had time to react. I'd plant myself in front of his desk and argue why I'd cut his orders short. The boy might give Jim pause, but he wouldn't change Jim's mind. To Jim, none of it would matter. A job was a job. Jim's law was the law. And his way was how he wanted it carried out.

"Ted?" Regina's voice jumbled my thinking, created commotion in Ted's bunk room, where he'd gone and shut his door.

"Yes?" Ted stepped out, careful to close the door behind him. I thought about slapping his pockets for the comb as he passed. If it still had those sharp little points to it, I'd enjoy it. He stalked through the barn to the open doorway at the front.

"Ted, it's getting too late to work the fence. Would you mind starting a fire in my kitchen stove so I can cook?"

"I'll take care of it." Ted's boots kicked over the hard brown ground as he hied to do what she said.

I waited. I could hear the widow in the barnyard, the doctor's footsteps along with hers. I could see in my mind what I'd imagined before, his tall gentleness a good solution to her problems, better than the ranch manager she had just sent to the house. She and the doc paused. I strained to hear, but if they spoke, it was quiet. Private.

"Fire's started." Ted was back outdoors. His steps stalled at her and Doc. I could hear the hesitation in his pause. I eyed the loft above his bunkroom. Maybe that was where I should sleep. "You have plenty to do," his voice took on a gentleness I'd never been able to master. "You're most likely tired. I'll rustle up some grub for us. Some dried beef and gravy. That'll be good for Jess."

I listened to the widow Howard and her two men. At least one would gladly obey the first half of Jim's command. Regina thanked Ted. He appeared at the barn door and stalked past me. He disappeared into his room, shuffled around, and reappeared with his arms loaded with utensils and grub. He managed to hold onto it all and close his door surprisingly well for a man with only one hand.

Regina thanked Ted again as he crossed the barnyard. I listened for the door to the house to close, and it did. Ted was inside, Regina and Doc were in the barnyard alone.

They were quiet. I'd never known that redheaded woman to be so still. I leaned against the low wall my saddle was normally slung over, stretched my legs out in front of me, and listened harder. The two of them were near Doc's buggy. I heard his soft voice. He posed a question, and before she could reply I came off the wall and stepped along the inside of the barn doorway. I peered through one of the gaps between the boards. Doc stood near her, very near her, looking down in a way the widow deserved.

"Thank you, Doc," I called and waved as I strode out where they could see me. Doc and Regina each took a step back from the other.

"No—thank you." Doc nodded, but I caught the baffled look on his face. "And thanks to your horse, there, also. Walter." He tipped his head toward Walter. I could see the ready in his eyes, the ready that would take care of Regina and Jess, whether they were ready or not.

I waited for Regina to chime in, say anything to either him or me, but she didn't. Her face picked up a sheen. A crimson flush that made her look right attractive where she was, here on a ranch instead of somewhere frilly back east. Red. I was way too fond of red. I felt a similar sheen creep up the back of my neck.

"Thank ya," I said again. I rubbed my hands along my trousers, making old memories sting. Doc needed to go. I dropped my hands. No, he needed to stay. I watched him and Regina. If I'd known the rules for moments like this, Becky wouldn't be Becky Carson right now. Doc was reserved, but he seemed to know how to stand and how to look. "Anything special I can do for Jess?" I called across the brown dirt to where they stood.

"Ben…" Regina looked my way. We stared at each other across that color of ground I didn't care for, her red on the other side like a rising sun. Doc should go. No, he should stay.

"Thank ya again, Doc." I knew I should hie it back into the barn. Doc would love that woman, but he sure couldn't lead. Ted would run over him every chance he got. So would she.

It was the look on Regina's face that gave me what I needed to leave them alone. I dragged one boot backward, and then the other until I was on my own in the barn's dim light. Walter nickered from outside the doorway as they began to speak again. To each other. Soft, so I couldn't hear. I went back to the low wall and bent forward, bracing myself against it with both arms. I leaned into my fists and listened until Doc Harris's buggy finally rolled away. Wheels grinding into the solid dirt, the crunch getting farther and farther from Regina.

"Ben…"

I heard her behind me, the step that said West as much as East, the clip of her deceased husband's boots stopping not far from my back.

I knew what I had to do. I drew in a deep breath and turned. She opened her mouth the same time I opened mine.

"Will you marry me?"

Chapter 18

"I do...do you?" "Yes...do you?" "Are you sure?"
~Regina

I stared at Ben. Closed my mouth the same time he closed his. Neither of us answered. Neither repeated what had just been asked.

Ben edged my way until we stood face to face. Toe to toe. A slight blush deepened the color of his already tawny neck, and a similar heat flared the skin of mine.

"I guess, then..." He glanced toward the door where his horse stood outside. Walter nickered. Ben listened as if Walter had offered a suggestion. "I guess this means that..."

"That we've reached an agreement...for the arrangement." I brushed my palms against Flynn's dungarees. They felt clammy. I ran them down my legs again.

Ben bowed his head. It was the slowest nod I'd ever seen. He lifted his hat as his head came up, and ran long fingers through that thick black hair. I caught the ebony of it, even in the low light, watched the way it carved a hole even in the darkness. His hair fell into place, heavy strands crowning his head, before he settled his hat back where it had been. "You'll have that name you needed..."

Yes, I needed a name. We both knew that. I'd said

so a thousand times. I watched his eyes, his mouth, and waited. *Say more.*

He raised his hand. I followed it, watched as he again removed and held onto his hat. "We could seal this the way some of the Indians do where I come—I mean, that I've seen passing through south of here."

He extended his other hand. Long fingers, rough skin. I'd felt the power of that hand and the texture of that skin the day he'd first arrived.

"That's what you want? That's how you suggest we do this?"

His hand wavered, my hand looking so fragile next to his—small, white, almost like china. He wrapped his around it. His skin felt as damp as mine as he lifted our hands in a single shake. "That's it. That means we agree to be wed." He loosened his grip.

I yanked my hand loose, latched onto one of his fingers, and gave it a sharp tug. "That's my answer." I hurried across the barnyard and let myself through the kitchen door. He didn't say more. He didn't do more, either. But he shouldn't. It was an arranged parting. I fell back against the rough wood as it closed behind me. *"Doggone you, Flynn. And double doggone you, Ben Miller!"*

Chapter 19

I really only needed to do one thing, and then I could go—hunt down the source of the ranch thieves. Now that one thing is complicated with another—the other thing I thought I really didn't want to do. ~Rex

Regina walked away. Not walked, ran. Hied, hightailed it, to her house. Walter nuzzled my shirt as I stayed where I was, next to him, as far as I'd followed her, and watched her go.

"I know," I muttered as the door slammed behind her. I stared at the house. "I should have hitched you to the wagon and taken her straightaway to Liberal instead of shaking her hand. Found a parson and given her my name. Even paid Flynn's debt on this place. Think Jim would foot that bill as part of my job?"

Walter snorted.

I rubbed my hands together. Hers had felt so warm. So tiny in mine. I turned to Walter. "Best give it a day. Maybe two. So she can adjust."

It was late. She shouldn't have expected more than a handshake this late in the day. I stared at the house, saw the tiny glow through the kitchen window. "Come on, Walter." I led him away from the barn's doorway, looked one last time at the widow's window, and headed for the stars.

****

The corral was empty when Walter and I returned. We'd taken a loop around the ranch in the early morning light, Walter collecting dew on his hooves as we waited for the sun to make it day.

I led Walter into the pen. "More feed for you without Boss here." I rubbed his back while I listened. No noise came from Regina's house. Her barnyard had never been so quiet. I glanced over my shoulder at the door. Closed. I needed Courage. I needed to ride more so I could think more. Get my thoughts back on the business side of this arrangement she and Jim had made for me. I laced my fingers through Walter's mane. I thought best from the back of a horse traveling across wide open spaces. Especially red spaces. Walter tossed his nose into the air and stepped away. I glanced back at Regina's house, then at Walter's back end as he abandoned me for his breakfast.

"You're no help." I went to the barn, opening and slamming the gate behind me. The two bottom rails dropped to the ground. "Neither are you." I shoved the boards against the gate post with my boot.

Walter stared from across the pen. "Well, what am I supposed to do? Go in and get her? Talk to her? Wait until she comes out? That might be never." I glanced at the wobbling fence behind him, the way it leaned, the poor quality of the wood it had been made with. "Built by an Easterner and maintained by a man who needs two hands. Well, I gotta do something." I marched deeper into the barn and scavenged around where I'd found Flynn's tools. Shiny. Too light. Not the sort of tools I would choose, but evidently tools that seemed right to a man from New York. I gathered up what looked like the best of them that weren't piled in the wagon, and toted them outside, around the end of the barn to the first corral post.

I looked at the house and listened. Nothing. I turned back to the fence. Maybe I should just kick it down. One good shove the right direction and the whole string of posts and rails would topple. I liked the idea of a loud breaking sound.

I dropped Flynn's tools into the dirt, set my boot against the first post, and shoved. Rails tumbled, wood snapped, a satisfying crack split the air. I flattened the first post to the ground, and gave it a good stomp.

"I beg your pardon. I don't mean to interrupt."

I turned, keeping the post pinned beneath my boot. Doc sat in the barnyard, he, his horse, and his buggy between me and the house.

"Where'd you come from?" I glanced around as if I could spot him sneaking up. I should have. If I kept wrangling with that redheaded woman, I'd go soft like Walter, and lose my rangering skills. "Why you here again so soon?" I stared at the man who should be saying, "I do," instead of me. "Did you forget to do something?" I looked at his jacket and wondered what he'd think if I latched onto his lapels and dragged him off his buggy and into Regina's house.

"I shouldn't have left yesterday… I mean, I need to check with Mrs. Howard."

I glanced toward the house, still as a morgue, then back to where he sat atop his buggy. *I'm getting ready to live your life, you coward. If you'd do what a man's supposed to do, then I wouldn't be here.*

I nodded toward the house. "I think she's in there." I disappeared into the barn, made it just inside the door, and stopped. I looked to the side and stared at the widow's pitchfork. She'd skewer poor Doc on that thing, and her boy'd be no better off than he was now. They might all three be worse for it in the end.

"Doc."

He paused and glanced back.

"She's busy. Got things on her mind. Maybe you could talk to me, instead." I sidled to the post and rails I'd kicked down. Flynn's tools lay in a heap at my feet, and Walter stood at the far side of the pen. Doc glanced from me, back to the house, then to me again. I walked to the second post. It was still standing—barely—and I laid my hand on its wobbly top. Doc Harris wasn't a man who would burn down a ranch when it needed to be. Slivers from the post jabbed my skin, irritating where my father's barn's splinters remained. Doc was a good man, but he wouldn't create wounds for memories. He wouldn't know how to use them to heal.

"It's her I came to see. I need to talk to her." His eyes had that strain of where he wanted to be.

"She's in the middle of a discussion with me. When we finish, then it's your turn."

Chapter 20

Silent. Men surely are too silent. Doc left without a word. Jess lies with his eyes closed.

Ted stalks about with a frown on his face. Ben stays outside, hammering away at my fence. And Flynn. One conversation would have spared me all of this. ~Regina

"Next time you decide to tear something of mine down, ask me first." I stared at Ben, at his back where his shirt lay damp against his skin. I brushed strands of red curls from my face, fluttering in my way, already loose from the combs and pins I'd spent twenty minutes fixing and re-fixing. Just in case.

"Ours. Not yours." Ben straightened from the stoop he was bent into. He swiped an arm across his brow, streaks of dirt smearing his forehead.

Trails of sweat ran below the smears, drips collecting in his brows and lashes as the rest cleared paths down his cheeks. He swiped his arm across his eyes again, then dropped it, taking a nice long gander from my head to my toes. At the skirt I'd put on, the blouse and its fine lace tucked tight at its waist. "Mrs. Miller."

"Not yet. In case you didn't notice, I look nothing like a squaw."

"Oh, I notice." He took a step my way, glistening

in the sun as he did.

"I'm going to town, Mr. Miller."

"Alone?"

"That's up to you."

He came closer, close enough I could smell the work on him, the sweat and the dust, the old broken boards. He stopped right in front of me, and stared down. "How about we make this a little easier for both of us. Get to know each other proper. You like proper." He swiped a hand down the front of his shirt, another streak of wet grime left behind. "I'm Ben. Ben Miller." He extended a damp hand. "I hail from a little bit of everywhere. Mostly south. I'm pleased to meet you."

"If this is another handshake deal, I can tell you Mr. Gulliver isn't the sort of banker who would consider such a gesture a legal document. And neither do I."

"No, ma'am, this isn't a handshake deal, and you ain't no squaw."

"Okay, then. I'm Regina. Regina Howard from New York. Well, from Liberal, Kansas, now. And I'm not shaking your hand, so let it drop. I'm going to town."

"What's this?" Ted appeared at the mouth of the barnyard—the way he always did when no one was looking or wanting him there—astride Boss, his good hand pointing at what was left of the corral.

"Going into town." Ben grinned down at me. "I'll finish when we get back." Ben watched my hair, the floating strands that flitted across my face, then glanced down to my skirt again.

"I knew if you stuck around I'd be cleaning up your messes. *Ben*."

Ben gave his hat a tug. Ted was wasting his breath. It was as if he wasn't there. Only I was in Ben's world. Me and town. "I'll go hitch up the wagon, ma'am."

Chapter 21

My stepmother always said we sleep in the beds we make. I'm used to sleeping on the dirt. ~Rex

Liberal wasn't so large I hadn't figured out where to leave the wagon so it would be easy enough to get to. Regina'd been quiet most of the ride, fidgeting with the bag on her lap, and watching ahead the first half mile or so. It was the looking to the side she did the rest of the trip that wasn't right.

Walter'd tossed his head in the air as we started out, making me think to talk to the woman that was about to become my arranged wife, ask her about errands she might need to run, dry goods to buy, or the bank—if we got done what we were supposed to.

The widow listened to my first few questions, the green of her eyes growing darker with each one. I brought up every single bit of shopping I could think of, even suggested an extra errand or two, until she turned those dark eyes to the side and kept them that way. I'd tightened the reins on Walter for causing me so much trouble. I hopped down when he came to a stop in town, walked to her side of the wagon, and extended a hand.

"You look right nice, Mrs. Howard." And she did. I knew the right dress—any dress—would set off that tiny waist and the rest of the shape she buried beneath her husband's…her first husband's…clothing.

"I can manage." She bent around my hand and managed those nice clothes, dropping to the ground in them without my help.

"That skirt didn't get in your way at all."

"I've never met a man so obtuse."

"Obtuse?"

"I'll see you back here. Later." She didn't look up as she marched off, but I nodded anyway. She turned to the right when she reached the boarded walk, her small frame, her fiery red hair, and that swishing skirt disappearing around the corner.

I walked to Walter. "You weren't any help at all. Otherwise Mrs. Howard and I would both be smiling. Be glad you're not a mare." I gave his back a smack. "If you were, I'd sell you today and get me another horse."

Chapter 22

If I could buy anything, anything at all, it would be time. ~Regina

"I'll see you when I'm good and ready." That's what I should have said as I left Ben behind. "I'm coming with you...we have an arrangement to take care of." That's what he should have said back. But he didn't.

I hurried to the postal office. That bank had better have something of Flynn's after all, and be ready to do some bargaining, since Ben wasn't going to be a bit of help to me and Jess.

"We got a wire in for you." Mr. Green pulled a note from the wooden slots behind him. "Looks like your father."

"Thank you." I turned from Mr. Greene and opened and read the offer my father made often—ever since Flynn's death and even before, while I was growing up—to take care of things. I read his usual words—strong, clear, precise, but loving—as he insisted again I let the ranch go. He offered to move Jess and me back to New York, settle us into a new home close to a good school. I stared at what he said was best. It would be so easy... No more Ben, no more Mr. Gulliver... Just let go... "No."

"Pardon?" Mr. Greene called from the counter.

"Sorry. Just talking to myself." I felt that familiar take-charge air in my father's instructions. Everyone wanted to take charge of me and my ranch, leaving me constantly saying no. Except to one man. The one I should have said no to, and stuck to it to begin with. Ben.

"I'd like to send a wire." I returned to Mr. Greene and ignored his raised brow as he slid me a form. "Doing well. Expect letter." I scrawled in cursive, then handed to Mr. Greene both the form and a letter I'd written that was full of promise regarding our situation. *Jess is happy. We're adding to the ranch.* Everything except the name it needed.

"That'll be ten...I mean, two cents," Mr. Greene said.

I parted with the coins, and thanked him. I gazed at what was left of my money in the bottom of my bag as I stepped out onto the boarded walk. Not enough for a horse and some cattle. *Doggone you, Flynn. If I had our money, I'd be buying my way out of this fix instead of needing to marry my way out of it.*

I glanced down the walkway. No Ben. Thank God. I headed toward the bank.

"Mrs. Howard, where's your wagon parked?"

"I beg your pardon?"

Mr. Wayne stood in front of his dry goods store. He leaned on his broom, his long, thin stature a twin to it. He smiled and waved me inside.

"I'm not here to buy anything. I was going to the bank."

"Of course." Mr. Wayne held the door. I stepped inside, a plethora of flour, fabric, hardware, and oils I couldn't afford meeting me. *I can live without new fabric. I can live without extra tools.* I caught sight of the candy jars along the counter. All of the colors Jess used to get when Flynn was alive. *How can my boy live without those?*

"Tell me where your wagon is, and I'll carry this out for you."

"But…" I stared at the glistening sticks. "I can't…"

"Is it close?" Mr. Wayne slapped his hand on a stack of flour, dried meat, and more things than I'd seen in ages. Far more than what a few sticks of candy would cost.

"Excuse me, but those things aren't mine."

"You're Mrs. Howard." Mr. Wayne smiled, dusted his hands on the front of his apron.

"Yes, of course, we both know that." I hated silly games. "But…"

"Some fellow came by and gathered all of this up and said to put it with whatever else Mrs. Howard bought."

Whatever else I bought. Colors shone from the jars. "I'm not buying anything, and whoever that fellow was, he can't expect me to pay for his supplies. He can get his own!"

"He did get his own. These are all bought and paid for. Gave me a little extra to help you tote it to your wagon." Mr. Wayne rubbed his hands together.

"Mr. Wayne…" I stepped closer to the pile that stood higher than my knees. "Who was this man? Was it Doc?"

"No, ma'am, though the doctor's kind enough to do this sort of thing. No, this fellow was tall, with black hair. Seen him in here the other day, just looking around. Kin of yours?"

"Not at all…but I'll be sure to thank him."

Mr. Wayne smiled as he loaded his arms with half of what Ben had bought. "Thank him good. I'll need to make two trips."

"I'll show you the wagon." I led the way, the fire in my cheeks growing with each step. Leave it to a man to be sensible about his meals he'd yammered about all the way into town and know nothing about… I stood to the side, watched Mr. Wayne stack both loads of Ben's supplies in the back of the wagon, a large heavy pan clattering in last of all. "What's that?" I marched to the end of the wagon as Mr. Wayne shoved the monstrosity toward the front.

"You don't have one of those?" He frowned. "Best skillet made."

"I would argue with that. My cookware from New York is excellent. Nothing like that beast. It looks too heavy to lift."

"No wonder you're so thin." He chuckled. "You need one of these to cook a real meal out here. I'm surprised you don't have one."

"Well, I don't. But I suppose if I can ever lift it, there might be a use for it." Like taking a swing at that tall varmint with the black hair.

Chapter 23

Shouldn't have to sniff twice to know there's a rat nearby. ~Rex

I watched from beside a nearby building as Regina marched Mr. Wayne to the wagon, and grinned when the frying pan hit the wagon's bed. Good thing I paid him, since there wasn't much gratitude in her thanks. Wasn't much kindness in her face, either, as she glanced around when the man was done. I stepped back and prayed she hadn't spotted me. Gave her enough time to decide I wasn't around, then peered around the building's edge and caught the back of her heading the direction of the bank. She wasn't supposed to be going there today, except with me. It was all that nervous talk that must have driven her to it. Walter'd never forgive me if the widow went in there and found out Ted was a better option than me.

I stepped out as she pushed through the bank's door. I hello-ma'am-ed and howdy-sir-ed my way to the bank's front. Bold. Like I wasn't terrified of the little woman inside. I knew better than to act shady around a bank. Too easy to get shot that way.

Regina was seated with her back to me as I stepped through the door. She was facing Mr. Gulliver, her bag and her hands in her lap. I kept my head down and my shoulders hunched, pausing at the center table in the lobby with the other customers who were speaking of the weather, waving paperwork, and signing their names. Maybe she already knew Ted could sign. Maybe shaking her hand, tearing down her corral, and making silly chatter on the way to town had made her madder than I thought.

I pretended to sort through papers as I eased around the table's edge, working my way close enough to hear what the widow...my arrangement...my wife-to-be... said. I stacked and restacked blank sheets, some with lines and places for dates, all of them with a spot for dollar amounts.

"Mr. Gulliver, my good name as Flynn's wife...widow...should suffice."

I wondered if her cheeks were the same color as her hair. Red. I wanted to look.

"For the moment, that is. After that, I have a proposal for you, Mr. Gulliver."

I glanced to the side as the banker leaned forward, elbows, arms, hands—all of it draped in wealth as he eased her way. "No, ma'am, you're mistaken. I have a proposal for you."

"Not before mine." I was behind Regina before Mr. Gulliver could propose Ted as her man, my hands on her shoulders, as I stared over her head into her banker's face. I leaned close to that red, as close as I dared. "There you are. Are you ready?"

She looked up, her eyes the size of something her banker would appreciate—dollars.

I slid to Regina's side as Mr. Gulliver came out of his chair. "My proposal comes before anyone's. You ready?" I extended my elbow. I'd done that only one other time in my life. Ages ago with Becky. The same night she told me she wouldn't be seeing me anymore. I held it steady and watched Regina's face.

Her small hand rose, her fingers inching around my elbow.

"I might still be interested in some land." I said it slow and easy, with only a quick glance to Mr. Gulliver as I watched Regina. Not the rush in which I nearly said it as the warmth of her hand took hold. "Like you talked about the other day. But first, I have more important business to take care of." I lifted Regina out of her chair. "I mean, me and Mrs. Howard have important business to take care of."

"You might want to reconsider." Mr. Gulliver planted his fingertips on his desk's glassy top and leaned into his arms.

"Don't look back," I whispered as I drew Regina away from her banker. "Stay with me."

I held onto her until we made it outside. I continued to hold and continued to walk, several steps of howdy-ing and helloing, until she let go.

She squared herself, and faced me. "Do you mean it? Or do you want to shake hands out here in front of the bank and see if Mr. Gulliver will turn over the deeds?"

"I meant every word. Mrs. Howard, it's high time you became Mrs. Miller, before you become something worse, like stowed on a train heading off to where you clearly don't want to go." Or yoked to a one-handed ranch manager that collects fancy broken combs. "And someday you're going to have to tell me about this other deed I keep hearing about. But not today."

I took her by the elbow and steered her down the walkway, the only aisle I'd ever known.

Chapter 24

On a train heading East or in front of a Justice of the Peace in Kansas. Not sure which is worse. ~Regina

The world became tiny. I shut out Jess and Flynn. My parents. Ted. It was just me and this stranger and the lie I was about to tell. A huge lie. Far greater than the finagling I'd been doing with the bank.

"And do you..." The Justice of the Peace's voice droned on. If I didn't hear that I'd love, honor, and obey, maybe it was okay if I said yes. I distracted myself with thoughts of New York, of restaurants there, of Boss and learning to ride, of the fights Jess and I had over the ranch. Of this. My plan. An arrangement, and nothing more, followed by a parting. I rehearsed my answer to the question and thought my most recent meal might end up at my feet.

"I do."

The Justice of the Peace's voice became a background drone. He was asking Ben now. I prayed Ben would lie, just as I had. Not pull anything sneaky when we were done, like deciding to stay, turn my ranch into something *he* enjoyed. The Justice of the Peace paused, peered at me over tiny spectacles. I glanced down. I wondered if I'd groaned. Or gasped.

Ben's boots were worn, miles dulling the leather, reddish hues tingeing them as if they'd been dyed. He was so much taller than I was, taller than Flynn. Flynn. We hadn't been particularly romantic in our marriage. But he'd been my vow. The one Jess still kept. The one that gave me the right to go back home to New York without complication, without explanation, without a penny in my pocket, and without judgment.

"I do." Ben's voice was strong. I glanced up to make sure he didn't mean it.

Ben didn't try to kiss me when the ceremony ended. He merely squeezed my upper arm and led the Justice of the Peace aside to discuss payment, paperwork, whatever needed to be settled.

Settled. More settled than I'd expected from this man after he tended my injured son out on the prairie. I gazed at the stark room as the two men sealed my ranch's fate. The fate I wanted.

"You ready?" Ben was at my side. The room began to swim, the walls to melt.

"A swooning bride," was the last thing I heard. After that, everything went black.

Chapter 25

For someone hard as nails on the inside, Mrs. Miller sure is soft on the outside. ~Rex

I propped Regina against my shoulder, red hair, clothing she did justice to, and the scent of a woman mixed with fresh air so close and powerful I garbled the guttural command for Walter to take it even slower than usual. He understood, in spite of my bungling, and eased forward. Somehow Walter understood women better than I did. Regina's head lolled back and forth, a sea of curls washing against my arm as the wagon lumbered toward home. Her home. Our home. I dropped her bag on the floorboard near our feet and caught combs and pins as they came loose, freeing more of her hair and its waves as she rolled against my arm and my shoulder...whatever she happened to touch.

I pondered my father and stepmother, wondered about things I hadn't noticed or cared about as a boy, as I balanced Regina against me. How did they behave as husband and wife? Even though Regina and I would never live the way they did, we had to put up a good pretense in front of folks. At least in front of the bank. Until we both got what we wanted.

Her head rolled forward, as I thought back to those secret parts of family life that remained a mystery to me. It slid off my arm, and dropped to my lap.

"Whoa!"

Walter yanked to a stop, jerking Regina farther forward.

"Not you, Walter, giddy-up."

Walter started again. I looped an arm around Regina, around her shoulders, and dragged her closer to my hips. I held her there, held and beheld a face crowned with a mane of red. Red. My favorite color. I ran a finger over her cheek. "Regina, are you with me?"

Her skin was soft, so soft I traced a line the length of her jaw, her face smoother than anything I'd ever touched. Her hair spread over her features and across my legs—so much red, like the sky during an Oklahoma sunset. I hooked my finger around a long strand and pulled it aside. I wanted to touch more of it…all of it…draw it through my fingers the way I did Walter's mane.

"Doggone it all, anyway. This is why I never got married. It's too confounding." I laid the reins across the seat to my left and pinned them under my thigh. With both hands, I raised her up, held her close, and patted the palm of my hand against her cheek. "Regina, wake up."

Her eyes fluttered. Green hit me in the late afternoon light. Her lashes lined that green, beautiful strokes like a painting again, arching around what was now my second favorite color. I propped her close and cupped her face in a hand. Those lashes closed, then opened, until at last recognition set in…a stormy sunrise…eyes widening and lashes shooting up. She shrugged out of my arms and looked around at Walter, at the passing scenery, and finally, at me.

"Did I fall asleep?"

"No," I dragged the reins from under my thigh. "You fainted."

"Fainted?" She stared at Walter's rump. I watched our wedding come back to her, a new sort of dawning, a crimson blush where it rose. "Oh, my."

I flicked the reins. Walter hied it a bit more. She laid a hand on my forearm. "No, wait."

"Whoa," I said again, this time to Walter. He stopped. The three of us sat, the wind in our faces, the grasses bowing our direction.

"We're married now?"

"You going to faint again?"

She shook her head.

"Then, yes, we are."

Her back bowed against the seat as she stared forward.

"So we did it. I told Jess this morning I'd do something."

I tucked the reins back under my leg. "Something?"

"Yes, something." More color returned to her face. "I wasn't sure what it would be, after your handshake deal, but... Oh, never mind. He remembers now."

I glanced at the woman that was now my bride. The red hair that billowed around her face. "Remembers us talking about getting married?"

"Yes, that. And since I didn't know if you were actually going to give me a civilized ceremony...which you came close to not doing...I had other plans in mind."

"Like proposing to your banker." I liked the way her face could turn the same color as that hair.

"Not that sort of proposal. I had to do something, though, since it seemed marriage was rather onerous to you."

I gazed at her, watched her curls toss in the wind. "Onerous?"

"Distasteful. Something you really didn't want to do."

I settled back on the bench seat alongside her and stared at Walter's rump myself. "I thought *you* really didn't want to marry. You needed a husband's name to hold onto this ranch, and I needed...well, I was needing to start a new life. We both got what we wanted. Right?"

Her head took a slow trip in a full circle, something I figured was supposed to be a nod. "Right. I guess we did both get what we wanted. I'm certainly glad you're satisfied."

Satisfied? If this was what marriage was supposed to feel like, then I wasn't. "Mrs. Howard—I mean, Mrs. Miller—you got what you wanted, and I'll figure my way, but besides us, there's Jess. And as far as he goes in all of this, my experience with trying to satisfy boys is that they like to be treated like men. They like to know the black and white of things so they can sort them out. He's going to want to know what this something you've done is." I watched her face, the green and the red, watched for the something that pertained to me.

Her brows drew together and leveled into a frown. "By all means, we want all of you men satisfied and treated properly."

"Properly? Well, then, if Jess, and Ted, and everyone else is to be treated properly, where do I properly sleep?"

I watched the red of her face, hoping to see her relax, the red of her lips, waiting to see her smile, and the red of her hair...most of all I was wanting to see her toss every bit of it back and laugh. Properly. Satisfied. I loved red. Just never seen so much of it in a woman before. Red like fire. Hot fire.

I gripped her face between my hands, watched her green eyes as I brought it to mine. Those lips were burning, stinging me with words as I pressed them against my own. Pressed them until the words stopped, and she pressed back. Her mouth, her shoulders, everything she had to offer melding into me. I'd only kissed someone once. Becky. A slight peck on the cheek. But in this moment it was as if I'd had lessons all my life and I knew exactly what to do. So did Mrs. Howard.

I mean Mrs. Miller.

Chapter 26

Nothing resurrects an old memory like a kiss from a handsome man. Nothing puts that memory to rest quicker, either. ~Regina

His hands were rough, powerful against my face. Flynn's had never been that way. Ben's were big; they were strong, almost as strong as the kiss he gave me. I swam in a sea of leather, of hands made rugged by work, of soap I'd never smelled before. The black of his hair, the coarseness of the stubble he barely kept shaved, the potency of a man who'd run the land with cattle and never let it run him, engulfed me.

The vigor I'd fought in this man was there, fueling the fervor of his kiss. I'd never known such power, such hunger, such fire. Time ignited right there in the wagon, exploding in a magnificent display. I immersed myself in the heat, relished its charge.

I pressed deeper, neither of us finding the bottom. His lips, my lips, our lips…

Then mine. Just mine as his softened. His relaxed, his mouth moved away.

I leaned further forward, searched for his kiss. His hands, so firm around my face, relaxed as his lips had, slid from my cheeks, over my shoulders, and down my arms. My skin prickled in waves behind them. Fire followed his touch in full flame until both of his hands dropped into his lap. I opened my eyes. I glanced down and stared at his hands, grabbed them up, latched on, and cupped his monstrosities in my smaller ones, holding tight, never to let go.

My lips burned. My skin crawled with excitement, my hands warm, my face hot. I wondered if Flynn saw. He hadn't answered even once when I'd challenged him from on top his grave. Maybe he couldn't hear or see what I was doing. Doing for the first time. I'd never been kissed this way before. Of course, neither had he. Poor Flynn!

I stared at Ben, swimming in his dark eyes. Passion roiled through me, a tumult that never wanted to stop.

"I'm sorry." He slid his hands from mine.

"What?"

"That wasn't part of your arrangement. I wasn't supposed to do that." He tipped his head back, stared toward heaven. "Unless things could be different…" He glanced down at me. I saw the question in his eyes that I wanted to hear *his* answer to, not mine. I waited, gave him the chance to say yes, things could be different. Waited and watched the question give way to an answer I didn't want. "Never mind. They couldn't." He rubbed his hands along the tops of his thighs. "I'm sorry. It won't happen again."

I was falling. I had no idea where from or where to, because I'd never been that high before. I looked below me, and there was no bottom, no place for a scream to stop, or for tears to hit when they fell. I gripped the seat and stared at Walter's rump, tightened my throat against the fist that wanted to wrench out my heart. "You're right." I spoke over the pain, my voice sounding odd and wrong in the prairie wind. "It won't happen again."

He made one of those infernal noises only Walter understood. A sound I'd be sure to use in the future. If I ever spoke to this man again.

Chapter 27

Morrissey, Morrissey, Morrissey. I'm a Ranger, I'm a Ranger, I'm a Ranger. ~Rex

Kansas grass looked greener than it had before. The wind felt fresher. Brown dirt sounded solid, like a road meant to be traveled on.

I shook my head. No, Kansas was all plains. Dull. Ruts didn't make a true road.

Her lips were soft, yet powerful. Warm, yet hot. Different from Becky's cheek. Responsive. Alive.

I stared at Walter's rear end as it lolled from side to side. This was a business arrangement. She'd get her ranch, and I'd get whoever was behind the thieves stealing ranches. And eventually I'd get Morrissey. She'd stay, and I'd go. Back home to my father. Back home to rebuild Pop's ranch. Back home to red—red dirt, not red hair. It was our understanding. We'd marry, then part.

I wanted to glance to the side. At her. At red lips and red cheeks. I made another sound, a noise with my tongue that told Walter to step it up a bit.

"What is that ridiculous noise you make at poor Walter? Does he really understand you? Wouldn't real talking be better? Surely the poor animal would be happier if you spoke English."

"English? Like obdurate? Onerous? Some of those

foreign words you toss around?"

"How about obtuse?"

I glanced to the side, at my arrangement, my wife, crossing her arms. The blaze in her eyes was obvious, even from the side. Red. Not a good kind of red. I looked at Walter. "Giddy-up."

She didn't budge other than to snatch that bag of hers from the floor, swipe all of the combs and pins she could into its top, and press it tight against her chest. The chest she'd pressed tight against me moments ago. Red. Her eyes were red around the edges. I'd never seen so much red. Except in Luke's eyes. And my father's, Adler's. And mine, when my stepmother died.

She yanked her head to the right.

"I said I'm sorry. I can't take that kiss back, and neither can you." I watched, hoping the tension in her shoulders would let down. Tension I'd caused. Walter should have stopped me. "Let's pretend it never happened. Just carry on with this business arrangement like we're supposed to." Those tiny shoulders that had felt so good moments before looked sharp and painful. "I'm sorry."

"I heard you," she shot. "Stop jabbering about it, so I can forget it happened. Be happy to forget it, too. Already would have, if you didn't go on and on about what a big mistake you made and how sorry you are. I heard you. I don't need to hear it again." The bulk of her hair spilled down her back, the wind lifting and blowing it behind us. Red.

I made another noise, and Walter stepped up his pace. A burst of air exploded to my right. Her arms crossed tighter over the bag. "Stop the wagon! Make one of your silly noises to tell Walter to stop!"

"Whoa," I said.

"See? He understands English."

"We get on good several ways." Maybe because he was a he, and had black hair instead of red. Maybe because I'd never been tempted to wrap my arms around him and...

"I'm walking the rest of the way home." She scooted to the right and swung her feet over the end of the seat.

I grabbed her arm. "Wait. You're not walking anywhere. I will."

She yanked her arm free and brushed where I'd held onto it. "Your hands are rough. You should be more careful where you put them."

I glanced down at my palms. At the one with red bumps where the barn splinters lay, looking even redder next to her white. She frowned from my hand to my face.

"Splinters. Just what your backside's going to look like if you keep sliding around on this seat." I jumped to the ground and handed her the reins. "I'll meet you at the house. You decide what you want to tell Jess. If you want to tell him nothing happened, and that we didn't get married, that's fine with me. I'll go along with whatever you decide. And I'll stay in the loft above Ted. But pick a story and stick to it. Men prefer facts, so what you say, every one of them will believe."

She took the reins. "Facts. What men like. Whether it works or not."

I saw myself in her eyes, and it wasn't good. I made that noise she hated, and Walter started forward.

Chapter 28

I didn't know men could be so heartless until I discovered my own. ~Regina

I didn't turn and look back. I hoped Ben got lost, even though that was unlikely for a cattle driver. I tried to make that noise he made so Walter would go faster, leave Ben farther behind. I clicked. I tried a low growl. Walter snorted and shook his head. I flicked the reins, and he stepped to, a smart little clip that would leave Ben in my dust.

Men liked facts. Phooey! I was sure Jess would like to hear his father's money had vanished. That we were penniless because of someone's mismanagement. That we'd lost everything—the money we'd brought, four years of good education for Jess, and…

Ben's lips. I could feel them again. I touched my mouth, running my fingers over my lips.

And all we had left—barely had left—was a tumbledown ranch house and a dilapidated barn.

I'd learned to ride, though. And learned to plant. Learned what it meant to tend animals, and preserve food. There was some good had come…

Along with the husband I didn't want.

I flicked the reins again. The ranch came into view, and I was glad to see it. Glad to have this wagon, glad Ben was way behind, glad to come up on my own, take care of Walter, unload the wagon myself, and get out to the pasture to work on that fence like I should have done instead of riding into Liberal to get married.

I edged Walter near the barn and tugged back on the reins. "Whoa." He stopped the moment I spoke English. I smiled. Maybe more of a smirk. I lifted off the seat to avoid splinters, climbed to the ground, and walked to Walter's head. "Good boy." I patted his nose, feeling the softness of it. "Mind taking me out to the pasture after I unload and change?" He raised his head and nickered. He was a handsome horse. Black, like his owner. "Well, most of you is good."

I glanced at the things Ben had bought, especially the ridiculously large pan, and carried my bag into the house. Jess would ask. I came through the front door and set my bag on the table. I ran my hands down the front of my skirts. I could blame his father. But I wouldn't. I could blame Ben. I wouldn't do that, either. I could blame the bank. Or my father for never telling me what I figured out anyway. About money, and what to do with it. Something he should have told Flynn.

I marched straight for my bedroom and opened the door. Facts. Jess lay facing me, his eyes closed, a gentle lifting up and down of the quilt draped over him. I could see Ted had been there, helping while I was gone.

Facts could wait. I backed out of my room and closed the door. I walked through the kitchen and out to the wagon, where Ben's things still lay. I looked at what he'd bought, what sort of items a man like him would choose. When other things should have been on his mind.

A sensation bubbled between my heart and my head, and it ran clear through me as I studied what was important to him…to Ben. I touched my lips. No. This was a business arrangement. His name for a time. Then we'd part.

I stretched and grabbed for the closest items, packages upon bundles tumbling to the side. "Ben Miller, where in the world do you intend to keep this many things?" I grabbed again, and red, green, and yellow flashed beyond my fingertips, shiny colors glistening deep within the disorder of what he'd bought. I rounded the wagon, keeping my eye on the colors, coming along its side, and stood on my toes.

Candy. I knew it. Shiny sticks like I'd wanted for Jess. I strained to the very tips of my toes, leaned into the wagon's side, and stretched my fingers, their tips just short of where the candy lay.

A hand, a rough hand, latched onto the bundle, tugging it up and out of sight. I jumped, I grabbed, I threw my head back, and watched the colors disappear. Under Ben's arm. He stretched over me again, grabbed a couple more of his items, and headed to the house.

"Wait! What are you doing?" I ran behind.

He went through the door into the kitchen, then to the pantry. He came back with a package wrapped in brown paper, and the candy. "For you." He extended the parcel to me. "And for the boy." He gave me the candy and nodded toward my room.

He walked back out while I stood there with three colorful sticks and a plain brown package. He returned with the rest of his purchases while I still stood there, and he toted them to the pantry, also, that heavy black skillet dangling from one hand.

I listened as he arranged and stacked all he'd bought in my tiny space.

He ducked as he came back through the doorway.

"I don't mind if you keep your things in there." I lifted my head and nodded toward the pantry.

"Our things. I'm half of this arrangement, and I plan to do my part." He walked across the kitchen to the door. "I'm taking Walter to the pasture as soon as I put my gear in the loft. I'll cut some posts and work on the fence."

"You're not fixing my fence."

"Our fence." He nodded toward the brown package, and closed the door behind him.

Chapter 29

She wears the trousers and I wear the apron. Never seen the like in my life. ~Rex

A man needed a map to figure his way around a woman. My stepmother always said God made woman to be her husband's helpmeet. I never understood what that word meant. I'd say for once Regina didn't understand a word, either.

"How was town?" Ted spoke from behind me. I didn't have to turn to know this wasn't a friendly question.

I steadied my foot on the bottom rung of the ladder I'd just come down, from the closest thing I'd had to a bedroom since I was a boy, the loft above his bunkroom. I gave it a shake; it wobbled worse than the fence I'd started to tear down. "You build this?"

"No, Regina's husband did. Her real husband."

That wasn't a guess I heard. And it wasn't a trick to get me to say I'd married his boss. I didn't have to say anything. It was clear he knew.

"The one with a name we honor, and whose memory I intend to protect." He nodded toward the loft. "Seems she intends to protect it, too."

I removed my foot from the rung and stretched to my full height. I never liked sleeping where a snake could crawl under me. Never trust them. Always watch them. Do them in if they get too close. I walked outside, straight to the wagon.

"Getting married don't make you the boss." Ted stood in the barn's doorway. I'd seen plenty of anger in my day and knew the results of jealousy. Ted's face and voice had plenty of both.

"That's exactly what it does, and since I aim to do the work myself, I guess there's not much use for you around here anymore." I hopped onto the wagon and clicked at Walter, the sound that said go fast. This arrangement was a job. Just a job. I headed to the nearest cluster of trees. Fast.

****

"I told Jess."

I looked up from the four posts I'd cut, the fifth dropping onto the toe of my boot. They were boy's trousers and shirt I'd bought Regina, but they fit her like no boy I'd ever seen. The boots, too, new and peeking out from cuffs that barely needed rolling. I wanted to whistle, but I didn't. All I could think was that Flynn Howard had been one lucky man.

"I said, I told Jess."

"I…" I cleared my throat, stuck on saying what I'd never been able to say to a woman. Maybe because my eyes were stuck on what I'd never seen so much of before, the legs, the hips, things I'd only been able to imagine.

The widow…my wife…reddened, like the red I loved in Oklahoma. "Stammering isn't a conversation." She jerked her chin up.

"I mean, I heard you. About Jess. Your ranch manager knows, too." I ran my arm across my brow. "Your wedding gift looks mighty nice."

170

She slid her hands down the shirt that fit in all the right places, cupped her palms around her hips as she slipped them to her thighs. "You should have let me tell Ted."

I nodded, watching those hands. "It wasn't me that told him."

"It had to be you. Unless he just guessed."

"Men don't like guessing. We like facts."

The green of those eyes flashed just before they got corralled under a frown. "Let's get this fact straight, now that we've initiated this arrangement. Your job was to provide a name. I'll manage Ted, just as I'll manage my son. And I'll do this fence, too." She glanced into the wagon at the extra roll of wire and tools I'd added.

"I told you it wasn't me that told him." I had my ideas how Ted might know Mrs. Howard was Mrs. Miller now, but I was surprised he'd known it so fast.

"From now on, just leave the ranch and all of its components to me."

Ted must be a component. Maybe that meant ranch manager in Eastern talk.

She bent over my stack of posts, latched onto the end of one, and gave it a tug, her pretty white hands straining as she pulled.

"Is that a component?" I nodded at the post. She dropped the end and walked to the other, lifted and shoved. "I mean, I'd help you, unless that post there is a ranch component."

"I don't need your help."

I watched my bride, hair as red hot as a spark. I knew from burning my father's ranch it took only one good spark to start a fire hot enough to take a building

171

down. "Let me get the other end. That's only half a component. We'll set it on the wagon together."

"I'll get this post; you can get the next."

The next seven. I figured I could have two more cut by the time she got that one anywhere near the wagon. Two more, if I could stop watching those boy britches. "Suit yourself."

I listened to her grunts, ladylike Eastern gushes of air as she managed to get that post up on its end. She waltzed it to the back of the wagon, making me envy that block of wood the way she wrapped herself around it and swayed through the grass. I grunted when she dropped it against the bed. Looked up when I realized my thoughts were the only sounds. Red was there. Red stare, red flare. I bent to the fifth post I'd made as she bent to and rolled the other three. I didn't watch as she worked each one to the end of the wagon, lifted her leaning post on top of them, climbed on the three herself, and hoisted her post the rest of the way in.

Red. I let the fifth log lay. Red looked good when it was wet. Red hair stuck to her forehead from the work she'd done.

"Bring me that one at your feet, and I'll load it, too." She swiped an arm against her forehead as she pointed to post number five.

"You did yours. My turn now."

"I changed my mind. I'll do it myself. I'm pretty good at it." She hopped down and marched to my post and kicked and rolled it to the wagon's end.

I watched this time. "This would go a lot faster if you'd just let me help. No sense you struggling with…"

"I'm not struggling, I'm contriving. Besides, these posts probably weigh half of what that pan you bought

172

today weighs."

"Skillet."

"Okay, skillet. I don't know how you expect me to cook with that thing." She hoisted one end of my log onto her little platform of posts.

"I don't expect you to cook with it. I'm probably a better cook, anyway, so I'll handle the skillet."

"I won't have you in my kitchen!" She planted her fists on her hips, hips plainly seen in those nice-fitting boy's pants.

"Well, if you don't want me in your kitchen, or your pasture, and certainly not your bedroom, Mrs. Howard…I mean, Mrs. Miller…then I guess I'll leave you alone. You can take over from here." I shoved log number five into the wagon, then loaded the three that made up her platform.

I looked down at the widow, my wife, wrapped my hands around a waist begging to be touched, toted her to the wagon's seat, and planted her on its top. Her mouth…her lips…were wide open as I made a sound Walter lifted his head to. "He'll get you to that pen you're going to build. I'm heading to the house." Walter hopped-to at my next sound, quick enough she toppled over—red, a flash of green, and pretty little arms and legs flailing to hold on.

Arms and legs I now knew more about than I probably should.

Chapter 30

Now I know what grub really is. But it's apparently the way Kansas cooking should be done. ~Regina

I rolled the wagon to my barn, bringing Walter to a halt. It was nearly dark, and I glanced around in the shadowy light, letting the wind cool my skin where my loose curls and my shirt were plastered with sweat. Every muscle protested as I stood, dull aches fighting me as I climbed down and settled Walter for the night, then dragged Flynn's tools into the barn, past Ted's closed bunk room door, where the too-quiet told me he wasn't there. Probably off for a ride. Or something. I dropped Flynn's tools near where he'd kept them. Ted said he checked on things. Flynn said that's what ranch men did. Probably checking on nothing, but nothing was what I was paying him.

I glanced around the barn, arching my back while squinting through the meager light at the nothing I owned. Lifting, dragging, rolling posts, digging holes, along with stringing wire, wore me out. But not as much as Ben did. If I could find what else I needed, besides getting his name, Mr. Miller would be paid off and out of my life. I stared around the main section of the barn where I'd already scoured the obvious places for Flynn's money and any extra deeds. Under boards, in knotholes, behind whatever I could move.

"Flynn, why did you have to go and die without telling me anything? Even if you'd just told me where our money was, I could take care of the fix I'm in now. Myself. My way. With a healthy boy at my side."

I glanced at the places Flynn had favored for his things—his saddle, his tools, his tins and boxes. "Come on, Flynn, show me." I moved around the interior, forcing every muscle to cooperate in the waning light. I checked around the lower floor and stared up toward the small loft above. Ben's place. He wasn't really a husband; he was just temporary. Just a name. A name who was sorry he'd kissed me.

I looked toward the ceiling, then at the door to Ted's room. I'd never been through that door, never even seen inside the bunkroom where he stayed. Flynn had said Ted kept it neat, stayed warm enough in the winter with a tiny stove he'd put in there.

I tapped a boot on the hard dirt floor and eyed Flynn's tools I'd just put away. I wrapped my fingers around the handle of a shovel and thrust its tip against the ground. It bounced back, every muscle shrieking in protest. "You wouldn't work this hard to bury something, would you?" I dragged the shovel to the barn door, thumped the dirt floor with my boot, and looked for places soft enough he would have been comfortable digging, or still loose because that was where he'd actually dug. And hopefully buried what I needed.

I pockmarked our barn floor in a steady rhythm, turning scoop after scoop of dirt over, and shoveling each back where it belonged when I saw nothing was there, leaving the ground looking like a prairie dog field. My muscles cried, but I kept digging. One of these gouges would surely pay off and get Ben off my ranch. "Your money is in here somewhere, and not out in the prairie or the fields. Right?"

"You talking to me?" A tall lean silhouette framed by what was left of the outdoor light stood in the barn's doorway.

"No, I wasn't talking to you." I pressed the shovel close to my side, stretched as tall as I could, so its handle wouldn't show above my head.

Ben stepped into the barn, his silhouette becoming more like a cowhand as he approached; steady, powerful, more capable than any I'd ever seen. He turned as he came close, edged to my left, walking near enough I could see one of my tea towels dangling from his hand. I inched with him, keeping my face his way and the shovel behind my back.

"You're in my kitchen cooking, aren't you? I told you not to, and now you need my help. Right?"

"You planting a shade crop in here?" Ben lifted his hat and scratched his head as he studied the ground around me, the craters scattered across the barn floor. "I'm handy with a skillet, but I'm more handy with a shovel. After we eat I could dig a few more holes in the barn for your shade garden. What did you say you were planting?"

"I'm not planting anything; I'm just loosening the barn floor. It's good for it. You go on with destroying my kitchen and our meal. I'll manage the barn."

He flipped my kitchen towel over his shoulder. "You need to come in and eat. The cooking's done."

"Cooking's not why you're here, you know, and I could do whatever you're doing, with a more sensible-sized pan."

Ben cut between the mounds of dirt. No longer a vague silhouette, he stood tall, a commanding man towering over me. "Mrs. Miller, nothing about why I'm here is the right way for things to be done. Not the way your husband would have intended, I'm betting, and not something I relish looking back on and feeling rotten about someday. I've never been married before, but one thing's for sure—I married a woman, and I intend to stay a man no matter what I do for her. And her boy." Ben slid my towel off his shoulder. "And whatever you do, and however you choose to do it, even after I'm gone—keep in mind that boy in there still needs a ma."

He draped the towel over the handle of the shovel behind me, stretching his arm above my head as he did. In his nearness, in his quiet, I stopped breathing. I waited, watched as he retracted his arm, knowing he could, he *should* say more. His lips parted, and his eyes stayed on me like two black holes in the night. I closed my own, tipped my head up, and waited for whatever his lips decided to do.

"Supper's ready." The shovel jiggled at my back. I opened my eyes as the towel he'd snatched from its top sailed past in his hand.

He went from a man to a silhouette again as he marched through my barn and headed for my house. Fast.

Chapter 31

They say three's a crowd. No matter how many there are, I'm always number three. ~Rex

I snatched the towel off her shovel and left Regina behind in the dark. Fuming, I'd suspect. No, not just fuming—something else, too. Something I saw in her eyes the moment she closed them. I kicked at the ugly brown dirt of her barnyard as I headed back to the house.

I'd never been a widow, and certainly never a mother, so how was I to know what was wrong or right? I'd been a man all my life, and I'd known plenty of hurt. A long ride in the open spaces took care of most of it, and Courage took care of the rest. I paused and looked back at the black hole of a doorway on her barn. Our barn. I slapped my palm with her towel. It stung. Maybe she and I both needed a little Courage.

I stepped into the kitchen and stared at what I'd made. Picked up one of her too thin, too tiny, too delicate china plates and heaped it with biscuits, chipped beef gravy, and potato fried in lard.

Jess's eyes grew bigger than the plate when I stepped through the bedroom door. "Sit up. Time to eat."

"Ma said I can't..."

"She ain't the only one wearing pants around

here." I stood above him. His gaze went to the heaping plate in my hands. "Had to pile it high since there ain't much room on these dinky dishes."

He kept his eyes on the food as he squirmed his shoulders, trying to snake upward on the pillow behind him.

"Looks like you need a hearty meal. Come on, get yourself a little higher up." *Run harder. Run faster. Don't let the smoke get you.* I held the dish just out of Jess's reach, watched his white face as he struggled to sit up. He coughed when he finally righted himself, dropping back against the pillow.

"Good man." I settled the plate on his lap. "Gonna get you up and out of that bed in short order, too." I saw his eyes swell, then narrow. I was the enemy in their family. But before I gave his mother the parting she wanted, I'd make sure this boy was ready to stand up and be a man.

Regina was there as I stepped back into the kitchen. She'd slipped in quiet, looked worn, inside and out, tiny in the soiled wedding outfit I'd given her.

"Fix a plate and go eat with him." I kept to myself what I'd rather say, and how I wanted to say it, as I nodded toward her bedroom door I'd left open.

She gazed at the food.

"You gotta be starved after building fence and airing all that ground in the barn." I reined in my tone. She looked so small. But still terrifying.

"It's part of my…" She stopped. "Never mind."

"Ted out there? He eat with you much?" I hoped not, to both questions.

She shook her head as she went to the washpan and scrubbed her hands. She patted them on the towel I'd

179

left wadded by the basin, then refolded it. "Sometimes he eats with us. Especially when Flynn was alive...around."

She filled a plate, taking more than I imagined a little woman like her could hold, and disappeared into her bedroom. The nice bedroom. The one with enough frills to tell me what that worn woman was really like underneath those trousers and the determined grit. Low voices came from her and her boy as I began fixing a plate for myself. Something about being married was messing with my appetite, making unappealing the cooking I knew was good. I set my plate on the table, leaving mother and son alone, and had laid a hand on one of the chairs to sit down when I heard a noise outside. Dirt, hard dirt. And metal.

I stepped to the kitchen window, stayed to the side, and listened, then slipped outside. I made my way to the darker side of the barn, slid low and slow until I was near the door. Someone was digging inside. I glanced back at the house. She hadn't come out without me knowing. She was too feisty to miss a chance to stop and tell me how awful she thought skillet cooking was. I glanced at the open window to her bedroom. The grunt I heard in the barn wasn't her. I knelt lower, removed my hat, and eased an eye around the edge of the door.

Ted was pretty capable with just one hand. He managed Regina's shovel just fine with his good arm and a foot. He finished a hole, broke up the clumps with his hand, then refilled it before he moved on. Maybe Regina really was airing out her barn floor. Maybe she and Flynn did it every year and the joke was on me. This was Kansas; maybe things were different with brown dirt. Maybe.

I started to slip backward and leave Ted to helping her, but he moved to the next hole. One she'd already dug. I watched him re-dig what she'd done, kneel down and sift through the dirt with his good hand while he pinned the shovel close to his body with the other arm. He grunted when he stood.

I eased away from the barn's door, staying low as I moved from the building. Whatever Regina had been doing earlier, Ted was redoing it now. My guess was he wasn't helping.

Chapter 32

Giving is one thing. Being taken from is another.
~Regina

Ben stood in the kitchen doorway, the door closed behind him, the length of him dwarfing it and everything else around. His size made my teacups look ridiculous rather than elegant like they were. Ben wasn't the sort of man who could sip from daintily designed floral china like Flynn could. Maybe that was why Ben stood across the room, leaving a full cup of coffee and a plate of food on the table.

I carried Jess's and my dishes to the pan I used for washing, Ben still at the door, his eyes following my every move.

"I'm cleaning up, but I won't throw your food away…" I nodded to the table where his full plate sat.

I waited for him to say something. I watched his lips. His lips. Warmth crept up from the neckline of my shirt. I looked down at the plates in my hands.

"I was out at the barn…" He twisted to the side and looked through the window.

My shirt swelled in my way as I looked down toward the washpan, at two plates nearly licked clean from Ben's cooking. "You should eat before it gets cold. It was actually very good." I looked over at him, at lips that were still now, at eyes pointed outdoors. At the barn? Surely he wasn't thinking… He *had* to sleep out there. Properly. It was understood.

One long finger rose and fell on the door frame, a series of taps. Ben looked from the outdoors to his finger as if he was counting its beats. When the last tap died, he looked at me.

"Ben…" I wiped my hands on the towel he'd soiled. "We both understood about this arrangement, certainly the beginning and end of it. I think it's right to clarify the middle."

He leaned toward the window and glanced back to the barn, then turned to me, a frown on his face.

"Clarify. To make clear."

"I know what clarifying is."

I nodded. Folded the towel again. "Okay, good. Then you understand we need to clarify the time between the wedding and the parting." I draped the towel across the dry sink. "We live civilly through the middle so we can part civilly at the end." I nodded toward the window. I meant the barn, knowing he'd understand. "That's why no matter what we do during the day, especially in front of others, you have to sleep out there at night."

The jaw squared, the muscles at each side bulged as his brows lifted. He looked at me, the bulge waning. He opened the door, and I watched it close behind him. Gone. Again.

The kitchen began to waver, its walls and all within it. Different from when Flynn was killed, but wavered just the same. I groped for a chair, scooted Ben's plate aside, propped my elbows on the table's edge, and dropped my head into my hands. I was used to hard work and being tired. That never made the room dip and sway. Maybe I'd eaten too much.

Or…maybe I was suffering some silly desperation that had come with Ben's blasted kiss. Some freshly widowed part of me that wasn't sure how to act with a man around. A tall man. A… My shirt heaved and sank again as I stared at the table.

This wouldn't do. I had a ranch to run, a boy to get back on his feet.

I stood, bracing myself with fingers perched at the table's edge. It had been a long day. I'd even married, earlier. That had to be it. I cleared Ben's food and coffee, washed my china, and scoured Ben's skillet. I wouldn't bother to learn to use it. He wouldn't be here that long.

Chapter 33

My stepmom said a seed is no good until it falls into the ground and dies. ~Rex

I lay awake in the barn's loft, morning in the air before the sun said it was so. The squeal of the pump shrieked through my thoughts and over the few birds that had started to sing. The same squeal that had kept me here, for the boy that had pumped water for my horse. The boy and his mother. The two I kept hurting. The squealing stopped.

"You want some breakfast?" Regina was at the opening to the barn, her voice rising to the loft, offering an invite I didn't expect after last night. "It's ready, if you plan to get up."

"I was afraid I'd fall in one of those holes you dug all over the barn floor. Hard to see them in the dark."

She was so quiet I thought she'd left. I listened to the birds, to my breathing, and for the voice I finally heard. "I made coddled eggs."

Coddled eggs? I sat up. "Does coddled mean they're not cooked in lard?"

"I never cook in lard. My parents send me oil from New York."

"Well, I cook in lard." I could feel her tasting last night's supper again.

"Mr. Miller, you're incorrigible!"

185

"Is that anything like coddled?"

Her feet, most likely in her wedding boots, stomped across the hard brown barnyard. I stood, slipped my shirt and trousers on, and laid a hand on the ladder's posts. My palm stung, reminding me where my father's barn's splinters were. It would sting even more if I took this hand to my wife's pretty backside. That would create a memory I'd never let go of.

I stepped through the widow's…Mrs. Miller's…kitchen door. I did it carefully, but loud enough she'd know I was there in case she'd changed her mind and taken her invite for coddled eggs back. Her back was to me, red hair pinned loosely on and around her head. I liked the way it tried to escape, snaky strands wiggling down past her shoulders, where that shirt was I'd bought her, and those boy's pants below that. I took a deep breath of toast and those eggs as I looked from her head to her toes.

"You just going to stand there?" Yesterday's—or maybe it was this morning's—fire burned in her eyes as I looked up from her boots that had turned my way.

"Smells good in here." I saw four plates lined up on the table. "Ted joining us?"

"No. He had something to do." She marched to the table and snatched his dishes away. "Well, he always seems to have something to do in the mornings, but I didn't like the way he left this time." She turned back to the stove, lifted a lid, and peered at the fire within. She dropped the lid with a clatter. "He said something about your…"

The sound of a horse brought her to a stop. Hoof beats in the barnyard, and Ted's gravelly voice as he slowed Boss. Regina glanced at the darkened window.

She returned his dishes to the table, less of a clatter for dishes I was pretty sure couldn't survive much commotion. "He didn't stay away as long as I suggested he might."

The door eased open behind me, I stepped aside as early morning air and Ted drifted in. "Morning," he said. I nodded. He was looking past me, to Regina. "Morning again, I mean."

"You can sit after you wash up. I'll take a plate in to Jess."

"How is he?" Ted asked. The gravel was still there, but tempered. A man carving his way back into a woman's good graces. She was sharp, and she was cold as she answered him with a shrug. Nothing like the blazing hot answers she gave me.

Ted went past her, mindful of the thin ice he was on, to her open bedroom door, and disappeared through it. I could hear him and the boy talking in there. He did it the way I'd always wanted to talk with a boy. With Luke when we were younger, when nothing I said ever seemed to be right.

"Smells good," I said again and looked at Regina.

She set three teacups on the table and filled each with black coffee. Flowers decorated every side, dainty saucers underneath.

I looked at my fingers and the tiny cup's handle.

"Oh, I forgot." Her hands shot beneath one of the saucers and she lifted it from the table.

"Wait, where you going with that?"

"Next time I go to Liberal, I'll buy you a mug."

"I still need coffee today, though."

She set the cup back on the table. "Just be careful." She returned to her cookstove.

I took a seat, wrapped my hands around her teacup, and lifted it to my mouth. It was hot, delicious, and black. I swirled the tiny bit of liquid, wishing it held more than a swallow. "No grounds in the bottom." I looked up.

"Of course not." She brought the pot to the table and refilled my cup, then fixed a plate for Jess. I sat alone where I was, holding a nearly emptied cup, listening to three voices in the other room—my arranged bride, her ranch manager, and my arranged stepson. Stepson. I could never do for him what my stepmother had done for me. Getting him on his feet would have to be good enough.

"The boy's looking good," Ted said as he and Regina came back through her bedroom door. He beat her to her chair and pulled it out. She thanked him as she sat. She did it proper, the way she and I were to act toward each other. Maybe I needed to take lady-handling lessons from her one-armed ranch manager before I went.

The house Flynn had built was small, and so was the Eastern furniture he and his wife had brought with them. She, Ted, and I sat too close to each other for my taste, filling our mouths with coddled eggs and toast until our plates were empty, mine scrubbed clean by the last corner of my toast.

Ted wiped his mouth with the cloth napkin Regina laid out, folded it into a triangle with one hand, and set it beside his plate. "So I guess we have a Miller family here, now." Ben-Whoever-You-Really-Are was there in his look, the one he gave me as he stared my way. Ted was a skeptical man. To be skeptical was wise. It helped a fellow live longer. But to openly challenge, like I saw in his eyes... Experience told me a man who did that had something to hide.

"This is business, Ted, not a family." Regina glanced at her open bedroom door, and lowered her voice. "This is an arrangement between Ben and me for the sake of the ranch."

"What good is this arrangement to him? To Ben?" Ben-Whoever-You-Really-Are now in his tone.

"None of this is your concern. I'll keep you informed what you're to do to help out, and the rest is up to me." She raised her napkin to her mouth. She kept it there, hiding those lips. Those lips that...

Ted stood. "Thank you for the breakfast...but a simpler arrangement could have been made. We could have held onto Flynn's land for you without a complete stranger being a part of it."

"You're wrong." Regina laid her napkin aside. "We couldn't have saved this ranch any other way."

"I'm afraid it's you that's wrong, no offense intended." Ted looked past me, the stranger they didn't need, and focused on Regina. "My name would have kept the ranch better than an unknown's."

"I'm not wrong." Regina said it like she believed it, but her eyes were too wide, her voice a bit rangy. Her ranch manager was planting seeds she didn't want. Error. Doubt. "I've done everything just as I planned, to hold onto this ranch."

"Everything except use my name." Ted took a step back. His chair snagged at the rug the table sat on. His good arm swung back, caught the chair before it fell. He glanced at my two good hands, both on the table, and righted the chair before he turned back to Regina. "You were too quick with your plan. It won't work and will slow us down. Enough time has been wasted, and we can't afford to waste more. We don't need him, it turns out, but we do need to plant."

"That's not right. That's not right what you just said." Regina's face was flushed, almost as red as her hair. She looked at me, Ben-Whoever-You-Are and Why-Did-I-Marry-You growing in her eyes. "Is it?"

"Only the planting part." If even that. I stood and stared down at Ted. He knew too much. And it would be best for this ranch and for him if he cared a lot less.

Chapter 34

I want one man to be where he's supposed to be, do what he's supposed to do, and say what he's supposed to say. Just once. ~Regina

I rapped against the wood of Doc Harris's door. Loud. And hard. I'd show my ranch manager how wrong he was and how right my plan was by satisfying the bank and its ridiculous rules. It was early. Doc should have been in. I knocked again, harder, stepped to the front window, and cupped my face to the glass, feeling like a child peering into a candy shop. The room was dark. Nothing. No one. Why didn't men keep sensible routines and plan as well as I did?

I put an extra stomp in my boots as I marched to the postal office next door. It was hard to put my plan to use if people weren't where they were supposed to be.

"Good morning to you, Mrs. Howard," Mr. Greene sang out when I entered. His grin stretched, then shrank as he eyed the pants and shirt Ben had given me. They were clean, and that was all that should matter to him, but Mr. Greene wasn't looking at clean.

"Good morning to you, Mr. Greene. I have a letter to mail." I stepped quick, pressed close behind the counter, and waved the envelope to get his attention. Mr. Greene righted, barely managing a smile over his startled expression. I'd never asked, but I was pretty sure the man wasn't married.

"You have some to pick up, also. And one for your ranch manager, Ted. Is he still working for you?"

"Yes, he is. Sort of. I'm doing a lot of the work myself." A one-armed man and a woman. I could see it on Mr. Greene's face as he glanced at the work shirt Ben had given me, his hands and arms busy at wooden slots behind the counter where envelopes and notes stuck out like white and beige tongues.

Mr. Greene slid several envelopes across the counter. I laid the one I was sending to my parents next to the pile, and two cents alongside it. He took the change and my letter.

"We seen you with that tall fellow the other day. Mr. Miller. Is he helping you, too?"

"Well, I…actually…" I was here to tell Doc about my marriage. I wanted him to know before the whole town, and telling Mr. Greene was telling the whole town.

Mr. Greene reached behind him and slid two envelopes out of a slot. "Got a couple for that Miller fellow, too. Came not long after we saw him last. Doc said he's out at your ranch quite a bit."

"Doc said that?"

"Well, we asked him, being the doctor and all, if he knew where Mr. Miller might be. Asked Mr. Miller myself how to get hold of him, but he was a bit withholding about his whereabouts, if you know what I mean. So do you know how we can get these to him?"

"I can take them," I said. "Just put them with the rest of our…I mean Ted's and my…mail."

"You sure it's no trouble?"

"I'll see him this afternoon. He's looking at a horse for me. Hard to get all that ranch work done with just one horse." Well, two, but Ben's didn't count since he was leaving.

"Doc was right, then." He laid Ben's items on my stack. I picked up the pile and slid it into my bag. "Might be out there right now, talking to Mr. Miller."

"What?"

"Doc left mighty early this morning. Your boy was on his list."

"Thank you." I wheeled from the counter and headed out the door. Doc needed to hear I'd married Ben, but I wanted him to hear it from me. My way. What was that word of Ted's? "Dang" just wasn't going to do it.

Chapter 35

Time to finish up with hell so I can return to heaven. ~Rex

"These are for you." Regina stood below me at the wagon's side, envelopes in her hand. Her small hand, the one I'd... "Mr. Greene gave them to me when I was there."

I leaned down from the wagon's bed, where I was stacking tools around the seed she'd evidently picked up on her quick trip to town, and took them from her, then hopped to the ground. "You see Doc along the road?"

Her eyes grew large, the green brighter than it had been. "Dang, I missed him. What did you say?"

"Me?"

"I mean, what did he say?"

"He said Jess was improving."

"Jess. Of course. That's why he came." She went from looking at me to looking at nowhere. Or somewhere down the road where Doc had gone.

"And..."

Her eyes cleared as she focused on me.

"And he asked where you were."

"What did you say?"

"I asked if he meant Mrs. Howard, and when he said yes, I said I wasn't sure."

"Ben Miller, you are incorrigible!"

I stuffed my envelopes into my pocket. "Mrs. Miller, I have a job to do, and I'm dam…danged well going to do it. I'm here to secure this ranch for you, so you'd better do your part and play along so your scheme works. The sooner you do, and do it right, the sooner I'm out of your way."

"This is not a scheme! And I'm not a schemer. For your information, this is the very reason I was in town. To tell Doc."

"That's a start. But I wouldn't have known it by the look on your face just now, and you need to do better than telling one person, or Mr. Gulliver will have you and your son on the first train back to New York." Or worse, have Ted signing his name next to hers. If Regina's eyes weren't so green and her hair so red, maybe I wouldn't care. No. I didn't care. This was a job, just like the other half Jim sent me up here to do, which wasn't getting done, either.

I strode into the barn while Walter nickered from the corral I was slowly piecing back together, that bossy sound of his pointing out I was doing something wrong, and it wasn't with the fence. I brought Walter out, toted my saddle from the barn, and tossed it over his back. I reached underneath him for the girth strap and hooked it through the ring and tightened it. No need to slap Walter's side—he knew the ropes—but I gave him a smack anyway.

"You're going somewhere?"

"Yep." I fitted the bridle over Walter's head, looped the reins over the saddle's horn, and climbed on. I needed to think. "Wagon's loaded for you. Be back later."

"If you're off to look at a horse for me, don't bother."

"Ma'am." I bent my head and touched the brim of my hat. I made one of those noises she hated, and Walter turned. This is why I never worked with a partner. Nothing got done quick enough or right. We hightailed it down the road.

The prairie was pleasant in the morning, the sun brushing across its top like orange dew. My thoughts began to clear as I rode, putting some distance between me and my wife. My irritation beginning to make less, and yet more, sense. Kansas certainly had the sort of terrain that let a man think. No obstacles, no sudden drop-offs, just flat land with no surprises except for the occasional hare or deer.

I rode past the ranch of the neighbor who first showed me the way to Regina's place. I eyed his barn, thinking of the trouble I'd had ever since his "favor." Naw. I patted my flint and steel and rode on, slightly northeast, far past everything familiar, even though it all looked the same. I let Walter slow as my thoughts leveled out, let him walk as Regina and her ranch manager faded behind.

A cluster of trees popped up in the distance. That meant water. Water for Walter. I thought of Jess lying in his mother's bed.

"Hyah." I reined Walter the direction of the trees, admiring the welcome change—the slope of the land, running water, wind that seemed less as we sank down to the line of trees. Prairie edged the small waterway and its long, narrow grove. A bare field lay to the south, its dirt a dark brown as a farmer worked it. He waved as I nudged Walter to the creek's edge and dropped to the ground. I waved back.

"You know what to do." I removed the bridle and looped it over the saddle horn, then walked to the nearest tree. I yanked a reed of grass from the ground, leaned back against the trunk, and chewed on the stem. The farmer went on with his business. He looked peaceful. Probably wasn't married.

I fished the envelopes Regina had given me from my pocket. The first was from Pop—Adler Duncan—penned in his own hand, my name written by him, also. I saw the tremble in his lettering. "I'm sorry, Pop." He would know his ranch was gone by now. More gone than just having Morrissey steal it from him. I prayed he didn't know it was me that done it, though. I read his name again. Adler Duncan. The sound of it never ceased to leave an impression on me, make me proud, warm inside…make me think of flames, of Luke, and the buried box I'd left behind.

I slid to the ground, my back grazing along the bark. I leaned against its rough ribs while Walter waded into the stream. Jim had addressed the letter, just like he always did for Pop when Jim knew where I was and no one else did. I opened my father's letter and unfolded the small piece of paper with fingers pulsing like my heart. I looked at his handwriting, at his few words. He called me son. He called me home. He didn't say why. I refolded the paper and slid it back into the envelope, thinking back to the last letter I'd sent him. I'd called him Pop, thought how I missed him, told him I was okay, kept to myself the things I'd save until I was there. I loved him, but never on a page. Just sealed it inside the letter, the piece of me I always gave him, and trusted I'd get back. Until he found out…

I gazed across the creek at the chocolate dirt the farmer turned over. Maybe Ted was right and it was time to plant. I didn't know much about it. Especially in Kansas. I glanced around the edge of the farmer's field, looking for bags of seed. There was nothing. He was just working the land. Less hurried than the rush Ted seemed to be in.

I stuffed my father's envelope back into my pocket and opened Jim's. It was long, surprisingly longer than any conversation I'd ever had with him. I started at the beginning, where he said he had more reason to believe I was in the right place.

Right place…that meant I should be spending less time on the widow's—my wife's—problems and more doing my real job. Jim described a pattern he was piecing together, and said that all indicators pointed north. I gnawed the inside of my cheek. Too bad he hadn't said I was in the wrong place, that he was sorry, and I could leave. I read through the scanty clues he shared with me, and the details of his suggestions, in addition to the reminder to marry the widow if I hadn't already, saying again it was good cover for the job, the best way to keep me alive. He'd find out when he got the letter I'd just sent that that was taken care of. I was thankful that discussion was done and would be out of the way until we settled with her.

Your half-brother won't be bothering you none, at least not soon. Morrissey's after him. Always thought of Morrissey as a bit of a coward, and now I'm sure of it. Taking after Luke instead of you isn't the manly thing to do. If you deserve the credit for burning down your father's ranch—your half-brother's getting the blame.

Jim's letter singed my hands. I squeezed it into a

hard ember like a chunk of hot coal.

I could see Morrissey. I knew how he would look, but I couldn't stand to imagine how Luke would after Morrissey was done. Or how my father's tears would spill down his face. For real this time, not just because of the fire. Every one of them would flood over me.

I felt the rope around Morrissey's neck as I pulled it tight, felt it tear at the splinters left over from my father's barn. Felt the terror Luke should feel, felt the hatred he harbored as he was reminded once again I was different from him. And felt the end of living that my father must feel. A wife gone, a life gone, everything he'd built—gone. Betrayed by the one son who was his spitting image.

I closed my eyes against the rising sun, the brown dirt, the farmer, and the prairie that surrounded me. A grassy prison holding me too far away. I belonged there—where Morrissey was, where Luke was, where my pop called me to. I squeezed Jim's letter until I couldn't feel it anymore. A tiny crushed ball.

I bent my head, dropped the wad onto the bank beside me. I stared at it. Wanted to smash it with my fist, grind Morrissey's name into the dirt until I had rocks and grit in my hand along with the splinters.

Walter planted his wet hoof next to the letter. "Better rest up," I said without looking up. "We're going to be riding soon, back to where we came from."

Walter's hoof moved away. I swiped Jim's letter off the ground, peeled it open one tight crease after another. When the page was open again, I flattened it as best I could against my thigh and looked it over.

Word has it your father's place is for sale. Morrissey's unloading it, and I don't think it has a thing to do with there being nothing on it now. My guess is that money he intends to make is for something else, something bigger. Still just my gut, but my gut's generally right. I got a man on Morrissey down here, and we're watching your family. You do your part up there. Follow the money. Or the stink of it.

Jim

The stink of it.

I could smell it from here. "Ain't no way I'm staying here. Morrissey's a snake. He's too clever to just be watched." I stood. Whistled for Walter.

"Howdy." The farmer was on the far side of the narrow creek. He swiped his forearm across his brow as he stepped to the water's edge. "Sweating up a storm even in the morning. Imagine if I'd waited to do this all later today."

I left Walter standing where he was and went close to my side of the creek, close enough I could see the streaks of brown where I wanted to see red. I looked beyond the man and his dirty forehead, to the south, far south to where there was red dirt, red rocks, and red fires to put out. I'd be there as soon as I said goodbye to the redheaded woman who was carrying my assumed name. "I suppose you'll be planting later today," I said, one eye on Walter so he wouldn't get too far away. "Looks like you're nearly done turning the dirt."

"Nearly done with this field, yes, but not planting yet. My name's Fred, Fred Albert. You own that piece of ground?" He nodded where I stood.

I glanced around me. The land all looked the same, and I wondered how anyone knew one piece from the other. "I'm Ben Miller. This somebody's ranch?" I looked back at Fred.

"Ranch? Probably not. Heard some fellow from back east bought it. Smart buy, but not for ranching."

"Back east?"

"That's what I heard. He was 'investing,' they said he called it. Heard he moved here from the East Coast, settled in, and started investing."

"You hear his name?"

Fred dragged a soiled rag from a back pocket and swiped it across his forehead and the back of his neck, spreading the brown and the grime until it blended with his skin. He bent his head like he was getting the kinks out. He looked down and shook his head. "Can't recall as I ever heard his name. If I did, I done forgot it."

I looked at the land around me. It looked the same as all of the other Kansas land except for the creek, the low level, and the string of trees. "What's to invest in here, if you don't mind me asking? Gold?"

Fred laughed. "Better than gold. Besides the water, it's the railroad. This, along with other land people thought was useless and had set aside for Indians or the poor homesteaders. Turned out some of it became worth more than gold. Why, if I'd bought that spot you're standing on instead of my patch on this side of the creek, I wouldn't be dragging around behind my horse, there, in the sun."

"Well, I'll be. Any more of that railroad land available?"

"Farther west, maybe, where the railroad's still plotting its way. But here? Some squabbling going on over what's left, but not as much. That's why I wondered if you were my eastern neighbor. I heard a lot about him for a while, and then it went quiet. Dead as can be."

Dead as can be. "Any other land quarrels going on around here?"

"Not like over railroad land. Wetland is worth something, but any land is high dollar if they put tracks over it. Like I said, my eastern neighbor there was smart. Well, nice to meet you, Mr. Miller. I'd best be getting back to work. That sun's getting pretty high."

I waved as Fred walked back to his horse.

I looked around. I had to be standing on Flynn Howard's land, the other deed I kept hearing about. Fred Albert was right about the high price on this land. It had cost Flynn everything. And now he was dead as could be.

"Walter, come on, boy. We gotta ride." I glanced to the south. "Soon, Pop. Soon as I take care of things here. Take care of the widow and her boy."

Chapter 36

If I hear, "Don't be taking on more than you should," again, including taking on pants instead of skirts, I'm going to spit! ~Regina

I envied men their freedom to spit. Nothing would have satisfied me more than to send a big wad of saliva behind Ben Miller as he disappeared down the road. Shouting *Doggone you, Flynn, Ben, and whoever else gets in my way* just wasn't going to do. I glanced at Boss. I could unhitch him and chase Ben down, spit right in front of him, and come back. Or I could just go finish my fence.

I laid Ted's letter aside and clambered up into the back of the wagon. Ben could have at least unloaded the seed and got it out of the way for me. I dragged each sack to the end of the wagon, sat down, and dropped to the ground.

"That the seed?" Ted tapped one of the sacks.

"Where'd you come from? You check the field?" I stretched my back, noted the dirt under Ted's nails. "And yes, it's the seed."

Ted pinched the sack, tugging up on it and making a point of showing how empty it was. "You should have got more."

"We don't need more. I told you just two fields. The rest is for hay."

"That won't work." Ted gave the bag a pat that was more of a smack. "Have you talked to Mr. Gulliver about this?"

"Mr. Gulliver? Why would I ask him what to grow on my ranch?"

"Not 'what' but 'if.' "

"There is no 'if.' I'm married now. I made a plan and did everything Mr. Gulliver said." I walked to where Ted's letter lay. I picked it up and handed it to him. Ted cocked his head to the side and peered at the front of the envelope. He studied the name and address with the look he was so good at—no expression—then stuffed the envelope under his bad arm.

"Did married get you a clear deed with Ben's name on it?"

"Not yet…" I looked the direction Ben had gone. Maybe I should have been a little more careful what I said, a little friendlier. "But I will. We just haven't had time."

"What's done is done, Mrs. Howard…I mean, Mrs. Miller…as far as you taking on a new husband. But besides the fact we could have taken care of things without him, there are other things you should know."

"Should know?"

"I've been looking into Ben, figuring out what he's been up to before now. He might not be good for this ranch, beyond being a name we don't need. Where is he, by the way?"

I glanced down the road again. "He was supposed to check into a horse for me…" If he'd taken care of that like he should, and I had that horse right now, I'd go find that man who was supposed to be my husband and take care of things that really needed taken care of.

"I'll find a horse for you. One gentle enough for you and Jess, when he gets back to riding." Ted looked over my head, stared behind me. "That Doc?"

Doc Harris, tall on his buggy, rode into my barnyard, smiling as I turned. Doc had a nice smile, and a soft bend in his posture, one that eased along with his horse wherever he went. Different from the black storm that had barreled out of here on Walter earlier. "Ben said he had been here already. Must have been really early."

Ted gave the sack another tap. "Regina."

I looked back at my ranch manager.

"We need to talk. Soon." Ted waved over my head at the doctor, then disappeared into the barn.

"Doc." I turned as he climbed down. He was graceful, for a man. Easy in his movements. "I went to visit you this morning at your office. Mr. Greene said you'd already gone."

Doc left his horse and buggy facing my house and strolled my direction, his hat twirling through his hands. "I should have warned you that with Mrs. Nelson down the road so close to going into labor I would be in your area at unusual hours, not to mention more." He stopped in front of me, his hat still turning. "She's at that age where having babies isn't all that easy… She may have problems, so…" His hat stopped. I looked into those eyes that reminded me of Flynn.

"Doc…"

"Please, call me Lester."

"I don't know that I should…"

"I want you to. And I want your boy to, also. Jess is doing rather well, by the way. I was here earlier. He was asleep, but if he's taking regular doses of that medicine I gave you for his pain, he will sleep. Keeps him peaceful."

"Ben told me you were here. Thank you for checking on Jess." I heard hoofbeats, a steady thunder coming down the road. Walter. I'd recognize his sound anywhere.

"I was wondering…" Doc's hat spun again, twisting in his fingers as he studied its brim.

The dark horse with the dark figure on it took form. Ben raced up behind the doctor in a cloud of dust. bringing Walter to a halt as the dirt plumed around them. I saw the warrior there again. Tall, striking a pose on a magnificent animal. In one sweeping motion, Ben dismounted, lit on the ground, and came my and Doc's way. I watched Ben's every move—the way he carried himself, the way he watched me as he approached.

"Mrs. Howard." Ben came alongside Doc and stopped, both men tall and slender, one sharp and determined, the other gentle and smooth. "Would you say your husband was an investor?"

I narrowed my eyes. "Is this a trick question?" Even through my frown Ben's eyes shone, the piercing darkness of them, an ebony sheen I'd never seen before. Ben. Might not be good for this ranch. That's what Ted had said.

"No, ma'am, it's not. Would Mrs. Howard say her husband, Mr. Howard, was a bit of an investor?"

"Flynn was a merchant by trade, but he was always keen with money. He knew how to strike a deal. He knew how to multiply what we had. That's why I find it so hard to believe…" I glanced at Doc. "I mean, not an investor by trade, but certainly talented that way."

"I'd like you to come with me." Ben's eyes danced,

a sparkle lighting the deep color. "And the boy, too."

"He can't be moved." Doc's hat stopped.

"I need him." Ben glanced at Doc. "We moved him once before. I think we can do it again, only in the back of a wagon this time."

Doc set his hat on his head. "He's mending, and we can't break whatever bonding has taken place in his bone. If we do, his recovery time will have to begin all over again."

I watched Ben's face, thoughts and expressions flipping past like the pages of a book, all going too quickly for me to read.

"Ted here?"

I nodded toward the barn.

Ben strode to Walter's side.

"I said he's in the barn," I called, wishing he'd come back. I wanted to see that dance in his gaze again.

He didn't come back. Ben was on Walter, wheeling in a half circle, his eyes never leaving mine. My heart skipped a beat, but it was gone. The dance and Ben were both gone as he clicked and rode away.

"Miller," I said to Doc. "My name is Mrs. Miller now."

The blue of Doc's eyes darkened as he stared at me.

"That's why I came to your office this morning. I wanted to tell you myself."

He backed away. He didn't ask why Ben had called me Mrs. Howard, like I would have. Instead he turned and walked to his buggy. He climbed into its seat and spoke English to his horse. "Let's go." Doc flicked the reins.

Doc didn't wheel; he turned a neat circle in my

barnyard. I imagined myself next to him, how it would be riding down my lane at his side. I would sit straight, and we'd hold an intelligent conversation while he gave his horse gentle and sensible commands. I glanced down at the ground—where Walter had been, where the dirt was kicked up as he and Ben had pivoted before they rode away. Or I could ride fast, in dungarees, behind a man who made no sense, and only chirruped and clicked at his horse. That made me smile.

****

"Doc?" Boss and I caught up to Doc's buggy. He hadn't gone far, but we covered the distance fast.

Doc looked my way, the blue of his eyes swimming in a watery glint.

"I'm heading to Liberal. Mind if I ride alongside you?" I asked.

He didn't respond but looked ahead. I slowed Boss to Doc's pace, a snail's pace, and I wondered if any of Ben's noises might work on his horse.

"Doc, I was going to lose the ranch."

He glanced at me, his expression reminding me so much of Flynn.

"I heard…" Crimson tinged his face. "I heard you might be in need of a husband. I know how it is for widows. I wanted marriage to be good for you. Better than just some arrangement, like most widows end up with."

I drew Boss to a stop, Doc did the same with his horse and buggy. The breeze pelted us both, threatening to whisk away whatever I tried to say. I wouldn't let it. Not this time. I'd made a plan, and I was sticking to it. Because I wanted to. Still wanted to.

"Thank you, Doc." What he offered was the very

thing I'd wanted to avoid. A husband who cared, who tried to be Flynn. I'd wanted one who stood far enough back I could keep an eye on him until he left, no thought ever there as to maybe finding I appreciated what I saw. "I'm grateful for your consideration. Your concern."

"Well, I…it's just that…"

"Thank you. But I should get on. I need to hurry to Liberal." To find Ben and settle with Mr. Gulliver, because Ted was wrong. It was in Ben's eyes. I saw that glow and I wanted to see it again. I kneed Boss so that his rump dropped close to the ground. Then we were off. Boss knew how much I loved speed, and he gave it to me. Almost as good as Walter would.

I made every noise I could think of in Boss's ears as we hied it to Liberal. Hied it. I'd add that word, Ben's word, to my vocabulary.

Chapter 37

I know there's a rat around here. I just have to figure out what's the cheese. ~Rex

"Rest for a bit." I stroked Walter's nose. He'd run hard back to Fred's field, and walked as far as the farmer pointed where the railroad was supposed to run. Fertile ground, plenty of water, the very path rich conglomerates said the line should be laid. After I'd thanked Fred, I ran Walter to Liberal. Pieces of Jim's puzzle were starting to sound like they fit up here. He was right, as usual, and if they did... If they did, then Regina needed more than a husband. She needed a guard.

A woman hopped up onto the walkway several buildings down. Red. Blazing red. Gunning for someone. "Pretend you don't know her, Walter." I ducked between two buildings, stayed flat against the wall, listening for the clop of her boots, praying she would pass. Why didn't she stay home where she belonged? Entertain Doc like she clearly wanted to?

Her steps came closer, brisk and determined, marching until she stopped not far from where I hid. Drat that Walter, he couldn't control himself. I heard her voice, heard her flatter my horse, her tone waving up and down like a song. I pressed tighter against the building, dropped low, and slid farther away. Her cooing slowed. She took a step. I could imagine her red head swiveling from one side to the other, no doubt wondering which direction I'd gone. I inched even farther from the walkway, stayed as flat as I could until my redheaded wife with the perfect pair of trousers passed. Courage. I'd had a nip the night before, and I'd need another tonight. Criminals weren't this much work. Except maybe Matt Morrissey, but even he didn't scare me the way Mrs. Miller did.

When her footsteps were completely gone, I straightened and let the wind out of my lungs.

When I was certain she wasn't coming back, I crept to the walkway, peered around the corner, and caught sight of her back as she disappeared into the postal office. I stepped out and hied it the opposite direction toward the bank but went on past it. There was a saloon not far on the other side. I doubted she'd come in a place like that—well, a normal lady wouldn't. I pushed through the doors, frowned in the smoky interior, and took a seat near the front window to wait her out. She'd give up and go on home eventually; then I could get back to my job.

I glanced at the crowd, letting my eyes adjust to the poor light. Mostly farm sorts, ranchmen, a couple of merchants at a table off to the side. I shook my head when the man behind the bar caught my eye. I needed to keep a clear head. The barkeep nodded back. I settled to wait until the way was clear.

"Sure you don't want anything?"

I looked up at a young woman, most of her hanging over her dress and my table.

"No, nothing. I'll be going in a minute." I slid her a coin for her trouble. She squeezed it down where I'd been trying not to look.

"Come back any time." She sashayed away.

The smart clip of boots made me forget the sashay. I tore my gaze from that walking cash box and glanced out the window. There Regina stood outside the bank, her head tossed back as she stared through the ornate door.

I ducked low in my seat as Regina looked my way. She stared at the saloon and beyond until someone called her name. I strained to see, but kept low as Mr. Gulliver stepped from the bank, and Regina turned. I peered over the bottom lip of the window, glad it was dark enough inside the saloon I could stay hidden while in plain view. Mr. Gulliver led Regina through the bank's fancy door. I watched until they disappeared. I was safe. But I wasn't so sure about her.

I scooted to the wall and pressed close to the glass.

"You're looking awfully nervous there. Sure I can't get you something to drink?" The cash box wiggled a drink between her thumb and forefinger at me.

"Sure, why not?" I scooted back to the middle of my seat as she set the drink on the table. I slid her another coin. Two of them, actually. One for her, the big one for the barkeep.

"Thank you. Enjoy yourself." She slid the little coin down where it could never clink, and sashayed again back to the bar.

"To Mrs. Miller." I lifted the glass to the empty walkway outside. "And the courage to see her through." The drink lasted only a second. I set the empty glass down and tapped on the table. With two fingers I had drummed out a whole song my stepmother had taught

Luke and me by the time Regina reappeared. I crouched as I watched her, but she didn't look up and down the walkway as she had earlier. She looked straight toward Walter, and it was his direction she went. Dang.

I patted Jim's letter, still in my pocket, along with Pop's. Follow the stink, that's what Jim had said. I stepped outside when Regina was far enough away, and turned into where she had been. The bank.

In one quick glance I was aware of who was there and who wasn't. I wanted the youngest one. Young, with that tinge of innocence holding on. Eager ignorance. He'd be the one that would talk.

"Pardon me." I dropped into a chair and extended a hand across the young man's desk. He was far enough from Mr. Gulliver I felt fairly safe, but close enough I kept my voice low and my back to Regina's banker.

The young man glanced up from the papers he was studying. He gave me a young pup's stare before he could gather himself. "Can I help you, Mr..."

I smiled. "Winston. Cal Winston. I'm new here."

"Pleased to meet you, Mr. Winston. What can I do to help you today?" The not-so-wily clerk shuffled his papers and laid them to the side. Maybe he was too young. He had that eager, boyish smile.

"Well, maybe not help me so much as my uncle. He's one of those...well, he's not like me. I'm a worker, but he's the guy that pays the workers. He knew I was coming to settle out here, and he asked me to check around for opportunity. Land, in particular. Or whatever else you might advise. He's back east and plans to stay there. He likes his money to do the work for him. Well, his money and men like me that mind the till."

The young eyes began to sparkle. He'd landed a big one. He rubbed his hands on his thighs beneath the desk, warming them up to reap some cash. He really was just a pup. Unfortunately, the big dog was nearby.

"Well, Mr. Winston, sir," he said. "Liberal is the right place for your uncle to invest his money. It's growing. Land is plentiful. This place has been a crossroads since its beginning, and the railroad is coming this way, too. Your uncle should come and see for himself what there is here. Liberal with opportunity, that's what I say."

I rewarded his cleverness with a smile. "Never known my uncle to travel much. Elderly. Old money, old bones. And lots of both." This would bring the old dog to point when this young man reported to him later.

"I tell you what. I'll come back in a couple of days, and maybe you can have some suggestions for my uncle. Some numbers, some names, some ideas I can look at." I stood, crouching enough I didn't tower over the crowd. The young man jumped to his feet.

"I will, sir. I promise. I'll have all sorts of information ready for you. Your uncle will be pleased."

"Good. That's what I like to hear." I reached across his desk and shook his hand. He pumped mine. "Be back in a couple of days." I tipped my hat, kept my face away from Mr. Gulliver, and strolled out of the bank. I resumed my posture once outside. I wanted to stretch, but I knew eyes were too close. I resettled my hat, and strode to Walter.

"There you are!"

"You been hiding between buildings?" I frowned at the widow Howard—I mean Mrs. Miller—as she sprang across the walkway at me.

"Never mind where I was."

"People do things like that around here?" I leaned to the side and peered down the narrow alley I'd been hiding in earlier.

"Never mind, I said," she repeated. "Where have *you* been?"

"I don't think that much matters to you," I said, unwrapping Walter's reins from the post.

"Well, it does. I need to talk to you, and I'd rather do it here than back home."

I stood at Walter's nose, eyeing the widow—I mean, my wife—slapping my hand with the end of the reins.

"That has to hurt," she said, frowning at my hand.

I looked down at the splinter spots, most still red.

"The posts do some of that?" she asked.

"No. These are a far worse memory than your fence and corral. Is that what you wanted to talk about?" I closed my hand over the reins.

"No. I may have made a mistake."

"You?"

"Turns out maybe I was wrong looking for a foreign husband like you."

"Foreign? You mean we're not really married?"

"I mean…well, Ted was right, no one knows who you are. The bank won't recognize you since you're an unknown, and they consider you a risk." She frowned, like I was a book written in a language with words she for once didn't know. "I should have asked more questions about you, I guess."

"More questions?"

"Well, yes. I know nothing about you, really, which suits me, but not the bank. Because of that, they're claiming only a local name will do on their deeds."

"Like Doc's?" I wasn't sure what I wanted her answer to be, but it wasn't what she said.

"Ted's. Mr. Gulliver said he'd take Ted's name on the deed even though I'm married to you. It would be Ted's name and mine. It's just that mine won't count for much."

"And mine for nothing. What about the other deed you're always talking about? And what about the debt they claimed Flynn built up? Oh, the hell they will!" I flung the end of the reins around the post. "I don't see you kicking up your usual fuss over this. You sweet on Ted instead of Doc?"

"Of course not! I'm not sweet on either of them, I'm… Not sweet on anyone." Red blazed across her cheeks.

She was lying. I could see her heart pounding for someone behind that crimson. "You just need a name on your deed, the right name. It's your beginning, middle, and end. All proper when it's done, and the way it's done."

The red darkened. "If we're talking business, about the deed and the ranch…" Her fists went to those hips. "Ben Miller, I need a name the bank recognizes. Tell me who you are, come up with a tangible background, and I'll go tell them."

"Tangible?"

"Solid."

"I'm Ben Miller, the cattle driver."

"That's not good enough. For them."

"Then, Mrs. Howard, I'd say you should get yourself another man's name, instead of mine. One that's recognized. Congratulations are in order, I guess."

"I'm not saying I want another man's name, and I'm not…"

"Not Mrs. Howard? I don't know what else you'd be called." I unwrapped the reins from the post. Again. Grabbed them in one hand and swung a leg over the saddle. I couldn't even look at her when I was seated. No more red hair, no more hips built for tiny fists, no more eyes that lit me up every time they flared. I clicked to Walter, pressed the reins to the side of his neck, and started away.

The widow ran alongside me and Walter, her boots clapping along the board walk while a string of clicking and grunting noises came from her mouth. Walter stopped, then he started up, but stopped again. I clicked louder than she did and dug my knees into his sides. She clicked and slapped her hands together, drowning me out. Walter jerked to a stop.

"Would you stop interfering with my horse?" I turned the widow's way. Those green eyes bore back at me, surrounded by the reddest hair and the prettiest face… I made a sound only Walter knew, one I reserved for special occasions. Like this one. He bolted forward, and I left red and green behind. Left her with what remained of my name if she wanted to use it, and left her with her own ways. I'd seen a boarding house outside of town. I'd get a room there, get my things from the ranch, and stay out of the widow's way. I had Luke to worry about. And Pop. Clearly she had plenty of others who could look after her.

"Rooms." I spotted the sign. Not a clever name for a business, but it was wisely at the opposite end of town from the saloon. "Whoa, Walter." He stopped, and I smirked. I dismounted. I'd sleep a lot better without Ted underneath me and my arranged wife a straight thirty yards away across her brown barnyard.

"Mister? Need me to water your horse?"

I heard the young voice behind me. A boy. I seemed plagued by them. First Luke, then Jess, now this one.

I tossed Walter's reins over the rail. "No, thank you. Only going to be here a minute." I turned, looked straight into brown hair streaming down over the forehead of that hopeful look. The one Luke had when he tried too hard, the one Jess had when he didn't know which side of life he stood on—painful childhood or frightening adulthood. "Turns out I think I'll be going now." I dug a nickel out of my pocket and tossed it to him. "You look like you would have taken good care of Walter for me if I'd needed you."

"Walter? That's a funny name for a horse." The boy grinned.

"You had to know the boy that gave him that name to understand." I hopped up on Walter's back. Someone had to know that boy, really know the widow's son, and get him on his feet. Someone other than Ted, even other than Doc. "Dag-nab-it," I said instead of what I really wanted to say, in case the boy could still hear. I never had so much trouble staying with or getting away from someone. "Back to the ranch, Walter. Back to the widow's—I mean, Mrs. Miller's—ranch."

Chapter 38

I was sorry Ben married me for nothing. Now I'm sorry I married him at all. ~Regina

I watched Ben's back as he galloped away. I was getting tired of this. If only he'd been forthright about who he was when we corresponded, someone the bank could clear. Someone who obeyed the way I needed them to. Someone who stayed. I hit the boards with the heel of my boot, stomped away any chance of tears I hadn't had time for. I could feel them. I stomped again.

Ben was a warrior retreating, his tall form, dark hat, and black horse tearing out of town. How could a simple arrangement become so complicated? I'd done nothing but vex that man since he came, almost as much as he had vexed me, and now the bank was vexing both of us. I turned toward the side street and clomped my boots all the way to the livery, where I'd left Boss.

Men's voices met me as I rounded the last corner. They were lingering there near the horses, a group of them wasting time with their feet propped up on rails instead of being off working somewhere. I wiped my eyes, pinched my cheeks, and tossed my head back. Men had become nothing but bothers ever since Flynn was gone. Maybe even before. No wonder crying was difficult.

If I didn't mind leaving Ben's name on a marriage certificate while Ted signed the deed, why should it bother him? It was part of the plan, even if that part didn't work out.

I stopped. What if he wanted a real wife? A family? What if someone was waiting for him? Some woman he would take care of while I was here reminding Ted I was his boss no matter where his name was signed. I stomped my boot, and the cluster of men turned.

I whisked past them to Boss, felt the path their eyes traveled over the shirt and pants Ben had given me. I glared at them. Their conversation stopped as I set the toe of my left boot in the stirrup and tossed my right leg over the saddle. Their mouths and eyes gaped as I made a clicking noise. Boss didn't move, so I punched him with both heels and laid the reins against his neck. "Bothers, all of you," I said loud enough for them to hear as Boss wheeled, understanding exactly what I wanted now. We sailed out of town.

Boss was heaving as we raced into my barnyard, creating a cloud of dust almost as big as the one Walter and Ben had left. I lunged forward when he came to a stop, loving the momentum. Boss was powerful, expensive according to Flynn, but he labored at the pace he'd kept up in the few miles he'd run, in a way Walter never would. He tossed his head and snorted. I felt like doing the same. I leaned over the back of his neck and hugged him, let the damp sweat of a horse wet my face. It felt nice. It smelled wonderful. I rubbed my cheek against his mane.

"You were in a hurry?" Ted was at Boss's nose, his hand around the bridle.

I sat up, tucked a wad of loose hair up with a comb, and wiped my hands down the front of my clothing. "I have a lot to do." I dropped to the ground and patted Boss's side. "Is Jess doing well?"

"He is. You have a moment to finish our talk?"

I undid the girth strap beneath Boss's saddle. "After I take care of Boss and check on Jess."

"I'll take care of Boss. You go on and see your boy." Ted tried to smile. Tried. "Then we'll talk. First chance you get."

"I'll let you know."

I walked to the house. I knew what Ted would say, at least I hoped it was that and nothing worse. The same thing Mr. Gulliver had.

There was nothing on Ben. Nothing good, nothing bad. He was a nonentity, whereas Ted was an entity. A known entity that could have saved me an arranged marriage. And parting.

Jess was propped up in my bed, his color better, his scowl less.

"Your leg feeling good?" I came to his side, touched his forehead, combed his hair with my fingers.

"I guess." He ducked his head away from my hand. "I can sit up faster."

"Don't get too adventuresome. Doc says you can't get up and around yet." Doc, who may never return to tend to my boy.

"I know what Doc said, but Ben said different. Doc said weeks, and Ben said soon."

"Ben was here? Never mind what Ben said. Doc said weeks. He's the doctor. Ben was here?"

Jess pushed himself higher with both arms. "Yes, Ma, Ben was here. You married him, didn't you? He came in and talked to me. He said he needs my help."

There was new color in Jess's face, new light in his eyes.

"Weeks," I said again. I glanced toward the window. "Ben was really here?" How'd he beat me? Walter. The warrior horse. He had to go farther, make a wide loop so I wouldn't spot him, yet Walter had done it faster.

"Yes, Ma, I told you he was."

"We need to make sure with Doc."

"Or Ted?"

I knew by the voice behind me and the steeliness of my boy's eyes in front of me who was there.

"Ted has nothing to do with this..." I stood and faced Ben as he filled the doorway.

But he left the doorway and was across the room in three easy steps, my elbow gripped in his fingers. "If you'll excuse us, Jess, your mother and I need to have a little talk."

"We sure do. I'll be right back," I added over my shoulder. I yanked my arm, but Ben held on.

"Tell her I'm ready to get up," Jess yelled.

Ben steered me out of my room, to the small stairs that led up to Jess's real bedroom in the loft.

"Up there." Ben tipped his head that direction.

"I will not! I told you, this is..."

"I know, purely a business arrangement. Ma'am, we need to settle a couple of things without an audience. Ted's ears pretty much fill up the outdoors, and Jess is suffering for lack of entertainment in there, unless he likes counting the holes in your lace curtains. So up you go."

His hands fit around my waist as he took me from

behind and started me up the stairs.

"I can do this myself. What are you doing here anyway?" I hissed as he followed. "I thought you were done here, the way you took off. Again." I paused and glared down at him.

"I did too, but Walter made me come back. Git on up there."

I took the last two steps and stood in Jess's sleeping area. I glanced around at what little my son had, looked at the bed, then at Ben. He was staring there, too. At my son's bed, my bed now, my own clothing and some of Flynn's draped across it. He looked at me, and extended an arm to Jess's only chair.

"Please sit."

I did.

Ben stood over me, his head bent forward under the low ceiling.

"You can sit on the bed." *But please don't.* My face burned as I gestured where I'd been sleeping. There were things there only Flynn had seen.

"I think I'll stand."

"As you wish." *Thank God.*

"I may have found your husband's...I mean Flynn's...other land. So maybe this deed you keep talking about really is somewhere."

I stood. I stared up at Ben. "How? How did you..."

"I need to be sure, and I think Jess can help."

"Jess never saw Flynn's land, if he really had it. And neither did I."

"Your boy listens, and I'm guessing he absorbs more than you realize."

"I listen."

"We can discuss that another time. For now, I don't

want you agreeing with the bank about Ted signing for your ranch." His head tipped farther…close, his eyes deeper and darker even than I'd thought. "You understand? Don't agree to anything."

I felt breathless, more breathless than I did lifting fence posts, as I stared into those eyes.

He reached for my shoulder, and I inched it his way. Little nudges, bringing us closer, until he paused, his hand stopping, leaving my shoulder where it was. Alone. He stepped around me and my shoulder, then, and went to the stairs. Air that was burning my lungs seeped out like a low-burning flame as he took the first two. "Don't forget, you're already under an agreement with me."

"The agreement was you'd stay out of my room." I glanced around for something to throw.

"Get ready to change rooms. That boy of yours needs to get up and walk. Soon."

Chapter 39

No use talking to women. Time to talk to the only other man I trust out here. ~Rex

I looked down at Regina's boy, pondered the excitement that mingled with the scowl on his face. I'd seen plenty of scowls from Luke. The difference between Luke's scowls and Jess's was that Jess had good reason. Two good reasons, in my mind, while Luke had none.

Jess winced as he pushed up in the bed. "Ma know you're in here?"

"You gotta be getting sore, just laying there all the time. Thought you might get up and outside for a little bit. If I had a horse down as long as you, I'd be thinking about shooting it. How about it? Want to get up?"

"I can't. Doc said." Jess mumbled to his lap, then he looked up. "Can I?"

I walked to the far side of the room and studied the frilly curtains. Those would be enough to sour my outlook on life if I had to stare at them day in and day out. I unstrung them and laid them aside on a trunk, opened the window wider, a wash of fresh air and sunlight flooding in. As well as a long black nose. "Well, I'll be. Guess this thirsty fellow is looking for you." Walter thrust his nose through the window, reaching for the front of my shirt. I glanced at Jess on

225

the bed. "What do you think your mother will say when she sees the backside of a horse sticking out her bedroom window?"

That made a dent in the boy's expression. A good one that didn't last long.

"So I suppose you'd rather have the curtains back up instead of looking at Walter?"

Jess shifted his face to the side, chewed the inside of his cheek.

"Nothing wrong with that. You're from the East, so lace may be your druthers." I stroked Walter's nose, leaned through the window, and patted his neck. "Git on now, Walter. Go get a drink. I'll be out in a minute." I smacked my hand on Walter's neck. He slobbered on my shirt and turned away. I retrieved the curtains from the trunk and studied the way Regina'd had them strung.

"That's okay," Jess muttered from behind me. "You can leave them off."

"Can't say as I blame you." I returned them to the trunk. "You tell your ma it was me when she complains someone took her curtains down. She's used to me getting in her craw." I made my way to his bed and looked down at the boy. He tried to straighten more and lift himself higher in the bed. "Your leg isn't ready for putting weight on it yet."

Jess pulled himself up even higher.

"You can straighten fairly well. Probably more than expected. That's good."

Jess nodded.

"Guess we won't have to shoot you after all."

The boy's eyes grew wide.

"Legs are a horse's livelihood. Laid up with a

busted leg, a horse is pretty well worthless. Of course that ain't true for men. We have other reasons to exist. Like being productive and helping in other ways, even though we're laid up."

"Like Ted?" Jess looked toward the window. "He's missing an arm, but he still manages to work."

Ted might be managing more than work. "I was thinking more along the lines of you, but yes, Ted is one example of surviving." Although not the best.

Jess frowned.

"Like, say, leather. You ever work with leather? You got two good hands there. I'll bet you could do some harness work I noticed needs done."

"I never did that before," he said.

"I could show you how. And you'd be a big help by doing it."

"Ted never mentioned needing no harness work done."

I shoved my hat back on my head. "Well, I imagine you kept pretty busy before the accident. Things are different now. You're in a position to work with your hands. And your head."

"My head?"

"Sure. Bet you can draw me a good map of your land. All the details. The shape of it, any fields, what sort of prairie, any water holes. Think you could do that?"

"Why?"

"Because that's the best we can do until you get out where you can show me."

Jess stared at me, his tongue working inside his mouth. "I suppose I know as good as anyone what our land looks like."

"Both sections?" I said it casual. I watched the flicker in the boy's eyes. I saw what maybe was left of his father, the last tie, the last thing his father did before he died. That other land. Whatever it was, wherever it was, Flynn Howard either did something very right in buying it, or he did something terribly wrong.

"I never saw any other land." Jess eyes still held that light. "I wanted to. My pa was going to tell me everything. It was special, whatever he had. He said so." I watched Jess's face fall, and I knew the rest.

"Think you'd know it if you saw it? If I could find it, think you could tell me for sure if that's what your father bought? When we get you up, that is."

"We?"

I stared at the boy. It was like getting gut-punched by Luke all over again. I was used to being on the outside of a family.

"The only 'we' that's ever going to matter to you and your mother is each other, and that's the way it should be. You need to think on getting up and out of that bed. I'm just here to help. She's going to need you."

Especially after she and I parted.

Chapter 40

One day you wake up and find you've been sleeping alone all along. ~Regina

"Mail from home, ma'am." Ted dismounted. He did it with one hand, lit on the ground the way Flynn had admired. I had to admit, Ted had mastered living with one arm and managed to do about everything as if he had two.

"This is home," I reminded Ted as he carried two envelopes to me.

"It still shows on you," he said with a nod. "The East will always be a part of you, and nothing wrong with that."

"Thank you for bringing the mail. How was Liberal?" I took the two letters.

"Quiet, as far as I could tell. Wasn't there long. Only had a thing or two to do, then came right back."

I wanted to ask Ted what he did in town. He came back with little, when he came back with anything at all. Most of the time he came back empty-handed, the same way he went. Like today, except for the mail. Like the mornings when he checked on things.

I glanced at the two letters in my hand. My mother's was one, and I knew it would include a "suggestion" from my father. The other from my cousin Clyde, at my father's bank. Timid. Unsure of himself. His handwriting was as unnoticeable as he was. Normally. It had an unusual kick to it today, as if he wrote it on the run. He must have done something silly and needed my advice again.

"It's time." Ted glanced across the prairie. "It's time we talked and got this ranch business settled."

Don't agree to anything. I glanced across the prairie with him.

"You need me to put my name on this place," he said. "You have to. Or this ranch is going to go under and end up in someone else's hands."

I tapped my two letters on the palm of my hand. "What do you know about that other land Flynn supposedly bought?" Not just any man's name. Ted's name. Why wasn't "Regina and Jess" good enough?

Ted's Adam's apple bobbed as he stared across the windblown grass, his eyes narrowing as if he could see that land far away. The crevices on his rugged face were like hard-earned gouges, deepening as he thought, furrowing as he shook his head. "What do you know?"

"I'm the boss here, and it would be my land we're talking about, so I'm asking you."

He argued what I said with an almost pitying shake of the head, followed by a shrug. "Not land to till, if he bought what I told him not to." He sighed. "That's the best I can guess. It was a mistake, if he did. A fool purchase that must have ruined him."

"Flynn was no fool when it came to money and investments." Investments. The word Ben had used.

Ted looked down, kicked at the dirt, then looked back up. "Maybe he got advice from someone besides me. Bad advice, if he did."

"Was he thinking of cattle, maybe?" I'd certainly

suggested it enough.

Ted shrugged. "Cattle would be worse, especially there, but he never said. Wish he'd told me what he done, or even told you." He raised a brow as he watched me. I said nothing but held my stance until the brow dropped and his usual bland expression returned. "Maybe he knew he'd made a mistake."

I couldn't stand the thought of Flynn carrying a regret, dying with it alone. If only he'd had time to fix it, or at least told me. "Where was this land? How could I find it?"

Ted ran his hand over his chin. "It was east and north of here, but I never saw it. Maybe he unloaded it before he...well, before he passed, and that's why the deed is gone." He glanced at me, a question back in his look.

"Flynn wasn't one to make big mistakes. Surely he had a reason for what he did, a better reason than someone's advice." I didn't want to think it was just another dream. This dream, this land, was a constant struggle, so maybe he thought another would be better, bring in a little more money to help support this one. "That's where he'd been the day he died, wasn't it?" He was so secretive about where he went. Secretive, but not so much that Jess didn't understand, according to Ben. Since Jess listened.

"Possible."

Maybe that land was where our money was. Maybe Flynn had taken it there the day of the accident. Maybe.

"I'm going to find that land, Ted."

"You're what?"

"And then I want to sell it." After I scoured it for things Flynn may have left behind.

"Sell it?" His face furrowed into one of those leathery frowns. "You can't just up and sell something you don't own. Even if Flynn still did. That's why you need to get my name on this place. And that one too, if it exists."

"If my name's on that land at all, I'm selling it. If it's just Flynn's, then it'll go to Ben." As payment for keeping his end of the arrangement. It had been written into my plan. "In any case, the land has to go. It's more than Jess and I can handle." Since we'll truly be alone.

"Look, I'll go to the bank with you. Now. You can have all of this settled today. Especially if that other property pans out."

Don't agree to anything. "No. Not today. I want to find that other land first."

"Tomorrow. First thing in the morning. I was going there anyway."

"No." I turned toward the house, the word I kept repeating to men hanging in the air. Trusting Ben had better be the right thing to do.

"Think about it. Sleep on it. I'll be ready in the morning."

I walked toward the house. I'd said all he needed to know. When I reached the door, I paused, made a loop, and cut into the prairie.

I tucked Clyde's letter into my pocket as I plowed through the grasses, opening my mother's as I went. I fell into the news from New York, the struggles from here vanishing beneath the large city's streets, tales of our neighbors, our family, and friends. I saw myself there. Jess, too. Back on those streets, me wearing a gown and carrying a parasol. I glanced up at the prairie around me. Ted was right; the East was still part of me.

Even part of Jess. But it wasn't home anymore. It was too relaxed, and life would be too simple back East. There would be no pushy ranch manager or bossy arranged spouse to contend with. I looked down at Daddy's note at the end. His worries over his grandson and daughter, his offers to bring us home. It was so like him. He made me feel five years old again. Which I wasn't.

I came upon Flynn's gravesite as I tucked my parents' letter away. I stared at the wooden cross, then glanced around the prairie, wondering if I should go ahead and get a stone without Jess.

"How did we end up like this, Flynn?" My voice sounded thin as I dropped onto the bare ground of his grave. Small sprigs of grass encroached where I sat, stealing away the freshness of his death. "I'm buying cattle." I bolstered my voice. "Not what you would have done, since you never tried my ideas. No one wants to, but since this ranch is mine, they have to." I untied my hair and loosened my combs as I stared at the ground between us, letting it blow with the breeze. Red ringlets battered my face. "Remember the calf I saved when you and Ted were gone? How I figured out, from giving birth to Jess, the way cows should give birth, and I did it right? Remember how filthy with afterbirth and dirt I was when you and Ted returned? You didn't thank me. Neither did Ted. You both fussed over the calf. But it survived, and that was thanks enough. I'm going to put everything I've learned to use now. If you're actually listening to me this time, and you have any power at all from up there, then do your part. Make sure my cattle ranch is a success, okay?"

I listened. I waited. There was nothing but silence,

only the wind whooshing past, maybe whooshing away any words he might say the same way it whooshed away mine—to everyone except Clyde. I withdrew my cousin's letter from my pocket. Clyde. My father would never have noticed Clyde in my shadow all those years he'd tagged along after me, except he was the rare male child in the family. Clyde almost fainted and I stormed out of the room when Daddy announced he was taking Clyde under his wing in the bank. My father might as well have chosen me after all, as much coaching as I'd been doing to keep Clyde number-savvy behind my father's back. I opened the letter. Clyde's penmanship on the letter matched the sharp angles he'd adopted on the envelope. He must be more desperate than usual.

Dear Regina,

Promise me you'll say nothing of this to anyone. Especially to your father.

I shook my head. All of Clyde's letters began this way. I could picture the panic on his face as he bent over this stationery in near darkness at his home.

You've always been so capable, Regina, and helped me whenever I asked. So I decided some time ago that it was time for me to figure things out for myself. That went fine—well, sort of fine—for a spell. But I'm afraid I've made a blunder now. A rather large one. One I'm not sure how to remedy.

When you and Flynn went west, I listened to the things he said about opportunity. The west was a treasure waiting to be mined. I know he loved the dream of farming, but he had bigger ideas, too. He spoke often of gain.

I laid the letter on my lap and stared at Flynn's marker. He had ideas before he even came here, generating them somehow from somewhere. "You didn't make mistakes, though," I said. "You were clever. Even my silly cousin knows that." I lifted the letter, and continued to read.

It sounded innocent enough at first, dear cousin, the venture I made. It was an investment, a word Flynn used, but it was in railroads. You know yourself they are cutting across the country in ribbons and webs, miles and miles of opportunity—at least I imagined it that way, the same way Flynn saw ranching. What I didn't realize, although probably I should have, was the roundabout way my money was being used.

Promise me again you'll say nothing. But the money I offered may have been part of a scheme. I found out by tracking it when I received a return from an area where no railroads are. Or are even planned for. I discovered it had funded a ranch far south of where you are. Several of them, actually. My money became a resource banks used to loan on land where ranchers eventually failed. Those ranches were then sold, at far more profit than I saw in my return, and the rest of the investment went to buying up railroad land, ahead of the rails, making the buyers rich.

The worst of it all is, Regina, I discovered some of those ranchers died, and then their land was turned over. What if there was foul play? I'm just sick to have had a hand in this. What if my money has done great harm instead of good? In the end, I haven't a piece of rail or land to my name. My return is nominal.

I'm thinking about traveling there, Regina, down to the areas where these ranches were. I know the names of the men I've been investing with. Met one of them, actually, here in New York.

I can find them. I'm sure of it.

Please write, but don't talk. Please let me know what you think. Did you and Flynn encounter anything like this in Kansas? You've always been my source of wisdom, and I need some now.

Forever in your debt...

My mouth hung open as I read the end. It stayed that way, even though I knew better. Schemes? Bank investments? Railroad land and ranches? Dead ranchers? I stared at the ground my husband lay beneath and fumbled with my cousin's letter, forcing it back into its envelope. Surely not. Surely, surely not.

Chapter 41

Leg up, lad. Leg up. ~Rex

"What's that?" Jess stared as I ducked through the bedroom door. Regina had gone across the prairie. Ted had ridden off. It was just me and the boy. Perfect.

"Crutches and a brace."

"What?"

"Crutches and a brace. I figure Doc doesn't want you putting any weight on that break, so we'll hoist it up with a brace. The crutches will take that leg's place when you stand up and walk."

Jess's eyes turned to saucers. Not as fancy but nearly as round as the dainty plates his mother used. I came alongside his bed, those big eyes scouring the crutches and brace.

"You up for this?"

"But Doc said…"

"I aim to be careful. And if it helps any, I've talked to Doc about this a little myself. I've seen these sorts of things used before, and so has he." I just hadn't let on I was making a set.

I could guess again what Flynn must have looked like as the boy's gape riveted on me. Regina was in his fervor, but someone else was in those eyes. And that hair. Just like Luke and the way he favored his mother.

Jess slid the light blanket that had been draped over

him aside. He jammed his fists into the mattress and edged himself up.

"No, just stay flat while I fit this brace to you. We want to keep that leg straight, so lay still. I'll tell you when to roll, if I need you to." The splint we'd made when Jess was first hurt needed to go. What I'd made now was sturdier, more functional. "When I have this on your leg, you need to use the side of the bed your good leg is on. It's your pivot leg. It's the one you'll use along with the crutches to get up. And out. Imagine using the outhouse again."

The boy blushed, but he looked thrilled.

I secured to his leg the wood and the leather I'd cut. "This is why we don't shoot men with bum legs. While you were laying here you could have been cutting this leather or making this brace."

"Yes, sir." Jess looked up. "I didn't know." He watched my face while I tightened the straps and hooks.

"You ready?"

His head yanked up and down.

"Okay, I'm going to hold your legs while you lift your upper half and scoot to the right side of the bed."

He nodded again. I managed his legs as he used his arms like spider legs, hoisting himself across the mattress until he collapsed at the other side.

"I'm out of wind." His color faded.

"Let me know when you're ready." I let him rest while I brought the crutches to the bed's edge, and leaned them his way. He grappled with the mechanics for a moment, until I jiggled the nearest crutch.

"I'm ready." He bit both lips between his teeth and laid hold of the crutch. He twisted and grimaced. I stayed near, ready to hold that leg steady. He perspired, but I sweat. He grunted, and I prayed. Every inch he advanced took an eternity. This boy had been in bed far too long. It had made him wobbly, and his ma and her doctor friend had made him afraid.

"You're doing good." I nodded. I held on. And with several more rocking motions Jess struggled to his good foot, his braced leg dangling toward the floor as he dropped onto the crutches. I gripped both and held him still. He breathed harder than I did when I argued with his mother. I held on tight while he swayed.

"You did it. You're up on your feet. Well, your foot."

I grinned at the mat of hair on the back of his head as he stared at the floor. "I am. I'm up." He looked at me, a grin stretching across his face. Staring ahead, he leaned forward, setting the end of the crutches not far from his good foot. He swung into them, until his foot hit the floor, his eyes growing with his smile.

"How's the leg? The one in the brace?"

"It hurts, but I don't care."

I knelt beside him, fitted the brace so there was no drag on the break in his leg, firmed the leather and wood so they did all of the work. "Now?" I glanced up.

He jiggled. "That's better."

"Okay." I stood. "Let's practice around the room for a bit, then that's probably enough for your first time up."

"I want to go outside."

"I kind of expected that, and I don't blame you. A man can only take so much lace and finery."

"My pa took it just fine." Jess scowled. "He never complained."

I glanced around Regina's bedroom. The one she

used to share with Flynn, she with the wild red hair, the fiery attitude, the perfect hourglass I'd seen formed by those trousers I'd bought her. I looked down at the boy they'd made, ventured a guess why Flynn never complained. "Your father was a lucky man. I mean he was a good man."

"He was. He should have never died. Not that way."

"What way was that, if you don't mind if I ask?"

That look of death I'd seen the first time I met Flynn Howard's boy returned. And with it some of the anger I'd seen.

"He shouldn't have been out there alone like that. Pa was proud of whatever he was doing for us. He told me he had something special, and I'm sure that was it. Land. That day, he was out there looking it over before he showed us. I know that's it. But he never made it back. Found him the next day. He fell off his horse and hit his head."

I looked at Jess. I slid around him and sat on the edge of the bed. "Ted know anything about the land?"

"Ted said Pa never told him anything for sure. He said he had no idea where Pa was when Pa didn't come home that night, and we went with Ted, guessing and looking all the wrong places. Pa shouldn't have gone out there on his own. If only Ted had been with him...or me. Or even Ma."

The boy's anger turned to tears. The "if only" that wouldn't let go. The "if only" that made him blame anyone and everyone around. Except Ted.

Chapter 42

I said a man who could take orders! ~Regina

I tucked my cousin's letter into my pocket while I stared at Flynn's grave. I kept my hand over the fabric and pressed both letters against my thigh as I sensed the earth beneath me. Flynn. The cold earth. I glanced across the prairie at the home he'd built horribly but with joy.

Surely not. Flynn's death was an accident. He wasn't at either end of a scheme—a perpetrator or a victim.

He was brilliant in New York. But a novice here.

I stood, my hand clamped over the pocket, wondering what exactly had turned his dreams into plans of opportunity. Maybe there was no plan, and no more money. Maybe Flynn had been duped and truly was a victim of a scheme. I shook my head. I couldn't believe Flynn could fall prey to a money trick. He was too bright.

So was I. I continued to stare at the hard earth between us, the grass slowly weaving a barrier, separating what was and what would be. Now I had to be even brighter.

"Goodbye, Flynn." My voice sounded strangled this time. I'd never told him goodbye. Not this way. There'd been no time for tears, but they came now.

Torrents of wet sorrow, spilling out, making their way down toward the earth where he lay—my tears, his land—the last communion we'd ever have. "I'm on my own. Maybe I always was."

It hurt. I glanced at the ranch house through a veil of shimmering wet, at the barn that amazed me as it continued to stand. I had to start over, look at things differently. A new way. A new road ahead. One without accidental deaths, bank investments, or plans others forced me to make. It would be my plan only. And I'd make it work.

I left Flynn's grave without looking back. I marched over the grass instead of through it, across the prairie differently than I had several weeks ago after Flynn's service. That felt like a lifetime ago. Jess had been well—unhappy, but well. I was in a dress. Shortly after, as I came across this same prairie, there had been a stranger in my yard. Tall, with a black horse. And my son.

Like now.

I stopped. Ben was impossible to miss. Tall and dark, rugged and sure. Walter was the same. I cupped a hand over my brow. And Jess? He was supposed to be in bed, but that looked like him hobbling around the barnyard. I squinted to be sure. That was Jess, and that was Ben beside him, hovering near, while Jess dipped and swayed like a seasick ship.

"Jess!" Drat the wind. He and Ben continued dipping and swaying around the barnyard. No one in Kansas could hear unless they were right in front of each other. I dropped my hands from my brow, hanging onto the pocket my letters were in. And I ran. Over the grass, against the wind, and into the yard where my son hobbled next to that man.

"Jess!" I raced toward him, he nearly toppling over, wheeling at the sound of my voice—the look on his face, the glow on his cheeks, the dance of his eyes, nearly toppling me. His new start.

"I'm walking! I got up!"

"But you can't. You shouldn't. Can you? Should you?"

"Yes I can, and I should. My leg doesn't even hurt. Well, a little, but Ben tightened the brace so it's steady. And there's no weight on it. Look how fast I can go."

"Whoa there, fellow." Ben put a hand on Jess's shoulder. "Save that speed. A little at a time, so you can build back to normal."

"Where did you get those...those contraptions?" I knelt at the sticks Jess leaned on, the new splint bound around his leg.

"Ben made them. They work just fine."

"Crutches and a brace." Ben looked down at me.

"Something you used on cattle when they went lame?"

Ben gave me a look that infuriated me, like he was barely keeping his thoughts to himself, none of them good. "You learn to do things out there when no one's around to help," he said. "Like how to mend cows, men, even fences." He nodded at the corral. Much improved since he'd been adding new posts and rails to replace the splintered ones Ted had propped back up. I thought of the day Jess had been injured, broken like the fence, because of Ben's careless whistle. How Ben had been in step with Doc Harris afterwards, even Doc himself suggesting Ben knew his medicine.

"Apparently you know your corrals, Mr. Miller.

And maybe even your boys."

Ben's color changed. There was no mistaking the paling of his face, the drop in his expression, the way his gaze waned as he glanced away from Jess. "If you want, I'll ride to Liberal and fetch the doc. He can check what I've rigged. Check Jess and say what he thinks. After all, he knows more than I do."

"I'll go to Liberal and ask Doc myself."

Ben stared down at me. "If you prefer to talk to Doc alone…"

"I was hoping you'd stay here with Jess. Ted mentioned he wants to go, so he'll have Boss. I could use Walter."

"We'll all three go. You, me, and Jess. In the wagon."

"Ben, I won't have Jess traveling until we're sure."

"He has to."

"He does not, he…"

Ben stopped me then. A finger in the air, and leaning close. With a voice worn deep by the wind, sweeping over me. "If your boy doesn't ride in a wagon, the next thing he's going to have to ride is a train. Back east. Unless the two of you want to hit the trail with an ex-cattleman."

Chapter 43

A man likes facts. Even when he's only twelve years old. ~Rex

I had struck Regina's little family with flint and steel the evening before. It sparked. I saw the shock on their faces—the heat of hearing they had more consequences than options. If I didn't torch what little they had to make things better for them, someone else would, but not with Regina and her boy in mind. I felt it in my gut. I'd seen too much in the Oklahoma plains of Indian Territory, and somehow this area was starting to feel the same.

The wagon was ready, dried grass packed into a bed in the back so my arranged stepson could go for a ride.

"Sorry, Boss," I whispered in the soft light of dawn. "You're gonna worry your boss for a little bit. Enough to put him under my nose where I can watch him." I hooked a burr under his belly, up below the shoulder. Just enough to make him squirm. I slapped him on the rump, stepped over the corral, and strode to the house.

"Good morning," I said as I came into the kitchen. "Boy up?" I poured coffee, wishing the cup was four times bigger. I took a sip, Regina's frown as hot as her coffee was on my lips. My lips. Her lips. I set the cup down. "Good coffee, by the way." I walked to her bedroom door, tapped, and pushed it halfway open. "You up, boy?" I went in, leaving the door ajar behind me, which her tiny figure immediately filled.

"Is this jaunt really necessary?" She followed me into the room.

"I'll try not to jaunt him."

"Jaunt means trip." Her spark was still hot.

"If we keep that leg straight, and the weight off it, he should be fine on our jaunt. Walter will take it slow and easy. To Liberal to see Doc, first, then to where Jess can show us Flynn's land. I hope." I held onto the crutches as Jess pulled himself up.

"I was going there when I got hurt." Jess looked up at me. "I always kind of knew from Pa's hints he had land out there." The boy hobbled past his mother and out of the room. Successfully. She didn't even stop him, so I decided to do the same, tipping my head as I passed her and hightailing it after her son.

"Something's wrong with Boss. What the..." Ted stood in the kitchen doorway blocking our way, but he pressed himself to the side as Jess brushed past and through. Lickety-split. Like me, when I was a boy. But not now. I stood back and watched Jess's hobbling speed that got him out of the house and out of range. Lickety-split. That's how my stepmother would have described his boyish rush.

"Watch your language, Ted. What's wrong with Boss?" Regina came from behind me and looked past Ted at her boy barreling toward the wagon. Ted was watching with her, questions in his stance as to how and why the boy was up.

"He's limping worse than Jess." Ted turned my

way. "Who has no business up."

I excused myself, squeezed between him and Regina, and hurried alongside Jess to study the bed of grass in the back of the wagon.

"Ben," Regina called from behind me. "Ted is going with us."

"All right, Jess, up you go." I'd accomplished what I intended—Regina and her son getting what was theirs, and Ted where I wanted him. And when.

Chapter 44

My cousin, Clyde. Yet one more man to maneuver around. ~Regina

"Here we go, nice and close." Ben brought the wagon to a halt in front of Doc's office. He hopped down while Jess worked his way off the grass bed, scooted to the edge of the wagon, and slid out onto his crutches as Ben held them.

Doc wasn't going to like this. Any of it.

My son steadied himself and swung up on the boarded walk before I could stop him, Ben right alongside Jess and pointing to gaps between the planks.

"I see them." Jess placed the tips of his crutches in the middle of the planks and headed toward Doc's door. Quick. He could at least look like he was being mindful of all the care Doc had given him. Even if I didn't.

"Wait. Slow down. I'm going in with you." I hopped up on the walk.

"I don't need nobody to come with me." Jess balanced on his crutches and one leg long enough to give me a scowl.

"Anyone. You don't want anyone to come with you, but I'm your family, and I'm going in with you."

"I want to talk to Doc on my own, Ma. I'm not just the boy on this ranch, anymore, I'm more. I'm also not so busted up I'm going to keep lying there counting

248

holes in your lace curtains until you shoot me."

"Counting holes? Shoot you? I'd never shoot you. Whatever gave you such a ludicrous idea?"

Jess glanced at Ben. "Like a horse, Ma. They shoot horses with broken legs."

"Cowhands sure do," Ted said from beside the wagon. He'd been quiet the whole ride, his only and last words, "I'll drive," right before Ben beat him to the reins and the seat.

"We'll meet you right here later." I turned to Ted. The bank was in the look he gave me, and a solid "no" in mine. I had my own questions for Mr. Gulliver, and I didn't want Ted around. Questions Flynn probably should have asked. Ted tipped his head my way and turned down the walk.

"Well, I'll be." Doc's door opened. The shock was clear in his voice until I turned. It traveled to his eyes, then, and changed to hurt as he looked from my son to me and then to Ben. "Well, I'll be," Doc said it again, quieter this time as he backed aside and held the door for Jess to clunk and drag himself through.

Ben and I followed.

"I can't believe my eyes." Doc looked at me as he spoke, then stepped past me and focused on Jess.

I braced for the anger Doc should rightly have, for the reprimand, the certainty Ben had ruined Jess's chances of ever walking normally again. And for the hurt I'd caused when I married another.

Doc circled my boy as he studied him, saying nothing terse, looking at Jess in ways even I hadn't. He considered my boy with a doctor's perspective instead of a mere man's, an eye for straightness, for posture, for strength. Nothing about how we'd insulted him.

Nothing about shooting Jess or comparing him to a lame horse. Doc ran his hand down the brace and touched the crutches. "These are as good as any I've ever seen. Where in the world did you get them?"

Jess tapped the tip of one crutch Ben's direction. "He made them. And they work just fine."

Doc glanced at Ben, then back at my son. "I hope you thanked him."

I saw Doc in a way I hadn't before. The way Ben saw him. Maybe more. Doc was good and gracious, humble and honest. I looked from him to Ben, who was watching me, the two of us staring at each other as I heard Doc walk Jess around the room, offering suggestions regarding his movements, and answers to my son's questions.

"Now this way." Doc took Jess the other direction, I turned from Ben and watched. Doc stayed with my son. Back and forth, around and around, close enough I could have touched them at first, but farther and farther away as Doc cut a path beyond my reach.

"You'll be like this for a while," Doc said to Jess across the room. They stopped, and Doc talked to my son about adjusting the brace, gauging his progress, and what was best as he healed. "No horse riding. Not for a long time. And stick to both crutches until I say you can switch to one. Or a walking stick. Don't try to hurry, either. And I'll give you some exercises to help strengthen that leg. Do everything I say..." Doc looked toward Ben. "And do what he says, too." Doc laid a hand on Jess's shoulder. "Then you'll be out running and riding again before you know it. Okay?"

"Definitely," I answered for my son.

"And how about you?" Doc asked Jess again.

"I suppose."

"I hope that means yes." Doc squeezed my son's shoulder.

"Doc." I stepped across the small office to stand in front of Doc as Ben followed Jess to the door. It was Flynn's blue-eyed gaze again, catching me as Doc turned toward me. Blue eyes I'd hurt in more ways than one. "I want to pay you. How much for today?"

I heard the door open and close as I stared into that faraway blue. What a different sort of arrangement it would have been with a man like Doc. It would have been a marriage, instead.

"This enough for starters?" Ben's arm stretched between me and Doc, money in his hand. I looked at that hand, the length and strength of it. I would have had a marriage with Doc, a nice gentle stroll into the next life, never touching hands like Ben's, never having them touch me.

"I should be paying you." Doc's gaze went from me to Ben, some of the blue fading from his eyes. "You did my job. Took over the one I especially wanted. So easy, the way you did it. Before I even knew it."

Ben laid the money in Doc's hand. "Trust me, nothing I've done here has been easy."

Both men looked at me.

"Well, I… Well, thank you," Doc said.

I looked from one to the other. "Honestly, I don't thank you. Either one of you." It sounded every bit as brusque as I meant it, and I was glad. "Come on, Jess, let's go." I marched to my son and took him outdoors.

"Can we go to Pa's other ranch now?" Jess asked.

"I need to mail a letter, and I believe your ma wanted to go to the bank." Ben answered before I had a chance, stepping behind me from Doc's office.

"I need to mail a couple of letters myself. Why don't you walk with me?" I spoke only to Jess.

"You mean all three of us? Like a family?" Jess frowned.

"Like there's important work to be done, and we aim to do it," Ben answered again before I had a chance to say a word.

"Work? Like a job?" I had my chance now, and I took it. "One that isn't easy? I know what you meant back there." I rounded on Ben. And if Doc stepped out that door, I'd round on him, too.

Ben glanced toward the closed door, probably hoping for help. "I doubt he was referring to you as a job."

"He was indeed, but he wasn't the one that made me sound like a chore."

"You're not a chore." Creases formed at Ben's eyes and mouth, giving away the beginnings of a grin. "Truthfully…" The creases were gone when he looked back to me. "You're an arrangement."

It wasn't a slap in his gaze, but it stung, and I felt it, just the same. He may have, also, the fun gone out of his eyes. Business. That's what Ben was saying. I *was* a job. Something he had to do. That's what this relationship was. Business. And a parting.

"Let's get going." Jess thumped his crutch the direction of the postal building and headed that way.

Yes, let's. I heard it in my head, but nothing came out of my mouth. I fell in behind my son.

I stood back in the postal office. A job. Ben handed two letters to Mr. Greene. An arrangement I'd set up, but he agreed to and was carrying out. I didn't bother to strain to see the names he'd written to.

"Your turn." Ben tipped his hat as he moved aside.

Making as broad a circle as I could, I stepped around him. "One to my mother," I said to Mr. Greene. "And the other to my cousin." Clyde. I thought of Flynn as Mr. Greene slid my cousin's letter across the counter. Flynn's gravesite and schemes. The questions I had for his banker.

"Wait. I should take that one back…" I laid a hand on the letter. Clyde shouldn't come out west. He wasn't man enough to survive. But I was.

"Ma'am?" Mr. Greene looked at me.

"I need to add something more." I turned to Ben. "Go on and do whatever *other* chores you need to. I'm going to fix this letter before I send it off."

"I'll go tend to Walter." Ben glanced out the window. "Ted's probably waiting for you at the bank anyway."

"I told him not today." Just like you advised, since I'm that work you have to do. I took my letter from Mr. Greene. "Go see to Walter. I'm sure he's not that much of a chore."

Ben nodded to Mr. Greene and gave Jess a look I didn't quite understand—some manly fact look, maybe, like the noises he made at his horse. I waited until, finally, he left.

"This will only take a minute," I reiterated to Jess. He tapped a crutch on the floor, impatient little beats while I told my cousin to stay where he was. I asked who he'd done business with and promised I would have them looked up. Just let me know, and I'd see to it for him. My cousin was cowardly. He would send me their names.

Ben was nowhere in sight when Jess and I stepped out onto the walkway, the wagon and Walter gone, also. "Let's go to the bank," I said. "Then we can leave."

I listened to the tri-thump of my son beside me. Two steps for me, three for him. Crutches, a slight drag, and a thump of his good foot. Jess looked strong, his color better. Impatient to see the surviving piece of his father. If there was one.

"Amazing coincidence." Ted appeared around the corner of the bank as Jess and I came to the door. He tipped his head and latched onto the handle with his good hand.

"If you have business here, it's your own." I shouldered close to my son.

"I don't mean to upset you, but I'm doing you a favor. You'd best see Mr. Gulliver with me. I just spoke with him. He caught me in there earlier, and I told him you weren't interested in having me sign. What he said wasn't good. That's why I'm back. Thought maybe he'd hold off before he did anything hasty, if we talked to him together." He tugged the bank's door open and held it for us.

"I told you, Ted, I'm here to speak with Mr. Gulliver myself." I walked through the door, Jess's thumps and slides behind me. People glanced up, and customers parted like the Red Sea as we entered. The thump and drag waned as Jess came to a stop.

"I'll wait here." Jess leaned against the tall central table, his crutches close to his side.

"I'll be quick."

"Just a minute or two, son," Ted added. He touched my elbow, but I drew it away, and walked ahead of him to Mr. Gulliver.

The banker stood when I reached the front of his desk. Mr. Gulliver's desk was clean, the top shiny and polished, clear enough his reflection stretched across in front of me. "Welcome, both of you."

I turned to the side, Ted there at my right. "I'm here on my own…" I began.

Mr. Gulliver smiled, gestured toward two seats that faced him. I settled into one, and Ted dropped into the other.

"Ted, I told you…"

"Is that your son?" The banker leaned across the shiny pool of his desktop. He gazed past me at Jess, at the uncomfortable way he propped himself at the table, ignoring passing stares.

I waited for sympathy, held my breath against something neither Jess nor I wanted to hear.

"He favors your husband," Mr. Gulliver said. Then he looked at me. "But he must have some of your courage. The two of you have borne a lot together."

"That they have," Ted agreed beside me.

The banker turned Ted's way. "So did the two of you decide it's best to settle the deed for the ranch the easy way? Today? Might be good to hurry. Looks like that boy needs to get off his feet."

I glanced back at Jess. Some of his color had drained. My boy. The ranch. My plan. "As I was saying, I'm not here with Ted. I have questions of my own that…"

Ted put a hand on the arm of my chair. "We're here about settling things as best we can. Then we're going to go look for that property Flynn must have bought before he…before he had the accident. Regina and me, her son, and that man who married her."

The banker's brows raised. "I don't think…"

"Mrs. Howard—I mean, Mrs. Miller," Ted continued, "feels it's time to find it, so she can decide what to do with it. Maybe we can get all of this settled at the same time."

"Mrs. Miller, no matter what you decide, there are rules…" Mr. Gulliver leaned back in his chair. "We'll have to go through this all over again. If only you'd listen to reason…"

"Ted is not here to speak or sign for me, Mr. Gulliver, and I don't need you to lecture me on things you've already said. I intend to secure all of the land that has been mine since Flynn bought it, and then I'll decide what's to be done."

"But the deed…" Mr. Gulliver leaned forward.

"I'd like to see it. Both of them. I no longer want just your word, Mr. Gulliver. I want proof."

Mr. Gulliver tapped his fingers on his desk, the reflection in the polish as clear as if he thrummed them on a mirror. "There is only one deed here, and that is for the land you're on. And as I've made clear, we're willing to waive all of the debt Mr. Howard accumulated against your ranch, with Ted's signature." Mr. Gulliver's fingers stilled. "Not intending to cast doubt on your choice for a mate, Mrs. Miller, but I have no history on that new husband of yours. Nothing. That may be all right for you, but when it comes to finances…"

"Mr. Gulliver, I've heard all of this before, and what you're saying isn't consistent." I came to my feet. "Flynn Howard was a stranger when he came here and bought land, and I don't recall him saying anyone balked at his name or signature in this bank. So balking at Ben Miller's name makes no sense."

"Mrs. Howard, in answer to your claims that we didn't balk at Flynn when he came here as a stranger, well, that was a much smaller debt than what he finally amassed. He left the bank in a rather touchy predicament."

Ted touched my sleeve, but I remained on my feet. "Let her see the deed," he said to Mr. Gulliver.

The banker gazed at Ted, then called for a young man seated several desks away. At a smaller desk, one full of papers and files. The young man stood, listened to Mr. Gulliver's instructions, and disappeared through a doorway. He re-entered with a piece of paper, set it in front of Mr. Gulliver, then returned to his own desk.

"Here it is," the banker said. "The only one we have." He twisted the document my way and I dropped to my chair. Swirls of cursive arched before me. It looked like art, a document in a graceful pen. Long and flowing lines creating waves, undulating like the prairie Flynn had bought. And at the bottom—his name. Flynn Howard. His name and mine, together, as owners of the land.

"Now, if you'd just let Ted sign for you," Mr. Gulliver said, scooting the document a little Ted's way.

I stared at Flynn's signature. It flowed like the Kansas wind. I could feel it, and I could imagine how he'd looked when he signed this deed. I wished I'd been here with him, but Jess and I were still in New York, waiting for Flynn to buy the ranch, secure the paperwork, and build us a home. Jess had asked every day if his father was ready for us yet. I could picture Flynn's hand, the smoothness of his skin, the long fingers meant for business, not for ranching. The mind meant for the intricacies of finances, not for finagling a crooked deal. "No…"

"Regina…" Ted began.

I could only see Flynn's signature and think how well he had always provided for Jess and me. How good he intended to be.

"Regina," Ted said again. "I'd only be a signature, making sure everything Flynn meant you to have would stay yours. And Jess's. My name would be on paper only. Ted and Regina."

"Make that Mrs. Miller. With Mr. Miller alongside it." A hand, a rugged hand, stretched between Ted and me. Fingers settled on the deed and swiped it away, quicker than Mr. Gulliver's reach. "Mrs. Miller and I are keeping this property. I'm her husband. I'm the rightful owner."

"Sir, are you still interested in other investments? I have some, if you are. Good ones."

I glanced at the young man who had brought the deed. He nearly bounced on his heels as he hurried toward Ben. Sir? He called Ben "sir"?

"I'll let you know." Ben nodded at the young man, and touched my shoulder. I looked up at a man Mr. Gulliver claimed he didn't know, and I truly didn't, either. With the deed in one hand, he took my arm in his other. And he turned me toward Jess.

Chapter 45

Be careful on the approach, and quick on the grab.
~Rex

I held the deed in the air, everyone's eyes on it except for one's. Her eyes were on me. This deed wed us more than the marriage certificate—my name and hers, joint owners of her ranch. She was beautiful. In her glance I felt a honeymoon.

Then I didn't. This was business. That's what she'd wanted, it was part of her plan. There would be "business" in her gaze as soon as we were outdoors. Something I really didn't want to see.

"Now, Mr. Miller..." Mr. Gulliver stood.

I held the deed higher. Ted rose to his feet. I looked down, as far down as I could. He didn't have a chance as he eyed the deed high above him. If he'd had two good hands, he would have been clenching two fists. I looked from him to Regina's banker.

"Now, I see no reason for another buyer. It would be wrong, don't you think, since she's married now?"

"The bank must protect its interests, Mr. Miller, and you are a gamble. Even with cash, that ranch is still a gamble, one we can't afford to carry again."

I rolled the deed and slipped it into my shirt pocket. "A simple 'yes' would have been the right answer." I glanced down at Regina. "You ready to go? We have land to look at, and I'd guess we can have this deed taken care of somewhere besides here."

She nodded. Then smiled. I liked the way she did it. If I'd drawn a sketch, when I was younger, of how my wife would look someday when I invited her to go somewhere with me, Regina would have been picture perfect. So perfect that the "Mr. Miller" I heard in the background didn't matter. I gave her my arm as if we'd been doing this—and would continue to do it—forever.

"Ma?"

"We're ready, son." We paused near Jess. "Time to go find your father's land."

The boy stole a glance at me, "father" too confusing a term after what he'd just seen. He faltered, dragged himself forward, and the three of us went for the door.

If I were Ted, I would have been quick to make it the four of us. If I were Ted and meant what I'd just said in there.

I reached the door first, let go of Regina's arm, and held the large oak monstrosity open while she and her son passed through.

"I'll be right there," I heard her ranch manager say in the background as I let the door close behind us.

"Shall we?" I looked at the bride I hadn't wanted, offering her an elbow, knowing our charade might be done now that we were outside. Or maybe it wasn't. A charade.

Chapter 46

I'd wanted a name, not an elbow. But Ben Miller's elbow looked mighty good. ~Regina

Ben's skin was warm through his sleeve, the feel of being alive emanating through the heavy cotton to my palm and fingers as I held on above his elbow.

"We shall," I said, peering into those eyes. Endless tunnels to something good. Surely. Good mixed with the occasional aggravation and obstinacy.

Jess took off faster than Doc would probably have preferred, his lanky body bobbing up and down as he charged forward on his crutches.

"Let him go," Ben said.

As Jess's thumps and bangs disappeared ahead of us, Ben and I were left to ourselves. "Rather an amiable moment for us, don't you think?"

"Amiable? Is that like what your son's doing up ahead?"

I looked at Jess swaying back and forth as he "hied" it away from us. He hadn't been amiable since his father died. "That's right." Even though what he was doing could more rightly be called ambling.

"Then we'll amiable right behind him."

"Since you've got the deed, I'd say you're right."

"Not *the* deed. *Our* deed."

We came to the end of the main boardwalk, and

Ben steered me to the right, where Walter and the wagon were waiting. Jess was already in the back, and Ted had the reins.

"I'm still doing the driving." Ben said it the same way he looked as he frowned up at Ted. "And I need Jess up close where he can see, with his mother behind us."

Ted's knuckles whitened.

"I take it you know where Flynn Howard's other land is, then." Ben stood beside the wagon, his comment a challenge, nearly an accusation, an opportunity for Ted to say "yes" or "no" to what he had already denied.

Ted stared down at Ben, the white disappearing. "No, I don't. Just trying to be helpful. It's what her husband hired me to do. The husband whose name is on that deed." Ted tossed the reins aside and dropped to the ground.

When he had everyone where he wanted them, Ben made one of those noises only Walter understood, and the horse started forward, my son on the front seat, me on a crate behind the two of them, and Ted behind—at the end of the wagon, his feet dangling off the back.

"Okay, Jess, I'm going to take you the direction I think this land is. I have a feeling you'll know if it's right."

Jess sat up a little straighter. His color was good, his eyes bright. Ben was the same, his posture strong, his eyes alert, his shirt the one he'd laid over Jess that night in the prairie. The night he promised to make sure my boy was settled. I raised a finger, touched the back of it, and grazed its surface.

"Got something for you." With the reins in one

hand, Ben glanced at my son, pulling two stems of grass from his pocket. He put one in his mouth and offered the other to my boy. Jess stared at the stem in Ben's fingers, then at the one protruding from between his lips. "Thinking weeds." Ben extended the grass Jess's way. "A man's gotta chew on one now and then."

Jess took the thinking weed, set it in his mouth the same way Ben had his, then gazed ahead. Just as Ben did.

"How long do you think it will take to get there?" I asked.

"If you're hungry, we can stop and eat under that tree over yonder. I packed us some food. Enough to satisfy even Jess." Ben smiled over his shoulder at me, and nodded to a greening oak to the right.

"You did?"

"All wrapped up under that crate you're sitting on, so sit still."

"I always sit still. If it won't take long to get there, we'll eat on the land."

Ben glanced at Jess. "You need to eat now? At least more than that weed?"

Jess swiveled the stem around in his mouth. "Thinking's okay for now. I'm watching, and not really hungry yet."

"Not hungry enough for this?" Ben drew a candy stick from his pocket. It was shiny and red, tempting even me as it glittered in the sun. The stem in Jess's mouth stilled as Ben ran the candy under his nose.

"Maybe I'm done thinking." Jess gave Ben a half smile as he watched the candy.

"I'll give you a few minutes off from thinking. If what I suspect might be your father's land really is, you have enough time for that candy before you get back to thinking." Ben handed the stick to my son.

"Thank you." Jess settled back against the seat, a fresh kind of contentment on my son's face.

We rode along in a peaceful silence, Ted watching the road behind us while Jess worked on his candy and studied the acres and acres of grass and dirt ahead and around us. An occasional homestead appeared, always poor, like ours. We wouldn't be quite so poor if I could find Flynn's money. I looked for landmarks so I could find my way back to Flynn's land on my own to look for that money, but there were none. Flat land, flat prairie, brown homes so far apart I couldn't tell one from the other.

"I can't believe Flynn would want land so far away," I said at last. I glanced back at Ted. He said nothing, stayed fixed where he was, watching behind us as we continued to the northeast. Far enough and wide enough of Liberal I'd never have enough time in a day to come all the way back here to search for hiding places Flynn may have chosen, and return in time no one would question what I'd been doing.

"You're going to need this." Ben handed Jess another stem of grass.

Jess perked up. He devoured the rest of the candy, looking around. "Yes." Jess said it softly, softer than the wind, but I heard it. He straightened, eyed a small grove of trees. Ben made a noise that brought Walter to a halt.

I looked where my son looked. More grass, a gentle rise and fall to the land, and trees. More trees than usual. "Is there a creek down there?"

"There is." Ben looked at Jess. He made another

noise and Walter edged forward, headed straight to the trees lining the creek.

"Walter sure was the right name for this horse." Ben grinned at my son. "Because of him I stopped at this stream the first time."

Jess felt the smile, caught the tribute, as he scanned the land close and far. For all the times I had tried to force Flynn Howard to speak from the grave, I knew he was speaking now. To his boy.

"This is it," Jess whispered. "It fits the stories Pa told me. He said he was making them up, but he wasn't. I knew he wasn't! He told me to keep learning. He was teaching me through all those tales he told."

Flynn. He was indeed a good provider. He'd made our son ready, even if there was no land.

Walter reached the stream and shook at the halter on his head. His language to Ben. The wagon teetered as Ben jumped to the ground. I listened to his deep rumbling tone as he freed Walter and gave him a love pat on the rump that sent the horse straight to the water.

"Let's eat." Ben snatched my son's crutches from the back and helped Jess down.

"Not really hungry." Ted slid off the back, and I scooted off behind him. "Gonna waste a lot of time, eating." Ted watched Ben remove a blanket from the back and spread it on the ground. Ben nodded for me to sit, lifting food from the crate and setting it at the wagon's end—stomach level for my boy. Ben handed Jess a tin plate, something I prayed was clean, since it had likely been his on cattle drives, and told him to do what my son had been dying to do—help himself.

Jess swelled with a grin, that big tin plate swelling with food as he balanced on his crutches.

"You might as well eat, Ted," Ben called from close to my son, ready to save either him or the plate.

"I said I'm not hungry." Ted's good arm shot into the air, sort of a wave, but more of a gesture as he tromped off through the grass.

"More for you." Ben shrugged at my son. Jess grinned and ladled more—more bread, more dried meat, more thick fried potatoes—onto an already heaping plate while Ben worked around him, snatching food for me and bringing me a plate. I'd fought this man for weeks, but this time I didn't. I stayed on the blanket and ate like a mother, and like a lady, while Ben stood at the wagon next to Jess.

I nibbled, and watched as the two of them pointed between bites, talking about the endless grass Flynn must have seen something special in. The water, the unusual lay of the land, the way everything in nature seemed to be coaxed its direction.

"We should head to that rise," Ben said after Jess's third helping. Ben stowed away what little was left. Methodically. Part of a ceremony that celebrated something Flynn had planned.

"Let's go. I can make it up there with no problem," Jess said. And he did. We walked alongside him against the wind as he combed his crutches and good leg through reeds and weeds, either or both snagging on occasion, but still he plowed through. The breeze was enough to undo my hair, and could have toppled my son, but somehow it didn't matter. We were on a piece of us, Jess certain he was touching something of his father. When we crested the knoll, we stopped, rotated together, hands at our brows saluting the endless Kansas terrain.

"Why this?" I asked. I didn't expect an answer. Flynn could have told me, although he didn't. Maybe he would now, if he had the chance.

"Pa called it Promise Land in his stories."

I frowned at my son. "I didn't know that."

"Especially right before...right before he..."

I wrapped an arm around my son's shoulders, squeezing his crutch between us. Jess looked over Flynn's Promise Land from my side. I did, too, above and around that straight light hair so like his father's. At land only subtly different from all of the rest of Kansas. If there was a promise here, it had to be our money. But where? I glanced at Ben. He was staring to the east, one hand rubbing his chin.

"How far does it go?" I asked. I couldn't imagine pock-marking all of this prairie the way I had the barn floor.

"I know who you can ask," Ben said. "He lives over there." Ben pointed to a lone settlement across a field. He poked the front brim of his hat up with a finger and looked from the homestead to us. "I say we ride. Looks a bit far for a walk."

"Let's go," Jess said. He spun on one crutch like a master and hobbled down the hill. Fast. The wind at his back, his father all around.

Ben re-hitched Walter to the wagon and helped my son and me into it.

"What about Ted?" I cupped a hand over my brow and scanned the land around us. Ted was nowhere to be seen.

"We're not leaving him behind. We'll find him before we go home. More likely, he'll find us."

Home. Ben called my ranch home. I eyed his

pocket. "Want me to hold the deed so it doesn't blow away?"

Ben laid his long fingers over his pocket as he shook his head. I glanced at my son. The day had been too perfect to strike up an argument. I'd wait until we got home.

The farmer met us as we rode into his barnyard. Like Kansas, he and his home looked the same. The same as other ranchers and ranch houses on a terrain that hardly changed.

"Howdy," he said as he looked us over. He narrowed his gaze, then cracked a smile at Ben. "Good to see you again."

"You, too. Regina, meet Fred Albert. And, Fred, this is Regina Miller. Was Regina Howard. And this is her son, Jess Howard. His father and her first husband was Flynn Howard. From New York."

The smile vanished as Fred turned his attention on Jess and me. A hand went to his chin where he scratched, a dry rasping sound carrying with the wind. "New York. You the folks bought that land over there?" He nodded where we'd been.

"They're not sure. That's why we came to talk to you. Flynn Howard died accidentally before he told his wife about the land."

"He told me, though," Jess piped up. "Not about it exactly, but some things. I think that's it."

"What do you know about the place?" Ben asked the farmer.

"Well, it's a long and narrow strip. Unusual, but I heard the owner...maybe Mr. Howard...insisted it be that way. About eighty acres. Goes about a mile that direction." Fred pointed west. "And another two that way." He pointed back east.

Ben looked north and south. "Guess the land around it must already be bought up. Or at either end?"

"Going fast." Mr. Albert shook his head. "With the railroad coming, this land is going fast, and what's bought is changing hands at even higher prices. It's usually Easterners or big money buying it up before the railroad gets it done. Smart buy for smart money."

Chapter 47

Death was in his stare. A different sort of death than had been in Flynn Howard's son's. ~Rex

Regina was quiet, stone quiet for once, as we headed back home. I glanced behind me to where she sat in the bed of the wagon, flat on her backside instead of on the crate, staring across the prairie as we passed. The last I'd heard from her was a slight gasp. It was Fred that made her gasp, not me. And she'd been silent ever since. I glanced to her son at my side.

"Now that you know where your father's other land was, we just got to find the deed to prove it. How about we take a shortcut from here to your home, so we can get started? You know one?"

"Ain't no need hurrying to find something we don't know exists," Ted called from the back. He'd found us, like I knew he would. Probably been lying and waiting like a snake in the grass. "Might as well spend what's left of the day riding."

I looked at Jess. "I was asking you."

"There is a shorter way…" The boy stared off to the right a slight bit.

"That-away?" I nodded where he stared.

Jess sank back in the seat, instead of answering me, his eyes on Walter's rump.

"Like I said, no need to hurry, and I need to talk to

our neighbor next to the ranch," Ted interrupted again. "Stay on this road so we can stop at his place as we go by."

I veered Walter to the right. "Don't worry, Ted, I'll run you by the neighbor's."

"You're wasting time cutting this direction. You'll just have to cut back again."

"I thought you weren't worried about hurrying."

"Ted, it's all right." Regina spoke. I glanced over my shoulder to see her sitting on the crate now, near Jess, one hand on his shoulder, the two of them staring ahead. I looked ahead, also, and waited for Ted's argument. He was quiet. The whole wagon was, except for the occasional groan from the wheels. Nothing from Ted. Nothing from the widow...I mean, my wife...either. Or from her son.

As Walter drew us farther into empty terrain, I was surprised to see trees and abutments of rock here and there. It was like God dropped the wrong piece of puzzle from the sky, something that wasn't supposed to be here in Kansas.

"Well, I'll be." I slowed Walter even more, nearly at a crawl for a horse that could make it across Oklahoma Indian Territory in a day and a half. "This place is downright interesting. Look at those rocks and the way the land spikes up through here." I pointed, stared after my own finger, amazed at this sudden near beauty.

Walter stepped onto a natural path. He was a Ranger's horse, skilled at finding trails of sorts where the grass was thin or even nonexistent. The land dipped, and Walter followed it, moseyed down an incline toward another abutment of rocks.

"This place is where a man should build and live," I said, admiring the scenery.

"This is where Flynn died."

Something touched my side. Soft. Gentle. I glanced down. Regina's fingers were there, on my shirt, near my belt. I followed them to her arm and up to her shoulder, then to her white face. There was no noise suitable for this sort of moment—I yanked back on Walter's reins.

"What?" My question echoed in the air around us, loss taking the fire out of Regina's face. I turned to her son, his face the same as hers. His eyes as red as her hair.

"Not a good place to be," Ted murmured from the back. "I tried to stop you."

I looked at the terrain that had enchanted me seconds before. This was Flynn's shortcut. This was where his life had come to an end. This was the only place Ted and Flynn's family had failed to look while he lay here. I studied the path, the way it bent around rocks, shrubs, and the occasional tree.

"How?" I turned to Regina, only thinking the question, but she understood. She pointed to the next formation of stones and I looked. Looked at the way the trail bent around them, at the stones on the ground.

Regina came off the crate and wrapped her arms around Jess. She held him close, his shoulders shuddering in her clasp.

I glanced back at Ted. He was staring the other direction, then down in his lap at his one good hand. "Seen enough?" he asked without looking back at me.

I'd been mighty foolish when it came to women and boys in my life, but this was more than foolish.

Taking them this way was blamed stupid. Regina stared at the rocks, at the ground, then looked up at me.

"Flynn was good."

I heard the question in her statement, behind us the "Easterner" left over from what Fred had said. "Easterner" and "big money" drained what was left of the color from her face.

"We need to get going." Ted was looking up now. Not at us, but across the land. I still saw it, though. A side of death Flynn probably didn't deserve.

I pressed the reins to Walter's left side, veering him to the right around the next stand of rocks. There was rubble on the ground, some of it strewn in the path where Flynn had evidently ridden. I studied it as we passed. White-gray edges. Fresh breaks. Clean and sharp.

I made that noise Walter understood and he hied it up. I had some tools to check. Nicks and scrapes. Tools back in Regina's barn.

Chapter 48

A name. Ben said Jess set store by them. Now I did the same. ~Regina

"You fixing to leave?"

The china cup slipped in my hands at Ben's voice and the way it raised behind me. I grabbed at the tea towel I had wrapped around it and scrambled to hold on. "This? No."

Ben filled my kitchen doorway, his head slightly bent, watching me pin the teacup to my stomach.

"Just packing some of my things." I finished wrapping the cup in the towel and set it in a small crate. *Would you take some Haviland China as payment?* I'd made the offer to Mr. Greene to pay for a wire I'd sent to Clyde, prodding my cousin to hurry and send me the names of the men he'd invested with.

"I was just getting used to holding onto those little cups. I don't suppose you want some tin mugs to take their place?" Ben crossed the floor and peered into my crate.

Tin mugs. I glanced around at the fine ware I'd brought from New York. Or what would be left of them when I finished using them for trade. "I never saw myself with campfire gear in my kitchen. How many do you have? And why didn't you bring one in to use before now?"

"One. Didn't want everyone squabbling over it. Want me to get it?"

I reached for another cup. "Tin I might get used to, but everyone sharing the same cup? Never. I want Jess to grow up with some decorum."

"I hope decorum isn't catching, whatever it is."

I looked at him, from the black hair on his head, to the worn leather of his boots. "Apparently, it isn't. Can you hand me the rest of the dishes on that upper shelf?"

"I will on one condition."

"And what would that be?"

"You let me handle the bartering."

"Bartering?" I looked away. Decided not to stomp.

"My guess is you've got some bills to pay, and this is how you're thinking on doing it until we find that other deed."

I looked down at the crate, at those tiny lumps of cups and saucers wrapped in my nicest tea towels. Not just the deed, but Flynn's money.

"Bartering's a man's job. It'll go better for me." He stepped alongside me. He laid out towels, brought down my china, lined each piece on top of them, and began to wrap.

"This is none of your business." I shoved Ben aside, knocking a saucer to the floor, splintering it into a thousand pieces, delicate pink painted roses turning to nothing but shards. "Damn!"

"Well, Mrs. Miller, next thing you know, that mouth of yours will be drinking out of a tin cup. After someone else."

"I...I... Oh, just go on outdoors while I finish this up." I butted against him harder.

"No, ma'am. I aim to take care of your bartering.

Besides these dishes, you got more?"

"I'll take care of it myself." Take care of what hurts. Take care of finding what I had to find, because eventually we would part, and I'd be on my own.

"A man's gotta know what he's bartering with. Otherwise he gets himself into situations that are tricky to get out of."

I stopped butting. I looked up at Ben, the sting of what he said like a fire across my face. "So that's why you're in such a hurry to get these deeds taken care of. I know you want out. I could have Ted sign and be done with all of this, if you want out that badly."

"Tricky to and wanting to aren't the same thing. This situation with you, Mrs. Miller, is tricky. Just let me know what things you want me to barter with. I'll take care of them when I go to Liberal next."

Tricky. I wasn't about to thank those dark eyes for whatever generosity Ben thought he offered by wrapping my china and saying I was tricky to get out of. Words worse than what I'd just said flashed through my mind, along with the flames on my cheeks. I turned toward the door. "Just wrap whatever it takes to make things less tricky for you." I was across the kitchen in fewer steps than it took his long legs, and slammed the door behind me.

Chapter 49

Sometimes you gotta learn more than how to run through smoke. Sometimes you gotta learn how to walk.
~Rex

"You going to town?"

I tightened the girth under Walter, Jess's lean shadow limping and tilted my way. I stared at that shadow, measuring how it had changed, as I shoved my hat back on my head. "I am."

The shadow hobbled closer. If it walked straight like it had the first day I'd seen it, I wouldn't be here. Probably.

I straightened and slapped Walter on the shoulder. "You ready, Walter?"

"I could ride a horse now."

I glanced down at Regina's boy. At the flesh-and-blood boy, not the ghost of him that covered this ground, missing his pa. His weight shifted toward that one good foot, the boy stretching as straight as he could. "Maybe if you rode sidesaddle like your ma should be."

"Sidesaddle? I'm not a girl!"

I rested a hand on the saddle horn and studied the boy. In another minute he was going to topple over if he stood any stiffer. "Let's see you walk." I nodded across the barnyard.

Jess scowled, but he pivoted, and took a step, doing his best to avoid leaning on his crutch. He staggered a mite, glanced back at me, but I nodded, urging him on. *Run, Little Brother...you can make it.*

Jess traveled several feet, then turned. "See, I can walk fine."

"Let's see you bend as far forward as you can until it hurts."

"What does that have to do with riding a horse? I said I'm ready to ride, not ready for a whipping."

"Whipping's your ma's business, riding's mine. Let's see you bend."

Jess gave me an even uglier scowl, but he did as I said and bent forward. He leaned on one crutch, bending low enough it looked like a bow. "See, I can do it."

"One more thing, and I don't want you to do this without leaning on your crutch. And stop if it hurts at all." I let go of the saddle horn and walked to the boy. "I want you to spread your feet like this." I moved my feet apart, half as wide as my shoulders.

"Easy. This is wasting time I could be riding." Jess inched his feet apart. His jaw tightened. I saw the flinch behind his glare as his boots plowed dirt to the sides into little heaps. "Ow."

"That's good enough. Straighten up and relax."

Red dotted Jess's whitened face. "You picked things easy for you to do. You knew they'd be hard for me."

You think you're better because you're taller and older. You think you're Pop's favorite. I heard Luke in Jess's fury. *It's for your own good.* I never said that to Luke, and I wouldn't say it to Jess.

"I could use your help today," I said.

Jess gazed through a grimace that didn't slacken at what I said.

"Tell your ma you're coming to Liberal with me. I'll hitch up the wagon. Got some supplies I should get anyway."

I left Jess's arguments behind. I went up to my loft and emptied the crate of dishes Regina had trusted me with. I toted it and my blanket down the ladder and filled the crate with leather straps, small broken tools, whatever I could find, then folded my blanket across the top. I carted it to the wagon and set it in the back against the seat.

"You coming or not?" I turned to Jess, still standing in the barnyard, his arms crossed over his crutches. I took my time unsaddling Walter and hooking him to the wagon. By the time I was done, Jess and Regina were both at the wagon, both of them frowning at me. "The two of you going?" She shook her head, eyeing the crate in the back. The green of her eyes that went so well with her fiery red hair looked wispy as she stared through the slats of wood. "Best get going, then. I plan to pick up lumber when we're in town." I slapped my hands together and looked at Jess. "You ready?"

Regina frowned. "More lumber?" She glanced at the crate, again, green dollar signs appearing in her eyes.

"Walter's been complaining about the conditions here. Promised him I'd spruce things up a bit. No charge to you." I mustered a smile.

"That's not…"

"You don't know Walter. He's always grumbling

279

about something." I looked down at Jess. "You ready, boy?"

Jess swallowed the half smile I was glad to see. He hobbled over to the wagon's side, and I hoisted him up. "You did that good," I said and nodded as he maneuvered on one leg until he was settled. A flash of pride came and went, and I walked to my side of the wagon. Luke had never showed me half smiles or pride at his accomplishments. He never believed he had any, probably not even when he shot at me to save our ranch the night I burned it down.

"You'll be careful..." Regina laid her fingers on my arm as I passed.

That touch, light as it was, reined me in harder than any whistle, sound, or yank ever could. I gazed down at her fingers, then up to those green eyes. "Yes, ma'am. I will." I hurried to my seat.

"Let me?" Jess asked as I choked the reins in my fist. My face was burning, my breathing a little too deep. The boy straightened himself against the sidearm of the bench seat.

"Go ahead."

Jess made a sound. Walter's ears perked up. He tried again, and Walter took a step. I handed the boy the reins.

"Good job." I said at the same time I heard the widow—my wife—say, "Don't let him..."

I waved behind me, kept my hot face forward. I settled back, and let Jess take us to Liberal.

****

"That box anything?" Jess asked after he made a dozen noises until he brought Walter to a halt at the livery. He looped the reins around the post near the seat

280

and glanced back at his mother's crate.

"Things I'll take care of. Some of this, some of that. How about we get you over to Doc's first and see what he thinks about your leg?"

The glow disappeared. Just like I'd thrown a bucket of water on an ember. A good ember, one I never wanted to put out. "So you can ride Walter yourself sometime." The ember flickered.

I walked to Jess's side of the wagon and helped him down. Side by side, once Walter's needs were taken care of, we amiabled to Doc's office, the way Regina would like. I would like her here amiabling along with us, but if she were, I'd never get any rangering done.

"I only half believe what Doc says," Jess muttered as we entered the office door.

"Then leave the other half to me."

I paid Doc for all his troubles and gave him extra for the arguments Jess kicked up at not being ready to ride yet.

"It's a miracle you're up and walking at all," Doc said as we readied to leave. "If it wasn't for that contraption Ben built, you wouldn't be doing anything." Doc gave Jess a smile. His eyes crinkled right, but not enough. There was still pain behind that smile. Saying another man's name in regard to the family he'd had his heart set on, hurt. I understood that. Becky had taught me that every time I saw her with her new husband.

I shook Doc's hand. "Jess knows more about that 'contraption' than anyone. You got other patients could use one?"

Jess stopped in the doorway, his eyes widening

beneath brows that had been stuck in a stormy vee.

Doc looked down at Jess. "You think you could come up with a few of those? With Ben's help?"

The storm waned as the boy's head dipped forward into a nod.

"Good. Make me a set that fits a man about my size and one that fits you. That will make a good start."

Jess nearly bounced as we told Doc goodbye and headed away from his office. His jabbering filled the air, reminding me of his mother, as plans and ideas for even more of these contraptions kept him busy until we stepped into the postal office.

"Well, hello to both of you." Mr. Greene's cheery welcome didn't slow Jess's ideas. They continued to spill out as I sent Jim and Pop letters and took what Mr. Greene had for me. And Regina. I glanced at one of the envelopes addressed to her. To Mrs. Flynn Howard, from New York. From a man's name I didn't recognize. "Regina owe you anything?" I whispered beneath Jess's rambling, his plans for far more sets than Doc had ordered. I pinched her envelope between two fingers. A letter. I considered holding it up to the light while Mr. Green whispered back a minute amount. I paid him. Double. She'd told me to give him a cup, and I'd tell her he refused. I stuffed the envelopes and wires into my pocket and led babbling Jess back outside.

"Think if I gave Mr. Wayne a list of what we need you could make sure he did it right while I go down to the bank?"

"Yes, sir." Jess hied it up even more. "I sure can."

I followed Jess into the mercantile store and left the wide-eyed clerk with a description of what the boy would need, plus a small list of supplies for the ranch.

Jess never even saw me walk out. He was leaning against the counter, not even looking at the candy as he repeated the supplies for crutches and braces, pointing to the boards and straps along his leg.

I dug my wire out of my pocket as I walked to the bank, rangering on my mind as I paused and read what it said.

Your brother's still gunning for Morrissey. And vice versa. Neither one's been seen. Jim

I shoved the wire into my pocket, tugged my letter out, and glanced at who it was from. Jim. I folded it in quarters and stuffed it back in with Regina's envelopes. I didn't need a bunch of instructions on top of bad news. My heart hammered the way my fist wanted to as I gazed off toward the south. "Little Brother, what are you thinking..." Luke was no match for Morrissey. If Luke was still alive.

I hustled to the bank and pushed through the door like it was hinged on a saloon. It withered behind me as it closed and I searched for Mr. Gulliver. His desk was vacant, the empty sheen reflecting nothing but lights and ceiling. I scoured the lobby as I stepped further in. I spotted him then, his profile, most of him hidden behind a low wall far at the back. I lengthened my stride and headed his way. He was talking to another man, and I kept a bead on them as I kept that direction. The other was a worn-out cowboy, the two of them keeping their voices low, each coming clearer as I approached. Clear enough I stopped. I recognized Mr. Gulliver's companion. I turned, hard but slow, keeping my head down, everything in the bank turning to ice.

Morrissey.

"What are you doing here?" Ted grabbed at my

arm as I pushed through the bank's door. Everything felt frosty, my heart hammering, working to break the freeze.

Morrissey. Luke.

"You got business in there?" I fired a question at Ted that was as much for Morrissey as it was for him. That's what Jim would want to know—why was Morrissey here? If I didn't find out, take the time to do this rangering job right, I'd ruin everything by dragging Morrissey out and hanging him right there in the street. Then Regina would know who I really was. Everyone would. Her ranch would be gone, like Pop's. And my job for Jim undone.

"What's it to you?" Ted answered the way I'd expect Morrissey to if we were in a crowd. Where he felt safe. Ted yanked the door with his good hand and disappeared inside. I stepped away from the front, leaned against the corner of the building, Morrissey still there in my mind, his guttural whispers strong in my ears. I edged to the window and watched Ted as he spotted Mr. Gulliver and strode his way. Morrissey watched alongside Regina's banker. Casual. No surprise on his face. He was slightly taller than Ted, but much younger. Young enough he had an overdeveloped swagger to go with his roughed-up clothing. All show.

Luke. Regina.

I slipped away from the window, stared down the boardwalk toward the mercantile store.

Jess.

I wove through people dotting the walkway, twisting my shoulders from side to side without a "hello" or a "pardon me" as I hurried to the store.

"We need to go." I laid a hand on Jess's shoulder.

He stood beaming beside a pile of goods high enough to outfit every invalid in Kansas. "I don't know if we can…"

"This boy did a fine job of clarifying what you need." Mr. Wayne's smile matched Jess's, his grin a calculation of what I owed.

I doled out the cash, fast. Too much of it. Luke. Regina. Jess. "I'll bring the wagon around back." I pointed to the rear of the store. "I'll load it from there." Where I couldn't be spotted.

"I can help you carry it wherever your wagon is, if you want." Mr. Wayne smiled.

"No, the back is easier." I gave a slight nod toward Jess. "Easier on the boy," I whispered.

Mr. Wayne let me go with a wealthy wink.

It was Morrissey's dark and rumpled hat, the sign of a man working too hard to avoid an honest life, that made me go for the wagon fast. He was in front of the bank when I stepped out of the store and glanced that direction. He was talking with Ted. I backed into the mercantile building and headed for the rear of the store. "I'll be right back. Maybe you and the boy could wait at the back door for me." I stuffed more money into Mr. Wayne's hands. "Maybe you could have all this stacked there by the time I get back."

I slipped to the livery. Morrissey and Ted. One gunning for Luke, the other for… My gut twisted into a knot.

I was quick, but not quick enough. As I hied Walter away from the livery, Ted stepped around the corner. He stood between me and the back of the mercantile building, absorbed in a conversation with Morrissey, not far from his side. Ted glanced at the lowdown thief as I slid off the opposite side of the wagon and crouched near the ground. Walter was easy to spot. So was the wagon. I stretched up and peered at the back of the mercantile store. So was Jess, and so was I. No pistol on me, no holster at all, since I was acting like a husband instead of a Ranger. I laid my fingers over my trousers pocket. Flint and steel. It had worked before.

Chapter 50

We all fall at some point. Some of us never get back up. ~Regina

Jess's eyes were brighter than I'd ever seen, glowing with each board, every strip of leather, every nail he laid out along the back end of the wagon.

"And look, Ma, these sizes fit together for a man." He leaned into his crutches as he grouped longer pieces into a pile. I ran my hand down the back of his head as he chattered on, his sleek hair and his excitement the dreamer that was so much of Flynn.

Ben unhitched Walter and led him toward the barn. The way Ben moved, the way he tipped an ear told me he was listening. He disappeared through the barn door while Jess made new piles and straightened leather into different groupings. My crate lay empty up near the front, even my tea towels gone, Ben's blanket all that was left. I felt I'd been punched. There had been too many goodbyes lately. And another coming soon. Ben reappeared from the barn. Another punch. One more goodbye.

Ben strolled to the house, disappeared inside, then came back out and walked to the wagon, resting his arms on its side as he leaned against it. Crinkles cut around a half grin as he listened to Jess. He looked pleased in the smile, but his eyes were sober. Maybe he knew he'd done wrong. He glanced at the barn, then my way, straightened, and reached into his pocket. I shook my head. It probably wasn't much anyway that he'd gotten for my china. And my towels, which weren't for sale.

I looked at the crate. Ben followed my gaze, and it seemed like "tea towels" may have finally registered, by the look on his face. He hustled around the wagon as I planted my hands on my hips, slid between me and my son, and bent over his piles.

"Ben," I said from behind his back.

"Yes, ma'am?" He didn't turn. He leaned farther over Jess and rambled on about wood and nails.

"Ben!"

One of those long fingers went up and punched the underside of the front of his hat, shoving it back on his head.

"Is everything I asked you to take care of gone?"

"Oh!" Jess nearly toppled. "We saw Indians! Well, not the Indians themselves, but smoke! They burnt something in town."

I laid a hand on Ben's shoulder, tugged at his shirt until he turned, a ruddier flush crossing his skin.

"Could have been anything." Ben shook his head.

"It had to be Indians. Walter ran fast to get back here. Ben made him!"

"Walter needed to stretch a bit." Ben's color deepened more. "He's been getting soft."

"Speaking of Walter, did you buy the wood for whatever it was you were going to build for him? Everything I see here seems to be for crutches and braces."

"Say, I almost forgot." Ben reached into his pocket

and drew out an envelope. "Some fellow in New York's looking for you."

"Clyde?" I snatched at the end of the envelope, coming away with nothing as Ben whipped it away from me. "That's mine." I grabbed again.

"You know this fellow?" Ben turned the envelope my way, Clyde's name, angular and sprawled across the corner, told me he wasn't any calmer.

"He's family," I said, grasping at the envelope. Ben let it go, and I folded it into the pocket of my pants. God, please let my cousin's news be good.

"A wire, too." Ben handed me another envelope.

Clyde again. And much slower than he should have been. The sound of hooves interrupted the thanks I was pondering to say to Ben. Pounding hooves, coming fast.

"Look at Ted," Jess piped, tugging at Ben, then at me.

Ted burst into the barnyard, Boss running even harder than he did with me. Ted was black from head to toe, the whites of his eyes standing out like two hen's eggs. He was off his horse in one motion, grabbing Ben's arm in his fist as he came to a halt.

"Where were you?" Ted yelled.

"Been right here the past hour or so." Ben made a circle with his arm, neat and quick, breaking Ted's grip.

"You know what I mean."

"Ted, no one knows what you mean. And stand back. You smell burnt." I covered my nose. "What in the world happened to you?"

Ted's blackened face turned my way, those white orbs like two moons with black holes in the centers. "A fire." He looked back to Ben. "You were there. You could have done something to help. Unless you set the fire to begin with. If that's your way. Like some."

"Indians set that fire, Ted," Jess chimed in. "We saw the smoke. We were way far away."

"Indians wouldn't set fire to a walkway. Nearly ate up the front of the saloon and a corner of the bank."

"The walk outside the bank?" I stepped between Ted and Ben. "No one would set fire to a walkway. It must have been an accident. A careless smoker or something. Was anyone hurt? Are the saloon and bank okay?"

"Thanks to a few good men, everything will be fine. Except for whoever set it."

"Probably be smart not to go accusing people of setting fires." Ben spoke above me, his words like hammers. Ted looked over my head at him.

"I ain't one to speak carelessly. Not like a young buck who can't shoot straight, not even with his mouth."

Fast and slow at the same time, Ben's arms appeared over my head. They plucked Ted from in front of me, from between Jess and me, and threw him face down to the ground. I saw the arms and the body, and I heard the air leaving Ted's lungs before I heard the horrible thud of his body against the ground. Fast and slow all over again, Ben planted a boot in Ted's back, a watery grunt, the last of Ted's air, gushing from my ranch manager's chest as Ben yanked and twisted Ted's good arm up behind him. I shuddered at the hollow draw for breath, the noisy battle Ted fought to gain air, all of it turning to curses and spittle full of dirt.

"Ben!" I screamed over my shudders, louder even than Ted, but my shriek was still lost under the cry of Jess's wails.

My son's crutches hit the dirt, he dove at the two men, grasped and hung onto Ben's arm. "Let him go! Let Ted go!" Jess lost his grip and tumbled backwards, fast and slow all over again. So slow I'd never forget the pain I saw streak across his face, and too fast for me to catch him before he hit the ground. I screamed again, different this time, at the dull thud I heard before Jess rolled to the side. My boy curled forward—I'd seen it too many times—clutching the top of his leg.

With his boot fixed in Ted's back, Ben bent forward and ground Ted's face into the dirt, drowning out the curses and the filthy spittle. Then he let go and dove toward my son. My hand was there midair, I was quicker than he was, and met his face before he lit. The slap rang above my son's groans, echoed over Ted's sputters and threats. My hand stung; it burned like fire as Ben stopped and looked at me.

"What are you doing?" My voice was high, out of control, its pitch piercing even my own ears. "You've hurt Ted and now you're hurting Jess. Again! Why don't you leave us alone!" My hand tingled. I wanted to slap Ben again as Jess whimpered in the dirt. I dropped to the ground beside my boy. "Can you straighten at all?" I tried to help, ran my hand down his leg, the back of his head, felt the tautness as he moaned all the more.

"You do it like this." Ben bent beside me. He righted Jess without a sound from my boy. Jess relaxed and straightened, propped himself on his elbows. "That's what Doc showed us to do today in case he ever fell."

Ted was on his feet, black spit draining from his mouth, clearing a channel through the charcoal on his face. "Mrs. Howard's right. Leave us alone. No cause you attacking me like that."

It wasn't Ted Ben looked at as he stood. It was me. He stared down as I glared up from near my boy. "Is that what you really want?" Ben asked. "To leave you alone?"

I looked at my son. I was sick of pain. I was tired of hurt on a face that had finally been glowing. I glanced at Ted, dirt, saliva, blood, and charcoal smeared like insults on his face. And the wagon, where the empty crate was. I looked back up at Ben.

"As you wish." He fished money from his pocket and dropped it into my lap. He disappeared into the barn, where I could hear him gathering his things.

"Ma?"

"Good riddance." Ted spit more dirt. "That man wasn't right. Never believed a word he said." Ted knelt down next to me. "You okay?"

The barn was silent. I listened, kept my hands on my son, until Ben's commotion resumed. I could picture him in there, tall and dark, in a handsome but devilish fury, preparing to go. An early parting.

"Can't believe he turned on me like that." Ted rotated his shoulder as he leaned toward Jess. "I'll sign so you can keep this place. Once we get that settled, everything will be fine."

Settled. "Ben took you to see Doc Harris today?" I looked at my son.

"Yeah. He did. Paid him, too." Jess took Ted's hand, and the two of them stood, Ted helping him balance once they did.

"What about my things in that crate? Do you know what happened to them?"

Jess brushed off his elbows and the seat of his

pants. Ted handed him the crutches. "Those weren't your things. I peeked in that box. Nothing but junk."

"What? No tea towels? No china?"

Jess snorted. "No, Ma, I told you, it was just junk."

I looked to the barn. One of Ben's noises came from within. This one was different—loud, strong, and powerful enough to send him and Walter out the side door and sailing over the corral. Ben leaned forward over the neck of his horse as Walter cleared the top rail. The horse lit on the ground as if his hooves had wings, and before I could think or cry, or say goodbye, they were gone.

"Wow," Jess gasped beside me. "I'm gonna do that someday."

I grabbed his shoulders, watched the road where brown dust filtered back to the ground, where Ben and Walter had disappeared. Parted. Gone. "No, you're not, son. No, you're not." I'd had enough parting, enough being left behind. He was not going to leave me like the two best men I'd ever known had done.

Chapter 51

It's hard to go north or south when, wherever you go, a little bit of you stays behind. ~Rex

South. Every bit of me, except one little part, wanted to head south. Back to red dirt to find my half-brother before he figured out Morrissey was up here, back to Red Rock Ranch to restore and rebuild before my father died of a broken spirit. Away from red hair that wanted me to leave.

But that one little bit of me refused to head south.

Run hard, Little Brother. Run hard and get away from that smoke. Luke was on his own.

I laid a hand on my shirt pocket. The deed Ted had hidden in that wooden box was there. But Regina's broken comb he hadn't been smart enough to let go of was in her house. Where I hoped she'd find it and ask the right questions, even without my help. I patted the deed. The deed to Flynn Howard's railroad land. In my pocket, right next to the one for Regina's ranch. Ted was a rat. I'd sensed it all along and wondered if Mr. Gulliver realized he was. Probably not, since Mr. Gulliver had nothing to gain by Ted owning those ranches. But Ted stood to gain everything by being cooperative and sneaky—two ranches plus the most enviable of women at his side. The woman whose comb he couldn't let go of. He just hadn't counted on her advertising for a husband other than him.

I spit. Then made a noise. Walter bent harder into his run. Ted would be figuring out quick enough I'd taken those things and made his plans worthless. I'd get both these deeds signed and back to that redheaded wife of mine before I said my final goodbye. She could deal with her ranch manager. In the meantime, north was the way to go. Back to Liberal, to catch that skunk Morrissey before he slipped out of town.

The boarding house came into view, the end of town farthest from where I'd seen Morrissey. I gave the building a wide berth, kept my face down, and eyed the horses tied outside. Morrissey used to ride a brown stallion. It blended in, like a snake did in the grass. I looped slow, beyond the boarding house, around that end of town, keeping Walter steady and my eye to the side, watching every movement, every man, every horse within range.

Jim's plan had worked good as far as giving me the front of a common ranch husband so I could go snooping around without raising brows. That plan was backfiring now. Too many people knew me, associated me with Regina and Jess, for me to barge in and take Morrissey by surprise the way I wanted to. When people found out Ben Miller didn't exist and was Rex Duncan instead, I wanted Regina to know before them. She deserved that much, and she deserved to understand why.

A few houses were scattered here and there along the north edge of the town as I made my way around the outside. A church, a school, things that stood far enough from the main street I hadn't paid much attention to them before. One house stuck out above all the others. Someone with money. A lone horse, plus a horse with a buggy out front, both standing at a white fence.

The far end of town, the saloon end where the bank and some other businesses operated, came up quick. The smell of dank, smoky wood filled the air. It hung as a reminder of what a fire could do. Of what flint and steel could do. A couple of big horses that could have been Morrissey's were outside the saloon. I looked them over as I kept moving. Two or three more were in front of the bank. Mr. Greene was right. Liberal was blooming. Blooming too much to make my job easy.

I circled around behind the saloon and bank, came along the rear of the livery and the mercantile building. The backside of the postal office and Doc Harris's office were next. Too many horses at the livery for me to make a quick judgment, and I wasn't about to drop in to see, in case Matt Morrissey happened to be there.

"You know the routine, Walter. You'd best not have forgotten how to be a Ranger's horse during your soft days at the Howards'. The Millers'." I edged Walter away from town. Found the nearest cluster of trees—heck, the only cluster of trees—and ducked inside. And waited.

By the time the sun was nearly set, so was my plan. I wanted one thing, and I aimed to get it. Morrissey. Nice and quiet, without letting anyone else see or know. As the landscape took on more gray than sunlight, I nodded at Walter. He nickered back. I slunk into town, and Walter stayed where he was.

Chapter 52

I can do this. I know I can. ~Regina

Gone. The road stretched empty between where I'd stood and where Ben had gone. A long strip cut through the prairie, going nowhere. Except to wherever Ben had come from, and what little piece of land Flynn may have left behind.

"Ma…"

It wasn't a marriage I'd had with Ben, it was a planned wedding and a parting…a plan that gained me a name but hadn't given me the ranch. Yet. Until I got the deed for this piece documented, even if I had to fill Ben's name in myself. And it had gained me a peek at what Flynn may have owned but hadn't given me that deed at all.

"You okay?" I asked Jess.

"I guess."

Gone.

Jess leaned on a crutch, sorting through boards, nails, and leather on the wagon. Quiet, never offering to hook them together or boast about how they would work. I went inside and sorted through the pantry, quietly did with Ben's contributions here what Jess was doing with those outside. I reclaimed it for Jess and me while Ted did his part reclaiming the corral. He labored over it near the barn, his sounds different from Ben's as they carried through the walls.

Gone. Ben shouldn't have attacked Ted that way over a fire that had nothing to do with him, and a silly comment that didn't even make sense. Young bucks that can't shoot straight? What did Ben care about them?

I packed away every remnant of Ben, glanced out the window at Jess and Ted, then took Clyde's letter and wire to the prairie. I was truly on my own now. I could do it. I'd planned for it.

Dear Regina,

I have to admit I'm relieved not to come out west. You're so much more used to the terrain than I am, surely you can figure out who and where these men are faster than I. But of course, if you need my help…

"Clyde, get to the point." I shook my cousin's letter, rattled it in the air the same way I'd shake him if he were standing here babbling at me. "Just spit out their names, you imbecile. And don't let Flynn be part of it."

I hid the paperwork in a file at the bank but moved it home once I discovered things weren't apropos.

I shook the letter again. "Clyde! Just tell me what I need to know!" I skimmed down through excuses, explanations, things he wouldn't want my father to know. "Oh, never mind." I stuffed my cousin's letter into my pocket and opened his wire, instead.

Carlisle and Morgan. Those were their names. Clyde

"Carlisle and Morgan?" I looked across the prairie, grasses blowing between the ground and my furrowed brow. "Are they a company?" I extracted the letter from my pocket, went to the second page, and ran a finger through meaningless chatter until I spotted their names.

I only met Carlisle, but I worked mostly with his and Morgan's representative. Those other two managed the money and it was their names on the small checks I received.

Carlisle and Morgan. I couldn't recall Flynn ever saying their names. At least not here. Maybe back in New York? I stared at the two names, then the rest of my cousin's gibberish, before folding everything and stuffing it all back in my pocket.

I turned to the house, the empty barnyard, and the vacant road that led to both. I walked this time instead of running.

Carlisle. I paused at the wagon to make sure Jess had put his hardware away. Nothing there except the empty crate and Ben's blanket. I turned to the house. "Morgan…"

"You need something?"

Ted, scrubbed enough he smelled less like a forest fire, stepped from the barn.

"No. I was just thinking about someone my cousin wrote about…" A Morgan.

"But you said my name."

"It was nothing. New York business. Family issues."

"I heard Morgan."

"Yes, I did say Morgan, but you know good and well I would address you by your first name instead of your last. I was talking about a different Morgan in New York. Rich, evidently."

"A rich Morgan?" Ted made the effort to grin, the remainder of the black soot crinkling between the furrows of his skin. "Need a few more of those."

"Rich people don't make their money on horseback. Or ranching." I glanced to the side at everything Flynn set his hands to. At least I couldn't see that they did.

"Speaking of money and ranches…now that your husband is gone…well, sort of a husband…"

Agree to nothing. That's what Ben had said. I ran my hand over my pocket. Carlisle and Morgan.

"Ben signed the deed. I have it inside." I lied. We hadn't done anything with it yet. Not together, anyway. I'd asked him to sign it, told him I wanted to keep it in Jess's loft, under his mattress, until we could take care of it properly. A distinct hiding place. No secrets. No guessing games. He'd better have done at least this one thing I said.

Ted stepped around the wagon, the faint aroma of smoke coming with him. "Mrs. Howard…I mean, Mrs. Miller…" He hooked his thumb behind his belt. "I don't mean to hurt you none, but Ben's name is no better than Flynn's. Especially now, since this husband up and left without covering the debt." Ted extracted his thumb. "Flynn was a good man. He made a mistake, maybe, but he at least tried to do right."

"And I want to do right for him. Give him the honor of respecting his name. I'm sorry, Ted, but I can't have just anyone sign that deed. It has to be someone in a family relationship to me and Jess."

"Family enough to run out on you? That fellow you call family didn't even argue when you sent him off. I'm here, and I aim to stay."

"I never called Ben family, but he married me, and that honors Flynn. And just like Ben, no one will stay here if I tell them to go."

The smoky smell came closer, near enough the heat came with it. "I'll be saying when I come and go on this land, Mrs. Miller, at your husband's—your real husband's—wish. And just remember, my name's the only one worth anything."

Chapter 53

Where there's smoke, there's fire. ~Rex

The saloon was the best place to find a man like Morrissey. I stayed to the back of the building, low and close. The ruckus inside was plain as day, but I wasn't—I was staying hidden in the fading light. The music wailed, then was gone. Coming and going. Sounds no better than a broken piano could make.

I leaned against the wall and listened to the voices in between the scattered notes. Giggles. Maybe the girl that had served me the drink I didn't want. Deeper laughter. The sounds of a card game, conversations so loud I knew they didn't matter.

I slid to the side of the building, came close enough to the front to look at the horses tied in a line there. The hitching posts looked charred, but they still stood. Someone had laid fresh boards over the burnt ones in front of the buildings. I glanced back at the horses. A bay, a palomino, and Boss. I eased into the shadows. I wasn't surprised this was where Ted went when it was quiet below my bed in the loft. I'd be even less surprised to find Morrissey in there with him.

I kept my back to the wall of the saloon, my thoughts louder than the chatter and music inside. For all the years Luke wanted to be tall like me, I'd gladly trade him sizes tonight. I edged to the front of the building, keeping low and swinging wide of the gaping doorway where smells and noises spilled out. I swung far enough to come at the horses from the rear, keeping with the dark of the street. I spoke gently as I came close and made my way to the one horse I knew.

"Hey, Boss." I wasn't much of a whisperer. I laid a hand on his rump, ran it along his side as I came to his head. "Easy, boy." I unlooped his reins from the hitching post, patting his neck while I backed him from the line.

The saloon doors swung wide when we were half a length back. I ducked even lower than I was, and pressed close to Boss's side. Two men. No, one man and a woman. A woman in trousers and boots. I crouched lower and peered between the legs of the horses still in line.

"Boss, what are you doing loose?"

Her boots came my way. Weaving between the forest of hooves, I scooted behind the horses and slipped between two farther down the line.

"You rode a horse this late?" That was Doc. I nearly ripped a muscle craning my neck.

"No, I have the wagon." Regina. "I borrowed the neighbor's horse. Ted rode Boss."

How did I miss her coming into town? Unless she came in the long way. But she shouldn't have.

"Come on, boy." Regina eased Boss forward to the post and re-looped his reins. "There you go." She patted his neck, then walked back to the new boards on the walk, where Doc stood. I watched from under the horses' bellies. It sure didn't take my wife long to recover from me leaving.

"Thank you, Doc. This should help Jess." She took

a small bottle.

"Just a little at a time. I had the barkeep dilute it. Sorry I didn't have any of the real pain medicine I gave you before."

"You had it diluted?"

"Of course. He's just a boy."

"But it was a pretty good fall he had this afternoon, and he's been complaining an awful lot." Regina sounded sweet, too sweet, and her story sounded wrong. Like an excuse to hie it into town and meet up with Doc. I crouched lower so I could see her better, see her lying red head, as I kept myself well away from the hooves of the horses I was annoying.

"Should I come look at his leg?"

"No. No, that won't be necessary." Regina shook her head, hard enough some of that curly red stuff fell loose. "No. But thank you."

If I wasn't so sure Morrissey was in that saloon, I'd stand up and make the widow—I mean, my wife—admit she was spinning a yarn. One the size of Oklahoma Indian Territory.

"Regina, I…"

"I know, Doc. And I'm sorry. But it's for the best."

A hoof came close as I pressed my face nearer to the ground. I wanted to see her eyes.

"Ben's a good man. He'll be good on the ranch." She was looking up into Doc's face, the tiny bottle in her hands.

"I'm…I'm sure he will."

Rotten music and loud laughter filled the gap between them. The gap Regina was pretending to put me in, while I was down here under a horse instead of up there by her side.

Doc took the bottle from her hands. "I'll get you something stronger, if you think Jess really needs it. But I advise against it."

The doors swung open. Boots scuffed the boards. Two sets of boots.

"You still here?" Ted stopped near Regina. "Kind of late for you to be out alone. I could ride with you."

"I was just leaving. Thank you, Doc, for the medicine for Jess." She snatched the bottle from Doc's fingers, her boots turning Ted's way. "I can handle myself, late or not."

The other set of boots made themselves comfortable near a post.

"I'll walk you to your wagon." Doc extended an elbow her way. Regina nodded. I sank lower, watching the man who wasn't, but probably should have been, her husband escort my wife away.

"That her?" It was Morrissey. He rearranged his feet near the post.

"Yup."

"Pretty thing. Looks better in those trousers than most women look in dresses. Not every ranch comes with one of those."

"Pretty wears thin when they're smart." Ted moved near the edge of the boards. There was no softness in his gravel, not like he used at the ranch. I ground my teeth. I had no use for a man who changed his story whoever he was with. "She's smarter than her husband was. At least quicker to figure things out."

"Wouldn't follow you on anything?"

"Has to question everything, then do it her way."

I thought of her broken comb. Glad I'd left it where she could find it. She needed to know what sort of scallywag Ted was when he came back and tried to act like her hero. She was bright enough to figure out it didn't appear there by itself. Hopefully bright enough to tie it to her ranch manager.

Morrissey snorted. "Why is it men are so easy to lead around, and women so much trouble? Never met a ranch owner yet that couldn't be sent on a wild chase with dollar signs in his eyes."

"We don't waste time asking questions, just get to the point. Just some aren't watching for what's behind that point."

Maybe like Flynn. Ran off, ran into an accident. Left a deed and a handsome widow behind.

Morrissey straightened. His feet shuffled Ted's way. "I laid a path a mile wide for the young buck I was telling you about that's been tailing me. Did everything but invite him to my house. He's still straggling behind. A real cowboy would have found me days ago; his brother would have. But not this fellow. I could have plugged him a dozen times. Too easy. Too stupid. Too much talk and not enough smarts. Taking all the fun out of having the last word with him."

So Ted had heard about Luke, even if he wasn't sure Luke was tied to me. At least wasn't sure before I laid him out on the ground. Next time I had Ted under my boot, he wouldn't get back up.

"Flynn wasn't slow, just green. He had a bunch of New York know-how that was no good out here." Ted laughed. I'd never heard him laugh before, and I never wanted to again. And I'd never give Morrissey the chance to insult my little brother that way again. Ever.

People spilled in and out of the saloon. Eventually one would want one of these horses I was crouched under. I eased backward, staying close to the ground, and moved into the dark street. Luke and Regina. I didn't like choices like that. I couldn't be both places at the same time, and I didn't want Luke to come here to make it easier for me. Because it wouldn't be.

I made my way to the far side of the street and watched. Too far to hear, but I'd heard enough. Ted left first. I watched him go, my gut feeling like I'd swallowed a boulder as he swung up on Boss, said something to Morrissey, then wheeled toward home. Home, maybe to tell Regina I wasn't Ben Miller, if he was sure. If I went after him, taught him a lesson that would drive him off, I'd likely lose Morrissey. Maybe even Luke. If I stayed… The boulder doubled in size.

Blood ain't thicker than water.

I stepped off the walk. I could catch Ted, even in the dark, even with his lead. I swung to the right, far outside the ring of light cast from the saloon. Walter was far enough out there to be hidden, but not so far I couldn't hie it to him. Luke would pay me back for this someday. Walking away from Morrissey was something I swore I'd never do.

"Come on out here and face me like a man."

Come on, face me like a man; get out here where I can see you. I stopped. I knew that voice. I'd know it anywhere. The same one that called to me from our father's burning ranch. I bent low and scurried deeper into the dark, wanting to run instead to the light where he shouted from. I half squatted, half ran, circling toward the side of the saloon. *Be quiet, Little Brother. Go home. Leave Morrissey to me.*

"I said get out here! Get out on this street so I can plug you."

I didn't care if Luke plugged Morrissey, even though I'd prefer the rat suffered longer than just a gunshot, but Luke most likely would miss. Then Morrissey'd plug him. Little Brother.

I edged along the side, up to the front corner of the saloon. Luke stood in the street, facing it, his feet spread far too wide, the tremor in his arms and voice evident even in the night. *Stop him, Ma. Can you do what I can't?* Her hair, that Luke had, was hidden under his hat. The light spilling from the saloon wasn't enough to show her eyes.

Morrissey leaned against the post, his back to me, staring at Little Brother. He spit into the street and crossed his legs at the ankles. The loop was off his pistol, his hip out where the gun would be easy to grab. I laid a hand on my pocket, on the flint and steel. Naw. Not this time. Luke never did master maneuvering through smoke. I flipped the loop off the trigger of my pistol, and positioned myself to shoot.

"Now, Luke Duncan. What are you doing up here in Kansas? You have to move since you got no place to live?" Morrissey spit in the street again.

Luke spread his legs a little wider. That boy had learned nothing at all from me.

The crowd gathered, yet cleared. More folks appeared on the street, but none came close. They moved back, like the ring in a pond when you threw a rock in.

I'd married the widow, and it looked like part of that ranch ring Jim wanted was standing right in front of me. All I had left to do was wring the other names from that part before I took it down and saved my little brother. My throat felt like I'd swallowed a knife as I looked back to Luke, praying him to be quiet and off the street. The widow'd be rid of me soon enough when I took Morrissey—or his body—back to Oklahoma. And rid of Ted, too, once she realized what a snake he was and I took care of her deeds. I straightened and leaned forward to take Morrissey.

"Here, here, I won't have any of this outside my saloon." The barkeep stepped out. Bravest barkeep I'd ever seen. "I run a civilized place, and I'll have the law on both of you if you don't move away from here." Or stupidest.

While Luke's and Morrissey's lock on each other was broken, I moved. Faster than a striking rattler, I was up on the walkway, Morrissey in my grip. Down we went. I heard a shot over Morrissey's grunt as the wind gushed out of him. Women screamed. Glass broke where Luke's wild shot hit. I rolled Morrissey while I had the chance, while the wind was out of him and the advantage was mine.

"Stop, or I'll shoot again." Luke moved with us as I kept turning Morrissey toward the dark. "Stop!"

Once I had Morrissey at the side of the building where Luke couldn't see, I brought him to his feet with one arm and took the rest of the wind out of him with the other.

That was when the next shot came. It followed my name. Rex... It hailed with Luke's scream.

Chapter 54

Plans weren't made to be broken. Only hearts.
~Regina

My neighbor had promised his horse could run like the wind. I snapped the reins from the wagon seat, made every noise I'd heard Ben make to Walter. Even came up with a few of my own, and yet this horse moved like its feet were plugged into the ground.

Carlisle, the name and where I'd heard it, had come back to me. After Ted left, long after Ben had gone, and too late to save poor Flynn. I had a plan. A better plan. And this time I wouldn't fail.

"Faster, you idiot!" I snapped the reins again. My house and barn materialized in the low light. Jess was with the neighbor until I returned for him. I rode straight to the barn and around to the far side, where I stood and yanked back on the reins. "Whoa," I shouted. The smell of horse, tired horse, was overpowering as I jumped down from the wagon and rounded the sweating animal. "You shouldn't be that sweaty." I tapped him on the nose as I passed.

I ran inside the barn and felt my way in the darkness to Ted's door. I fumbled with the handle, twisted and lifted, but it didn't open. I'd never noticed if he had some trick to getting in and out of his room. I settled my fists on my hips and wondered if it was

locked from the inside. My heart lurched. If it was…
"Ted?"

I listened at his door. I didn't breathe, as I stood silently praying Ted hadn't beat me back. My neighbor's horse nickered outside the barn's wall. I crept close to Ted's door and planted my ear against the wood. Nothing. Ted couldn't have been that quick. My neighbor's horse stomped a foot. Well, Ted could have. I ran my hands along the seam where the door and wall met. There had to be a way…

My finger bumped over something cold. A tiny latch. I eased it up, and the door swung open. I paused, listened to nothing but the wind, then entered, and closed the door behind me.

Ted's room felt cold. Colder than the outdoors. A chill ran up my arms as I groped through the dark until my fingers brushed the base of a lamp. Running my hand along where it sat, I found matches nearby and struck one, creating an eerie orb of light in the small room. I trimmed the wick, lifted the lamp, and set about inspecting Ted's sparse but neat quarters.

I searched the obvious places first—under his cot, beneath his tight blanket, on a small shelf, in his spare boots. Nothing. The second obvious place was the large box. I brought the lamp close, set it on a nearby crate, and opened the lid.

Carlisle. Of Carlisle and Morgan. It was back in New York I'd heard that name. He'd talked with Flynn about ranching. He'd claimed it was an open door, and what Easterners like Flynn didn't understand about homesteading, other men did. Men out here. Like Morgan. But which Morgan? I intended to find that out.

I tipped the lid back as far as it would go and dug

deep, Ted's tidy piles falling into disarray as I scavenged to the bottom—ending at nothing. I stacked everything back the way it had been and straightened. I needed something with Carlisle's name on it. Or the other deed. Or Flynn's money. Something, so I could carry out my plan.

I stepped back to the door, cracked it open, and listened. The wind howled, as always, a coyote along with it. I closed the door, returned to the box, and closed its lid. I held the light high and looked behind it. Black shadows and nothing more. Latching onto the back corner, I tugged and twisted until Ted's enormous box scooted out from the wall. I brought the light to its back, and saw it, then. A rim of white sticking up from a false back. My arm was slender. Thin enough I snaked it behind the box, pinched the white edge with my fingernails, and lifted.

My hands trembled, but I held tight. If this was what I needed, I'd load Jess—and the bottle of medicine I'd tricked Doc into giving me so Jess could travel without pain—and we'd go. Back to New York with the deed and this evidence. I'd undo whoever else was tied to Carlisle and Morgan, and come back to claim what was mine.

The wind changed, and I listened. It wasn't the wind I heard. It was a voice. A voice and hooves. I tugged hard at the papers. Only one came. I shoved the box back, leaving the rest behind, and blew the lamp out.

Chapter 55

Blood is thicker than I thought. So thick, a heart might stop. ~Rex

"Rex!" Little Brother's shout echoed in my head along with the shot. The music was gone, the crowd was still. Everything was quiet except for Luke's voice, the shot, and the fire raging through my veins. I had Morrissey up off the ground with a fist, and I dragged him to the street as I barreled out to look for my brother. My half-brother.

I spotted him. Spotted Luke in the middle of the street, lying there like he was all gone. Morrissey hung from my fist like a rag doll. I looked down at Matt and landed a fist on him again. For Pop, for Luke, for the ranch I had to burn down.

I dragged and kicked Morrissey through the street, dropped the rumpled bag of wind in the dirt beside Luke. Beside my knees where I knelt at Luke's chest. Luke was bent like Jess had been in the prairie that day, half mooned on his side. Lying all wrong.

"Little Brother." I laid a hand on Luke's ribs and an ear against his chest, blood turning his shirt thick and warm. If I'd heard a man drown, this was what I imagined it would sound like. Froth blocking the cries for help until they were wordless gurgles. Then nothing. "After all I taught you."

313

I looked up at the crowd. "Where's the sheriff?"

The barkeep ran off. "I'll get him."

I'd stayed away from the sheriff until now, kept as far from him as I could, as Regina's husband. Things were different now. I grabbed a loop of rope from a nearby horse. The men in the circle moved back.

"I'm a Ranger. This man's under arrest." I nodded toward Matt Morrissey, his limp figure in the street. No one argued I'd taken their rope. I bound Matt tighter than necessary, then thrust him up against a hitching post and tied him there. No one questioned whether I was really a Ranger. The cowhand lie didn't even make them doubt where I'd really learned to manage a rope.

I scanned the crowd and spotted Mr. Greene. "Make sure the sheriff takes him to jail."

"Yes, sir, we will." Mr. Greene pushed through the crowd. He stood close to Matt, hanging over him like a vulture.

I hied it to Luke, swept my brother off the ground, and ran, breaking through the men who were fixed in a circle, racing through the dark to Doc's.

Doc responded the way he had with Jess. He was more than a man doing a job. He was a man who cared, who had Luke on a cot and his shirt cut away before I said a word. Doc bent in front of me, hovering over Little Brother and the bullet hole through his chest. I stood back and shivered. Tried not to scream. At Luke, for Luke. For the smile that couldn't die, the one that looked like my stepmother's. My shirt stuck to my skin, turning cold, as I shook above Doc. I glanced down at the dark, cooling stain. Little Brother's blood.

"I'll be back." I didn't know if Doc heard. My voice sounded like it did at the ranch when I burned it down. Like a boy's voice, one so full of hurt he couldn't talk.

The door slammed behind me. I looked to the left, down the boarded walk where the saloon was. Only a knot of men remained where Luke had fallen. Mr. Greene and Morrissey were missing. No one seemed alarmed by that, so it meant the sheriff had Matt. I turned to the right. Time to visit the jail. Officially.

****

"I'm sorry." Doc's hand was gentle as he touched my arm when I came to his door. He stepped aside and ushered me in, pointing me to where Little Brother lay.

The sheet over Luke was mostly white, darkened only with a large oval of red below where it covered his head. Red. For the first time in my life, I hated red. I dropped to the chair beside Little Brother, adding spots of my own to the white. Wet spots. Wetness that couldn't put out the fire or cut the smoke. Doc left me alone as I finally cried.

Chapter 56

It takes one to know one. I never believed that until now. ~Regina

The horse stopped. Whoever had ridden up to the ranch pounded on my kitchen door. Warm fumes of burnt oil filled the air. I grabbed the lamp and took it with me as I slipped from Ted's room; I set it in the back of the barn to cool.

"Regina!" Ted hit the door to my house again.

"What is it, Ted?" I walked as far as the pump and stopped in the dark barnyard behind him.

"Why are you out here? Is it Jess?" He came toward me, his boots marking his advance where I couldn't see.

"No, Jess is still at the neighbor's, where I left him while I went to get that medicine."

"I'll go get him for you."

"No, don't. They were going to play a game. Something quiet, that he doesn't have to run in. I thought I'd give Jess some time there; he needed the change."

Ted was at the trough, his steps on the ground coming around to my side. Too close to the barn, the wafting scent of the extinguished lamp I'd left out, and the paper I'd slid under loose hay for me to retrieve later. "I've got news. Bad news."

I thought of Ben. I thought of Doc. I slapped a hand on my chest, my heart pounding the way Ted's fist had hit my kitchen door. "What? Who?"

"There was a shooting. No one you know, but it does affect you." Ted looked toward the house. "Would you like to sit?"

"No, Ted, just tell me. Who was it?"

"Don't know his name, but I know his brother's name. Rex Duncan's the brother. You might know him as Ben Miller."

I sat. I tried to stay on my feet, but I backed to the trough and dropped onto its edge.

"Sorry you had to find out this way. I knew something was wrong about that man. I just knew it."

"Ben?" My voice was barely a whisper, barely audible over the night breeze.

"He's not Ben, he's Rex. His marriage to you was a hoax. He's a Ranger from down south. I found it all out."

My marriage. A marriage I hadn't considered real…wasn't. "Ben isn't Ben." The dark made the information confusing, more unbelievable.

Ted dropped down on the lip of the trough beside me. "Sorry, Regina. He lied about everything."

My life passed before my eyes. The life I'd had the past several weeks. The life that was made of images of Ben. With me, with Jess. In ways even Flynn hadn't…but it wasn't real.

My chest rose and fell. I couldn't see it, but I could hear my breath as it surged. In. Out. How could Ben lie that way? How could he accuse me of lying about hiding a son from him? He was right. He was no good with women or boys. He didn't even care. Every breath weighed more than I did. Each one burned as it turned to fire.

"I'm going for Jess now." I rose. "Come with me, please. Ride alongside with Boss so he can pull the wagon back and my neighbor won't have to." So you can settle Jess in the house while I tend to Boss. Tend to your lamp. And the paper, hidden in the barn. My plan.

"Yes'm. That I will. You can count on me."

Chapter 57

Now I was lost in the smoke. My stepmother was right—what would happen if I fell? ~Rex

I thought three of us would be going back to Oklahoma—two of us, at least the right two of us, alive.

Doc stood in attendance as we loaded into the back of the wagon the pine box I'd bought, the box that held Little Brother. I strapped it down, but not as tight as I strapped Morrissey. He was bound and gagged, because I was fed up with listening to him, propped with his back behind the seat, and tied into place.

A gunshot exploded in my mind every time I looked at that skunk, the loud boom, and the voice that cried my name for the last time. *Rex!*

I slapped my hand on top of Luke's box. It sounded like another gunshot. The one that heralded in Luke's other words, the ones he shouted through the thunder of our ranch's blaze—*Come out where I can see you. Come out and face me like a man.*

"Thank you, Doc." I shook his hand.

"So you're not Ben Miller after all."

I shook my head and let go of his hand.

"That's how you knew so much about medicine, how to do what most men don't."

I looked at my half-brother's box again and at the man beside it I held responsible for Luke's death even though I knew Morrissey didn't shoot him. He couldn't have. He was unconscious. But if Morrissey hadn't swindled our family, Luke wouldn't be dead. As far as I was concerned, everything was Morrissey's fault.

"Apparently, I don't know enough." I slapped Luke's box again.

Doc followed me around the wagon to the side of the seat. I climbed up and took the reins to Walter in my hands. My gut felt empty, carved out as if someone had shot a bucket-sized hole through me, leaving it black…only a flittering unease left inside. I looked down at Doc.

"Do me a favor?"

Doc nodded. "Anything."

"Tend to Regina. I'm going to stop by there on my way to Oklahoma. I'm hoping she hasn't heard by now I'm not who she thought I was. But she ain't going to like it, no matter who tells her."

I couldn't say more. I didn't need to. Doc nodded again. Those were eyes I could trust to take care of her. I flicked the reins.

Chapter 58

*It was our parting. We'd planned it, just not this
way. He had to go. I wouldn't look back. ~Regina*

"Go in the house." I shooed Jess toward the kitchen
door. I cupped a hand over my brows and stared at the
wagon heading our way. At the tall, unmistakable
figure and the black horse bringing him near. "Go on."

"Is that Ben?" Jess stuck at my side.

"I said go in. Please. He's not going to be happy."

"Why?"

I looked at my son, the color in his face, the brace
and crutch that let him stand the way he did. "His
brother was killed."

"Oh." The color left him the moment I said it.
Killed. How stupid could I be?

"Please, just go inside."

Jess pivoted and dragged himself away. Death
still too near. Walter's hooves set an equally slow
cadence on the hard ground. My heart pounded with
every step. Heartache was too near, also. I was done
with heartache.

Ben...Rex...didn't hurry or slow when he spotted
me. He kept Walter steady until the wagon was in front
of me. Ben made a noise, and Walter stopped. A man in
the back twisted to the side. He leered above a bandana
that stretched his mouth to a fish-like gape. I shuddered,

clasped a hand over my own mouth. He was bruised and swollen, filthy, his face distorted.

"Turn back around," Ben barked. The man leered through puffy eyes, then jerked toward the back again, focused behind the wagon.

Ben stepped down, looped the reins over the seat post, and came around Walter to my side. "I want to talk." He jerked his head toward the man who was looking away. "Private."

Ben's brother's pine box lay in the back of the wagon, long, yellow, identical to Flynn's. The strange man was pressed between it and the wagon's side. Ben's pain was there. It felt like mine. I had seen it on his face. I turned from the box, and looked at Ben. But I saw Rex, instead. The fake. The liar. The one who intended to callously break my heart.

I turned and walked to the edge of the prairie. Far enough from the house Jess couldn't hear and far enough from the stranger he couldn't, either.

"Where's Ted?" Ben...no, Rex...looked down at me when I stopped.

"I sent him to Liberal." To get him away while I readied to go. Go, like Ben was doing, him to his Ranger life and me to New York. With a letter from W.C. to Ted. It had to be Carlisle, a commission to take on another ranch. Just two weeks ago. Carlisle and Morgan. Ben and Rex. Deceivers, all of them.

"You've heard."

"Yes. You're not Ben at all. You're some Ranger who didn't come here for my sake but your own. You used me!" My voice ranged out of control. High enough maybe even the wind couldn't wipe it out for once. Loud enough that far wasn't far enough from the stranger's or my son's ears. I didn't care. Flynn brought me here for his dream, and then died. And now Ted and W.C.—possibly W. Carlisle—were wrapped up in dreams of their own, my ranch likely being part of them. But Ben was worse than all of them. He'd never cared. He'd never dreamed. He came. He lied. He got what he wanted, and now he was going.

Ben stepped closer. "Yes. I did come here as a Ranger. But…"

"And now you're leaving as one. I don't need your 'buts.' I needed a name. I was honest about that. I also said I was perfectly capable on my own. That was true, too. But you weren't honest with me, and the name you're leaving me with is a fake. You're leaving me with nothing but a lie."

"There's more to it than that. It was all worked out ahead of time by my boss. He answered your ad. Yes, he made me come here, but it was for your good, too. He's going to do away with Ben Miller. You can keep the name, he'll make sure you get the ranch, but I'll be gone." Ben's lips tightened into a straight line. "If that's what you want."

What I want. What I had wanted. No one had cared what I wanted but me. "I want you out of here." I pointed to his wagon. "Now."

He turned. Looked at the ranch house, then back at me. "Don't trust Ted."

"'Don't trust Ted'? How can you lie to me the way you did and tell me not to trust someone else?"

"Something's not right. I'll make sure this ranch is yours. Just don't trust Ted."

"Well, he said the same thing about you, and I can see he was right. This arrangement is over. We intended

to part anyway. I just never knew it would be like this."
I dropped my arm to my side and turned toward the house.

I didn't look back. It's what we had intended. It's what we had arranged.

Chapter 59

We planted Little Brother in red dirt. Nothing's growing there. ~Rex

Red dirt. Red bluffs. I'd dreamed of this for ages. Now, looking over all that I'd loved, I dreamed of red hair.

Jim never disappointed when it came to the right he believed in, and he treated Morrissey no better than I did when I took him in. Morrissey was locked in a tiny paddock near the back of Jim's office, with all the finery he would have had if he'd gone ahead and lived in the ashes of Red Rock Ranch I'd left behind. I told Jim everything I knew from my job in Kansas, gave him Mr. Gulliver's name at the bank, shared what little the young bank clerk had told me, and described the railroad land and what Fred explained about those who bought and sold it. "And then there's Ted..." I mentioned Regina's ranch manager, with his name and memories of him stuck in my craw. "I don't have anything concrete to tie him to any scheme, except he had Flynn's deed somehow. But he worked for the man, and my guess is he was holding out for Flynn's wife." My wife. Jim thanked me. The same way he always did when I finished a job and finished it well. He gave me a nod and paid me more, far more, than I expected.

Jim knew without me telling him the pine box in

the back of my wagon held my brother. Pop knew it too, the minute I walked up to his door. Tall, like me, but stooped with age and disappointment, he was a misfit in that little house near a trading post, a place not even a shadow of the ranch he'd built for all of us. His dark eyes went from relief to despair as he looked from me to his other son. Or rather, the box that held him.

Luke had been long enough above ground. Pop never even had time to weep before we had Luke out at the Red Rock Ranch—or what was left of it—and buried beneath its red dirt. Friends came, as did a girl Pop said was Luke's intended. Her hair was black, like mine, her eyes dark, and she was tall and slender. I shook her hand, shook everyone's hand, and took Pop back to the house he didn't belong in.

Neither did I.

I roused Pop early the next morning, hooked Walter to the wagon, and took Adler Duncan, the man I'd always admired and wanted to see live again, to the bank. With the money Jim had paid me, I restored Red Rock Ranch to my father. Exactly what Mr. Gulliver had wanted me to do for Regina. Except that was a job, my part of it over. Jim would take care of her now. The black of my gut darkened.

Pop sat quiet beside me as I took him to the nearest sawmill and bought what we needed to rebuild a ranch house for him and me. He was too old to be cutting his own boards this time, and time was what I wanted to give him. Along with a house for the two of us, just like we'd started out in years ago.

That day, and from then on, we built. Pop and I rebuilt over the black char that was smeared across the ground. He never asked, and I never explained.

Every day felt the same under the red sun that beat down on the red dirt. It was like shoving Kansas and its brown dirt aside, like Luke's funeral never ended. Each day I felt that knot of dark inside and that niggling uneasiness, all of it housed in a sweaty body, caked with red dust, as I rebuilt my father's house with his help. I promised myself that when it was done the empty look would disappear from Pop's eyes, along with the empty feeling inside my chest. I made each nail and spike a memory, hammered and buried them all so hard and deep I'd never see them again. Neither would Pop. No one would take this house from us. Not this time. No one would destroy my father's ranch. And hopefully not Regina's. I slammed the hammer again. Harder and louder.

****

"Who shot Luke?" Jim leaned back in his chair the way he had ages ago, the way he always did. I stood at the front of his desk, just like I had when he told me I'd be marrying the widow Howard.

"I don't know." I looked out the window behind him. There was too much red. Red dust on the glass, red dirt beyond. Red hair stuck in my mind.

"Not Morrissey, though." Jim pressed the tips of his fingers together in a tepee.

"No. Maybe someone scared, trying to stop my brother from shooting wild."

"Can't pin Morrissey with murder, then. Got him for other stuff, though, but not sure I can hang him. Yet."

"If you don't, I will."

"Then Adler will have two dead sons. You finish that house. I'll take care of Morrissey." Jim shoved papers across his desk at me. "Got the papers written up to send to the woman you married. I've explained everything to her, said we'd pronounce Ben Miller dead, and she's free to marry for real, if she wants."

Tend to Regina. Doc would. I stared at the papers. Tried not to swallow in the too-quiet.

"That Mr. Gulliver was as guilty as Morrissey, it turns out."

I looked up, *He was?* written on my face

"We got him. Part of the whole scheme that was indeed up north. As for the woman you married, I just need the deeds for the land you told me about, and I can make the land officially hers. Then we'll be done with that part."

"I have them."

Jim's eyebrows peaked. "You have them? You should have told me."

I should have, but I hadn't. I'd been holding on to them while I hammered one nail and one board at a time. Rebuilding here while I let go of there. "I didn't trust that ranch manager of hers, so I grabbed both of them. Stole one out of his bunkroom and took the other from her bank. Didn't leave them with her, even though I'd intended to." She'd probably assumed I left the one under Jess's mattress but likely knew better by now. Another reason not to trust me.

Jim grinned. "You're turning into me. Good job. Bring them in, and we'll get them official for her. In the meantime, I'm wiring her to expect these papers. She'll be a proud ranch owner as Mrs. Whoever-She-Wants-To-Be soon."

"That would be Mrs. Harris." Doc's wife.

"What?" Jim looked up.

"Nothing."

Jim leaned even farther back in his chair. "You okay?"

"I'll bring those deeds in tomorrow. She needs to get on with her life. And so do I. When can I get back to work?"

Jim stood. "Finish your father's house. No work for you until I say so."

Chapter 60

A man can mess up my plan when he's here. How can he still mess it up when he's gone? ~Regina

I slammed the drawer to my dresser and glared around my room. Where in the world was that deed Ben...Rex...took from the bank? It was supposed to be upstairs, but it wasn't. It had to be somewhere here. Maybe he wasn't even a Ranger. Maybe he simply preyed on me, like Ted first thought.

I went to my trunk and lifted the lid. The little bottle of "medicine" I'd finagled out of Doc for Jess was still there. Ready. He'd need it to travel as soon as I tricked Mr. Gulliver into giving me a copy. I'd come up with some reason for him to. *Drat that Ben! Rex!*

I marched to the kitchen to see if whichever-one-he-was had created some sort of hiding place of his own in the stones around the hearth. Like Flynn. I beat on every rock, and nothing budged. I was fed up with looking for men's hiding places. Why didn't they just do sensible things, like plan ahead and let everyone know what those plans were? I scoured the cabinets, emptied shelves, and even looted the pantry. Nothing. Scallywag!

I climbed the ladder to Jess's loft to check more carefully one last time. Flynn's clothes I no longer wore lay scattered where I'd tossed them across Jess's room to look under the mattress.

I lifted the mattress again and dropped it back into place when I saw nothing under it. Again. I ransacked my own clothes and Flynn's, as well. Again. Jess's also. Ben must have stolen my deed, and it would be nearly impossible to wrangle a copy out of Mr. Gulliver. I didn't have enough money from what Ben had got for my cups and saucers and tea towels both to bribe Flynn's banker *and* buy our train tickets to New York.

I kicked one of Flynn's boots across the room. Why had Ben, the liar, bothered to give me money anyway? Guilt, no doubt, since he'd done God knows what to my dishes and towels. I kicked Flynn's other boot. It hit the chair and spun, something shooting from its top. Something sparkling and rattling as it skittered across the floor. It was small and shiny, definitely not my deed, but I chased after it anyway, and bent to pick it up. My comb. Its broken teeth. I turned it over. The comb I'd lost the day of Flynn's funeral.

I looked around Jess's loft, clamping my comb in my hand. He couldn't climb up here. And I certainly hadn't dropped the comb into Flynn's boot. In fact, I'd worn those boots since the funeral. I sank down onto Jess's bed. How? Who else but Ben? I threw myself backward. Ben. What a clever thief.

I sat back up. Of course. His loft!

Holding onto the comb, I clambered down Jess's ladder, hurried outdoors to the barn, and scaled Ben's, climbing it furiously until I reached the top. There I stopped. My eyes level with his floor, I stared at the place Ben had slept. At his bed. At the hay he'd bunched together, with a shirt lying nearby. I climbed on up and stood where he used to lie. I gathered his shirt and bunched it into a ball, held it over my mouth and nose. Everything smelled like him. His scent was there, even more powerful than that of dust and hay. I dropped down onto a pile of straw, hit something hard with a crunch, and toppled off to the side. I rolled to all fours and stared at the lumpy straw where I'd sat. With Ben's shirt around my hand, I brushed golden stems and blades aside until blue shone through. And white. Fine strokes of red and green on each piece. I blew at the straw, swiping away the rest, my cups and saucers showing through, even my tea towels. I fell back to my haunches and stared at my treasures.

Ben hadn't sold them. Or he'd bought them himself—but left them behind. I laid out his shirt, gathered my china and tea towels within its long back, then bundled them like a sack. With Ben's shirt in one hand and the broken comb in the other, I managed the rickety ladder and made my way to the barn's floor.

"What's all that?"

"You're back?" I looked at Ted.

"Where'd you get that?" Ted reached for my comb.

"It's my comb." I twisted, keeping the comb out of his reach. "The one Flynn gave me, that I lost at his funeral."

Ted glanced to the barn behind me. "Where'd you find it?"

Don't trust Ted. I knew myself now that Ted couldn't be trusted. "It's no concern of yours."

"And what's that?" Ted nodded at Ben's shirt hanging from my other hand.

"My china." I lifted Ben's shirt, thinking of the way the loft still smelled like him.

"He stole it from you?"

"No. He sold it for me; he paid me for it."

"Probably not as much as he got."

More than I expected, truthfully. Ben had done well.

Ted pointed to the comb. "Not right. Not right a man would keep something like that around."

I tucked the comb into my pocket. "You're right. No man should. But I never said Ben did."

Chapter 61

When the smoke clears, a man can see forever.
~Rex

"Son, you building this house or destroying it?"

The ping of my hammer rang across the red dirt and plains, looking for a place to echo, but there was none. I straightened from the board I'd been nailing and swiped my shoulder across my brow. More red. Red dirt streaked and stained my shirt.

"Sorry, Pop." I walked to his side. The two of us stood there looking at what we'd done. Together. Years ago, when Pop built the real ranch house, he'd done the hammering. Loud, like me now. The echo of his agony I hadn't understood still rang in my memory. He'd wiped red sweat from his brow while I dragged boards and carried nails. I looked at my father. He must have hammered frustration out then, like I was hammering it out now.

"I miss Luke," I said. Every board that rebuilt this house reminded me of him. How awful he was at hard work, how he complained, how he struggled to keep up yet stayed behind where he was comfortable. "I miss her, too." I meant my stepmother. Pop and I stood in the quiet, the echo of hammers in our minds. He crossed his arms. I knew the discussion was done.

We'd worked around the one building left

standing. The shed. Neither of us mentioned it. Pop never even offered to store our tools inside it. Maybe he knew what his wife used to do for me there. Maybe he was afraid, because it was the last thing he'd built left standing. He stooped to grab another board.

"We'll build the barn back, too," I said. I didn't turn and look at the enormous black char on the ground behind me. Pop grunted as he dropped the next board where I could hammer it into place. That meant yes. I understood Pop's noises the way Walter understood mine. They said just enough. But not enough.

As I hammered the next and the next boards, I tempered the strength I put behind each swing. Instead of the endless ping, I heard Luke, his constant harangue, his boyish chatter that needled me when it was aimed my way. Jess chattered when he was happy, grumbled when he hurt. I slammed the last nail hard, harder than the rest. The hammer vibrated, bounced out of my hand, and skidded through the red dirt.

"Son, you need to get away. Go ride. Go take a breather." Pop needed a breather, too. Looking into his eyes, I saw hard hammering that never stopped.

"I can finish…"

"Go on. You need it."

I let the hammer lie, hopped on Walter, and rode. I didn't look back as Walter and I headed across red buttes and plains, but I knew what that hilltop would look like if I did—half a house, a man who looked…and felt…just like his son. This son. Not the one he and I had buried next to his ma, and both missed.

Walter and I rode a big loop through land we knew as well as our own. We'd covered this ground many times going to and from assignments, checking in with Jim and Pop, then leaving again.

The building Jim used for an office appeared below a long grade. "Come on, Walter. Let's go see if Jim is about ready to have us back."

Jim had a spark in his eye when he met me at his office door, the kind that said something good had come of his ways. "Sit down. Got news for you. Good news I'm going to pay you more for."

I never sat in Jim's office. I always stood, ready to go…except when he sent me to Liberal to marry the widow. I stood that time, too, but I wasn't ready to go. I sat this time. Part of Pop's breather I needed.

Jim rounded a desk covered in red dust and stacks of papers and dropped into his chair. He twisted my direction, tipped back, and grinned like a cat that had just cornered a mouse.

"You did good up there in Liberal," he said. "Even better than you thought." He leaned forward, rested his elbows on his desk. "Found the main guys, I'm pretty sure."

I raised my brows. "Gulliver?"

"Naw, he was important, but not the most important. But he talked. Kind of a worm, wanting out. Willing to cooperate."

"So, who was it?"

"It was a they. Carlisle and Morgan. They're the heart of this scheme."

I straightened.

"Little ranches were merely means of cash. So were investors from the East. And ranchers who didn't know any better. That money went not just into their pockets but also toward the railroad land. Bought up or stole more and more, turned it over for a pretty profit."

"You mean my pop's ranch really was just for cash?" The house I'd burned? The barn and the rest of it? For nothing? For a place Morrissey never admired or intended to lay his head at all?

Jim nodded. "Yep. Bitter. Raises a man's hackles to know some thief saw what had been a homestead and hard work as nothing but disposable."

I saw red. Red fire, red flames, red words my little brother shouted at me as I ran from our burning ranch.

"Got dibs on Carlisle. He's back east."

Morgan. I was on my feet, spilling Jim's chair over backwards. The dark finger that hadn't stopped niggling through my black and empty gut coming to light. "Ted. Ted Morgan. I'm heading back to Liberal." I saw red again, red hair, red danger. The man who had most likely killed Flynn. And Little Brother.

"Sit back down. You're not going to Liberal. Already got men on the way."

I stayed on my feet. Red hair waving through my mind. Ted and I had both ended up at the Howards' place, with opposite goals in mind. Except neither of us wanted to marry the widow after all. That was then. I knew better now. I fixed my feet in the stance that said I was ready to go.

"You build that house for your father. I have other jobs for you coming up. For now, you're to do as I say and stay put."

"How close are your men? Would they be there by now?"

"Close enough."

I wasn't made to just stand there when my guts burned inside. I strode back outside to Walter. Walter, because he liked water. I looked to the north as the door to Jim's office opened behind me. I turned to look at him as I latched onto Walter's reins and my saddle horn.

Jim was leaning against the door jamb. "You need to collect yourself," he said. "We're getting your man, and I promise to take care of that one in the back." Morrissey. The ruts and gouges on that weathered face deepened as one side of his mouth kicked up. I knew Jim would.

I mounted Walter without a word to Jim or a noise to my horse, and rode straight to my father's ranch. Hard.

The ranch was quiet when Walter stopped in a cloud of red dust. Pop was gone, likely for a breather of his own. I dragged the saddle and bridle off Walter and slapped his rump to let him roam free, cool off, get a drink from one of the buckets that had survived the fire.

I stared north as he amiabled away. One of Regina's words. I knew she meant amble, but I'd never told her I did. I stared through the house that was more than half built but looked half unbuilt. Unfinished business. Like Regina and her ranch, and other things I never told her. And the shed right here that stood not far away. "I can't, Ma." I shook my head. Too many memories that hammered nails hadn't solved. Of her, of Luke, of the night I should have gone in there and dug up whatever it was she left. The tin box was probably disintegrated by now.

I walked to the pile of lumber, long boards waiting to be hammered into place.

The shed. I turned. It was as if Ma was tapping my shoulder when Liberal was on my mind. The shed.

"Dang it, Ma."

I left the boards where they were and walked to the shed. I stood in the doorway, glanced around the square open space, light in long slits striping the floor and walls. The corner, the one my stepmother always used, lay flat and bare, two slivers of light making a cross on the spot.

Pop had brought a shovel from his house, along with other tools he didn't store in this shed. I went to his pile and snatched the shovel off the ground. I bounced its tip on the hard dirt with every step—leaning into it like a crutch. Until I entered the shed. Stepping where the cross marked Ma's spot, I dug a wide circle around where the tin used to be. The ground was softer in this old space, but still it resisted. I felt her smile, that motherly insistence as I kept at it until the dirt came loose. Setting the shovel aside, I nearly smiled myself, seeing Regina's barn floor, all the holes she'd dug for some reason. Maybe for a treasure. I knelt near the rim of the hole I'd dug and pawed away the rest of the ground until I felt it. Tin. The box. The last token of my childhood.

I carried the box out of the shed and to the half-built house. I dropped to the ground, settling it in my lap, and stared at Walter nibbling on whatever he could find. "Okay, Ma. Sorry it took me so long."

I pried open the old lid, the metal soft and crumbling. Inside, instead of toys or tokens, like she usually hid, there lay a stack of papers. Mostly envelopes, everything yellowed, the top piece just a folded page. I chewed my lips until they hurt. My heart hammered in the cavern of a chest where Luke used to be. And her. And Becky. My hands trembled as I lifted the page, the paper wavering, her handwriting ambushing me when I saw it. "Ma." I set the tin box with the envelopes aside and pressed her letter against my lap.

Son. I waited as long as I could to set this box out for you one last time. I knew this last time was coming. It's near enough I dare not wait longer.

Your father has no idea I'm leaving these letters to you. The hard truth is, he wouldn't want me to. They've been hidden where he thought no one would see, but I've seen. I've seen them in his eyes and your heart.

Nothing I could ever do for you, or give you, could do what these letters will.

They're from your mother, your real mother. To Adler, and sort of to you. About you. Read them as you can. I learned on my own she is gone now, may she rest in peace. And may you find peace, also. I'm not sure your father ever will.

From your second mother, one who loved you as if you were her own.

Tears turned her name into something unreadable. Ma. That's all I ever called her, and it was exactly what she was. I refolded her note and swiped my sleeve across my eyes. The tin box sat on the ground beside me. My other mother was in there. The woman I'd always feared I'd somehow driven away.

When my eyes began to clear, I lifted the stack of envelopes, put them in order by date, and began to read, one at a time. Pages and pages unfolded inside me as I read, more around me, and all in my hands. A young woman who'd loved and lost was there. Loved Adler, until she was wrenched away by her father, a wealthy eastern man far more conscious of social status than he was of the heart. Propriety was his love. Aghast when he discovered his daughter had fallen for a common rancher, he'd let propriety take over.

She was sent back east where she'd come from, and forcibly married to another. She was carrying me, she wanted me, but yet above all she wanted what was best for me. She arranged for me to be given to Adler. He came for me, and she explained my absence by carrying out some elaborate scheme that I'd died. Her husband and her family never knew whose child I really was or that I was still alive. But she did. She kept in touch by mail. And I could tell by what she said and how she said it that Adler never answered her.

I leaned my head back against the side of our second ranch house. I could see those arms crossed over his chest, hear the hammering that never stopped, stare into eyes that never cried, and I understood needing a breather.

The look of death I'd seen on Jess's face the day I met him must have spread over mine. His face had been a mirror. And the look of love I'd seen every day on my stepmother's face was there in Regina's, the eastern woman who refused to go back. Who stood where she wanted. And who loved. Loved her boy with everything she had.

Love was as powerful as death. More powerful. Love overcame it.

I stacked the envelopes, laying my stepmother's letter on top. I made a noise for Walter. He tossed his head my direction. "What I meant to say was, come on. We got things to do." Right, this time.

Walter looked baffled for a moment, but when I stood, he understood. We met at his saddle, and I threw it on him. "You better be rested up. Got a long fast ride ahead of us."

I left the empty tin near our tools and tucked the envelopes and letter into my saddlebag. I'd swing by Pop's and tell him I had a wife that needed my help. And a stepson, too.

Chapter 62

Cleave is a funny word. A husband is supposed to cleave to his wife. Yet cleaved is how I feel. Split, not joined. ~Regina

"We just got a wire for you, ma'am," Mr. Greene said, as I stepped to his counter.

"Is it from my father?" I'd wired him, told him to expect me and Jess. *Tell people your plans. That's what Flynn should have done.*

Mr. Greene shook his head. "No, from Oklahoma. I think from the same fellow who wired that man you had around. Miller. At least we thought that's who he was." He pulled a folded paper from its wooden slot.

"Oklahoma?" Oklahoma meant little, but the name Miller meant a lot. I stared at the paper Mr. Greene slid in front of me.

"You gonna read it?"

Maybe it was a confession. Or an apology. Neither one of which would make any difference. I had everything gathered at home. Jess and I would leave first thing in the morning for New York. With very little evidence, but a lot of prayer. Mr. Gulliver was gone, the bank saying nothing of where he went, the clerk nearest him claiming to know nothing about getting copies of deeds. Doc had insisted I should stay, promised to help with whatever I needed, but I refused.

I couldn't, and he shouldn't.

The wire felt like fire beneath my fingers. "As soon as I read this," I said to Mr. Greene, "I'll send one myself."

He nodded. I walked to the far side of the room and opened the note.

Deeds to your ranch and other land signed and official. Both are yours, free and clear. Deeds and legalities coming by mail. Calling Ben Miller deceased. You are free to remarry if you wish. Jim Handley, Oklahoma Indian Territory Rangers

I stared at the wire. Deeds. Both? I re-read it again. Ben gone. Willingly. Pronounced dead so he could get on with his life. He'd meant to do this all along. How could our planned parting have meant anything to him when he had a parting of his own in mind? He'd done me as a job, but he'd done it well. Both deeds. I had no idea how he'd managed it, other than coldly. No wonder he treated me as he had. I ran a hand over my face, touched my lips. The kiss. He hadn't meant that, either, but he'd done it well. Like a job.

"No wire," I said to Mr. Greene. He said something in return, but I closed the door between us. I'd let my father know tomorrow that Jess and I weren't coming after all. The ranches were mine. Everything was over.

****

Ted stepped out of the barn and met me at the wagon as I brought Boss to a stop near the door. "It's mine." I looked down at him, the reins still in my hands. I'd said it over and over on the ride home, loud at some points, to make it sink in. "This ranch. The other land. Both are mine."

"You mean ours?" He unhooked Boss from the

wagon, his movements tight and sharp.

"No." And I meant it. I looped the reins around the post and scooted to the end of the seat, ignoring any splinters as he walked Boss to the side and set a halter over his head. "Mr. Gulliver is gone. Did you know that?" I stared down at Ted.

It was like seeing Ted at Flynn's funeral all over again. Staid. Stolid. "Someone else will take his place," he said. Boss's saddle was there on the fence, as if Ted had been waiting. With the same abrupt movements, he had the saddle on his horse, cinched, and ready to go. "Trust me."

Don't trust Ted. "They haven't yet."

"They will."

"Doesn't matter to me. I won't be dealing with them. Ever. Ben—I mean Rex—took care of everything. Both deeds are signed and legal, in my name along with his. But he's leaving it all to me."

"Both deeds? That ain't right. He's lying to you again." Ted's voice matched his face—no longer staid, but taut.

"I have it on authority other than Ben's—I mean, Rex's. No matter what you think of him, Ted, this much he did was good. I'm grateful he did, even though I'm equally grateful he's gone."

Ted had more strength in that one arm than I'd ever imagined. His fingers clamped around my wrist, and he yanked me to the ground.

"Ted!" I tumbled against the hard dirt, my arm twisting, the wrench making me cry out.

"Since that lowdown thief managed to steal those two deeds, what did he do with the rest?"

"The rest?" I tried to sit, turned with the pain, and

rubbed my shoulder.

"Yes, the rest." Ted let go, and I rolled to my haunches at his feet.

"Ma?" Jess came up behind me.

"Go on to the house, Jess. I'll be there in a minute." I struggled to my feet.

"You okay?" Jess was eyeing Ted, the hair that fell over his forehead not hiding his frown.

"Git on, boy. This is between me and your ma."

"Jess does what I say, not what you say." I turned to my son. "You go on, finish what I asked you to do." Finish packing, even though we weren't going. But Ted was. I wheeled to tell the last man on my ranch goodbye.

"Where are the other deeds?" He was close, closer than he'd been.

"I don't know what you're talking about. But I want you to get out. Get off this ranch and stay off."

Ted wrapped his fingers around my arm again. He squeezed and twisted, I bit back a wince, another scream, as he tugged. "I seen you digging all over this place. Surely you found them by now."

"I wasn't digging for deeds. I was looking for Flynn's money."

"Ma?" Jess's eyes were wide, the color of Flynn's. Brighter.

I shoved against Ted, but his fingers tightened as he spewed in my face. "Flynn spent every penny. He bought up railroad land, just like I told him to."

"You told him to?" I broke loose and stared into his eyes. "Carlisle and Morgan—that's you. I'd expected a suit. Culture, wealth, not this. Not someone down in the ranks getting his hands dirty. I suppose

Carlisle is the neat one."

"Where are those deeds?"

Jess hobbled close. He grabbed a fistful of my shirt at my back. I felt the fabric tighten.

"Pa would have told me if he had more land. He told me everything." Jess leaned forward, his hand still clenched.

Ted laughed. It was ugly. Then he spit to the side, a ball of wet, brown dust rolling away.

Jess knotted more of my shirt in his hand. I felt the tug as his other crutch came up, fast and wide, a long stick aimed at Ted.

Like an opposing weapon, Ted's good hand struck quick. He snatched the crutch out of the air, yanking my son forward. Jess teetered against my back, both fists holding on, one to me and the other to his crutch. "You're right," Ted whispered, jabbing the crutch and yanking my son. "I bet he did, even if you didn't understand. Where are those deeds, boy?"

I felt the calculations inside of Jess. While he teetered, I could hear him churning thoughts and memories, conversations with his father, hints Flynn had passed on regarding his heritage. Promises. Dreams. Visions that Flynn's son understood better than anyone.

Jess stopped weaving then. He relaxed. Whatever Flynn had covertly shared, dawned. Ted saw it, too. He yanked Jess's crutch, his bad arm splicing between my son's hand and my shirt. I clawed at the air, missing Ted's arm, the force throwing Jess off balance. Ted latched onto my falling boy before I could, and dragged him to Boss.

I lunged, dug my fingers into the back of Ted's

shirt, pinched skin and fabric as I yanked. "Let him go!"

The arm with no hand, the useless one, wasn't useless at all. It fell like a club. Ted swung it behind him, and I saw it coming. I heard Jess scream, but then I saw and heard nothing.

Chapter 63

There'll never be hell again. Not here or there. Only heaven, when I am done. ~Rex

Walter and I bypassed the farmer who'd first pointed me to Regina's land. He was out in his barnyard, one hand raised as I passed. Fast. I waved and was gone, glad for the wind in my face this time. Focused on the dilapidated barn and house I was headed toward.

The place was quiet as we barreled close. Still house, stagnant barn. A heap of something on the ground in between. As Walter brought me to the mouth of their entrance, the heap took shape. Blue shirt, dark trousers, hips I'd never forget, and red. Red curls spilling out all around her head. I was off Walter the way she'd dove off Boss when we found Jess lying in the prairie. I understood that passion this time. I thought I'd spent it on Luke, but it was back, and even stronger, as I covered the distance quicker than my horse.

"Regina." I dropped at her back, skidded close, and leaned over her, brushing the hair from her face. A purple lump rose on her forehead, brighter than it should have been against the bloodless color of her skin.

I gathered her into my arms and carried her to the pump. The handle let out the squeal I'd never forget as I pumped up water and splashed it on her face. "Regina. Wake up."

There was movement in her brow and behind the closed lids, until finally those green eyes fluttered open. Dazed and hazy, their focus too far away, she frowned at me. "Jess."

I looked around at a barnyard that was far too quiet. Jess might be sullen sometimes, but he'd be out here to protect his mother or tell me to get off their ranch, if he were home.

"Where's Jess?" I brushed more hair from her face.

She spotted me, then, the green darkening along with her frown. She fought to sit up, arms flailing as she tried to roll away.

I grabbed for arms, for shoulders, for whatever I could, but she slipped away from my grasps and fell to the ground with a groan. "Regina. Stop. Hold still." I knew I was wasting my breath. This woman never listened, and she fought like a wildcat to get her way.

"Let go of me." She rolled to all fours, then was quick to settle back to her backside, holding onto her head.

"Regina, where's Jess?"

She came back to all fours and staggered to stand, battling off my hands as I reached to steady her. "He's...he's..." She pinched her face between both hands, tears turning the green to red. "Ted..."

"Ted hit you?"

She frowned, she nodded, she looked where she'd been lying.

I jumped to my feet, wrapped my hands around her tiny waist, and brought her close. "Walter, hie."

Walter tossed his head over his shoulder, then

trotted my way. I had her on him in a second, seated in my saddle. He felt my energy, even though I was sure he had none of his own. He pranced. I reached in front of Regina, grabbed the saddle's horn, and sailed up behind her. "Let's go. And this time, I'll do the holding on."

And I did, with both arms around the tiny woman I never intended to let go of. Walter burst forward as I leaned into his run, Regina close and leaning with me.

"What's Ted want with Jess?" I asked through her hair.

"More deeds to railroad land. He says Flynn had them somewhere." Her voice faltered. She had to be hurting, inside and out.

"And he's looking?"

"He won't have to look hard. Jess knows where they are. At least he's pretty sure." Her voice dwindled to nothing. She pressed even tighter into my chest.

"Come on, Walter." Walter seemed to understand English as well as he did grunts and clicks. I let him run as hard as he could toward what railroad land of Flynn's we knew of, Flynn's widow—my wife—in my arms.

We cleared the distance in no time. I scanned the creek area where Walter and I had gone that day, then the fields and the prairie, looked toward the knoll where I'd stood with Regina and Jess. Boss was nowhere in sight. Neither was Ted, nor Jess. I reined Walter the direction of the knoll. He understood and barreled for the top. When we reached it, I brought him to a stop. Still full of energy, Walter spun in place. "Whoa, boy."

"I don't see them." Tears were evident in Regina's voice as we covered a circle, scouring every direction.

"Hold on," I said near her ear. "Come on, Walter, let's go." I dug my knees into his sides and he was off again. Down the knoll to the shortcut Jess and Regina had showed me.

"Why are we going this way? Do you think they're back at the ranch?"

"No, I don't."

I'd checked Flynn's tools, and one pick had fresh gouges with traces of limestone. Either Flynn or Ted had dug at rocks, most likely in the place where Flynn had been found dead. My guess was both of them had used it. Flynn first, to bury his deeds as a future surprise for his son, and Ted second, to break off a rock to kill Regina's husband so he could lay claim to as much as he could. I dug my boots tighter against Walter's sides.

I gave Walter a tug to slow him as we came near the small hills where Flynn had last been alive. I listened over the sounds of his hooves and the wind he was trying to gasp. "Easy, boy," I whispered. I stretched around the woman who was my wife and patted his neck. Soaked with sweat. Walter meandered through the twists and turns of the rock formations. I studied the ground, Regina twisting in front of me, holding her head, and looking in every direction.

"Whoa, Walter. There." I pointed to the dirt where Flynn had been killed. Hoof prints, boot prints, both big and small. "See that gouge?" I pointed at a dig in the dirt.

"Jess's crutch?"

"Maybe." The rocks were broken, scattered, but I wasn't sure they were different from the way they had been the first time we'd come through here. "Stay on Walter." I slid to the ground. "Stay in the saddle and keep hold of the reins, but keep low," I whispered. Green eyes, wide with worry, gazed down at me. I held on to the reins with her; I wanted her hand near mine as long as we could.

"Thank you," she said. "Thank you for being here. And for declaring yourself dead, just so I could have the ranch."

"But I'm not dead." Far from it. I squeezed her hand, let go, and knelt to the ground. I studied the rock chips and the prints in the dirt. I'd tracked men before, over harder and grassier ground than this. I looked up and pointed the direction they were heading. There were several abutments of rocks in the direction Ted had gone. "Stay here," I told Regina. "We'll get Jess and your deeds."

"I don't care about the deeds. I don't care about any of this. Just Jess."

I patted her leg, and she let me. I crouched low as I crept forward, easing against and around each spire of rock. It was the whimper I eventually heard that brought me lower, the sound of a shovel that caused me to stop. I pressed my back against a wall of rock and listened.

"Stop your whining."

I scooted to where I could peer around the edge. Jess was on Boss, straddling the horse, one crutch across the saddle, his face white as he leaned away from his healing leg, trying to take the strain off it.

"Shut up." Ted was on all fours, digging under a low shelf of rock. I loosened the loop off my trigger and waited, watching Jess's face tighten as he moved.

Ted leaned into the crevice, grunting. Jess stiffened, propped one foot in a gun loop beneath the saddle, and slapped Boss's neck with the flat of his hand. Boss gave a lurch and jerked forward. He veered in a sharp cut to the side, barely missing Ted, with Jess holding on, plastering himself against Boss's neck.

Papers flew as Ted rolled to the side and came to his feet. He was quick, his pistol out and pointed at Jess in one fast move. Amazingly fast for a one-armed man. But I was faster, and it had nothing to do with having two hands.

"Drop it, Ted."

There were two shots, the first at me, the second at Jess. The bullet near me grazed the rock beside my head. Shards of limestone shattered in my face as the bullet ricocheted away. Jess tumbled with his. Boss dipped. And Regina screamed.

The third shot was mine. Ted staggered backwards, and the one-armed ranch manager hit the ground.

By the time I reached Jess, Regina was there. Blood spilled onto his shirt as she wrapped her arms around him.

"Jess," I shouted, taking his head in my hands and holding it up. His eyes fluttered.

"Ben? Ma?"

"Where you hit, son?" I looked down at his shirt, his legs, using one hand to cover every bit of the boy I could see.

"I'm not. It's just my leg."

I ran my hands where the break had been. I felt the dislocation. "Hold on, I'm going to adjust your brace. It's going to hurt."

Regina helped me this time, leaning close and holding on to her son to steady him for the pain. I slid my hands beneath the splints and straps of the contraption, set them at both sides, and pressed. Jess jerked. He let out nothing more than a moan. "Hold on to him," I said to his mother. I glanced down at her as I grabbed at the straps and splints to tighten them. Blood splattered where she leaned over Jess. 'Regina?"

I took Jess's mother by the shoulders and turned her to face me. Blood ran down her face, mixing with tears. Red. More red. Too much red.

"You're hurt!" I grabbed her close, ran my hands over her face, feeling and searching for where Ted's bullet had gone. "You didn't stay where I told you to stay." Of course she didn't. Regina wouldn't. No mother would.

"He's got to be okay," she whispered. "My boy's got to be okay."

"Ma?"

Regina pushed my hands away, tears thinning the blood as they splashed onto her son. "Fix Jess."

Helping a boy was helping his mother, even his stepmother in some cases, the woman that mattered. The look in those green eyes told me what I'd known all along.

I bent over Jess, keeping close to his mother. I drew every strap tight, made sure each splint of his brace was in place, slow and fast at the same time.

When each was, I held her. Drew her close with one arm and kept her there as she lost the strength to hold on herself. "Regina..." I whispered her name, but it felt like a shout inside as my other hand plowed through her hair, checked her neck and her face, and searched for the damage Ted's bullet had done. "Regina. Hold on. We're not parting, not this way." Her eyes closed and she bled into my hand. Red blood through red hair. I looked at her boy.

"Can you manage, son?"

Jess was on his feet before I had his mother up in my arms, his hands full of the papers his pa had left behind, his eyes full of the love that was stronger than death. I wouldn't leave the boy behind with a dead man who had probably killed his father in this same spot. I helped Jess onto Walter—sidesaddle, but he didn't argue—and I held onto his mother as I climbed into Boss's saddle. Jess made a sound, the right sound, and Walter moved. I kneed Boss, and together we hied it to Doc.

****

Red. I made this arrangement. The final one. I took my redheaded wife and her son to the red dirt of Oklahoma, where I married her again. I'd wired ahead, and Jim had everything ready—Pop, some of our friends, and a real preacher waiting at that half-built house on the rise.

"Pop, I want you to meet Regina and Jess." I helped my family down from the wagon and watched Pop's face, the widening of his eyes, the memories that wanted out.

Pop stepped forward, studying the woman that was to be his new daughter-in-law, the trousers she wore, a shirt that fit, and his new grandson.

"They have land up in Kansas. Lots of it."

Pop shook Jess's hand, the one Jess wasn't using to hold his crutch, and then he turned to Regina. "My son always was partial to red." Pop smiled. He didn't mention her trousers, or the bandage around that pile of red where Ted's bullet had hit but thankfully not stayed. I hadn't seen Pop smile in ages. "You remind me of someone," Pop said still looking at my wife. Maybe it was the Easterner in her, or the Easterner that had gone out of her. "That was a long time ago, but looking at you makes it all clear."

Pop looked at me, then. More red. Red swimming in his eyes.

"We need to build on, Pop. Just like we did the last time we put up a house. Gotta make room for the new wife and the son. Again." I wrapped an arm around Regina and pulled her close. "And you'll be the new Mrs. Duncan. As soon as we say, 'I do.' Again."

A word about the author...

Born and raised in the Midwest, Colleen earned a four-year degree in Medical Technology and used it to travel and explore other parts of the country while working in the field of science.

Outside the laboratory she delves deeply into literature, both reading and writing, her interest piqued by tales involving moral dilemmas and the choices people come up against.

A lover of the outdoors as well as a comfy living room, Colleen is always searching inside and out for the next good story.

Visit with Colleen at:

https://www.facebook.com/ ColleenLDonnelly

http://www.colleenldonnelly. com/

https://twitter.com/ColleenLDonnell

Thank you for purchasing
this publication of The Wild Rose Press, Inc.

If you enjoyed the story, we would appreciate your
letting others know by leaving a review.

For other wonderful stories,
please visit our on-line bookstore at
www.thewildrosepress.com.

For questions or more information
contact us at
info@thewildrosepress.com.

The Wild Rose Press, Inc.
www.thewildrosepress.com

Stay current with The Wild Rose Press, Inc.

Like us on Facebook

https://www.facebook.com/TheWildRosePress

And Follow us on Twitter
https://twitter.com/WildRosePress